P9-DGB-421

6-13-00

MURDER
IN THE
MUSEUM
OF
MAN

Novels by Alfred Alcorn

THE PULL OF THE EARTH

VESTMENTS

ALFRED ALCORN

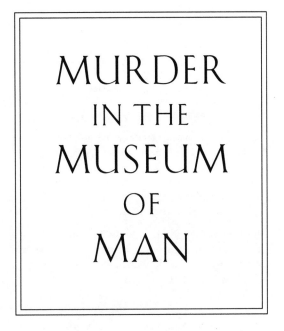

MURDER
IN THE
MUSEUM
OF
MAN

ZOLAND BOOKS
Cambridge, Massachusetts

First edition published in 1997 by
Zoland Books, Inc.

384 Huron Avenue
Cambridge, Massachusetts 02138

Copyright © 1997 by Alfred Alcorn

PUBLISHER'S NOTE

FIRST EDITION

Book design by Boskydell Studio
Printed in the United States of America

03 02 01 00 99 98 97   8 7 6 5 4 3 2 1

This book is printed on acid-free paper, and its binding
materials have been chosen for strength and durability.

Library of Congress Cataloging-in-Publication Data
Alcorn, Alfred.
Murder in the Museum of Man / Alfred Alcorn. — 1st ed.
p.   cm.
ISBN 0-944072-77-1 (alk. paper)
I. Title.
PS3551.L29M87   1997
813'.54—dc20   96-37558
                                                    CIP

For Margaret and Sarah

The following account by Norman A. de Ratour, constituting unofficial entries into the Log of the Museum of Man, was entered as evidence in Middling County Superior Court, and while in the public domain as such, is reprinted here with the consent and cooperation of the author.

MURDER
IN THE
MUSEUM
OF
MAN

It is with great relief and some reluctance that I begin these unauthorized and unofficial entries into the Log of the Museum of Man. I say "reluctance" because, as Recording Secretary here at the MOM for more than three decades now (if you count the nearly year and a half I was assistant to the ailing Miss Vogel before her retirement), I have endeavored to be meticulously objective in my maintenance of the official and authorized records. In these thirty-odd years I have heard no more than one or two complaints about the minutes of the innumerable meetings I have kept. No one has ever questioned the Annual Report that I submit to the Board of Governors or the way I have organized the records and the biographical files or my editorship of the *MOM Quarterly*, a publication that began at my instigation when Dr. Commer became director. But matters of late have taken such a turn that no "official" record will do them justice. I refer, of course, to the strange and disquieting disappearance of Dean Cranston Fessing. A one- or two-day absence is one thing, but the good dean has been gone now for a week, and concern is mounting for his well-being. Moreover, I find the dean's absence symptomatic of a deeper malaise afflicting the Museum of Man. We are like some great crippled beast about which the scavengers have gathered. In a manner breathtaking in its boldness, Wain-scott University is attempting nothing less than to take us over, lock, stock, and barrel. Of a piece with these dark happenings is Malachy Morin's usurpation of nearly all executive power at this venerable institution.

Before I go any further, however, I want to make it clear that I have no intention of letting this *ex officio* journal (which I plan to keep under separate code in the mainframe memory and the printouts in a locked drawer of my desk) degenerate into a mere compendium of complaints about Mr. Morin. Above all, I do not wish to sound querulous. (I would like to point out, incidentally, that I am making this entry after hours, on my own time, when the last lingering visitor has left this marvelous place to me and old Mort, the key-jangling security guard. And, of course, to Damon Drex, whom I can hear five floors down cavorting with his charges in the Primate Pavilion.) No, I am determined not to be reduced, in this ad hoc journal, merely to venting my frustra-tion with that man. But the fact remains that Malachy ("call me Mal") Morin has lately made my life here at the MOM nothing less than hellish. His offenses are so legion I scarcely know where to begin.

With effort I have been able, just, to abide the man's presump-tuous familiarity, his jockstrap jocularity, his calling me, with that laugh of his, Bow Tie to my face and Stick behind my back. And it's not just his larger-than-life person and persona, his six feet, six inches and four hundred pounds or thereabouts of corporeality, much of it soft lard that bulges everywhere. It is not even his questionable grooming and the peculiar acridity in which he billows about this place. After all, keeping that much flesh clean on a regular basis must be something of a chore, particularly for someone who is by nature slovenly. It is not even the way, starting as Dr. Commer's executive assistant, he took advantage of that aging scholar's infirmities, machinating his way around the Board of Governors, making a mockery of the Rules of Governance with his so-called executive committee, which he stacked with his cronies from the Wainscott jockocracy — to drag in a suitably clumsy portmanteau word — until, as Administrative Director, the reach of his meaty hands knows no bounds. (Even as I write, the hoots and howls of chimpanzees rise from the new exercise yard that Damon Drex had built at great and controversial expense in the old courtyard, which used to be graced by an ancient rhododendron and some prim lilacs, a development, quite frankly, that Malachy Morin should have prevented rather than encouraged.)

But it is not even that. It is not even that he had no right whatsoever to appoint me "press assistant" for the MOM, thereby loading on me a spate of spurious duties, telling me that I should simply tape all of the pertinent proceedings in the museum for the record. The fact is — and these rules have yet to be officially altered — I still report directly to the Board of Governors. And for good reason. With all due respect to Dr. Commer and his distinguished predecessors, the position of Recording Secretary was established at the very founding and incorporation of the museum as a distinctly independent office in order, and I quote, "that the Board of Governors as constituted above should have on an annual basis and at such other times as deemed appropriate clear and objective accounts of all important undertakings of the museum and its officers." Nothing could be less equivocal. The fact is, as Recording Secretary, I report to no one but the Board of Governors, to the institution, and, in my own small way, to history.

But how, I ask you (you being the intrepid researcher, the field archaeologist of archives, who a hundred years from now will no doubt ferret out these little addenda), am I to fulfill my responsibilities as Recording Secretary, how am I ever to write an edifying history of this unique institution when, as "press assistant," I must speak to one insistent journalist after another about the apparent disappearance of Dean Fessing? About the attempt of Wainscott University to swallow us up. About the restoration of Neanderthal Hall and the diorama of Paleolithic life Professor Pilty is so determined to create there. About the rumors issuing from the Genetics Lab; about why the Primate Pavilion is not open to the public. About the rise in the price of admission; about the greenhouse effect. About the destiny of the human species. I am not exaggerating. It's quite extraordinary how journalists think everything is their business. One impudent young man of the modern type with rimless spectacles, hair slicked back, and an oversized overcoat, was so bold as to ask me about Dean Fessing's sexual preferences. I responded, rather wittily I think now, that I was sure he had some. Another one, the science reporter for some television station or another, asked me if dinosaurs will be included in the diorama of Stone Age life. No, I said, but perhaps a journalist or two. Such invincible ignorance.

The fact is I have never refused in all the time I have been here to provide reporters and others with what I know about the history and operation of the museum. But I was not even asked if I wanted to "handle" the press. Malachy "Stormin' " Morin (he's famous, of course, for blocking that last-minute field goal attempt by Middlebrough in the "game of the century") merely summoned me to his office last week and said I was to take press calls because I knew the place "inside out." Naturally, I remonstrated with him, implying that as Administrative Director he should know the institution at least as well as I, that he should, when necessary and in Dr. Commer's stead, represent the MOM to the public. "You're it, Bow Tie," he said. "You're our front man. I want you to take the heat." Take the heat. The man is a veritable fount of clichés. And he finds my seriousness risible.

Oh dear, I'm afraid I'm off on precisely the complaining note I wanted to avoid. Because in some ways it's not even these faults of his that I find ultimately noisome. It's not even the man's sexual incontinence, the way he leers after anything in a skirt, the way he importunes with his bulging eyes, the knack he has of divining just how far he can go, which women will not only tolerate his more flagrant advances but (ghastly thought) submit to them. Even that is forgivable and, quite frankly, none of my business, except where it reflects on the museum. We all have our foibles, after all.

What is not excusable, what rankles to the marrow, what is intolerable, is that Malachy Morin cares not one whit for this institution as an institution. The man is sublimely oblivious to the grandeur all around him. He could as easily be running a mortuary supply warehouse or a laundry. His eyes visibly glaze over when, on an obligatory tour for important visitors, we pause by, say, the pre-Columbian exhibit with the marvelous sitting figures from Oaxaca or the wonderful terra-cotta figurines in our admittedly small Greco-Roman display. The Solomon Islands canoe in the Oceanic exhibit with its majestic bow points and shellwork along the gunwales leaves him cold. The Hominid Collections on display in Neanderthal Hall, charting the miracle of human evolution from Lucy to Albert Einstein, are for Mr. Morin little more than a jumble of old bones. Once, to my acute embarrassment, when we were showing our extensive collection of Paleolithic coprolites to a touring delegation from Romania, he picked up one of the larger and better-formed specimens (which is strictly forbidden by museum regulations) and said, believe it or not, "talk about shitting a brick." The Genetics Lab, of course, is utterly beyond his ken, a maze of rooms filled with serious people about whose work he has scarcely a clue. And doesn't want one. His ignorance is *willed*. He is very nearly proud of it. Indeed, the only part of the museum he finds congenial is the Primate Pavilion, where he gladly leads important visitors, where he mugs at the monkeys and talks to

Henry, the old gorilla. And the beasts respond, as though recognizing one of their own. (Speaking of which, I am definitely going to lodge a complaint about Damon Drex and his hooting chimps. It's like hearing the echoes of the bestiality from which we have so painfully evolved.) It is that ignorance, that obliviousness to the palpable evidence of man's capacity, nay, instinctive compulsion, to create beauty, that I find intolerable. It's an awful thing to say, but Malachy Morin's very presence desecrates this temple.

Well, chagrin and all, I feel better already having made this account of the true situation. Indeed, I feel positively purged. And I've even worked up something of an appetite to take to the Club, where, I believe, the special tonight is poached salmon. I might try it, perhaps, with a *demi-bouteille* of that dry Graves I helped the Wine Committee select last month. Izzy Landes tells me it's rather disappointing, but then Izzy can be finicky when it comes to wine.

WEDNESDAY, APRIL 1

It wasn't easy, but I confronted Malachy Morin again today over the press assistant issue. He tried to dismiss me, saying we had already discussed it, but I persisted. I must say I was in something of a lather. I hate confrontation. It makes me nervous. It makes me angry and I am not one of those people who enjoy anger. But people like Mr. Morin respond to power, and anger is a kind of power. When he tried to tell me that the matter was closed, that he was busy — I'm not sure the man knows what the word means in any real sense — I said if we don't discuss it here and now I will be obliged to take it to the Board. I then read him the appropriate sections in the Rules of Governance, pointing out not only that my position is a constitutional one as far as the museum is concerned but that I report not to him but to the Board of Governors.

Well, after much blustering and standing and sitting, he acceded to my demand. He said he would put a notice in the Seaboard *Bugle* for a press assistant and promised to have someone onboard within two weeks. I refrained from pointing out that he might consider doing the work himself instead of adding to the bureaucracy (the new assistant will no doubt need an assistant before long) because he grew so effusive, saying that he would henceforth regard me as part of his "management team." In this spirit I agreed to help him interview candidates for the position. I said I would also be available to help advise him or her, probably the latter, given the man's propensities. In the meanwhile I am to continue "handling the press."

Marge Littlefield, the comptroller of the MOM and a dear friend of many years (she always saves me a dance or two at the Curatorial Ball), told me afterwards, when I related the meeting to her, that I am not to trust Mr. Morin in the least. She recounted for me a set-to they had had not long after he assumed virtual control of the administration of the museum through his rigged executive committee. She said he asked her in so many words to "cook the books," i.e., spread the expenses of his office around the other departments, especially the tabs he runs up dining out and traveling to see things like the "Super Bowl," whatever that is. He also caused a stir down in Purchasing when he said he wanted to "vet" certain suppliers. (The finances of the MOM are becoming quite warped enough with allocations from the Onoyoko Institute.) Well, Marge was having none of it, of course, and she told him so. When he began to insist, she told him in no uncertain terms that if he persisted she would feel obliged to report his requests to Dr. Commer with carbons to the members of the Board of Governors. And that, according to Marge, made him change his tune immediately. He said that she had misunderstood him, that he really wanted her advice on budget matters, where, he pretended to confess, his experience was limited. He also asked her to join his management team. Well, not long afterwards, she learned from a friend in the Wainscott administration that Mr. Morin had tried, through various reorganizing schemes, to have her position "integrated" out of existence. My little triumph, in short, is qualified with caution.

But it is still a triumph, and I find myself taking an almost irresponsible delight in it. It will be such a relief not to have to talk to the press about what the museum is doing, or rather not doing, to find Dean Fessing, whose disappearance grows more ominous with each passing day (not to mention what the rumor mills are churning out). It is futile to try to explain to members of the Fourth Estate that the museum is essentially doing nothing in the case other than cooperating to the utmost with the appropriate authorities, because museums as a rule are not equipped to find missing persons, our expeditions to uncover long-buried mummies or hominid remains notwithstanding. (And these individuals, you might say, are found but not missing.) I mean, how am I to know if foul play is involved or not? It would not surprise me at all if the man simply grew tired of being a dean. He certainly ran into a buzz saw of opposition around here. Perhaps he just *left*. It's something I've contemplated myself, though not in any ultimate sense.

But what a pleasure it will be to tell Damon Drex that I will no longer be in a position to grant him an institutional imprimatur for his monkey business and that I am no longer the conduit for the media attention he so desperately craves. Ever since my appointment as press assistant, the man has grown positively chummy in his obsequiously aggressive way. I suppose I should have disabused him right from the start of the strange notion that I am impressed by or interested in his "work" with the chimpanzees in his care. I have always considered the addition of the Primate Pavilion to the MOM — however muddled the affiliation — just after the Second World War a mistake for several reasons, not the least of which being that apes are animals: they belong to zoology, not to anthropology and certainly not to archaeology. (Thank God there's a fine early-spring rain misting the air, or the beasts would be out in their yard sending up their usual clamor.) Nor have I ever cared for the pavilion as an institution. It looks jerry-built, and with its bars and drab laboratories and that smokestack that rises over its crematorium, it has always reminded me of those beastly German camps. Nor do I understand the cult of cuteness that attends these animals, what with their dull, brutish faces, their blighted eyes, their lank, mangy hair, their mocking antics and revolting exhibitionism. I mean, has not humanity spent millions of painful years evolving *up* from that state? Of course, when one thinks of those death camps, one wonders.

Again, in reviewing this entry into the Log, and glancing over the first one I made, I realize I must sound quite negative about the museum. Nothing could be further from the truth. I do not wish to complain. The fact is, I have spent a singularly happy professional life here at the MOM. While "Recording Secretary" may not sound like much, it is a position of considerable reach and responsibility when exercised as it was originally intended. At a small reception on the occasion of my twenty-fifth anniversary in this position, my good friend Izzy Landes raised a glass and dubbed me the Curator of the Curators, a sobriquet I have worn with pride ever since. Lately, in fact, I have been giving considerable thought to the possibility of writing the history of the museum. I think it's time that someone told the story of this wonderful place, and to this end I have begun to locate and collect the necessary records and materials. (I didn't mention this when I met with Malachy Morin today, as he doesn't strike me as someone who is interested in either the past or the future. I mean, how do you explain to someone like him the impulse to write history, to render an account for the judging God of future generations?)

The fact is, when I leave in the evenings, I almost never take the little rattling elevator at the end of the corridor; instead I walk the other way to the main core of the building, a glorious atrium that is lit from above during the day by a domed skylight of wrought-iron tracery worthy of Kew Gardens. There, starting with the Greco-Roman/Egyptian-Sumerian Collections on the fifth floor, I descend through the galleries that encircle and open onto the atrium. A rich hush emanates from the delicate potteries, ivory work, and silks of the Far East that take up much of the fourth floor. On the third, of course, is the cream of our justifiably famous collection from Oceania — the canoe, of course, but also the wood carvings, the jade-bladed weaponry, tapa cloth, the fabulous, grotesque masks. There I linger as well over the African display, the Kongo figurines, the incised wooded vessels of the Kuba, the Masai beadwork. The second floor is given over to the Americas, and our strength here, as even the most cursory visit will attest, is the pre-Columbian Mesoamerican display. I walk around each case, sometimes pausing to absorb the beauty of millennia, until I reach the ground floor, which undercuts the galleries. This floor comprises Neanderthal Hall, even though the material displayed here extends back some three and half million years. Imagine that, three and half million years! And we always think there is so little time. Most of the specimens are casts of what Professor Thad Pilty calls the usual lineup. There's Lucy, of course, a gracile australopithecine lady little more than three feet tall, along with some of her robust cousins. There struts early man, *Homo habilis,* the first, perhaps, to fashion some of the beautiful, bifaceted stone tools, the start, as some have said, of aesthetics. *Home erectus,* of course, and then *neanderthalensis,* who are represented by several heavy-browed models based on the Gerasimov reconstructions. I mean, here is the evidence, lovingly labeled and displayed, that where you find man, however primitive, you find art, proof that we are not merely creatures but creators, that we partake . . . Well, there goes the phone.

Oh, dear, dear. That was the Seaboard Police Department. Dean Fessing, or pieces of him, at any rate, has been found, and I must go.

THURSDAY, APRIL 2

I have just had the most awful day of my professional life. Poor Cranston Fessing, as I reported last night, has been found. Or rather, what remained of him was found yesterday afternoon next to a Dumpster behind Atwood Hall, the gender studies building.

I am not good at public relations. And, as though sensing it, the vultures of the press lost no time in descending on me. They came flapping down as if out of the sky with their scrawny necks and glistening faces. Or they loped right in, big jawed and brazen. I threw them what few bones I could (forgive me that, Cranston, wherever you may be, in whatever well-regulated heaven or hell deans go to for their final reward), but the Seaboard Police Department is keeping a tight lid on details.

And I was left virtually alone to deal with the situation. Everyone who might have helped quite simply disappeared. The Wainscott Public Relations Office, an entire floor of nice but very nervous people over in Grope Tower (a suitably hideous erection of concrete and glass), referred all questions to the MOM on the pretext that the dean was on assignment here, was, for the current academic year, on official leave from the university. Someone over in Grope told Amanda Feeney, a reporter from the *Bugle*, who has already misquoted and misconstrued me twice on previous stories, that the dean had been cannibalized and that expertise in such matters resides here. Which may be true but is surely irrelevant. It's clear that the university simply wanted to dissociate itself from the grisliness of what has happened. Malachy Morin was no help whatsoever; he had left by nine-thirty after bungling a phone call and acted, if you ask me, quite suspiciously. But then, he always acts suspiciously. I gave the press and the police his home number, not, I'm sure, that he was there. And when I tried to tell Dr. Commer the news, the poor man thought I was arranging for him to have lunch with the late dean. I did manage to gin up a press release, including a paragraph of boilerplate from President Twill's office praising the dean in terms one usually finds in encomia to retired or deceased faculty and administrators.

I did take some small satisfaction in keeping certain details from the press. It appears that the dean, after having been murdered (presumably), was butchered and cooked quite expertly before being eaten (presumably). The coroner, Dr. P. M. Cutler — a familiar figure here at the MOM, having used for forensic purposes specimens from our considerable collection of human remains — took unseemly relish, I thought, in relating to me some of the details of the autopsy. Indeed, he sounded more like Rick Royick, the *Bugle*'s food critic, than a coroner. The dean's buttocks, it appears, were baked with a cinnamon honey glaze; there was a veritable roast rack of dean, complete with those little paper caps, one of which the doctor kept twisting in his hand; there were (I am paraphrasing Dr. Cutler) medallions of thigh dressed in a basil curry *beurre blanc* that had been served with a thyme-infused purée of white beans and black olives in a marinade of citrus and fennel; there was evidence of a *bourguignonne;* and the dean's head, while intact, had been partially emptied, with gross violation to the foramen magnum, where traces of nutmeg were found. I must say that if the doctor was indulging in levity at my expense, it is a levity I find in the worst possible taste, and no pun is intended. But in fact, I believe he was being entirely serious. When I betrayed the least incredulity, he asked me if I wanted to see the evidence firsthand. I said no, thank you. It appears the remains had been ravaged by dogs (Seaboard still does not have a leash law) and perhaps raccoons, judging by gnaw marks on some of the bones.

I did arrange to have four of us take questions at a hastily convened press conference. We were obliged to cram into Margaret Mead Auditorium on the second floor of the museum after the university refused permission to use one of their larger lecture halls. Someone in President Twill's office told me he didn't think a press conference an "appropriate use of university property." I am going to write a very strong letter about this matter to President Twill for Dr. Commer to sign, with a copy to each member of the Wainscott Board of Regents. Cranston Fessing was, after all, a Wainscott dean, and while I would normally be among the first to keep the press at a distance from any university business, I thought in this case that anything smacking of a cover-up would only make matters worse. And matters are bad enough as it is.

The press conference turned out, despite my best efforts, to be something of a travesty. Before I knew it, there were coils of cable lying all about the place and glaring lights and glaring ignorance. Perhaps it's just the arrogant, knowing way in which reporters ask the most banal of questions. I took their questions along with Chief Francis Murphy of the Seaboard Police Department, Dr.

Cutler, and Professor Cornelius Chard. Corny Chard, as most people know, is the Packer Professor of Primitive Ethnology in the Department of Anthropology and a public advocate of anthropophagy. A compact, cocky, red-faced man with a short, grizzled beard and a head both balding and closely shorn, Chard is best known for two popular (in the sense of nontechnical) works, *The Cannibal Within* and *An Anthropophagic Credo: Let Us Eat What We Are.* I had not realized when I invited him to answer questions at the press conference that he was (and remains) a principal suspect. With unusual acuity, one of the wire service reporters pounced on that possibility with an insinuating question. Chief Murphy parried it adroitly, saying that no one was above suspicion. (To me afterwards Professor Chard remarked that he would never eat an old dean like Fessing, what with all that vitriol building up in him over the years.)

What possible motive could someone have for killing and eating the dean? The coroner shrugged and said, "Hunger?" He explained that one couldn't determine from the evidence that the dean had been either murdered or eaten, only that he had died and been cooked. In other words, he went on, it was possible, but not very probable, that the dean had died of natural causes and been subsequently "scavenged." After a thoughtful pause he added that most of the meat we eat — after processing, hanging, canning, et cetera — is the equivalent of carrion.

When someone asked if the dean had enemies, I responded, paraphrasing Winston Churchill I think, to the effect that any good man has enemies, but none, I hoped, to this degree. Matters were not helped much by the presence of Amanda Feeney, who fancies herself literary and covers the university as part of her cultural beat. She all but accused me of being "locked in conflict" with the dean over the "university's efforts to buy the MOM." I explained as well as I could that the museum was not for sale to anyone; that I differed with the dean about the terms and extent of future relations between the university and the museum; and that having differences with someone did not necessarily make that person an enemy. My response did not mollify Ms. Feeney in the least. In what might be called the journalistic voice — accusative interrogatory — she said, "Isn't it true that Dean Fessing was delving into some very sensitive issues at the museum and may have come across something that could have proved embarrassing had it become public?" I replied as civilly as I could that the dean, with the consent of the Director of the museum, was evaluating the possibility of incorporating the MOM as an integral part of the university. I pointed out that Dean Fessing, in his Interim Status Report to the Select Committee on Consolidation, had not alluded to any matters that might be construed as embarrassing to the museum.

The question of how the dean had been cooked was brought up by a young woman from National Public Radio deploying a curiously toneless accent in vogue in that organization. Chief Murphy took that one, saying that, for investigative purposes, certain details were not being divulged. Dr. Cutler did answer an inquiry as to how the remains had been found. It seems a retired doctor had been out walking his dog, and when the animal came back to him carrying one of the dean's humeri, he recognized it as human.

A reporter from the local television station asked if the Adventurers' Eating Club, which has a loose affiliation with Wainscott, was being investigated. Chief Murphy said that all parties would be investigated impartially and that, for the moment, members of the eating club were under no particular suspicion. I added that while it's rumored that certain members of the club had enjoyed the dubious pleasure of consuming human flesh while abroad (a very private club in Hong Kong, I'm told), the bylaws expressly forbid the preparation and consumption of human remains on the club premises.

When asked what in fact was left of the dean, Dr. Cutler replied, "Scraps," and on that rather irreverent note I declared the conference over. I suppose it was arbitrary on my part, but I think they would still be there listening to themselves if I hadn't cut it off. I'm sure the whole thing will be covered in all the papers tomorrow and on the television news this evening. I find it difficult to imagine that I will be on television. I have an old black-and-white set that my dear mother was watching when she died. I should probably dig it out and try to keep myself *au courant*. It is all too tedious.

It's been a sad day for the museum and for the university. And of all nights, I suppose this is one when an appearance at the Club is most necessary for the sake of appearances. I can only hope they haven't run out of the vegetarian special.

FRIDAY, APRIL 3

As a matter of routine, I supposed at first, I had a visit this morning from a Lieutenant Tracy of the Seaboard Police Department. It turned into a most disturbing encounter. Dark haired, square jawed, ruddy faced, the young man evinced a demeanor both respectful and skeptical as he said he wanted to ask me a few questions in the privacy of my office. I tried to be as straightforward as possible with the plainclothesman (actually he was wearing a well-cut tweed jacket and a silk tie hand-painted with linked triangles) when he asked me about my relations with the late dean. I readily admitted that I had disagreed from the very start with the objectives of Dean Fessing's mission to the MOM. I explained that the assignment of a "Visiting Administrative Dean" to an institution already associated with Wainscott has come to signal the start of a more formal consolidation.

Wainscott, he might remember from news accounts, had been publicly criticized for its so-called anomalous relationships with affiliated institutions, and this had become a matter of some concern in light of the auditing that attends federal funding, not to mention the sensitivity to adverse publicity given the plans for a major capital campaign. I recalled for him that a visiting dean had been at the Thornton Arboretum just before that fine institution was trimmed back to a mere sprig of Wainscott's Department of Botany. I told Lieutenant Tracy, who was all the time taking meticulous notes, that I was not opposed in every case to this practice. Wainscott's acquisition of the old City Observatory made sense as the place had become decrepit, and the university does have an established and well-respected Department of Astrophysics. But, I said to him, did anyone really think it was in the public interest for Newhumber Conservatory, a financially sound, well-administered school of music (I was on the board of trustees), to be reduced to a mere appendage of the Wainscott Music Department? I admitted to him that I am no great admirer of the present director, Arnie Beaumont, whose little confections I find scarcely transcend the category of random noise.

Lieutenant Tracy took all this down, and I went on to explain to him that the MOM is still not technically part of Wainscott, however complex and intertwined the affiliation has become over the years, particularly between the university and the Genetics Lab. For complete union to occur, the Board of Governors would have to dissolve itself by unanimous vote, and even then it would be possible to challenge the matter in court. I said I had spelled out my objections to the consolidation in several memoranda to Dr. Commer and to the Board itself, pointing out the clause in the Rules of Governance enabling the Recording

Secretary "from time to time and in an appropriate manner [to] inform and advise the Board relative to matters he [the Recording Secretary] deems important to the sound operation of the museum." I told Lieutenant Tracy that I had been very frank, in a cordial way, of course, with the late Dean Fessing regarding my views. And I believe I had more than a little influence on his. I showed Lieutenant Tracy the dean's Interim Status Report to the Select Committee on Consolidation, which, while citing continuing concern for the financial situation at the MOM, especially its growing reliance on the institute founded by Onoyoko Pharmaceuticals, also indicated that a way should be considered to maintain, and I quote, "the unique character of the museum, which makes it a place attractive to scholars and public alike." Those are, in fact, my own words.

The officer appeared to contemplate all this for a moment before asking who, besides myself, in what he called "the museum complex" might not want the university to take over.

To answer that I had to explain how the Genetics Lab and the Primate Pavilion were really only affiliated institutions of the MOM, that is, theoretically under the Board of Governors but in reality constituting a kind of academic free zone between the university and the museum.

The lieutenant lifted his chin just a fraction, and I thought I could detect a glint of significance in the steely, noncommittal blue of his eyes. "What do you mean by 'academic free zone'?"

"Well, for instance," I replied, "many of the researchers in both the lab and the pavilion are Wainscott faculty. But when it comes to fund-raising, say, or benefits, bonuses, patent rights, they use their extramural affiliation to do pretty much what they want to. Quite aside from that, the resulting budgetary process is skewed, I'm told, beyond the reach of chaos theory. It's the real reason, I think, the university wants to take us over. And frankly, sir, they are more than welcome to both of the other institutions, but the museum, *qua* museum, cannot be absorbed without a unanimous vote by the Board, as I've said."

Lieutenant Tracy took a moment to record all this before asking me several probing questions about Cornelius Chard and just how "active" he was in promoting cannibalism.

I began my response by trying to disabuse the officer of any correlation between what an academic advocates and what an academic practices. Wainscott, I said, abounds with the usual gaggle of tenured radicals for whom rhetoric of one sort or another constitutes a reality all its own. As perhaps it does. But I'm not sure I entirely convinced him that while Professor Chard might think it wise for some hypothetical population to eat its dead, he would probably never really consider the consumption of human flesh himself. I don't know what it was, perhaps the lieutenant's silence and the way he lifted one eyebrow, but I felt a shiver of suspicion myself about Corny Chard. The man has never seemed entirely stable. He's certainly been known to test the limits of what might be called acceptable eccentricity.

As the lieutenant scribbled diligently, I remarked, not entirely facetiously, that I thought he would make a good recording secretary. He didn't seem to find it very complimentary. Indeed, at that point he turned noticeably officious and said he would like to have copies of all the correspondence between myself, Dean Fessing, and the Board of Governors. I said it would take some digging through my files but that I would send them over to him by tomorrow evening. I also said, deputizing myself, I suppose, that I would keep a sharp lookout for anything out of the ordinary.

The lieutenant scarcely acknowledged my offer of assistance, and indeed the entire interview from that point on took a decidedly nasty turn. Did I know, he asked, what the late dean's "sexual preferences" were? I replied that I believed Cranston

Fessing to have been gay, as they say, but that he was the soul of discretion regarding his proclivities save for an incident with a graduate student some years ago that the university handled rather badly. (The student was, after all, well beyond the age of consent.) Did I know anyone the dean might have been having a "relationship" with at the time of his death? I repeated that the dean was most discreet, and that in any event I was not privy to his social life. The lieutenant glanced up sharply and asked me: "Mr. de Ratour, have you had or were you having any kind of relationship with Dean Fessing other than what related to your work at the museum?"

At first I didn't realize what the officer was insinuating. I said I had seen the dean at social functions, of course, and we were members of the Club, but he didn't play tennis or attend any of the Club's special activities, such as the annual New Year's party. With an almost admirable lack of embarrassment, the officer asked me, "What I mean, Mr. de Ratour, is have you ever had or were you having a sexual relationship with Dean Fessing?"

I shouldn't, I suppose, have been so surprised, but I was in fact utterly dismayed. When I had regained some composure, I told the lieutenant that I had had no dealings with the late dean that were not in every sense professional. I continued that while my own orientation in such matters was, strictly speaking, my own business, I led, in fact, a celibate life. I tried not to sound defensive, but I know I did. This whole issue is a real sore point with me. When a man in my situation decides to live alone and not socialize with the fair sex, it is taken these days as *prima facie* evidence that he is heteroclitic. (I happen to know that Malachy Morin has made slurs about me to this effect on more than one occasion.) The problem is compounded by the fact that I have more than one friend who is more or less than what's taken for normal, and by the fact that, however instinctively normal one's own predispositions, one learns, over time, to be tolerant where the inclinations of others are concerned. (In this matter I have come to subscribe to the dictum of my good friend Izzy Landes, who contends that the only perversion is the neglect or abuse of children.) There is something else: to pronounce oneself orthodox in a convincingly enough way, one has do so with an emphasis that can be inferred as a denigration of what is heterodox while at the same time inviting, in nearly direct proportion to one's vehemence, skepticism as to one's own real stance. I felt, in short, that my freedom of speech, or more pointedly, my freedom of silence, had been violated. I certainly was not going to go into my failed romance with Elsbeth Merriman, which occurred so many years ago, although I can admit in the privacy of this journal that that deep and tender wound feels as fresh as ever.

I could not determine whether or not I had convinced the officer of my noninvolvement with the dean, and I had by that time ceased to care. If he wanted ours to be an adversarial relation, I was quite prepared to accommodate him. He closed his notebook, signaling the end of what I realized had been a rather expert interrogation. He then took out his card, handed it to me across the desk, and said he would appreciate it if I would call him if I were planning to leave town. I nodded, took his card, and was holding it before me when it came to me with a nasty shock that I was a suspect.

"Lieutenant," I said, "surely you don't suspect *me* of perpetrating this outrage?"

It quite unnerved me the way he gazed impassively at me for a moment before saying, and I quote him verbatim: "Is there any reason why I shouldn't suspect you, Mr. de Ratour?"

Now I am familiar enough with the modes of detective fiction to know that to have protested my innocence too vehemently could have been taken as indicative of guilt. But I could not keep myself from telling him just how absurd was the notion that I had had anything whatsoever to do with Cranston Fessing's death. "Really, Lieutenant," I said, "I don't even know how to cook, except for the toast and five-minute egg I have each morning with my coffee and grapefruit. And I would never *knowingly* eat another human being. In fact, I routinely eschew red meat, as Carlos, the waiter at the Club, will tell you. Most evenings I take the catch of the day, although very occasionally I will indulge myself in a well-done joint from the standing rib, but more to go with a good wine than anything else."

The officer listened with an expressionless face as, taking out his notebook again, he recorded what I had to say. He stood finally to put on his trench coat, which made him look every inch the detective. And while he didn't shake hands, he left me with some slight assurance by asking me to let him know immediately should I see or hear or remember "anything to do with the case."

Still, I have yet to rid myself of the awful, soiling sensation of being a suspect in such a heinous crime. It somehow makes me, through the mere possibility of guilt, guilty. I certainly hope others don't start suspecting me. It's extraordinary how easily one can become a pariah in an academic community, where everyone is supposed to be so broad-minded.

TUESDAY, APRIL 7

The fog has rolled in, but the day started off beautifully, a brisk, chappy morning of juncos and jonquils, blue sky and white cloud. My matinal walk to work, which I do at a fitting cardiovascular pace, takes me through Thornton Arboretum, where, except during the most inclement weather, I go the long route, by the wooded side of Kettle Pond. There I stopped for a moment to look at the alders, their black-barked, still naked branches doubled in the sunstruck water, and there, from a certain angle, the oiled green heads of courting mallard drakes deliquesced into the brilliant reflections in a burst of shimmering motes that left me half blinded. In a calmer light, the narrow ring of white at the bottom of the drake's neck has often put me in mind of Anglican clergy. As a youth I had thought at times of taking the cloth. I'm glad now that I didn't as I have found that I have never been able to separate entirely the people I like from the people I love or must love.

But enough of this. The phone started in almost immediately with more press calls about Dean Fessing. Most of them, thank God, I was able to refer to Cornelius Chard, who not only is a veritable fount of cannibal lore but appears to be enjoying his notoriety as a suspect. I do this in part to annoy the Wainscott public relations establishment, which both objects to Chard's grandstanding and insists on referring media inquiries to the museum.

At eleven I went to Dean Fessing's memorial service in Swift Chapel. On these occasions I have begun to suffer the illusion that I see exactly the same persons in attendance each time, less one, of course, and we sit and stand and murmur the responses as though waiting patiently for our turn. And in fact I again noticed that what Izzy Landes calls the usual suspects were present. I nodded to Izzy himself and his charming wife, Lotte, as well as to Marge Littlefield and her husband, Bill, whose law firm handles some of the university's legal work. There was Thad Pilty, somewhat of a newcomer to this group; President George Twill, of course, along with a scattering of older deans and administrators; Joyce Earl, the editor of the *Wainscott News*, the university's *Pravda*, as one wag called it. Father O'Gould is also a regular, but not usually in a pastoral role except when the departed is of the Roman faith and he dons a surplice and joins the Reverend Lopes on the altar.

This morning, though, I noticed some new faces — quite aside from a gaggle of obvious sensation seekers, the kind of people who congregate at bad accidents to gawk at what has not happened to them. I mean, for instance, Malachy Morin was there, probably to show, I'm sure, that he and the late dean had no real differences regarding the finances of the MOM. I was astounded to see Damon Drex shuffle in wearing a jacket and tie. He was accompanied by the assistant he hired some months ago, a tall, ungainly young man who appears, perhaps because of pronounced upper teeth, to be constantly smirking. And I can't imagine what Corny Chard was doing there, except, perhaps, to give yet another interview to one of the reporters who are still hanging around. Speaking of which, Amanda Feeney bustled in late, nothing being sacred to the press. Being in church I tried to restrain these and other uncharitable thoughts, but it was difficult.

The Reverend Alfred Lopes certainly gave a stirring elegy. The Plumtree Professor of Christian Doctrine in the Divinity School and Minister to the Chapel, the Reverend Lopes, or Alfie, as I know him, is the first person of color to hold that position. He spoke most eloquently of Dean Fessing as a casualty in the war on ignorance. The dean's murder and its grisly aftermath were a reminder, he said, that we should not take our civilized order for granted, that we are vulnerable to lapses into unimagined barbarism, as the history of our sad century makes only too clear. I must say it was good to hear the point made so forthrightly. The Reverend Lopes, being black (actually, he's a rich shade of *café au lait*), has the freedom to be old-fashioned and even curmudgeonly in his views and practices: he forbids cameras and tourists in the chapel and holds a worship service each morning at eight during the school year. I daresay he would make attendance compulsory if he could get away with it. Without Alfie there's no telling what kind of a circus the chapel would have been turned into by now, as a white man would have had to bend to every prevailing wind or be castigated as a racist, sexist, and so on.

But as a matter of fact, the chapel remains much the same as it was more than thirty years ago, when I returned to Seaboard after Yale and a year at Oxford for my graduate studies at Wainscott. (I returned also to be with Mother, who had gone a bit batty after father's death.) Swift is quite a beautiful building — of Bulfinch Georgian graciousness with a double march of Palladian windows that lets in the enlightening sun without obviating the aura of a place concerned with more transcendent matters. I have often sat there mesmerized by the play of sunlight on the tablets of white marble ranged on the walls between the windows and incised with the names of Wainscott's war dead. They go all the way back to the French and Indian War, to an Ezekiel Hosmer and his dog Zeus. Sometimes, starting with Ezekiel and Zeus, I feel compelled to read all the names from all the wars. I think of their faces, their voices, the heartache occasioned by their deaths. Otherwise, I think to myself, what's the point in having their names there? Several were added who died during the Vietnam War, and there is, alas, plenty of room for more. Swift, in fact, is where I had always imagined that Elsbeth and I would be married, even though my tastes run to the high church edifications of Saint Cecilia's in town, where I am a communicant. I had imagined a quiet ceremony followed by a tastefully modest reception at her parents' home or at the Club and a honeymoon, perhaps in Tuscany. And even while I sometimes think it best we never married, I still rue a future that never was, an alternative life never lived.

Ah, well, poor Fessing. He was a vague sort of fellow in baggy tweeds and mustache who came into meetings with a perpetual air of impending defeat. For all that he was an able administrator, a decent man, and I did say a prayer for him if only by trying to imagine what meaning his life and awful death might have in the larger scheme of things. If there is a larger scheme of things. I certainly hope that the person or persons responsible for what happened to him are quickly apprehended and brought to justice.

Speaking of which, I experienced a curious, premonitory shudder when, at the end of the service, I turned and noticed Lieutenant Tracy by himself at the back of the church. He was standing and watching us all with the attentive circumspection of a Hercule Poirot.

MONDAY, APRIL 13

I have just gotten up and closed the window, even though it is one of those absolutely gorgeous nights when the air has its first vernal softness, which usually comes late in these latitudes. Those damned chimps. I have never felt particularly pongicidal, but tonight I swear I could walk into that place with a gun and . . . Well, I probably couldn't. They are our cousins, after all, however distant. It's simply that they don't belong here, locked up and toyed with in the name of science. They belong back in their tropical glades, picking fruit off the trees and doing whatever it is they do to each other.

Speaking of which, Damon Drex accosted me this afternoon as I was lingering in the Mesoamerican exhibit admiring some of the Aztec material, especially the array of knives and fonts which, wrought so wonderfully from chalcedony and obsidian, were used for human sacrifice. Anyway, the man seized my arm with a powerful grip and all but pinned me against the case. "I have large news, Norman," he said, torturing the language in his strange, deep monotone, his dull, yellowish brown eyes animated with an excited glee. (He is, I believe, a refugee from some Balkan or Baltic hinterland. But then he also seems one of those unfortunate types who would be a displaced person no matter where he was.) "Really?" I responded, extricating my arm from his grasp. "Oh, yes, yes," he went on. (I am quoting from memory, which, when it concerns words, is nearly photographic.) "Our experiment starts soon for interest of universe, Norman. It overtakes suspicious randomism with great jump forward for primate pedagogy." Then he laughed his toothsome laugh. "You know, Norman, ha, ha, the chimpanzee and the man keep ninety-eight percent the same DNA, ha, ha. You know how that means, Norman. It means, ha, ha, God makes man by his image, then, ha, ha, ha, God must be chimpanzee! But you must not breathe words to souls, Norman, then time ripens."

I remained, of course, noncommittal, except to say out of ordinary politeness when he pressed me, that I would consider a visit to the pavilion to see the changes in the physical plant and to see what they were doing. There is something about the man. His large teeth, perhaps. I pictured him, for a horrifying moment, as a cannibal, feeding with fiendish glee on human flesh. He is certainly the most hirsute person I have ever seen. I mean, the hair of his forearms comes down well over his knuckles. He's one of those men who shave from one hairline to another. Of course, in a jacket and bow tie at a departmental meeting, he doesn't look all that different from his colleagues.

As far as that goes, I don't know of any credentials he has as a trained primate trainer. He began at the pavilion, if I remember correctly, as an assistant in charge of feeding the chimps and gorillas (we had several more of the latter in those days) and cleaning their cages. He has a knack, apparently, for teaching the animals various tricks, and through some highly publicized stunts (he taught an old female chimp how to knit — but not purl), he has parlayed an essentially janitorial job into something approaching academic respectability, whatever that means these days. He is now, believe it or not, the Ruddy and Phyllis Stein Keeper of Great Apes in the Museum of Man. I would have thought my own position as Recording Secretary warranted endowment before one that involves little more than animal training. But then, I have not sought publicity the way Damon Drex has; nor have I stooped to the kind of genteel beggary needed to shake money out of the sort of people who launder their reputations at places like the MOM. But I am being catty. Our benefactors include many wonderful and disinterested people.

Still, as I stood there listening to him and watching his eyes, I could not rid myself of the notion that Damon Drex might be the culprit. The man certainly looks the part, and I'm sure Cranston Fessing made inquiries about the finances of the pavilion. But isn't that the insidious thing about a murder like Fessing's? After a while you start to suspect everyone — Corny Chard, Thad Pilty, Damon Drex, the poor apes themselves. I know a few people probably even think *I* did it. Just yesterday, Marge Littlefield, whom I have known forever, gave me a long, searching glance and then shook her head as though to say, *Not him.* I mean really.

Well, enough of this. I certainly am not going out of my way to provide Mr. Drex with a forum for his chimp show, however cunning the stunts. And, to judge from the interviews Malachy Morin and I conducted this morning with candidates for press assistant, it seems I will be in that position for some time. What pathetic ignorance permeates the world today! One young man, the lobes of his ears arrayed with rings, his hair dyed orange, allowed how he really "grooved" on the idea of working for a "museum of anarchy." When I corrected his misunderstanding, he nodded knowingly and said, "Yeah, man, I hear what you're saying." So Mr. Drex is going to have to put up with me for a while longer. More important, I'm afraid, is that I will not have the time to devote to working on the history of the museum. Strange, isn't it, to feel that if I wait much longer it will be too late to write such a history.

Well, enough of this. But Drex's laugh ... it's the stuff of nightmares.

Speaking of which, I found an anonymous message from someone in the Genetics Lab waiting for me in my e-mail when I returned from lunch today. I am punching it up, as they say, right into this journal:

TO: detour@mom.wain.edu
FROM: worried@genlab.wain.edu

Dear Mr. Detour: [Sic! Someone in UNINET, the university-wide e-mail system, gave me that designation, a slipup I have been trying without much success to get remedied.]

I'm sending you this message because I saw you on television after they found Professor [sic] Fessing and you seem like a nice person. I'm sending this message tracer-proof not because I don't trust you but if it got out that I told you I could lose my job and my pension and everything. There's stuff going here that's very hush-hush. One of the technicians told me that they've put hidden cameras in sensitive areas that are on 24 hours a day. And Dr. Kaplan who is usually a very nice man got mad at me when I accidentally closed the safe where they keep the protocol note-books because the safe locks automatically when it closes and they need two people to get it open. I know Dr. Kaplan was one of the senior researchers that didn't want to contribute to the sperm bank Professor Gottling set up in the specimen lab. I heard Dr. Kaplan complaining about it to Professor Gottling but when Professor Gottling asks you for something it's like an order. Charlene who's the secretary at the specimen lab says a lot of the older guys take a long time and don't come up with much. But she tells them not to worry because she can get some of the maintenance guys to fill in for them. I don't know if any of this has anything to do with Professor [*sic*] Fessing's murder but someone ought to know about it. I have got to go now but I will let you know if I find anything else.

Worried

There have been rumors for some time now, somewhat better punctuated and spelled, I hope, than this one (which I cleaned up for the record), that Stoddard Gottling has been bending if not breaking the formal and informal restraints normally placed on genetics research and applications. But I don't see what that would have to do with the murder of Cranston Fessing. Unless . . . Unless the consolidation would mean the termination of some project . . . No, it's too fantastical. Or is it? In crime as in art and science and life, one must consider all the possibilities.

I suppose I should send a copy of this communication over to Lieutenant Tracy. But, frankly, I doubt very much that it has anything to do with the Fessing case, about which I can report no breaks. Amazing, isn't it, how quickly interest in the most hideous of crimes fades away. I haven't heard from the lieutenant in a week, and life around here has resumed its unpunctuated equilibrium.

Speaking of the late dean, there have been some rather tasteless jokes circulating about his fate. I hear someone has come up with a "Decanal Cookbook" and is soliciting recipes over the e-mail network. Even my friend Izzy Landes has not been impervious to this ghoulish ribaldry. Last Friday I ran into him in the Club library. Over coffee we got to talking about the dean, and about what had happened and what was happening, when he asked me, with that mischievous sidelong glance of his, what I thought "they served Fessing with."

"What do you mean?" I said.

"The wine, Norman, the wine. Was it a red or a white? Red I would think, a Bordeaux, but not a *premier cru*."

I tutted at him, but his face was a moon of mirth. "Really," he went on, "what are we, after all, red meat or white meat?"

I tutted again and told him he had been spending too much time with Corny Chard.

Well, I must say it's good to get back to this unofficial Log after nearly a week. I feel as though I could go on writing for another hour. Perhaps, though, I am simply reluctant go out into that good night, which will, I know, remind me of Elsbeth, and I will arrive at the Club in a maudlin state and perhaps drink more wine than is good for me.

THURSDAY, APRIL 16

Despite a contretemps today with the egregious Mr. Morin and the worthies of the Wainscott Public Relations Office, I have been in an absolute dither of aesthetic bliss since yesterday afternoon. Perhaps I should describe the unpleasantness first.

Upon arrival this morning I learned that the university has appointed someone named Oliver Scrabbe to succeed Cranston Fessing as Visiting Dean to the Museum of Man. All well and good. (Although I had hoped that the university might desist in its plans after what happened to Fessing, not that good should come from evil, although it often does.) At any rate, a Mr. Bells or Balls in the Wainscott Public Relations Office called to tell me that he was faxing over Dean Scrabbe's CV and that I was to draft a press release announcing the appointment and send it over to them for approval. I refused on the simple grounds that I do not report to anyone at Wainscott and that the appointment is being made by the university and not by the museum.

As I should have expected, they went over my head to Malachy Morin, who came lumbering into my office with a "what's this about our not writing the press release for the new dean?" I told him quite simply that I don't see why we should do their work for them, especially since they, along with everyone else, deserted me when there was a real public relations crisis. I insinuated that his toadying to the Wainscott bureaucracy was a form of cowardice, especially for someone as big and strong as he was. It was enough to make him beat a quick retreat, and I nearly felt sorry for him when his secretary, Doreen, an attractive but hard-faced, gum-chewing type, brought me a page of the most pathetic copy. Apparently he had tried to get her to write it. I finally decided to help them. It would have been just like him to put the thing out under my name, and I don't want to get off on a poor footing myself with Oliver Scrabbe, who must be a brave man, considering Dean Fessing's fate.

I don't really know much about the man. He doesn't play tennis, as far as I know, and I haven't seen him at the Club. It would appear from his *curriculum vitae* that he is another scholar turned administrator. The title of his Ph.D. thesis, "Elements of Philo-Semitism in the Writings of Adolph Schicklgruber: A Deconstructionist Reading of *Mein Kampf*," indicates he is some kind of language theorist. I assume he will be going over the late dean's files, including copies of my memoranda to Dr. Commer and the Board. Somehow I will have to call his attention to my views on the proposed consolidation in a way that doesn't sound repetitious. Perhaps I could talk Dr. Commer into a response to the Interim Status Report, which I will write, of course, and in which I will stress our wholehearted endorsement of the late dean's recognition of our unique status *vis-à-vis* the university. Perhaps I can get to it next week, although I will be spending more time with Malachy Morin, interviewing another batch of candidates for the press assistant position. All this busywork. I simply must find time if I am to start work on the history of the museum.

But I also have some good news. I received by registered mail yesterday morning a miniature Ming Buddha carved in ivory. It's no more than an inch and half high in a full lotus position, and the ivory has aged beautifully, giving the Gautama's genial face an old and wise aspect. And while it's going to cost me a small ransom (I have it on spec from Remstein's of New York), I have such a perfect place for it that I will simply have to have it. The wonderful thing about collecting is that one can indulge and invest at the same time, although I cannot conceive of cashing in a single one of my precious things before I cash in myself. Anyway, I showed the piece to Esther Sung Lee, whose office is right next to mine. I know it is genuine, of course, Eliot Remstein being who he is; but I don't think I have seen Esther so enthusiastic about a piece of mine since the white Qing snuff bottle with a dragon carved in blue overlay that I acquired some ten years ago. (Esther also knows that my collection will go to the museum.)

I left work early and hurried home with my treasure safely tucked under my arm in its packing box. I knew exactly where I was going to put it. For several years now, I have been nurturing a small grove of red cedar bonsai arranged in a semicircle at one end of a redwood planter measuring roughly two by three feet. The sides come up about six inches, giving it the appearance, what with soil, moss that passes for grass, and sand that simulates gravel, of a walled garden. Not long ago I found for it a shallow dish of milky jade that I set into a bed of tiny pebbles so that it looks exactly like a goldfish pool. Well, I cannot tell you how exquisitely my little Buddha fits in, seated just on the lawn in front of the trees contemplating the pool. If only I could find some tiny, tiny goldfish!

The arrangement is such a success I have placed it on the gateleg table in the window alcove of the living room. I think it calls for a dinner party. On the other hand, perhaps it doesn't. I already think of my little garden as a refuge, a place in my mind where, serene as Buddha, inhaling the fragrance of cedars, I contemplate the peace of the void.

Speaking of voids, the fog appears to have kept Mr. Drex and his beasts at bay for the night. And there's a concert at the Conservatory to look forward to, even though the Newhumber Players will more than likely make a hash of the Dvořák Piano Quintet in A, and there's the obligatory piece of noise by a student of Beaumont, and then one of those infinitely sad, infinitely beautiful late pieces by Brahms. Strange, when I think of it, how Elsbeth never cared much for Brahms.

TUESDAY, APRIL 21

A gorgeous cardinal and a flock of neatly bibbed chickadees, which looked in contrast like clergy of a lesser rank, curates, perhaps, graced my bird feeder this morning. One of those quirky late-season storms had mantled the scene — porch railing, feeder, rosebushes, and hedge of hemlock — with an inch or so of snow. And as I sipped tea and contemplated it from the kitchen table, a wonderful tranquillity descended on me. My back garden is one of the things that keeps me in this old place that Mother bought after Father died. It's really too large for my personal needs — I could easily do most of my entertaining at the Club. But there's my collection, and I feel I've grown into the place, a modest enough Federalist structure at heart that came out of the Greek Revival of the mid–nineteenth century with a colonnaded entrance, pediments galore, and half-moon windows set into the tympanums at either end of the house.

My Neoclassical tranquillity didn't last very long. By the time I started for work, the sun had turned the snow to slush, and I arrived to find Lieutenant Tracy standing in my office perusing on the wall opposite the bookcase some of the awards and citations I have received over the years. (In 1977 I was named Recording Secretary of the Year by the American Association of Recording Secretaries, and in 1982 I received the much-coveted Order of Merit for Undocumented Excellence, just to name a few.)

The door was open, he said to my rather frosty good morning. As a professional lawman he remained apparently impervious to any sense of trespass. I had scarcely hung my overcoat on the coatrack that stands sentinel near the door when he had his little spiral notebook out and had started in. It all seemed quite routine, the blandness and repetition of the questions, I mean. I nearly yawned when he flipped back through pages of his notebook, paused, then said, "You told me, Mr. de Ratour, that you don't cook except for a boiled egg and tea in the morning."

Although not a shrugger, I shrugged. "I can make a tuna fish salad sandwich, and I know how to heat a store-bought chicken pot pie in the oven," I replied. I glanced at my watch to indicate the *soupçon* of irritation I was beginning to feel.

The lieutenant remained nonplussed. "I've been told you give very good dinner parties."

"Oh," I said, getting the drift of his questions and controlling with an effort a welling sense of dread, "but I don't do any of the cooking, any of the real cooking." I explained how Marge Littlefield sometimes drops by beforehand to help out, or, if I'm having more than a few people in, how I get Yvette and her husband, Gideon, to come over. They're excellent cooks, especially of this blackened Cajun stuff, although they do leave quite a dent in the sherry. I said I have used caterers, but I find the food, despite all the froufrou, a bit insipid.

The lieutenant, tweedily enough dressed to suggest he was trying to go undercover in academia, took this down and flipped again through his notebook. "I've been told you make a very good pesto sauce."

For a moment I didn't know quite how to respond. I was both gratified to hear my pesto praised and appalled that someone, presumably a friend, would tell the police about it. The dread grew to a kind of nausea. I became acutely aware that I was being "grilled" as a suspect, that this other person — however much it was his duty — thought it possible that I was a murderous cannibal. And as I hadn't told the lieutenant earlier about my pesto sauce, I began to feel perversely guilty, not of murder or cannibalism but of withholding evidence. I tried to frown but laughed guiltily instead. "Lieutenant," I said, attempting to sound nonchalant, "making pesto is more like mixing a drink than cooking." I explained to him how I use nothing but a few handfuls of fresh basil, which I render with olive oil in the blender to a kind of green slurry. To this I add grated pecorino, crushed walnuts, a touch of pressed garlic, salt, pepper, a squeeze of lemon, and — my secret ingredient — some finely chopped dried tomatoes.

He took this down, nodding as though with approval, as though he were going to try it himself. "What kind of a food processor do you use?" he asked.

"Oh," I said, trying to be helpful, "just the old Waring blender my mother had." Only then did it occur me what he was doing. Extraordinary, I thought, the way a detective's mind must work, the way suspicion gets raised nearly to an art form.

A forlorn art form. When the lieutenant finally left, going in the direction of Malachy Morin's office, I fell into a state of what I can only call nervous depression out of which nothing — my

Buddha, my collection, the museum, thoughts of friends, the work on the history — nothing could rouse me. The very air seemed blighted. Not only my own life but all life seemed a beastly, futile attempt to rise above itself. That another person, even though it was his duty, could consider me capable of such depravity left me crushed beyond words. I answered the telephone — a routine call about scheduling a meeting — and spoke like an automaton. I shriveled inwardly until there seemed nothing left of my spirit but a dying ember of anger.

It didn't die. I wouldn't let it. I nursed it to a flame of real anger, a kind of unfocused rage against the slings and arrows of outrageous misfortune. I quite worked myself into an elated anger, or perhaps an angry elation, during which I resolved, with a solemn inner vow, to find the murderer myself. I got quite carried away with the idea. In classic style I saw myself assembling the likely suspects in, say, Neanderthal Hall, or, better, the Twitchell Room, where, with my clues and evidence marshaled and with ineluctable deduction, I would expose the foul miscreant. And then, having allowed myself the sour pleasure of this fancy, I felt committed to undertake what at first glance I am not in the least suited for. I doubt, for instance, that I have the lieutenant's knack for suspicion. Nor do I have what's appropriately called "the killer instinct." I have neither a badge nor a gun, which is to say authority. On the other hand, am I not a trained archaeologist, that is, an investigator, one given to literally digging for evidence, sifting for clues, even though it probably was, in my case, a sublimated search for beauty?

With an agitation now invigorating, I stood and began to pace the diagonal of my office, which is exactly ten of my indoor strides. I moved as though to keep up with my mind as it pondered more deeply the murder and mutilation (which is what cooking is, after all) of Dean Cranston Fessing. Why the good dean? Why the elaborate disposal of his remains? Why no attempt to effectively hide the remains of his remains? Was he simply the chance victim of some demonic cult? Or was it done to make it look that way? Or — and this is when I started to feel truly excited — *both!* I began, like Inspector Morse, to see the outlines of a design, a kind of fearful symmetry, a perverse beauty wherein not merely the dean's demise but the manner of it was precisely what his mission to the Museum of Man had, perhaps inadvertently, threatened. In murdering and disposing of the dean the way they did, the perpetrators had, so to speak, their cake in the very eating of it.

I sat down and began to compile a list of suspects, if only because suspicion is my weak suit. To suspect someone of such depravity, after all, takes a kind of imagination, a kind of creative paranoia. I began with Corny Chard because he is, conventionally, the most obvious suspect and therefore the least likely to be guilty. Moreover, he lacks, as far as I know, a motive in the specific case of Dean Fessing. I certainly put Damon Drex down, but without a whole lot of conviction. He's too obsessed with his apes. . . . Although any consolidation with the university could have adversely affected his operation. And the culinary aspects. Unless he's some kind of closet gourmet. Then Thad Pilty. Again, my powers of suspicion failed me. And yet, of all of them, Thad has the most to lose from merger with Wainscott. The late dean had put all major projects on hold, including Thad's plans to turn Neanderthal Hall into a dioramic monument to his own research. I listed Malachy Morin as well, but more out of spite than conviction. I can, if I really try, imagine Morin and his pals sitting around like savages with cans of beer and feasting on the dean — had he been, say, roasted whole on a spit. Otherwise the cuisine is all wrong.

I concluded the morning in a state of rare self-satisfaction. I determined not to let my "investigation" interfere either with my regular duties or with my plans to write a history of the museum.

I determined to become, in the tradition of all amateur sleuths, a deal more sensitive to seemingly irrelevant details, to keep, in short, my eyes and ears open.

And speaking of Mr. Morin, I must confess to indulging in a bit of backhandedness. Just before he left this morning, the lieutenant asked me if I could recall anything, any incident, any remark, that seemed suspicious to me. Well, after a moment's thought — under normal circumstances I wouldn't have done this — I told him that on the morning of the news conference Malachy Morin had left the office early and had not returned until the following day. I pointed out that considerable concern had been expressed by the late dean in his Interim Status Report to the Select Committee on the accounting procedures in Mr. Morin's office, enough concern, in fact, to "warrant immediate attention." Now I did say that I thought it unlikely, though not impossible, that Mr. Morin, while a man of large and low appetites, had anything to do with Dean Fessing's fate. I said that the Administrative Director's absence more likely stemmed from moral cowardice and habitual sloth — a good deal of work, after all, was involved in "managing" and disseminating the news on that day. I told the lieutenant that Mr. Morin, as Administrative Director of the MOM, knew, or should know, a good deal about the workings and finances of the museum and that it was possible that a certain amount of interrogatory pressure might be fruitful. The lieutenant thanked me cordially and set off in the direction of Mr. Morin's office.

FRIDAY, APRIL 24

I learned today a piece of startling and what may be significant news: funding for "The Diorama of Paleolithic Life" was granted final approval yesterday at a meeting of Malachy Morin's "executive committee" convened in an "executive" session, which means I was excluded from taking its minutes. It's clear as day to me that Professor Pilty is acting on his pet project before the new Visiting Dean can get established. Which means that in a quite tangible way he has benefited from the murder of the late dean. Now this is not to accuse Thad Pilty of complicity, but, as I noted in the black notebook I have begun to keep on my own investigation, it does give him a strong motive.

There is another consideration. I do not want to sound a captious note, but it happens that any "executive" sessions are in direct contravention of the museum's Rules of Governance. The Rules explicitly state that "no meeting regarding significant expenditures of monies within and by the Museum shall be held without said proceedings being duly recorded and entered into the Log by the Recording Secretary." The only "executive" meetings allowed are those by the Board itself and only for certain matters as are spelled out in the Rules of Governance as amended November 12, 1923, at the Board's annual meeting.

I want the record to show that it is not simply the professional insult to me with which I am concerned. This is not the first "executive session" in which large expenditures have been approved. The Genetics Lab within the past year has hired new staff and expanded into the old Punnett Annex after considerable renovation and enlargement of that venerable building. And, from what I have heard, Damon Drex, besides destroying the old courtyard by turning it into an exercise area for his animals, has revamped the entire first floor of the Primate Pavilion and called it, believe it or not, Pan House. I am more convinced than ever that the increasing presence and influence of Edo Onoyoko and his minions throughout the MOM does not bode well for the future of the museum. As I pointed out last year in my Annual Report to the Board, we are witnessing the emergence of a budgetary process that, whatever its temporary advantages, will prove less than salutary in the long run.

It's common knowledge that I have been opposed to the Paleolithic diorama from the start. In several memoranda to Dr. Commer with copies to Professor Pilty, I pointed out that while the current exhibit (which Pilty dismisses as "Alley Oop under glass") could use some updating, it did not warrant turning the entire ground floor of the atrium into a Paleolithic fun house. I didn't use those words, of course, but I may as well have. I noted that if the entire space is usurped for the diorama, there will be little room left for temporary exhibitions, although we are not mounting as many of those as I think we should be. Finally, I pointed out that the ground floor has traditionally been used for the annual Curatorial Ball. I know this doesn't sound of great consequence, but in fact the ball is the one event we have each year that brings the entire museum together, and the sense of morale and united purpose that it provides is not to be discounted.

I should explain, perhaps, that each year between Thanksgiving and Christmas we decorate the hall with ribbons and crepe streamers. We deck out Herman, the alpha Neanderthal, in a Santa suit. We chip in for a champagne bar and hire the Wainscott Warblers, who play all the old favorites as well as Christmas music. It is a most beautiful occasion, at which we all let down our hair, as they say. I get to dance with the ladies, especially Margery Littlefield, who on one very memorable occasion . . . But I won't go into that. Suffice it to say that I have been driven home from more than one Curatorial Ball, but then everyone is a little abashed the following Monday. And while there are other possible venues, it simply would not be the same. Moving the ball elsewhere will, I fear, destroy the special meaning this event has for all of us just at a time when we need all the morale we can get.

Because this Fessing business is getting to everyone. There's a poison in the air. I had the distinct feeling when I went into the cafeteria this morning to fetch my usual cup of coffee that people lowered their voices. How to explain to them that Lieutenant Tracy's visits to me are "routine"? All the more reason, I find, to pursue my own investigation and to keep up an honest, brave front.

MONDAY, APRIL 27

Is writer's block, of the short-term kind at least, nothing more than memory block? I had been sitting here watching the sunset — a glorious shelfing of clouds underlit by ethereal reds and somber mauves — and feeling heavy with the accumulated events of the day, which the practiced diarist needs discharge into words. Only I could remember nothing. Or, to be precise, I could remember nothing when I took keyboard in hand, so to speak, and tried to write. I had to reconstruct my day, starting with breakfast, my morning walk through the arboretum (where a goldfinch, my favorite bird, flew in its roller-coaster flight from a clump of forsythia, as though a part of the bush had broken off and taken wing), then my cup of coffee from the cafeteria, which, as usual, provoked a productive visit to the men's room, at which point in my retrospective musings, I was quite deluged with recollections of the rest of the day.

As part of my own inquiry into the murder of Dean Fessing, I made an appointment to follow up on numerous requests to tour Pan House, as the troglodyte floor of the Primate Pavilion is now called. Although I have never thought much of all that Freudian business (bad science and worse art), I may in fact have repressed my memory of what happened because of what I saw and heard in the south wing of the Museum of Man.

I was met at the entrance to Pan House (What next, a coat of arms?) by a smilingly unctuous Damon Drex ("Norman, Norman, my friend, how good you come"). He was accompanied by his assistant, the same youngish man I saw him with at the service for Dean Fessing. Frans or Franz Snyders, as he introduced himself, has, I heard somewhere, some kind of connection with the Wainscott English Department. He shook my hand and spoke in a slow, toneless voice in which I detected a note of insinuating knowingness. I found something vaguely disturbing about his strongly featured face — nose, eyes, and teeth all prominent under a shag of dark hair — and the way his ostensible seriousness appeared to mask a kind of malignant facetiousness, making him seem an amused, toothy Svengali.

"Franz or Frans?" I asked. "With a z or an s?"

"Either." He smiled.

Well, small wonder eyebrows have been raised of late about Mr. Drex's spending. Gone are the dismal cages where the poor beasts used to hang forlornly on the bars. This was more like a suite of offices. A fluorescent-lit corridor led between glassed-in cubicles, each equipped with a kind of chimp desk, to which was secured a keyboard much like the one I am using now except larger. I could see the animals busily typing away with great seriousness, pausing only to glance up at color monitors filled with all manner of moving signs. In fact, it wouldn't have appeared much different from any number of business offices I have been in except for, well, mostly, the droppings.

We paused outside the cubicle of Howler, where I noticed that, at a certain signal on the screen, the ape would inspect a small compartment with a hinged door next to the keyboard. The assistant explained that the animals love M&Ms and that one or two of these candies is programmed to fall into the compartment

when they do something conducive to the production of literature. For instance, he told me, simply by spending enough time
"typing" on the keyboard, animals will receive an M&M every
half hour. They are also rewarded if, at suitable intervals, they
press the space bar. If they press it too much, of course, they are
not rewarded. But, he continued, as though amused by it somehow, if they learn to alternate vowels and consonants, they are
further rewarded. Certain combinations, such as *ate, ead, pre,
tion, ack, eck, ick, ock, uck,* and so on, garner small windfalls of
M & M's, as does the typing of actual words. "In a way," he said
with a sly smile, "it's not all that different from how nonchimp
writers work."

We stopped at another "office," where a large and ferocious-
looking male was bent over the keyboard. "This is Royd," Drex's
assistant said. "He's the alpha male, and we have great expectations for him."

As you might imagine, I was quite aghast at all this. I am not
exaggerating when I say that the reconstruction, with all the new
lighting, glass work (actually, shatterproof plastic), and electronic systems, must have cost hundreds of thousands of dollars.
Who paid for all this? I wanted to ask. Where is oversight when
we need it?

The corridor opened onto a "rec" room equipped with a
television set, in front of which some of the residents sat quietly
watching reruns of *I Love Lucy.* Franz or Frans told me that they
limit the amount of television the chimps are allowed to watch.
"We are concerned," he said, "about the adverse effect exposure
to television, especially the prime-time shows, could have on
their intelligence." Again the faint, goofy, sidelong smile, leaving
me to feel as though I were walking through the middle of a bad
joke. We watched a couple of animals playing a game of table
tennis that he called, with open amusement, "pong-pong." Right
next to the rec room was a food preparation area that looked to

me like any large and well-stocked kitchen. Marge Littlefield has mentioned that the pavilion has held, at considerable expense, catered dinners for its residents.

As we were about to move along, a door just in front of us swung open. A maintenance worker brought a dolly loaded with boxes across the threshold, and I managed to glimpse a remnant of the old pavilion. I could see a truncated double row of dim cages with their inmates gazing numbly through the bars, a veritable dungeon compared with the fluorescent dazzle of the renovated area. In front of the cages I saw a gurney on which lay what appeared to be a draped form. Not far beyond, I realized as I got my bearings, was the crematorium. The assistant quickly shut the door. RESTRICTED, a sign on it stated in red letters. AUTHORIZED PERSONNEL ONLY. I nearly asked if the unfortunate denizens of that place were authorized personnel. "What goes on in there?" I asked instead.

The two men exchanged glances. "It's AIDS work."

"With the Medical School?" I asked.

"Yes."

"Strange," I said. "I've not heard about us doing any research on AIDS at the MOM."

"It's very hush-hush," the assistant said, and with a key he opened another door to a driveway outside, where a large vehicle was parked. "That's what we call our Pan Van," he went on, obviously to distract my attention. "We use it to take the writing group for outings." And he gave his miserable laugh.

"It stirs their brains," Drex said. "Most extraordinary, yes," he went on as we entered his office, which I took at first to be another, somewhat enlarged cubicle for one of the chimpanzees. "But you must protect with your hat, Norman."

"My hat?" I said.

"Keep it to yourself," the assistant interpreted.

"Keep what to myself?" I asked, preoccupied by a previously

unconscious prickling of recognition nearly emerging as a tantalizing realization: Drex reminds me of someone I know but can't quite place. Drex is on the squat side, with a longish torso, long arms, and short, powerful legs. His skull slopes down to bushy eyebrows that beetle over prominent supraorbital ridges, under which his eyes seem to have withdrawn as though into caves. Then there's a lump of a nose, a wide mouth full of big, square teeth, and a weak chin, but maddeningly, neither could I then nor can I now recall who it is he reminds me of.

He took my arm just at the elbow and said, "Our project, Norman, our project. We show the world how random is random. We show . . . How you say . . . ?"

His assistant interceded again, the flattened tones of a professional translator not quite concealing the note of manic glee. "We are in the process of demonstrating that random text creation by a finite number of text-producing entities using state-of-the-art text-recording equipment can, within acceptable parameters, produce enough textual material from which to reliably extrapolate the amount of time and producers it would take for the production of the entire literary canon as it is variously described."

It took a moment to sink in. "You mean the old monkeys and typewriters thing?" I was appalled.

"Not monkeys," Drex said.

The assistant smiled.

"Whatever will be your criterion?" I asked, incredulous.

Drex released my arm finally. "We settle standards, yes, Franz?"

The assistant nodded. "We are using a combination of actual text and mathematical extrapolation. The output from each of the writers is being fed into the mainframe, the same one we all use. Each morning Dr. Drex and I go over the output from the day before. We have a text-recognition program that underlines anything that looks like it might be from the canon." Then he quickly added, "Of course, the canon isn't what it used to be, so it shouldn't be that difficult. The Modern Language Association has already expressed an interest in publishing the results."

"But what is the point of that?" I asked, incredulous as ever. The dull gleam of Damon Drex's narrowed, remote eyes had an edge of mania. "Point, Norman? You ask point?" Then he laughed. "Point, ha, ha, how you say, a fun pun, is break the balloon of man's prideness."

"But it will just be random," I protested.

"Yes, yes, random."

I laughed myself, deprecatingly of course. But when he took my jeer as assent to his craziness, I shook my head. "But literature is not random." I groped for meaning myself. "If anything at all, literature is an attempt to render coherent the seeming chaos of life." I know I sounded like a Sunday school teacher, but in the face of such mocking nihilism, I didn't know what else to say. "I mean, literature at least *tries* to give form to what happens — from the founding myths of the world and its tribes to the little domestic melodramas of today. Literature encompasses our most noble thoughts and sentiments. . . . It gives purpose . . . and pleasure of the most exalted kind. It's what makes us human."

Damon Drex's large, grotesque head went from side to side, and I recoiled from his repellent smile. "Oh, Norman, my friend Norman," he cooed, his condescension like an oily ooze in the air, "we make you to see the light."

"A dim light," I replied. "More like the darkness."

He liked that. He poked his assistant. "Yes, yes, Frank, ha, ha. . . . We make Norman to see the darkness."

Because I could not keep the disgust from my face, I turned away. I gestured out the door. "How are you getting funding for this . . ." I nearly said "nonsense."

The man's brows furrowed for a moment, and his eyes went

hard and suspicious before he recovered his unctuous affability. "We have our means. But we are only begin, yes, Franz? Monkeys and pigeons do same. But no. Franz will say, how, we make history real . . ."

The younger man's nod was like a shrug of modesty. "Dr. Drex is alluding to the second, concurrent stage of our experiment. Once the writers have learned to manipulate the keys and built their vocabularies, we will start teaching them to write their own sentences."

"Why?" I asked. With what I was hearing, with the smells and the animals screeching about something right next door, I truly felt I had landed in a madhouse.

The assistant shrugged again. "Actually, it's nothing that new. Chimps were taught to use computers back in the seventies."

Damon Drex was nodding vigorously. "Yes, yes, Frank is right. Remember you Lana, a chimpanzee schooled in Nevada. She make sentence, 'You green shit . . .' "

"But that's not part of the canon," the assistant interrupted. "Not yet, anyway."

"But we land beyond, yes, Frank?"

His switching of names made it seem he was speaking to two or more people. And in the craziness of the moment, it all seemed part of it.

"Oh, of course. We expect to get nothing less than chimpanzee poetry, short stories, novels, screenplays, murder mysteries, even theory and criticism. We expect to produce nothing less than a pongid literature." That mocking, toothsome rictus again, and yet he sounded utterly convincing as he added, "We are even thinking of starting a creative writing program."

"What in the world do you think they will write about?" I asked.

He appeared to speculate for a moment. "I guess they'll probably write a lot about their relationships with other chimps.

Chimp love stories. Chimp coming-of-age stories. Oh, you know, accounts by young male chimps of how they worked through their relationships with their fathers. I imagine the female chimps will also write about relationships, failed love affairs and parenting and grooming and their relationships with their mothers. I see chimps writing about how tough it is to be chimps."

"Yes, yes," Drex was saying, bouncing on the balls of his feet. "Yes, Franz, tell Norman plans for —"

But Frans or Franz or Frank was shaking his head. "Later," he said.

Drex had me once again in his grip. "And we number on you, Norman, when time arrives. I mean for presses. We do some leaking, for, how you say, for wetting hungers."

I was utterly at sea. I merely looked at them and asked, "Why?"

"Why how?" said Drex.

"This whole undertaking."

The man's eyes narrowed and withdrew again as he seized and released my arm once more. But he was speechless. He turned to his assistant, who merely shrugged. "Think of it as an exercise in randomness. Or, as Beckett said, who cares who wrote it?"

"But, but," I stuttered, "it still matters what gets written."

"We're not entirely sure of that anymore."

"Well," I said, "I'm certainly at a loss for words."

"You have lost words?" Drex seemed alarmed.

"More than words," I replied. "To be perfectly frank."

"Perfectly Frank?" The Ruddy and Phyllis Stein Keeper of Great Apes scowled for a moment, then gave his awful laugh. "You are funny man, Norman, funny man."

And sitting here now, listening to the latest literary crowd yapping and howling in their compound below, I have to admit to a morbid fascination with the whole thing. I mean, if they ever do get a chimpanzee to bare his soul, what do they expect to find?

More to the point, I wonder what all this might have to do with the murder of the dean. Old Fessing would have rolled his eyes at that circus and smelled a rat. I mean, where has Drex been getting the funds to finance his preposterous boondoggle? Was Fessing investigating that? Why do I feel suspicious just being in that place? If my suspicions were more acute, I might trust them more. But I have to remember I am still only an amateur in this business.

THURSDAY, APRIL 30

There has been a development that may or may not have a bearing on the Fessing case. I learned quite by happenstance today that Thad Pilty has agreed to allow the university's Oversight Committee to hold hearings on the form and content of his proposed diorama of Paleolithic life. This is the first time I know of that this body, the University Oversight Committee on Sensitive Issues, to give it its full thwacking title, has been allowed to meddle in the affairs of the museum, where it has no warrant. I say "meddle" even though at least two of its members, Izzy Landes and Father O'Gould, are friends of mine. (They joined to give the committee some balance after it voted, at the insistence of the Science for the Masses group, to ban *sociobiology* from the list of approved words in the Wainscott Language Code.) And I would be less than honest if I did not admit to a certain conflict of feelings in that part of me wants the committee to come in and scuttle Thad Pilty's little project, something, I am told, it is perfectly capable of doing.

There's another aspect of this oversight business that puzzles me exceedingly: Thad Pilty has long been a vociferous champion of the museum's independence. While he holds his professorial appointment at Wainscott along with the rest of the faculty who are associates or curators at the museum, this has not kept him from supporting me in my sometimes lonely battle to preserve the integrity of the MOM. I know he objected at the highest levels to the appointment of Dean Fessing, knowing very well what that appointment would eventually entail. I know he shares my fear that if the university takes over, the exhibition space will get whittled down to nothing and he will no longer have a venue for the well-publicized exhibitions of his field research that he has mounted over the years. Surely he understands that to allow the Oversight Committee to review his diorama is to allow the university to get its heaviest foot in the door of the museum.

It has made me reach for my detective cap (figuratively a deerstalker) and want to summon a hypothetical Dr. Watson with whom to share my darker speculations. For instance: If Thad Pilty is involved with the Fessing mess, might not the acceptance of the Oversight Committee's purview be a ploy, a way of showing he has nothing to hide? Or does it show, *au contraire*, that he has nothing to hide and simply wants that fact established? No one, after all, other than the half-mad Chard, has enjoyed being a suspect in this case. Perhaps. What I can't shake is the intuition that this oversight business fits into a larger picture of the whole grisly mess that flits and fades in the nether reaches of my consciousness.

I should say that it is only reluctantly that I question Thad Pilty's character. I have long admired his work, despite a good deal of muttering among his peers as to the significance he assigns his various finds. He is, of course, the Pilty who discovered and excavated the well-preserved remains and artifacts of Lucille and her family in a cave in the Dordogne. His subsequent book, *Lucille: The Human Dimension*, although I do not agree with its main premise, is a thoughtful, thought-provoking attempt to define what we mean when we say human. He expatiates at great length that it is not just tools but a panoply of tool-making tools, tool-using activities, and what he calls a "tool ethos," constituting a paleotechnology that enabled early man to develop agricultural civilization. Izzy Landes pointed out the limits of this approach in the piece he did for *The New York Review of Books*. He sees Pilty's hierarchy of values putting a premium on gadgetry. As Izzy remarked, "[Pilty's thesis] might have us believe that the Hollywood hack, hunched over his 'state-of-the-art' word machine, is superior to the Bard scribbling away with quill and inkwell." I couldn't have said it better myself.

I should say also that I like Thad Pilty personally. He is a large, squarish man with a sharp, eager face. He sports an Amish-style beard, bow ties, and well-cut tweeds, and remains one of the few people around here with tenure who still looks like a professor. (The younger generation, I've noticed, affect leather jackets and Bertolt Brecht haircuts while cultivating curt, vile manners.) Pilty in short is a gentleman and a scholar, and he plays a spirited if somewhat distracted game of doubles.

But then, Professor Pilty is ambitious. He wants, I believe, to embody his ideas in this diorama, to erect, in short, a monument to his research. And to get his precious diorama, he appears willing to sell out the museum, if not his soul. Which is what makes me speculate.

Putting a stop to the diorama is not something, unfortunately, I'm in a position to do myself. I have checked back through the Rules of Governance and the founding documents of the museum, and while it is nowhere stated explicitly that the ground floor of the atrium should be reserved for temporary exhibitions, tradition and precedent surely have established that to be the accepted practice. But tradition isn't what it used to be. Thad Pilty's project involves nothing less than the usurpation of common space by the Hominid Collections. Quite frankly, were the Director and the Board of Governors operating as they have in the past, i.e., responsive to my occasional and, I like to think, pertinent memoranda, this never would have happened.

I have tried, through indirect means, to alert the Council of Curators about what the diorama will mean to opportunities for them to mount exhibitions in their own specialties. But except for Baldwin Jones, who, as a curatorial assistant, takes care of the African Collections, no one has heeded my warnings. And Baldwin's acknowledgment sounded more like his usual politeness than any voicing of real concern. The curators, of course, want to cultivate their own little gardens, restoring, preserving, labeling, and researching the artifacts of their specialties. I can understand, sympathize with, and even envy them their narrow passions. I would no doubt be the same. But the very magic that enchants them is something that should be shared with the world. That is why museums are places for the public to visit. That is why, ultimately, the curators are curating what they curate.

Of course, the moment the diorama is installed they will start complaining bitterly that they no longer have space for the special exhibitions they are so reluctant to mount in the first place. And when the time comes for the Curatorial Ball, they will all be wondering aloud why it has to be held in some drab rented hall with no Herman to play Santa Claus. It's not the same, they will say, as they lift their champagne glasses and grouse to one another about the lack of planning and administration at the museum. And they will be right.

Be that as it may, Malachy Morin must also share some of the blame for allowing the Oversight Committee into the museum. It is another instance when he should have stepped in on behalf of the MOM, but I think he sees little or no difference between the MOM and Wainscott. I have heard, in fact, that he is bent on becoming a university vice president. (I must say I took some low pleasure in the look on his face after Lieutenant Tracy got finished with him last week.)

But then, I do not pretend to understand Mr. Morin in the least. Yesterday when I was in his office, having been summoned there on one pretext or another, he began to regale a friend of his from Wainscott Administration with a story about the Queen of England being on the BBC radio show *Twenty Questions*. I remember listening to it myself, years ago, on the wireless I had in my digs at Jesus. As everyone knows, the audience on this program is given the answer to the question, which in this case, according to Mr. Morin, was "blackcock." The contestant, of course, has twenty questions to ask of a panel of three judges in order to ascertain the answer. All of this Mr. Morin explained to his friend and to me, as I was standing there, with a hilarity I could not in the least fathom. According to his account of the broadcast, the first question the Queen put to the panel was "Can you eat it?" Now that struck me as a perfectly reasonable question, but it was one which had Mr. Morin and his friend, through a kind of contagion, nearly inarticulate with laughter. So much so that the former, his whole bulk quivering and shaking, could scarcely tell the rest of the story, in which the three judges, after a brief conference, answered yes. Her Majesty quickly asked, "Is it blackcock?" getting the answer with only two questions.

I told them both that I failed to see the humor. In fact, I said, the Queen has no doubt had numerous opportunities to eat blackcock as the bird is surely found at Balmoral, where the royal family goes to shoot. And blackcock is, I added, a considerable if somewhat gamy delicacy. I informed them that it's also quite a stunning bird, and there is a marvelous Audubon painting of a covey, which hangs, the painting that is, I believe, in a Harvard library. Well, by then they were both nearly weeping with a laughter of the silly schoolboy kind. I finally left them to their foolishness. What I simply cannot understand these days is why everyone thinks the Royal Family is such a joke.

FRIDAY, MAY 1

Suspicion, I've decided, is something like temptation: One naturally inclines to give in to it. It is not an entirely enjoyable state because ordinary decency forfends one from enjoying the perverse excitement of nearly but not quite knowing that someone, especially someone one knows, has done something very, very wrong.

It began earlier this evening when I joined the Landeses for a drink at their table after dinner. I had been describing my visit to the Primate Pavilion over a postprandial concoction that Kevin, the Club's excellent barkeep, has been trying out. (Gorillas in the Mist I think he called it — a mixture involving coffee liqueur rising from the chartreuse depths of a chilled glass. Sounds like a hangover, the good Lotte remarked, and kept to her brandy.) Well, when I recounted my encounter with the chimp masters and what they were attempting, Izzy could not decide whether to be appalled or amused and succeeded in being both, his eyes starting, his face opening with incredulous laughter. Chimp-lit, he called it, saying it was about the silliest thing he had ever heard about and wondered aloud if it was just age that made him think the world had gone bonkers. Lotte simply shook her head and smiled wisely.

I told them with a lowered voice that I had visited the pavilion to see if there were any indications that Drex and his minions might be involved in what happened to Cranston Fessing. In a cursory way we touched on what the consolidation process might mean to the pavilion and how, in this instance, the killing of the messenger might have been a message in itself. It was then that Izzy made a remark that left the hairs on the nape of my neck standing. "If I were investigating this thing," he said matter-of-factly, "the first person I would make inquiries about would be Raul Brauer."

"Raul Brauer," I said, "the expert on early Polynesia?" A sick excitement began within me. "I thought he had retired, had moved out there."

Lotte snorted. "That old goat."

Izzy held his drink up to the light, sipped and nodded, and said, "He still gets back here. He has a house of sorts out beyond the bypass."

"Really," I said, keeping my voice low, "you don't believe all that stuff about that . . . cult?"

Lotte smiled, and Izzy regarded me over his half-moon spectacles with a skeptical, knowing gaze. "That, Norman, is the conventional wisdom, based on the dubious assumption that some things are too grotesque to be true. I've always thought there was more to the Brauer cult than fantastical rumors."

I sipped my drink again and found in its clashing taste something that appealed to me. I glanced around at the genteel furnishings of the Club — the glassy chandeliers hanging from the corbel-edged ceiling, the glinting brass sconces on the fleur-de-lis wallpaper between the oil portraits of distinguished, long-gone personages, the layerings of linen on tables, on side tables, and on the arms of waiters, the well-groomed men and women talking and dining, and the heavy drapes swagged back to show it all richly reflected in the windows, as though part of the darkness beyond. It is one thing to entertain theoretical doubts about colleagues, it is quite another to have the force of real suspicion fall on one like a hammer blow. I shook my head. "No, Izzy, not in academia."

He merely smiled at me and murmured, "You have the gift of innocence, Norman."

I have had to return to the office to pick up my house keys, and as I sit here in the quiet (Mort just checked in to see if everything was all right), I have been brooding about Raul Brauer. Come to think of it, I have seen him around lately. He's unmistakable, being a tall, heavyset man with a massive, voluptuously bald head and the pale, staring eyes of a predator. I never got to know him beyond the conventional pleasantries, and though getting long in the tooth now, he still moves with the aggressive, forward-leaning stride of a younger man. His museum office was directly under mine when he was curator of the Oceanic Collections. Back in the late sixties and early seventies, he achieved some small fame as a proponent of what he called "re-creational" experimentation in anthropological research. The role of the anthropologist, he contended, involves more than just digging up objects and analyzing the past; he must try as well to comprehend it in all its living aspects through a vigorous re-creation of life patterns, including rituals, food, tools, and art forms.

He is an authority on the life and rituals of the Rangu, a tribe occupying the beautiful island of Loa Hoa in the Marquesas group. The area figures prominently in the founding of the museum and was the locus of the Schortle Expedition in 1892, the museum's first serious collecting/research venture. Schortle returned with vivid accounts of the loose amorous arrangements among the Rangu, their predilection for sporadic warfare with neighboring tribes, their taste for what they called long pig, and the ease with which they cultivated breadfruit (whatever they are). I remember vaguely a *National Geographic* article devoted to Brauer's work at a site far up one of the deeply clefted valleys that divide the island. There was a picture of him in a loincloth, his torso heavily tattooed, as he instructed several graduate students in some native custom with the help of a local chief. In some quarters he was dismissed as a charlatan. But that could have been academic pique at the amount of publicity he was garnering for his work and for himself. He used his so-called methodology, it was said, to recruit his graduate students, including several young females, for participation in a dance that included public copulation and culminated in a general free-for-all. More disturbing was the persistent rumor that, during one of these expeditions, Brauer and his understudies got carried away with their methodology to the point where they sacrificed one of those hapless, unaffiliated types that show up out of nowhere and volunteer at digs. The rumor has it they not only sacrificed this young man but cut him up and ate him, according to the custom of the Rangu. There has been talk over the years of a Brauer cult, maintained by him and his students who were present at the alleged murder and cannibalism. They meet, supposedly, and do things that cults do. I have never subscribed to the rumor myself. It strikes me as apocryphal, one of those tasteless jokes that gets started around the campfire and takes on a life of its own. Besides, I can't imagine academics letting something like that go by without someone, somewhere, publishing a paper on it.

Now I have my doubts. Now I have my suspicions. But suspicions, however compelling, are not proof. I will need to do some digging, to go into the archives and go over the original files of those expeditions.

Well, on other matters, quickly, before I take my yawning self home to bed. My e-mail has certainly been busy of late. I arrived this morning to find a note from Oliver Scrabbe announcing that he has established himself in the late dean's office and will be meeting with each of us individually "to bring us up to date on the consolidation process." It would seem that for him the take-over of the museum is a foregone conclusion. I was tempted to write him (I never use the e-mail, it seems so ephemeral) a response pointing out that a final decision had yet to be made but decided against it, at least for the moment.

MONDAY, MAY 4

I walked this morning through a bird-loud world enveloped in a veil of gauzy verdure of just-leafing trees prinked here and there with the pinks of the blossoming cherries and the unequivocal yellow of forsythia, which is common as blue jays and quite as beautiful. From the woodland path I saw on the shore of the pond a pair of Canada geese with a brood of tawny puffball goslings. Being a voyeur of nature, I stopped to admire them, the scene so affecting I could understand why a painter or a poet would want to grasp and hold it with the delicate, powerful grip of his art. These noble creatures mate for life. That way, we are told by naturalists, they don't have to spend valuable time and energy on yearly courtship rituals. But is it not possible, I have often wondered, that they simply fall in love?

Ah well, despite such a beginning, my natural ebullience withered as soon as I crossed the Lagoon Bridge and the museum came into sight. What heretofore had been a cause of delight — the view of five stories of elegant brick rising above the blush of budding sycamores on Belmont Avenue — filled me with boding instead. I suffered the awful presentiment that Cranston Fessing's killer was not merely in the Museum of Man but of it, an endemic sickness, part of our killer genes.

It didn't help to find that Lieutenant Tracy had called. I tried to call him back, but he wasn't available. I don't know why it should make me nervous that he called. I know I am innocent, at least of Fessing's murder.

Indeed, as part of my own investigation of that murder I went down to the archives in search of the files of Raul Brauer's expeditions to Loa Hoa in the late sixties and early seventies. Imagine my surprise, my foreboding, my excitement, to find the whole section missing! I summoned Mrs. Walsh, the archivist, a woman notorious for her lack of organization, and she could give me no satisfactory answer as to where they might be. They could be out on loan, she said, with the incipient panic of the naturally disorganized, rummaging around her cluttered desk. I signed out some files on the early history of the museum, calmed Mrs. Walsh into a state of coherence, and asked her would she, with utmost discretion, make inquiries for me as to what happened to the materials from the Brauer expeditions.

I returned to my office in a perturbed state of suspicion. I could understand if, say, one or two of the files had been missing. Or, say, if some legitimate researcher had signed them out in good order. Or had they been misfiled, perhaps under Polynesia or Oceania. They belong, rightfully, in the extensive Marquesan section, which is arranged chronologically. But they were simply gone. I am loath to raise a ruckus about the matter because to do so might alert certain parties that I am on to their game. And quite aside from not wanting to tip my hand, I do not look forward in the least to sharing Dean Fessing's fate.

My state of mind wasn't helped much to find another of those anonymous messages from the Genetics Lab in my e-mail.

Dear Mr. Detour [*sic*]:

I was hoping something would happen after I sent you that first message. I was serious when I told you something is going on over here that someone should hear about. Maybe the Pope was right when he said it was wrong to use artificial fertilizers. You know when they take an egg from a woman and a sperm from a man and mix them together in a test tube. When they were doing it to find bad genes for diseases I thought it was okay. Now I think they're doing something else, but I don't know enough about it to tell you. All I know is that Professor Gottling stays here even more than he used to and is even more grouchy than he usually is. He works nights and keeps things secret even from Mr. Onoyoko and Dr. Bushi. Dr. Bushi is very polite and bows a lot but he doesn't smile as much as he used to. I found out one person has been fired because they recorded her on one of the secret cameras using the phone in Professor Gottling's lab without permission. They also have a whole section of tape showing Dr. Hanker and Charlene doing it on the couch in the office with the safe. Charlene must have taken him in there to help him get his contribution to the sperm bank because she had one of those little collection cups, but it doesn't look like a whole lot got into the cup. One of the technicians made a copy of the tape and has been showing it on the monitor in the basement. It's about twenty minutes long and there's no sound but you can really see everything and all the different positions they tried even though they didn't take all their clothes off. It surprised everyone because Charlene is kind of fat and has a funny little mustache and Dr. Hanker's wife is supposed to be very pretty and rich and thin. I don't know if telling you this is whistle-blowing or not, but I'll let you know more when I find out.

Worried

I'm not sure what to make of it as there have been so many grumbles and rumbles and rumors coming out of the lab over the past couple of years. Marge Littlefield has told me that ever since Professor Gottling and Onoyoko Pharmaceuticals established an independent institute within the Genetics Lab the place has been running virtually on its own, institutionally ducking, so to speak, behind the MOM or behind Wainscott, as suits its purposes. I've printed the communication out and clipped it into my Fessing notebook, though how any of this fits into a larger paradigm of suspicion is beyond me at present. The assumption of university control over the museum would entail the same for the lab and the Primate Pavilion followed by some rigorous and perhaps retroactive oversight and regulation. A motive, perhaps, for doing away with the dean? But why all the *haute cuisine?* Is the culinary aspect part of an elaborate smoke screen or an attempt to embarrass a university all too sensitive to its public image? How might all this fit in with the Brauer cult? Why do I sense in this whole affair a mad imagination at work? Or am I letting my own imagination, fired by suspicion, run away with me?

Well, to change the subject completely, I've often wondered what our children would have been like had Elsbeth and I ever married. I mean, we were something of a contrast, perhaps even a mismatch: she is scarcely five feet and I am well over six. I was and remain quite lean, and she, alas, always quite generously endowed, has gotten a tad plump since marrying, although I haven't seen her in fifteen years, not since that disastrous visit I made to Philadelphia. And while I am pale eyed, blond, and thinning on top, with a nose of Roman dimensions, Elsbeth has dark, alluring eyes, lustrous, nearly black hair, and generally pretty if somewhat blunt features. I imagine the boys would have had my long legs and slender frame. Of course, they could have turned out short and stocky, like Elsbeth, while the girls, had we any, might have gangled like me. Or perhaps something in between. One of them surely would have had my mother's russet coloring, the strawberry redness of her hair tingeing so delicately the features of her face. Poor Mother never quite approved of Elsbeth. "Don't you think she's a bit *common?*" she once said to me. "I mean, her father is a car dealer." Mother, I'm afraid, was a bit common herself, common, I mean, in her consideration of social standing. And a bit mad as she got on. She didn't want me to marry Elsbeth or anyone else for that matter, but she did complain in her dotage of not having grandchildren. I told her you couldn't have one without the other, not in those days anyway. These days it happens, I'm told, even among respectable people, as we slide back toward some state of nature. I suppose it won't be long before people start coupling in public, like dogs.

Speaking of which, I mustn't forget the first of the Oversight Committee meetings on the Paleolithic diorama is set for Thursday. Thad Pilty came in late this afternoon to ask me to sit in on the meetings and record them. He can be quite disarming when he wants to be, but there was a disingenuous note in his voice, a kind of false confiding when he told me that "political considerations" had prompted him to agree to the committee's request for the hearings. He said, his eyes not really meeting mine, that in the wake of what happened to Dean Fessing he felt any resistance to the committee's request would be seen in the wrong light. Still, had he followed my advice, contained in a memorandum sent to Dr. Commer and copied to him, the issue might have been limited to the legitimacy of the committee's purview, rather than the form and content of his precious diorama. At the very least the issue would have been the venue. But Professor Pilty conceded even that, and the hearings are to be held in the Twitchell Room.

This happens to be a more serious matter than he realizes. Mason Twitchell, a pioneering giant in the field of ethnopaleosiphonapterology, which is the study of fossil fleas, was a benign presence at the MOM for many years and a powerful advocate for its independence even as he occupied one of the university's most venerable chairs. His portrait, a very good likeness in splendid academic plumage, showing his kindly but intense blue eyes, his persuasive jaw, and the backward sweep of his abundant white hair, dominates the round table in the room named for him. Of course when I knew him (we sometimes had coffee together in the wonderful old cafeteria on the second floor, which has since been turned into offices), he was getting on in years but still had that twinkle in his eyes and was quite gracious to everyone. But I'm sure he is turning in his grave at the thought of the room being used for a hearing by an oversight committee from the university.

I am still trying to arrange a dinner party in honor of my little shrine. What immense, vicarious peace that tableau affords me! Strange, the little things that keep us going.

WEDNESDAY, MAY 6

Unannounced, dapper as ever, Lieutenant Tracy appeared in my office just after eleven this morning, and, with a politeness that produced a small moment of melodrama, asked if he could shut the door. I acquiesced, and he sat before my desk and requested permission to smoke. I nodded, and he took out a cigarette, lit it with a flick and snap of his lighter, and, exhaling toward the ceiling, said, "Tell me, Mr. de Ratour, "what do you know of the relationship between Professor Pilty and Dean Fessing?"

"Pilty and Fessing?" I repeated. I shook my head most emphatically and told him that I had had on more than one occasion the pleasure of meeting Theresa Pilty and their two lovely children. But knowing how little appearances count for these days, I threw in some gossip I had heard about Pilty and a female graduate student with whom he apparently had a fling during one of those long, arduous forays in the field, when any kind of comfort is at a premium.

The lieutenant was in turn shaking his head before I finished. "I mean strictly professional. What do you know of their differences over some kind of exhibit Professor Pilty wants to build?"

I informed the lieutenant that the dean had attempted, upon his appointment, to forestall the initiation of any major projects pending the completion of his one-year term and his final report to the Select Committee on Consolidation. I said that this stance had generated resistance from those departments — principally the Primate Pavilion and the Genetics Lab, but also the MOM proper in the person of Professor Pilty — that had begun or were about to begin major undertakings. I noted that I had played a small if complicated role in some of these tussles by sending Dean Fessing carbons of my memoranda to the Board and Dr. Commer.

"Complicated in what way?" The police officer was watching me closely and taking notes. I had to resist an impulse to produce my own notebook and do the same.

"I say 'complicated,' Lieutenant, because while opposed myself to the dean's mission, I was also opposed to the installation of the diorama on Paleolithic life and did not particularly welcome support from what I consider inappropriate sources."

Lieutenant Tracy finished a note he was making of my remarks before reaching into a trim attaché case and extracting a folder of correspondence between Pilty and Fessing that he had culled from the latter's files. Well, I must say, the memoranda showed the fur really flying between those two. While the dean began politely enough regarding plans for the diorama, it wasn't long before Thad Pilty sounded rather like I sound, saying that the dean's mission at the MOM was "evaluative and as such should concern itself with neither museum policy or [sic] administration." Mind your own business, in other words.

I told the lieutenant I felt curiously vindicated but hardly saw in these exchanges, notwithstanding the dean's less than veiled threat "to take the matter to a level of authority in such a way as to make the diorama problematic even in the long run," a cause for murder.

He made the tolerant nod of a professional listening to an amateur and asked me how valuable I estimated the diorama to be to Professor Pilty.

I hesitated to respond, all the time aware that hesitation signified the contrary of what I really thought rather than what I had to say. I took a deep breath. I said, "The diorama is very important to Thad Pilty. Through it, I believe, he wants to dramatize his discovery and interpretation of Lucille and her family, a Neanderthal group from the middle to late Paleolithic. But I can't see . . ."

The lieutenant was still watching me closely, his cigarette smoking on the ashtray, his pen poised over his spiral notebook. I tried, not very successfully I'm afraid, to dissemble a rush of disquieting thoughts, not just about Pilty but about what I had, or rather hadn't, found out about Raul Brauer. I'm not sure now why I told the officer nothing of my suspicions. Loyalty to the institution? A sense of the information being proprietary? The fact that I really had nothing to go on but rumors, conjectures, will-o'-the-wisps? He finally stubbed out his cigarette and stood up. "What's surprising, Mr. de Ratour," he said, stopping at the door, "is how little we sometimes know about the people we think we know. Give me a call if anything occurs to you about Professor Pilty that might help us."

His words had their desired effect. I sat in the wake of his singular scents — aftershave, cigarette smoke, gunmetal oil — having doubts about Thad Pilty. The man is extraordinarily ambitious. He may have perceived Fessing as a threat. He wouldn't be squeamish about carving up a body as he is an expert on human anatomy and has been called in by the state police to lend his expertise to some very messy cases. And he did concede rather easily to the demands of the Oversight Committee to hold hearings. And the lieutenant is right, isn't he, about how little we sometimes know about each other.

THURSDAY, MAY 7

I can only report that if the first meeting of the Oversight Committee provides any indication of what's to come, Thad Pilty is in for some very choppy times with his diorama of Paleolithic life. I do not wish to gloat, but I cannot deny a certain grim satisfaction at what happened today.

It has cleared since this morning, when a spring storm lashed us with a bright rain, producing in the corridor outside the Twitchell Room a flowering of taut umbrellas and a few small puddles under the coatrack. I arrived a bit late to find the attendees already inside and still animated with the exhilaration of weather as they settled in. Some were pouring coffee for themselves from the urn at the side table or saying cheery hellos to those they knew.

The meeting itself began equably enough. I took my seat, as customary, facing Mason Twitchell's portrait. Someone suggested that we introduce ourselves, and so we did, going around the table clockwise for self-descriptions the length of which varied according to status (the more important the personage, the shorter, I've noticed). Constance Brattle, the rather hard-bottomed chair of the committee, began by describing herself as Director of Gender Studies at Wainscott. (Professor Brattle, who serves on many committees, is the coeditor of *Blame: Source and Resource,* a compendium of scholarly articles about a subject on which she is a nationally recognized figure.) Next to her was Randall Athol, a specialist on ethics at our sad little Divinity School. Dr. Commer, at his turn, simply sat in the vacant silence that attends the declining old until Athol tugged at his sleeve and whispered, "Who are you?" Dr. Commer, ever the gentleman, shook the educator's hand and whispered back, "Dr. Commer." But we all heard it. Next was Dr. Gertrude Gordon, an oncologist at Wainscott's small but excellent medical school. An impressive woman of middle years, she wore the impatient expression of someone who has better things to do. I then introduced myself and explained what I was doing. Thad Pilty sat to my left, followed by Cornelius Chard, whom everyone seemed to know, then Professor John Murdleston, a shaggy-haired little man who is Curator of the Ethnocoprolite Collections in the MOM. These latter two, like Dr. Commer, were in attendance as representatives of the museum. (I had expected Malachy Morin there in that capacity, but he has a knack for avoiding these kinds of meetings.) Marlene Parkers, a black woman of considerable presence, represented the university's Office of Outreach. I was surprised to see, sitting next to Ms. Parkers, Mr. Edo Onoyoko, who was introduced by his translator, Ms. Kushiro, a winsome young woman of his nation, who then introduced herself. Bertha Schanke, quite preoccupied with the plate of donuts in front of her, simply stated her name followed by the word *bitch,* standing, I think, for BITCH, a coalition of local victims' groups. Next to her was the ubiquitous Ariel Dearth, the Leona Von Beaut Professor of Situational Ethics and Litigation Development in the Law School. Then my friend Israel Landes, Smythe Professor of the History of Science, who was sitting next to his good friend Father S. J. O'Gould, S. J. Father O'Gould holds a joint appointment in paleontology and philosophy and is well-known for his revival of the ideas and ideals of Teilhard de Chardin, a fellow Jesuit. Last year Father O'Gould came out with his long-awaited *Wonderful Strife: Natural Selection and the Inevitability of Intelligence.* One reviewer, I remember, castigated him as "an out-and-out unreconstructed neo-optimist," but the book was, surprisingly, well received.

Professor Brattle, following a perfunctory note of gratitude for the use of the room, went on to make it clear that the hearing would be anything but salubrious for Professor Pilty's project.

The committee, she said, reported directly to President Twill, who, she added, dropping her chained glasses for effect, took the committee's findings and recommendations "very seriously." Prim and proper in brooched blouse and no-nonsense business suit (the shoulder pads did make her look a bit like a bespectacled football player), Professor Brattle stated that, as chair of the committee, she had been distressed to learn about the plans for the diorama at such a late date. She said the form and content of the diorama represented "an area of profound sensitivities" and that the Museum of Man, "the very name of which makes it suspect from a genderist's perspective," had acted without regard for "significant and increasingly powerful marginalized constituencies within the university community." She even dragged in poor Cranston Fessing, insinuating that the "climate" at the museum had had something to do with the dean's fate and intimating that the committee might be compelled to extend its purview into areas beyond the project under discussion.

Attention to her remarks was somewhat blunted, I think, by the distraction provided by Bertha Schanke. As the chair spoke, Ms. Schanke consumed a good number of the two dozen or so Dunkin' Donuts heaped on a platter which, while centrally located on the circular table that takes up much of the Twitchell Room, appeared locked in the force field of Ms. Schanke's scowl. I don't think I was the only one who tried not to stare as the woman broke into pieces and ate, in rapid succession and with a cup of coffee, first the Old Fashioned, then the Frosted, and finally the Boston Kreme. (I admit a fondness myself for those vile concoctions as often, on Sunday mornings after church, I stop by the Dunkin' Donuts on Linnaeus Avenue to indulge.)

She was working on the Toasted Coconut when some of the other committee members ruffled up their feathers and made opening statements as well. Professor Athol said he wanted to make sure that the diorama did not become one more "white male fantasy." (I have placed it in quotes in the official Log as well.) He then reached for the high ground with pronouncements such as "When we look at early humankind we look at ourselves . . ." and "We are not dealing just with models but with role models . . ."

Ariel Dearth, who last year published his autobiography, *Ariel Dearth by Ariel Dearth* (by Ariel Dearth), had, surprisingly, little to say. Perhaps it was because he was sitting next to Ms. Schanke. She seemed to agitate him, especially when she picked up the Sugar Cruller and began, in a rather disturbing manner, to lick the end of it before biting it off and aggressively masticating it. Professor Dearth usually goes around with the pinched expression of someone who is smelling something foul. He seems to like the sound of his own voice and to be continually casting about, as though looking for the cameras. There was a considerable flap not long ago when Spike Manacle, a columnist who emotes regularly in the *Bugle*, referred to Dearth as the Von Beaut Professor of Situational Ethnics. Professor Dearth accused Manacle, who claimed it was a typo, of committing an ethnic slur.

Father O'Gould, a tall, slender, handsome man who speaks in the lilting cadences of his native Cork, said he hoped there would be some outward sign that early man did not live by bread alone. "And," he added in that shy, deferential way of his, "I am not referring only to diet."

Mr. Onoyoko, the founder of the pharmaceutical empire that bears his name, listened to the translations with much smiling and odd flares of mirth. I am frankly puzzled by his presence at the meeting. His company provides most of the support for the Onoyoko Institute, but that organization, as far as I know, has confined itself principally to underwriting research in the Genetics Lab.

I very nearly protested when Ms. Schanke reached for the Blueberry Filled, which I could distinguish by the purple-stained smudge at one end. I watched covetously as she ate it with unusual relish, nibbling her way toward the violet blue, clotted, semiliquid center, tilting up her chins in an attempt to prevent the inevitable dribble.

I might have said something, but just then Marlene Parkers was striking a most positive note, thanking Professor Pilty for taking time to meet with the committee. She praised the museum for being one of the more accessible parts of the university to the general public. Ms. Parkers stated that she simply wanted to make sure that access for the handicapped and provisions for the visually impaired would be considered in planning the diorama.

Professor Pilty told Ms. Parkers that the visitor paths through the diorama would accommodate wheelchairs and that eventually there would be audio sources of information for use by both the sighted and the unsighted. Indeed, I must say that Professor Pilty comported himself at all times in a most gracious manner despite manifest provocations on the part of certain individuals on the committee. Indeed, I found his forbearance puzzling, not to say out of character. Like most people with a well-developed sense of their own importance, Thad Pilty is not known to suffer fools gladly.

And yet, when the opening remarks concluded, he welcomed the committee members to the MOM and told them he would take their recommendations very seriously indeed. With the help of handouts and illustrations and much patience, he described for them "an interactive diorama of Neanderthal life set in a permanent encampment somewhere in Europe sixty thousand years ago, i.e., contemporaneous with Lucille." Visitors would enter the camp through a darkened passage "to give the illusion of stepping back in time." This passage would emerge at the mouth of a wide cave formed from the overhang on one side of the second-floor gallery. The diorama itself, taking up the entire floor of the atrium, would be enclosed in double-walled partitions painted in a continuous mural depicting a late Pleistocene landscape "with flora and fauna typical of that time." From the near distance a small group of hunters would be seen approaching the camp, carrying on a pole the carcass of a deer. Before exiting through a doorway cleverly painted into the mural, the visitor would walk on a path among the twenty-five or so individuals "representing a cross section from the newborn to the very old," who would be engaged in a variety of tasks, from "cooking and tanning hides to weaving baskets and making stone tools typical of the Mousterian culture."

Professor Murdleston interrupted briefly to mumble something about siting a "Late Stone Age latrine in the diorama." (Murdleston is best if not particularly well known for his *The Ethnocoprolithic Record: An Enduring Legacy,* a work irreverent students have dubbed "The Origin of the Feces.")

Professor Pilty nodded politely at his colleague's remarks and then went on to hand around sketches of the models that are being designed for the diorama by Humanation Syntectics of Orlando, Florida. He said the models would be of the "classic" Neanderthal type, with short, powerful bodies, large faces, and heavy brows. They would, he said, move *"in situ"* as they performed their various tasks. Special emphasis is planned for the "making of tools to make other tools based on our excavations in the Dordogne." There are plans, apparently, to make the diorama interactive by giving the models the ability to simulate some kind of speech with which to answer questions about life in man's early history.

It was at this point in the professor's presentation that Ms. Schanke, working on the Chocolate Frosted, spearing with wetted finger the bits of glaze that fell to the table, interrupted him. "Isn't it true, Professor, that you're only able to do this because the Neanderthals are powerless?"

I should explain, perhaps, that Ms. Schanke is a familiar, nay, an unmistakable presence in the greater Seaboard area. A year or so ago, she received national attention when she led a successful campaign to have Wainscott set aside in classrooms, lecture halls, and so on seating six inches wider than standard to accommodate morphologically challenged persons. Ms. Schanke, in short, cuts, if that is the verb, quite a figure, what with the boot-camp haircut, earrings that look like handcuffs, a studded leather jacket, and army surplus trousers tucked into her combat boots. The undershirt she wore today was lettered WHY SO MANY MALES?

Professor Pilty, after scratching the shaved part of his chin, responded with a condescending smile that Neanderthals were not just powerless they were extinct. He qualified his statement to the effect that some researchers have reported isolated groups of Australian aborigines that manifest cranial morphologies and dentition characteristic of European Neanderthals of fifty thousand years ago. He was about to qualify this qualification in the manner of an academic when Ms. Schanke accused him of "imperializing the past with white male sapienism." Shaking his head, Professor Pilty allowed that she had "lost" him. Ms. Schanke snapped the French Cruller in half and retorted that she had lost him long ago. When Professor Pilty shrugged and said something about a lack of coherence — showing an edge of the Thad Pilty I've witnessed in other meetings — Ms. Schanke called coherence "just another white male power projection." At this point, Dr. Gordon, in excusing herself from the meeting, turned to Ms. Schanke and said that to characterize sapienism and coherence as the domain of white males was to lose her cause before she even began. Undeterred, Ms. Schanke returned to her attack on Professor Pilty, saying that he would be extinct someday as well. Raising his eyebrows at that one, Izzy Landes turned to Ms. Schanke and said she sounded "awfully hopeful" about the prospect. At that point, the background buzz of Ms. Kushiro's translation and Dr. Onoyoko's amusement became quite apparent.

Before Constance Brattle could bring down her verbal gavel, so to speak, Ariel Dearth, his voice squeaky and portentous at the same time, opined as to how there were precedents in law for defending groups *in absentia*. Well, that also got a rise out of Izzy, who said he doubted there were any "rich and famous" Neanderthals for Professor Dearth to represent in court. On the contrary, Professor Chard chimed in that facetious manner of his, the species is alive and well, and he mentioned Donald Trump and Mike Tyson. Clearly irked by this badinage, Ms. Schanke accused the museum "of making puppets of people who aren't around to defend themselves." She said it was another example of "the patriarchy seizing the past to control the present and the future." Professor Pilty, with remarkable self-possession, I thought, replied that while he didn't know in what sense Ms. Schanke was using the term *patriarchy*, they planned to leave the organization of the camp ambiguous because they didn't know much about Neanderthal social life. They presumed, he added, that it followed the pattern of surviving hunter-gatherer groups. Scowling, her voice rising, Ms. Schanke said by *patriarchy* she meant the dweems, an apparent reference, I learned afterwards, to dead white European males, and "living white males who are messing up the planet for everyone else." For some reason Mr. Onoyoko found this outburst particularly hilarious, provoking Ms. Schanke to rise angrily from her chair and all but scream, "Will someone tell that f--cking little Jap to shut up!"

Constance Brattle finally did bring about order of sorts, and a rather tedious discussion ensued about whether white males were criminals because of nature or nurture and whether sapienism is a form of racism or sexism or both.

Now, before I say what I am going to say, I would like it in the record, however unofficially, that I seldom have much sympathy for the causes that Ms. Schanke and her kind espouse. It strikes me that they have made disgruntlement into a profession and spend much time and energy searching for things to complain about. However, in this instance, Ms. Schanke may have a point: who are we to impose our ideas on how our forebears lived. Given such scanty evidence, is not any attempt to re-create the conditions of such a distant past doomed to be highly speculative at best? Think of what future archaeologists and anthropologists would make of our culture if they had so little to go on? They might think we worshiped soup cans. Finally, is it really the role of the MOM to indulge in such speculation? Paleoanthropology, after all, is a science and not, as some might have us think, a form of entertainment.

There are other issues as well. I was sorely tempted to step out of character for a moment and point out to the committee a few other more tangible consequences of proceeding with the project: the occupation of the entire ground floor of the atrium by the Hominid Collections for this diorama would leave no room for temporary exhibits and would mean the end of the annual Curatorial Ball as we have known it. Of course, I said nothing, as I still think it highly inappropriate for the committee to be holding hearings on anything to do with the MOM, especially where the real issues are concerned.

What afflicts me, though, as I sit here listening to the pithy *littérateurs* at play in their yard below, are persistent doubts about Thad Pilty. There was something about his demeanor today. I have never seen him so solicitous, so tolerant, especially in response to some of Ms. Schanke's comments. It's as though he would do *anything* to get his precious diorama. I certainly had not realized the extent of his conflict with Dean Fessing. I am not saying he had anything to do with what happened to Fessing. I am simply saying that I cannot rid myself of lingering . . . suspicions. But then, that's the nature of suspicion, isn't it? I mean, the way it lingers, like the smell of smoke.

Well, I think I will go over to the Club. This business about donuts has given me quite an appetite.

TUESDAY, MAY 12

Well, small wonder Edo Onoyoko was in attendance at the Oversight Committee hearing. Small wonder Thad Pilty is allowing that body to meddle in the affairs of the museum: the Onoyoko Institute, I learned at lunch today with Marge and Esther, is funding the diorama! Or most of it, anyway. Marge told me that Thad had "pitched" his idea to the Japanese billionaire in January, emphasizing that the focus of the diorama would be man's early development of technology. It seems Mr. Onoyoko liked the idea and agreed to underwrite the diorama provided a version of it could be installed in a museum in Tokyo and that it be done in a politic manner.

The news gave me so many disquietudes I scarcely knew which one to entertain first. For a few moments I pondered the Onoyoko link between the Genetics Lab and Thad Pilty's project and how it might relate to the Fessing case. But it made no sense except as coincidence. Any large funding source, after all, is bound to attract beneficiaries. To posit that Mr. Onoyoko, in league with Thad Pilty or through his minions, hired a gourmet anthropophage "hit man" to "take out" the dean to protect his investments borders, I think, on paranoia. But then, I am not schooled in creative suspicion. I am, frankly, more worried now that Thad Pilty will be quite willing to let the university have its way, to let them take the museum and demolish the rest of the exhibit space once he gets his own permanent exhibition.

There are people, I know, who wonder why I remain adamant

about the independence of the museum *vis-à-vis* the university, especially when it seems that nearly every other institution in the Seaboard area has succumbed to the collegial embraces of Wainscott. I'm sure there are those who think I simply want to keep my position, which, if consolidation were to occur, might be considered supererogatory. And I admit such an eventuality is a concern. No one wants to find oneself redundant, as the British so nicely put it. But my professional fortunes, frankly, are a distant second to a real danger: the complete submergence of the MOM within the Wainscott system would mean, essentially, its disappearance as we know it today. No one would plan it that way, of course. But bit by bit, room by room, floor by floor, the MOM would be turned into office space, which is just about what happened to the Humboldt Museum.

When I was growing up in Seaboard, my good Aunt Agatha, who had no children of her own, would often walk me over to that venerable institution, long before it had been taken over by the university. It had several floors of stuffed animals, some of them, admittedly, rather moth-eaten. There was a silent, still aviary, and the fossil collection, to be honest, comprised mere leftovers compared with what other museums have. But the Humboldt had a charming old-fashioned diorama of wildlife in winter, with a cutaway showing, beneath leaf cover, deep snow, leafless trees, and a sky of dusty purple, various small animals in the blissful drowse of hibernation. All that is gone now, disposed of, God knows where, and replaced with fluorescent-lit offices peopled with perfectly nice people in nice clothes who drive in from West Seaboard and the South Shore to create, as far as I can discern, paperwork for one another. What's left is a few bits and pieces, a truncated hall where they have on permanent display, believe it or not, pictures of the old spacious halls and their exhibitions. At the moment it's occupied by some sort of beetle extravaganza, including a tank of dermestid beetles busily cleaning the flesh from the skeleton of some small animal or another.

Short of consolidation, I happen to know there has been talk at Mr. Morin's "executive committee" meetings of "renovations" that would, for instance, include taking the fifth-floor atrium space for offices, i.e., boarding over the skylight and mangling in one blow the whole exquisite design of the exhibition space.

The thought of the MOM being vandalized in this manner depresses me beyond words. You see, I can scarcely describe the subdued, delicious shiver of revelation I experience when I linger alone among the collections. I love the orderliness of the objects in their cases of glass and polished mahogany and the manifest reassurance they provide of our slow and painful rise from brutishness to civilization. I stand enchanted when, say, the light pools in a certain way on the ebony smoothness of the great Haida raven. I very nearly start each time, which is daily, I confront among the African Collections the reliquary guardian figures carved from blackened wood. I perfectly understand that what's represented here, of course, is a construction, in most cases a reconstruction, of our artfulness. (I have often thought the public would appreciate all this more if they could go into the various workshops to watch, as I have, conservators piecing back together the fragments of a black steatite rhyton more than three millennia old. It is like seeing the shattered past lovingly restored to something whole.) But reconstruction or not, everywhere I look in this sacred place I see a beauty that brims. And in this art I see and sense something deeper: that the spontaneous, gratuitous, and infinitely delighting human impulse to create beauty is nothing less than proof of our divinity. We are creators as well as creatures.

I know, of course, that such sentiments would not go over very well with the administrators at an administrative hearing, replete with architects and their blueprints, gathered to consider a "reorganization plan to meet staffing requirements." These are, with a few exceptions, people who cannot see the forest for the trees, who cannot even see the trees. Which reminds me, I must get to work on the history of the MOM before, like so much else, it is gone.

Speaking of which (in a roundabout way), I spent a good deal of the afternoon in the company of Malachy Morin interviewing another group of candidates for the press assistant post. What sublime, wonderful ignorance! It is clearly the age of Dionysus. One applicant, accoutred in cartoon clothes, dense sunglasses, long ponytail, and pointy beard, wanted to know if he could use the museum in the evenings to practice with his band. Even Mr. Morin had doubts about that, and neither of them got the joke when I suggested to the young man that he try the Primate Pavilion for such purposes.

The women, I have to admit, seemed much better qualified than the men. Still, it got embarrassing when Mr. Morin turned on all his blustery charm, especially with the better-looking ones. I think he shook hands three times with Elsa Pringle, a slight, comely young woman who has worked on suburban papers and spent a summer as an intern reporting for the *Bugle*. She certainly knows how to write a sentence and even a paragraph, to judge from the folder of clippings she brought with her. She's without doubt the best candidate for the job, except, perhaps, for her self-confidence, which didn't measure up to her competence as a writer. Malachy "Stormin'" Morin was quite smitten with her. She was scarcely out the door of his office (all cheap-looking paneling and a huge framed blowup of himself blocking that field goal attempt by Middlebrough) when he turned to me with that helpless laugh of his and boomed, "You know, Norm, outside of every thin woman there's a fat man trying to get in."

I admit I was attracted to her myself, to the fetching way she tilted her head and the nearly comic seriousness with which she listened to what we were saying. She reminded me, in fact, despite some differences, of Elsbeth. But then, it is one of those fog-rolling-in, sea-racked days when Elsbeth haunts me, even though I used to think that I had, years ago, exorcised her ghost. I never did. Sometimes, like right now, when time seems a mere illusion, I think it is myself who is the ghost, one haunted by the living.

FRIDAY, MAY 15

Late this morning I underwent a most distressing experience. Armed with a search warrant, the Seaboard Police did a thorough search of my unprepossessing if commodious home on Bridge Street. Lieutenant Tracy did have the courtesy to call me at the office, and I arrived at my front door in time to open it for a forensic team from the police department. Lieutenant Tracy also told me it was routine; they had already searched the homes of Professors Chard and Pilty, those of several members of the Eating Club, and Malachy Morin's. Still, it's a shock to arrive at one's house and find two police cruisers and an unmarked car parked in front, as though some kind of disaster had happened. I could practically hear Mrs. Norris, a busybody of venomous smile who lives across the street, calling around to make sure no one missed the spectacle. How to explain to them that it was only "routine." Not that I socialize much with the neighbors, although I am unfailingly polite and friendly enough. One likes to think one doesn't care what they think, but one does.

At least I keep a tidy house (Yvette comes in once a week to give it a thorough cleaning), and the officers were most careful with my quite valuable collection. Indeed, I was gratified to hear a couple of them exclaim over my little arrangement of bonsai and Buddha. But really, to see drawers and files opened and inspected, the contents of the kitchen cabinets minutely observed, and samples taken from the ice in the freezing compartment of the refrigerator. Did they really think I might have kept pieces of Cranston in there? And then to have the clothing in my wardrobes gone through was as much an invasion of privacy as I could stand. I tried not to act guilty, which, I'm sure, only made me seem more guilty. I wanted to protest my innocence, to tell them they would find only evidence of a blameless, perhaps too blameless, life. They did turn up a pair of kidskin gloves I thought I had lost years ago and a catalog from a New York art dealer I had misplaced. They even went over the venerable Renault I keep parked in the side driveway for occasional weekend excursions, although I have never liked driving and am not very adept at it to judge from the reactions of other motorists. I can't imagine what they expected to find in it. I was tempted to scoff, but I didn't deem it wise to confront the police, especially in front of the whole neighborhood.

The matter might have remained "routine" had they not uncovered my father's old Smith & Wesson tucked away in an attic chest filled with memorabilia. The gun was still in its case and looked not only well kept but as though I had used it lately and hidden it there. I told Lieutenant Tracy that I did not have a permit for the gun, as required by state law, because I had quite forgotten that my father had possessed the thing. I explained that my father, the late Alexander de Ratour, had been a mining engineer, an occupation that took him to remote and dangerous places and necessitated his carrying a weapon. I said my own interest in archaeology had been spurred on at an early age by the kinds of artifacts he brought back from his travels.

This account appeared to satisfy the lieutenant, but another officer in plainclothes, a rumpled suit in fact, a Sergeant Lemure, interrogated me in a manner that bordered on the abusive. Standing in my kitchen, leaning against the sink counter as though he owned it, he had the impertinence to suggest that I "hid" the revolver in the attic and suggested I might want to have a lawyer present. I informed him I had hidden nothing in the attic or anywhere else. I answered him in a dignified manner as he repeated his questions. Where did the gun come from? Why was I hiding it? Why had I not applied for a permit? It took me a while to realize that he was subjecting me to nothing less than a crude travesty of the technique detectives use when they try to get someone to contradict his "story."

I finally said to Sergeant Lemure, in a tone that suggested his questions were a trifle foolish, that I thought it should be a simple matter to have the weapon tested to see if it had been fired recently. I followed up with some questions of my own: What exactly did they expect to find that might implicate me in the presumed murder of Dean Fessing? Why had they waited so long? Surely if I had committed the crime I would have gotten rid of any evidence by now. When the sergeant tried to bully me again, I said in an even voice that I was not in the least intimidated by his manner and that if he could not conduct his investigation with intelligence he could at least conduct it with civility. When he mentioned something about "going downtown" (actually police headquarters have been relocated to a new building out near the bypass), I responded that to do that he would have to arrest me and that he had no grounds whatsoever for doing so. I said if he did arrest me I would embarrass both him and the department with a civil suit of exceedingly large dimensions.

At that point Lieutenant Tracy intervened, saying that Sergeant Lemure was only doing his job and that it would be a simple matter to have the gun examined. He took me aside and, in a tone as apologetic as police use, told me they were operating on an anonymous tip received on the 911 line.

"A tip?" I said. "Who made the tip?"

"We don't really know. Someone calling himself 'Panglosser.' "

"Panglosser?" The odd name, obviously a pseudonym, struck several faint bells, but I could make nothing of their distant, tantalizing chiming. "But you said it was routine," I objected.

He explained that it was routine to follow up whatever leads they had. I was not reassured. My home, my castle, had been legally burglarized and rendered alien to me in a way I cannot describe. It's as though it, as well as I, has been besmirched. And while I know, as much as anyone can know anything, that I had nothing to do with the dean's demise, the thought that others suspect me, had even called the police department about me, has left me with a vague, nagging anxiety akin to guilt. I suppose I am naive, but I had begun to think that Lieutenant Tracy trusted me, even counted on me to help him with his investigation. It's as though, however innocent we may be in one instance, we are all capable of the crime we are suspected of.

When they had finished, he gave me a receipt for the revolver and, by glance more than anything, apologized, I think, for what he had to do. We parted on amicable terms.

But I had hardly gotten back to the office and begun to regain some kind of inner composure when Amanda Feeney called from the *Bugle*. In that awful voice of hers, she demanded to know why the police had searched my home. When I tried to explain that it was routine, that others had had their homes and offices gone through, she brought up the gun. (Lemure, to get at me, probably told her about it.) When I again tried to explain, she twisted my answers around horribly, put words in my mouth, and made me sound defensive. I can just imagine the story she's going to write. I'm sure she would have loved to have a photographer there to see me led away in handcuffs. And what I find most offensive is the undisguised relish she takes in maligning the museum through me.

This assault on my privacy and dignity has had one salutary effect: it has reinvigorated my own investigation of what happened to Dean Fessing. I have gone over my notebook several times. I called Mrs. Walsh to see if she had located the missing files, but she could report nothing. I pondered connections. While the Onoyoko money trail leads all over the place, might not the real connections here be between the Primate Pavilion and the Genetics Lab? I mean, if those communications have any substance at all . . . And the more I think about Raul Brauer . . . Those eyes, I mean. His is the home that should have been ransacked.

I have begun, in fact, to contemplate bold and perhaps dangerous steps. I am thinking of doing some hands-on work of my own. After hours, I mean. Mort and I go back decades, and more than once he has fished through his impressive array of keys to grant me access to restricted areas. And I have put in a call to a friend at the Medical School to see if, in fact, the pavilion is involved with AIDS research there. Or any real research for that matter. Still, I must confess to being quite at sea. It always seems so easy in those detective novels where the amateur sleuth picks up on seemingly inconsequential details and weaves out of them a dark and beautiful tapestry of crime. All I seem to have are random bits and pieces that I might sew into an abstract, not quite plausible quilt.

Well, I do have some good news. I am finally going to have that dinner party to introduce my shrine to my friends. The Landeses, the Littlefields, Esther and her husband Norbert, a professor of chemistry, and Alfie Lopes can all make it next Saturday. Esther, who is well-known for her Chinese cuisine, is going to cook, while I am going to do the peeling and chopping. What would we do without friends?

TUESDAY, MAY 19

A strange transformation has come over Malachy Morin. Of a sudden he appears to be edgy and subdued at the same time. The boom of his voice issuing from his office on the third floor and echoing up through the exhibitions (a counterpoint of sorts to the hoots and hollers rising from the chimps in their exercise yard below) has all but ceased. His very presence seems to have shriveled: he slumps even while standing, and there's something haunting and askance about his eyes when he looks at you. I don't think it's the heat. We're in one of those greenhouse heat waves that has everyone around here panting. Personally, I rather like extremes of weather; at least they're memorable, when so much of life isn't. Perhaps the thickening atmosphere of fear and suspicion is getting to him. Perhaps the police have ransacked his life as well, and he is a more sensitive soul than I imagined. Perhaps he's ill. Perhaps he has been to the clinic and been told that he has some anomaly, some lump, some shadow behind the heart, some indications that indicate . . . One forgets that the Malachy Morins of the world sometimes suffer.

The fact is I've never seen the man so considerate without wanting something. This morning he came into my office to ask me if I had gotten any more police inquiries. About what? I asked. Oh, he said, nothing in general. You know, the Fessing murder. I told him that I hadn't heard much lately about our murdered dean other than what could be garnered from the newspaper. And that, judging from the way the *Bugle* played the search of my home, wasn't especially enlightening. ("Museum Official Denies Complicity in Dean's Murder." I mean, really.) He asked me if I had heard from Elsa Pringle, and I told him I hadn't. He lingered around, as though trying to make up his mind about something. He kept inventing questions. Had there been any more calls about the press assistant position? I said no, and added with perceptible impatience that I thought he had decided to offer the position to Ms. Pringle. At that he appeared to turn pale. Yes, he said, he was working on that angle. If she didn't pan out, he said, he would put another ad in the *Bugle*. All this time I had the uncanny feeling he wanted to ask me something specific or wanted me to do something. Just what, I cannot begin to imagine.

Finally he said that if the police ask any questions about any other missing persons to let him know. Was anyone else missing? I asked, and he quickly said no, not that he knew of, and added that perhaps we should have a policy about police inquiries should anyone else turn up missing because the person or persons who had done in Dean Fessing might strike again. What sort of policy? I asked. Mr. Morin said he meant to say that the policy should be to consider a policy. When I looked dubious at that response, he said he meant we should get a press assistant onboard as soon as possible, and was I sure that Elsa Pringle had not called or written, or had anyone else called or written on her behalf? He went on in this vein until I scarcely knew what the man was talking about, and I'm not sure he did either.

At the end of it, he stood up (he had been standing and sitting by turns during this entire exchange), shook my hand with something of an uncertain grip (he usually breaks your knuckles), and told me that I was doing a wonderful job, that I had an important role to play at the museum whatever the eventual status of the place in relation to Wainscott, and that he was someone I could count on when push came to shove.

It wasn't until after he left that I realized I had not acted like the detective I need to be if I am going to solve this mystery. I ought to have questioned him about certain aspects of the Fessing case. For instance, what did he know of Raul Brauer's whereabouts at the time of the dean's disappearance? What did he know of certain experiments going on in the Genetics Lab? Of course, the chances are he would know nothing. But I can't help thinking that he knows *something*, that he's hiding something that might have a direct bearing on the dean's murder.

I mentioned my impressions of Mr. Morin to Marge Littlefield, and she said we weren't the only ones to notice. Doreen, his secretary, told her that her boss had called in sick yesterday, saying he was to be called immediately should anything important arise. "I've never seen anyone change so quickly," Marge told me. "I've never seen the man so subdued before."

In this regard, I would like to think that my own example and some of the quiet but pointed remonstrances I have made to him, particularly in the recent past, have taken their effect. We sometimes underestimate the power of principle and the chastening effects of seriousness where important matters are concerned. Mr. Morin may finally be learning that you cannot bluff and bluster your way through the world.

However ineffectually, I have continued my own investigation. Today I phoned Mrs. Walsh again about the missing archives. It's a painful experience. The woman is so apologetic and unhelpful at the same time that I feel both sorry for her and frustrated in my attempts to track down what should be so readily accessible. On the other hand, is not this very inaccessibility significant, as a clue, I mean?

THURSDAY, MAY 21

I have suffered all day from a nagging melancholia that I can ascribe to nothing in particular. The morning began brightly enough. I left my house at my usual brisk pace, with happy thoughts about Saturday's dinner party. But then, as I was walking by the pond . . . I don't know, it might have been the flat smell of the water, the midges in the sun, or the call of a red-winged blackbird, which seemed to come from long ago when I was young and easy under the apple boughs. I tried to cheer up, but even the bower of wisteria that graces the entrance to the Marvell Gardens seemed little more than limp lilacs. I remembered it was the anniversary of the first time I met and talked with Elsbeth.

It seemed like yesterday and yet so long ago. We were both on the ferry to Kirk's Island. Elsbeth had braved the brisk chop to visit her grandmother, and I had joined a group from the Waxwing Club, although it was a bit late for warblers. I noticed her immediately. She had tied her hair in pigtails in pink ribbons that didn't quite go with the bright yellow slicker she wore. Imagine my surprise and delight to see her take from her rucksack a copy of Waugh's *The Loved One*. It seemed little short of destiny that we should both be reading the same book, she for a course on the modern English novel and I for my own amusement. We smiled acknowledgment at each other. And, being close enough to talk, we began a spirited conversation as to the merits of the work. While agreeing with her that it was a good laugh, I maintained that its literary accoutrements didn't save it from an essential nihilism.

As I write this now, I cringe at the thought that, in learning about our present difficulties, Elsbeth may think me implicated. Why that should worry me I don't know, but I find it spurring me on to find the culprit myself and thereby free my name from any possible taint.

Then there was the meeting with Dean Oliver Scrabbe. He called around midmorning, practically summoning me to his office on the third floor. I'm not sure what to make of the man, who seems in a constant state of bristling. He is in his early forties, I would guess, with sandy gray hair that recedes far back over a wide, freckled pate and fringes, as a beard, a long hawkish face. During our interview, he appeared distracted and intense at the same time, pulling at his chin whiskers and glancing away with grimaces that revealed a pair of pronounced canines. I thought at first he had asked to meet with me at the instigation of Malachy Morin, who I assumed had warned him that my interest in preserving the integrity of the museum requires at least minimal acknowledgment — a five-minute lecture and dismissal.

The dean quickly disabused me of that notion. Hardly had I sat down when he asked me in a tone that sounded like sarcasm born of exasperation, "What exactly does Malachy Morin do here at the museum?" I was tempted to shrug at the man and his unpleasantness, but it was one of those occasions when I couldn't resist being candid. I said I didn't know with any detail what Mr. Morin did at the museum, but I was under the impression that whatever it was it wasn't much. Dean Scrabbe regarded me for a moment with a baleful stare, as though Mr. Morin's shortcomings were my responsibility. He went on to vent the opinion that the Executive Director "appears to lack the most elementary understanding as to how this institution functions or how its finances operate." I said I could not answer for Mr. Morin insofar as I had been increasingly and in direct contravention of the Rules of Governance excluded from meetings where financial matters were decided. That did little to mollify the Visiting Dean. I began to think that it was perhaps the arrival of Scrabbe that had reduced M. Morin to such a jittery mess.

Quite abruptly, the dean changed tack, dumping the wind out of his own sails, so to speak, in assuming a less accusatory tone. What, he asked, did I know about the Onoyoko Institute? Again I wasn't much help. I said I had not been made privy to the institute's workings, its disbursements, invoicing procedures, et cetera, as it was a private body with no formal connection to any part of the MOM. I assumed, I said, that it had been established to fund what is called technology transfer. "But isn't it in fact funding all sorts of things?" the dean asked. It would appear that way, I answered, in a tone meant to convey that I found his question stupid. Why don't you ask them? I said. There must be records. "Oh, there are records and records and records." He pointed to several cardboard file boxes stacked next to a filing cabinet. "We have a regular paper trail of invoices, disbursements, expenses, grants, refunds that appear, from initial glance anyway, to go in circles."

I asked, "Is this something Dean Fessing was working on?"

The dean regarded me for a moment as though trying to decide whether or not to take me into his confidence. "Did Cranston talk to you about this aspect of his work at all?" Before I could shake my head in the negative, he had spun the video screen of the computer around in my direction. "Let me show you something," he said, working the keys so that a list of files appeared on the screen. He pointed to one labeled "ONOBILPRCDS/FST." Then he called it up. It was blank. He did the same with another one called "GENDREX/INV." It too was blank. Then again with "EXPNS/SCL." He kept a skeptical eye on me as he handed me a printout. "This is a hard copy of Cranston's program file he printed out a week before he disappeared," he said. Underlined were all of the programs brought up on the screen. The first showed it had used nearly thirty thousand bites of the disk capacity, the second more than seventy-five thousand, and the third about forty thousand.

At that point I took out my small black notebook and jotted down some notes. Scrabbe's eyebrows gave an inquiring lift. "A little investigation of my own," I said. "No backup?" I asked, distracted by the screen and a file labeled, I think, "RATOURISM." Of course, it could have been "RE:TOURISM." My eyes are not what they used to be.

"Nothing I've been able to find," he said and pivoted the screen back to where it was.

"Have you told the police about this?"

"I mentioned it to one of them, but he didn't seem interested. He told me to keep him posted."

We lapsed into the kind of silence that signals the end of a meeting. I was about to bring up the future of the museum when, as though remembering something incidental, he told me he had read my memoranda to Dr. Commer that had been copied to the late dean. In a rather dismissive way, he gave me some *pro forma* assurances that, whatever the future relations between Wainscott and the MOM, the museum would remain open to the public. But on what basis, I asked? Ten hours a week to let people wander through a couple of rooms festooned with a few bits from the collections? This, I told him, was not what the founders had in mind and would not meet the requirements of the charter; which, I reminded him, were subject to the law.

That got a Dracula grimace out of him and the observation that nothing lasts forever. Except bureaucracy, I countered, and told him it would be little more than cultural vandalism to turn the atrium into dull little offices for the creation of paperwork.

Well, he really showed me his fangs on that one. Did I have any idea, he asked me, what a financial mess the MOM was in right now? Did I realize that the museum was operating under at least five separate budget systems? He ticked them off for me, taking evident relish in describing the mess: there was the old MOM budget, dependent on income from a shrinking and badly managed endowment and declining admissions. There were the parts of the museum underwritten by contracts with Wainscott, an arrangement confused by separate accounting systems for archaeology/anthropology, primatology, and molecular biology. And that was all quite aside from the MOM's tangled relationship with the Onoyoko Institute and other funding sources.

Despite what appear to be heroic efforts by Marge Littlefield and her staff, he went on, none of the accounting procedures conforms to federal regulations, which daily grow more byzantine, with the result that grants from NIH, NEH, NSF, and IMS are all in a paperwork limbo of extravagant complexity. "The danger, Mr. de Ratour," he said, leaning toward me with his amazing fangs, "is that the MOM, unless Wainscott steps in, will simply go bankrupt and disappear." And he added, "I can assure you that that is a distinct possibility."

I was, as you can imagine, quite taken aback by all of this. It often amazes me how different reality is from the way one imagines it to be. Not that I haven't known the MOM's financial arrangements to be complicated. We are part of the university's telephone and computer network, after all, and our employees, depending on their health plans, are allowed to use Keller Infirmary, all of which is quite aside from the hodgepodge of systems whereby the museum is paid for lab space, use of the collections, and so on. But over the years I have relied on a financial statement of some detail from Marge Littlefield to include in the MOM Annual Report.

With as much dignity as I could muster, I retreated from Dean Scrabbe's office and made my way down to Accounting, where Marge and her two assistants attend to numerous forms in an eye-blinding fluorescent glare. Margery and I go back to when she was Margery O'Donovan, one of five gorgeous O'Donovan sisters, and before Bill Littlefield came along . . . But then I've always been a little slow where women are concerned. She must be fifty now, and I still find myself having thoughts, although I'm not sure I like the way she's done her hair of late — cut short so that she appears, despite her freckled snub of a nose and her quick green eyes, rather mannish. Maybe it's the shoulder pads.

I poked my head into her glassed-in cubicle. "Got a minute?"

She glanced up from a folded coy of the *Bugle*. "Norman. Of course. I was just taking a break with the crossword. I'm stumped. What's an eight-letter word for three of a kind?"

I didn't even try. I shook my head. "I don't have a clue."

She put the paper down and dazzled me with a smile. "So what brings you here, dear Norman?"

I wasn't sure how to begin. "I'm told there's reason to be concerned about the museum's financial condition."

"Oh," she said, with that delightful little hiccup of a laugh, "you've been talking to Scrabbe. The poor man has no accounting experience whatsoever. It's all Greek to him. His background is literary something or other. He likes to make things complicated. He's also an academic *manqué,* and quite bitter about it. I think he was Dean of Student Affairs or some such thing before he came over here."

"But are we on the verge of financial collapse?" I asked.

"Oh, Norman, we've been on the verge of financial collapse for twenty years, ever since J. C. Pullman talked the Board into putting a sizable chunk of the endowment into a South American fur-farming operation."

She was holding an unlit cigarette and waving at the air in front of me, and I was thinking what a lucky man Bill Littlefield was.

"Then what Scrabbe says is true?" I asked.

She shrugged her padded shoulders. "The big problem, Norman dear, is the Onoyoko Institute. We have no control over its disbursements, its billings, its purchasing, or any of its accounting procedures." The situation, as she related it to me, was that funds from other private sources that heretofore had gone through her office were being funneled through the Institute without any real accountability. And in fact federal regulations did change practically on the hour and grant writing, which already took more time than the research it was meant to support, had become an arcane specialty. She waved that away and smiled and asked, "So what's new with you?"

"Oh, the party, Saturday night," I said, making her smile. But as I sat there, making noises, looking at her pretty face, I realized there really hadn't been anything new with me for thirty years.

MONDAY, MAY 25

Lieutenant Tracy dropped by this morning to tell me I should come down to the station, apply for a permit, and reclaim my father's revolver. I took his gesture as a small vote of confidence, but I'm not sure I really want to. I have this feeling that once you introduce a weapon, in life as in art, the Chekhovian dictum applies. The lieutenant sounded a rather apologetic note regarding the whole affair. I assured him that I did not take his participation in the ransacking of my home personally. He informed me in strictest confidence that there may be a break in the Fessing case. It appears that some young man, another former student, had blackmailed or attempted to blackmail Fessing for indiscretions allegedly committed while this young man was in his charge. The lieutenant mentioned a name and asked if I knew anything about this individual and where he might be located.

I took out my black notebook, which he eyed with a covetous glance, and wrote down the name. I reiterated in a tone meant to convey my disappointment in the paltriness of the "lead" that I did not move in those circles. I assured him, however, that I would make inquiries as best I could. I think this time he believed me, and I thought I detected in the young man's sharp blue eyes a glimmer of appeal. Indeed, I had the distinct impression that the investigation had run into the proverbial blank wall and that he was asking me to help him in ways beyond those expected of an ordinary citizen. Mind you, the appeal and my acquiescence were so subtle — I merely leaned forward, returned his gaze, and nodded briefly — as to be easily denied. At the same time I resisted, out of practicality and hubris, bringing up Raul Brauer or suspicions about the Primate Pavilion or the communications I had received from the Genetics Lab. I wanted to be able to present the lieutenant with something solid, a piece of evidence, a real motive, some convincing circumstantial proof. I like to think that, as he shook my hand in leaving, he understood that he could count on me to do some real behind-the-scenes digging and to let him know when I had come up with something solid.

On quite another subject, I would like to report a development that has brightened my whole existence. At my little dinner party — which was an unqualified success, by the way (everyone just loved my little Buddha and Esther's steamed buns and braised shrimp with broccoli) — Izzy came up with a brilliant suggestion. I had been grousing, as is my wont, about not having enough time to work on the history. Nonsense, Norman, he said, there is always time for history. Why not, he asked, devote the next few issues of the *Quarterly* to more or less finished drafts? In fact, I could simply devote the considerable time usually spent assigning, assembling, editing, and laying out the various profiles of MOM people, reports on research, accounts of expeditions, the rather thin "MOM Calends," and so on to researching and writing the history. I am going to put out an announcement to this effect in the next issue, which is nearly ready to go to the printer. That will simultaneously alert the readership, which has been declining of late, and commit me to the enterprise.

Not that I needed committing. Indeed, I have been in a state of delectable excitement ever since I came in yesterday to start organizing my research. I already have some of the archives right here in the office, and there are materials in the basement that have yet to be sorted through, never mind cataloged. Not only is the museum at a crossroads in its destiny but of late it has suffered from what is called bad press, and the time is propitious, I think, for an unbiased account of its rich history. Such a book, amply sprinkled with portraits of the founders and chief personages, as well as with illustrations from the collections, all carefully executed by Wainscott Press, would keep our course straight and true. The only extant work on the subject that I know of is a rather sketchy monograph penned in 1911 by Phinneas McIsaac, the museum's fifth Recording Secretary. This little publication, written in an archaic style, does little to illuminate a neglected but important chapter of the nation's cultural history.

The origins of the MOM are in fact quite picturesque, involving as they do the Remicks of Remsdale, a prominent seafaring family in these parts. (Robert Remick is on the Board of Governors, but he lives in the Virgin Islands, and I seldom hear from him.) Very early in the nineteenth century, the original Remick, yclept Othniel, an original as far as the MOM is concerned, left the family farm in the upper reaches of the Newhumber Valley to try his luck as a seaman. In the summer of 1814, Othniel shipped aboard the *Rapier,* a converted privateer that, bearing a cargo of dried cod, set out in the direction of the West Indies on a voyage of trade and barter that was to make its owner, Spaulding Goodfellow, a deal of money. Over the next few years the young Othniel accounted himself very well, rising through the hawsehole, as it was said, to become a captain and part owner of a ship by the age of twenty-four. By his early thirties, he was "one of the established merchants of Seaboard," to quote from McIsaac's little tract, with a house of "generous and graceful proportions on Upper Market Street." Indeed, the house, a Neo-federalist clapboard mansion graced with an elegant widow's walk, still stands and houses, if I am not mistaken, a drug rehabilitation program and a refuge for shattered women.

Othniel in the meanwhile had married Goodfellow's daughter, Sarah, and their considerable issue over the next ten years included three sons, two of whom, Nathaniel and Eben, followed their father down to the sea. (The third son, George Washington Remick, attended West Point, answered Lincoln's call to arms, and fell at Antietam.) Nathaniel, alas, also died young, when he was shipwrecked in 1854 off the coast of Loa Hoa during a typhoon of great magnitude. The sole survivor of that tragedy told a tale of such savagery and cannibalism on the part of the native inhabitants that he was judged somewhat less than *compos mentis* and restrained in an asylum, where he raved into ripe old age.

According to McIsaac, it was in 1876 that Eben, in part as a memorial to his two brothers, donated the land, ten thousand dollars, and a veritable warehouse "full of curios, artifacts, and objects of wonder from the four corners of the world" toward "the erection of an institution where these objects may be properly appreciated, classified, and studied." The other merchants and seafaring families of Seaboard not only proved generous in their subscriptions to what was originally and somewhat alliteratively to be called "The Museum of Man in His Many Manifestations" but also found in their own warehouses, cellars, attics, and sheds treasures from a century of worldwide trading and importing. For decades these shrewd sea captains, with an eye for beauty as well as worth, had been bringing back in their ships porcelain and jade from China, scrollwork, netsuke, and kakemonos from Japan, Javanese batiks, native carvings from Borneo, statuettes from Africa, a whole gamut of material. Hannibal Richards, "the Bernini of Seaboard," was commissioned to design the building. His gentle conflation of neo-Gothic and neo-Grecian flourishes has not been entirely ruined by the bastardized wings. As the amount of money and material grew, so did plans for the museum. After debates worthy of the Continental Congress, the Rules of Governance were agreed upon and a self-perpetuating Board of Governors selected. On a "drizzling day" in April of 1879, Byam Parkhurst, the first Recording Secretary, took the minutes of the first meeting of the Board and entered them into what was called, in a gesture to the seafaring tradition, "The Log of the Museum of Man."

And that is only a sketch of the origins. There was an attempt by Wainscott in the course of McIsaac's tenure to take over the museum, a development that caused a schism among the leading families of Seaboard. Still, a fruitful affiliation did spring up in which the museum and the university's departments of anthropology and archaeology (I've always preferred the archaic spelling of that latter word) cooperated on various digs and collecting expeditions. And I think this affiliation has remained fruitful precisely because the museum has stayed independent, a theme that could be developed quite without bias.

I will need considerable time if I am to give this project the attention it deserves, and if I am going to get to the bottom of this Fessing mess. I also need Malachy Morin to follow up the interview we had with that competent young lady so that I can be relieved from talking to the press. Alas, when I mentioned it to him again this morning, he started to burble incoherently, and for a moment I thought he was going to weep. Oliver Scrabbe seems to have utterly cowed and demoralized the man. Still, I will not be deterred. Strange, isn't it, how you need time to go back in time, to escape to the past and thereby achieve some perspective on the present.

I suppose somewhere in my history I'll have to include accounts of the Genetics Lab and the Primate Pavilion. Of course, both could be handled in appendices, but that in a way would simply be a distortion of a distortion. At any rate, I am not going to let their existence ruin a perfectly good story.

Speaking of which, I found another of those anonymous messages from the Genetics Lab on my e-mail this morning. Again I have entered it into this record and noted it in my little black book.

Dear Mr. Detour [*sic*]:

I'm sending you another trace-proof message because things are not getting any better over here. Last week Professor Gottling announced that Project Alpha had been concluded and that the lab would now move on to other things. And at first everyone believed him. But just yesterday when I went into Dr. Kaplan's lab to recalibrate the centrifuge he was sitting at a bench crying with his head in his hands. It wasn't at all like Dr. Kaplan who is very nice but very dignified. He's not the only one I've seen crying but all the senior researchers walk around like it's the end of the world. I stayed late last night to use this keyboard to send you this message and I heard Professor Gottling telling Dr. Kaplan who doesn't want to contribute to the sperm bank that they wouldn't use any of his on the chimps which are his exact words. So it may have something to do with the pavilion but I don't know for sure because everything is very secret. I know that Professor Gottling found out about Dr. Hanker and Charlene and is very angry at Dr. Hanker because they're afraid he could be blackmailed if that tape ever gets out. I know you can't do much without some real proof. I could probably get you a copy of the tape of Dr. Hanker and Charlene doing it on the couch in the room with the safe because the technician who showed it has made some extra copies but that's not really proof of what's really going on over here except for the sperm bank which is supposed to be hush-hush. I will keep sending you these messages anyway because it makes me feel better.

Worried

While I have always considered anonymity in such matters to be a sign of cowardice or mendacity, I am beginning to wonder if these little missives don't fit into a larger scheme of things. My source at the Medical School informs me that no animals in the pavilion have been made available for AIDS research despite many requests. The situation, in fact, has generated a good deal of ill will. Why would Damon Drex and his assistant lie about such a fact? Perhaps there's more to these communications than I give them credit for. In perusing it a second time, I get this uncanny sensation of a larger design, an inkling of connections, an intuition nearly of beauty. A dark, perverse beauty to be sure, like the sleek lines of a well-made gun.

THURSDAY, MAY 28

I believe Lieutenant Tracy has come to think of me as a colleague in the investigation of this Fessing business. Again this afternoon, after I had written up the minutes of the morning meeting of the Council of Curators and was getting ready to spend some time on the history, the police officer came by. He brought me my father's revolver with a special six-month permit. He told me that he had gotten it cleaned and adjusted and that I should keep it around to protect myself. I might have taken some comfort from the inference that I was no longer a prime suspect were it not for the concomitant suggestion that I was a potential victim. The thought of being killed and eaten by cannibals provoked in me a most morbid curiosity: what would I taste like?

I thanked the lieutenant and put the revolver in the top drawer on the right of my desk, which I keep locked. For a moment the officer sat there, a study in good grooming and tasteful haberdashery, his hair neatly parted and combed and his suit of dark seersucker crisply pressed. He appeared to be thinking carefully about what he was going to say before he spoke. Finally, after taking out a cigarette, tamping and lighting it, he asked me in a seemingly offhanded manner just how active did I think Cornelius Chard was in the Adventurers' Eating Club.

I, too, was silent for a moment, resisting an impulse to reiterate, because I am no longer convinced, that too much stock should not be put in what Professor Chard said or did or said he did. I informed the lieutenant that I had been a member of the Eating Club years before, when the emphasis had been on eating rather than adventure. In those days we considered a hot curry adventuresome enough, unlike the fare today, what with *pâté de foie de chien,* amanita soup, giraffe heart, baked stuffed elephant trunk, fermented seal flipper, monkey hands, that sort of thing. Attempts at sensation in matters culinary, I said, are bound to disappoint or disgust or both.

The lieutenant paused a moment before he said, "Are you aware, Mr. de Ratour, that every other month the club holds a 'mystery dinner' that is provided by one of the members?" Did I know, he went on, that immediately following the meal there is a round of guessing as to what they have just eaten and that the person guessing correctly wins a bottle of fine port? I nodded, saying it was precisely that sort of thing — a chewy meal of baked aardvark, in fact, in a sauce of diced ants, palm oil, and black olives — that had led me to resign from the club when I did. The lieutenant leaned forward as though to impart something of a highly confidential nature. "On Thursday, March eighteenth, not long after Dean Fessing was reported missing, the club held its semimonthly mystery dinner. The member in charge of the dinner that night was Professor Chard."

I sputtered a bit and shook my head, faltering again when it came to suspicion. "Do you really expect me, Lieutenant, to believe or even suspect that Corny Chard killed Dean Fessing, cooked him gourmet style, and fed him to the other club members? I simply cannot believe they would ever eat a sitting dean. Certainly not a whole one."

Lieutenant Tracy took another document from his attaché case and pondered it for a moment. "According to the club minutes, prepared by its secretary, Sheffield Brownaway, Professor Chard was in charge of the mystery dinner on the night in question. Let me quote: 'No one present, except, apparently, a special guest, could guess what had been prepared for us, and there were loud groans and some protests when Professor Chard told us we had just eaten, as an exercise in "virtual cannibalism," a large male chimpanzee.' " He let it sink in. I took out my notebook. "Not only that, Mr. de Ratour, but the descriptions of the various dishes are remarkably like those in the coroner's report." I was still shaking my head, but doubts were hovering. Lieutenant Tracy went on: "Professor Chard is unable to document where and how he got the chimpanzee. He said he procured it on the sly in contravention of various state health regulations."

Appalled, I said, "Was the chimp dead, I mean when he procured it?"

"Who knows? Chard says it died accidentally in the zoo of a large midwestern city."

I was, to say the least, dumbfounded. I felt again the inadequacy conferred by a belief in respectability. That is to say, I could not suspect with any conviction a person of Corny Chard's position of committing a crime so dastardly. "No, Lieutenant," I said, "it can't be Corny Chard. He is . . ." One of us. I didn't utter the words, although I may as well have.

The officer shrugged. "Human beings are human beings, Mr. de Ratour. You would be amazed at what the most respectable of people get up to."

"Have you confronted Professor Chard with this yet?" I asked. I could see looming another public relations disaster, the reporters swarming, the headlines. "Professor Claims Eaten Dean Was Chimp."

"We had him at headquarters last night."

"And what did he say?"

"He denied everything. He's something of a tease. He told us he was used to working with evidence and we really didn't have any. He said that while he did serve a sort of 'rack of chimp,' he did not use the little paper caps reported by Dr. Cutler and that he served more of a *ragout* than a *bourguignonne*. Of course, even if he could prove that he received the chimp carcass, it doesn't mean he didn't dispose of it and use Dean Fessing in its place."

"Do you have any real evidence then?" I asked.

The lieutenant gazed by me, out the window. "Not really. But he remains under very active investigation. There are a lot of holes in his story." After a slight pause, he reached into his attaché case again and produced a list of the members of the Adventurers' Eating Club. He asked if I knew any of the people on it.

Extraordinary, I said, glancing over the list, how few of the names I still recognized. All these new people. (There are always new people, I've found.) "Who was the special guest?" I asked out of curiosity.

The lieutenant checked his notebook. "Raul Brauer," he said, his whole face tensed for any reaction I might betray. "Does that name mean anything to you?"

Again I felt a shiver of excited foreboding, but I successfully maintained, I think, a poker face. "An anthropologist, retired now." I was acutely tempted to blurt out what I had heard about a cannibal cult centered on Brauer and about the missing archives. I kept silent instead, tormented by conflicting scruples. What if there was nothing to it? What if someone like Amanda Feeney got wind of it? We would never hear the end of it. I did not want another man's good name sacrificed to the media's insatiable lust for sensation.

When the lieutenant stood up to go, there was a skeptical glint in his eye. "I want you to spend some time thinking and trying to remember everything you can about the last few weeks before the dean disappeared. If you remember anything, anything at all, that might shed light on this case, please call me immediately." At the door, just before he opened it, he told me that whoever had killed Fessing was probably still around and would likely strike again. He told me to be very careful.

The phone immediately started ringing with calls from members of the press. Someone had leaked the chimp story. I'd had enough. I dialed the central switchboard and told them that all press-related calls henceforth would have to be put through to Malachy Morin's office because I was no longer taking them. I then went straight down to Mr. Morin's office to tell him what I had done. Getting in to see the Pope might have been easier. His door was closed, and Doreen had to buzz him twice before he came and opened it, peeking through to see if it was really I who was there to see him. I told him that there was a messy new story connected to the Fessing case and that I no longer had time to deal with the press. He sat down, stood up, sat down again, all the time nodding, his eyes shifting around the place as though looking for something. When I mentioned that he ought to interview other applicants for the job if that young woman we had agreed upon was not available, he went into a near palsy and kept agreeing with me, but in a manner that gave little assurance he would do anything about it. When I left, I was in such a state of perplexed frustration that I caught myself thinking about the gun up in my drawer and how satisfying it would be simply to bring it down and point it at this man and make him do what he's supposed to do.

Well, if only to get away from the noise of the chimp literati in full voice five floors down, I think I will wend my way over to the Club bar. I'm very much in the mood for a double Scotch, no ice and easy on the soda, the way I learned to drink it at Jesus.

SATURDAY, MAY 30

I have happened upon a very, very interesting bit of information regarding the Fessing case. I found it in, of all places, the MOM Library, which wraps around the exhibition space on the north and west sides of the second floor. It was all by such happenstance that it makes me doubt my abilities as a detective. Indeed, when I arrived this morning to work on the history, I was resolved to put that whole sordid business aside for the nonce. I confess to being in a mood to escape the present into the lost possibilities of the past. On my way to the museum I chose a path that took me by what used to be the women's dormitories of Wainscott. Ah, such scenes, such tender regret stirred in my heart as I walked by Bramble Hall! It was months after I came back from North Africa before I could even walk through Marvell Gardens. Elsbeth and I spent so many memorable hours there, especially during her junior year, when she took a course on landscaping botany and studied the differences, for instance, between white oak and mockernut hickory. It was in autumn, and the foliage had just erupted into an inferno of flaming maple, orange oak, and yellow beech, with the lowlands daubed with scarlets and burnished purples. Elsbeth collected leaves, which she pressed into the notebook where she had sketched the vase shape of the doomed elm, the muscular bole and limbs of the beech, and the sycamore in its camouflage fatigues. Together we walked hand in hand through autumn's dazzling, untidy beauty, and I thought then that it would ever be thus.

In winter, when Kettle Pond froze over, we joined other merry-makers in skating parties. And though somewhat ungainly, I used my long legs to good advantage as we raced together in the biting air. Indeed, I was not above striking poses — hands clasped behind my back, nose in air — and Elsbeth once had, perhaps still has, a photograph of me remarkably similar to Raeburn's painting of the Reverend Robert Walker skating. Elsbeth was an excellent skater, and I was quite moved to watch her spin off by herself, twisting and jumping and sashaying backwards in her form-fitting slacks. I'm not sure the pond freezes over anymore, what with our mild, unnatural winters of late. Most of the skating is done at the Wainscott Rink, where, even in summer, there are piles of dirty artificial snow melting outside.

Bramble Hall, Elsbeth's dormitory, opens out onto the rose arbor of the Gardens. It was, I remember, a genteel sort of place. In those days a gentleman was expected to wait in the roomy parlor for his date to come down, and he was expected to bring her back at a respectable hour. No more, I am told. When I walk by there now, a kind of syncopated doggerel, said to be music, issues from high windows. And even the bathrooms, I'm told, are shared by men and women, who each year, I must confess, look more and more like girls and boys when you can tell them apart.

In my day, in one of the reception rooms, on one of the love seats placed discreetly in one of the alcoves, we would read together. Elsbeth was an English major, and I remember her reading to me from Hopkins. I can't say I listened to the words as much as to the sound of her voice sweetly telling the lines. " '. . . all things counter, original, spare, strange . . .' " She laughed. "Just like you, Norman, strange, counter, spare." And she laughed again when I tried to steal a kiss. "Not here, you silly, not here."

I especially remember the music room, where, as I plonked away on an old upright Vose, she would sing in her tremulous soprano from a book of lieder. She used to tease me with Schubert's *Die Unterscheidung,* her eyes bright and mischievous as she sang,

Und willst du mich durch Küsse lehren,
Was stumm dein Auge zu mir spricht,
Selbst das will ich dir nicht verwehren
Doch lieben, Norman! kann ich dich nicht.

How the memory of that music mocks me now! Teach me with
kisses what my eyes speak! That, she would not deny me, but love
you, Norman, that she couldn't do! Was I naive to think then that
exactly the reverse pertained?

I very nearly proposed to her the night of the senior prom.
We had left the main party at Union Hall to walk by Bramble
into the rose arbor, which had been decorated with Japanese
lanterns. There, within earshot of the big band flourishes from
the dance — Lester Lanin's, I believe — we sat on one of the
benches, a frilly old thing of cast iron painted white. There we
inhaled the sweetness of alyssum, which presaged the bouquet of
the budding rosebushes, and dreamed of our future together.
Other couples were doing the same, but the maze of hedges kept
all of us virtually alone, and tradition has it that a good many
Wainscott marriages were proposed and not a few prematurely
consummated in that fragrant place.

I remember our own night there so vividly, it nearly makes me
weep. The perfume of the tiny flowers, the softness of the air, the
distant sound of some popular love melody, Elsbeth's hand in
mine, the low cut of her ball gown showing off her creamy
shoulders, gorgeous neck, and, I must admit, quite unnerving
décolletage. We sat as in a dream on one of those antique benches
in a bower of our own. I told her how beautiful she looked, how
her eyes were like dark jade, how . . . "Kiss me, Norman," she said
with a finger to my lips. And we leaned toward each other and
kissed. "No!" she expostulated, drawing back. "Really kiss me!"
And with a sensation I had not experienced till nor since then,

her tongue pushed into my mouth and entwined with mine. I confess I lost all restraint. Fed upon, I fed back. My hand dropped to her breast, down over it, nudging (how easily those formidable-looking garments give way!) until the incredible fullness of it was in my hand. I'm not sure what would have happened had not another couple, somewhat drunk, burst into our magic nook and begun, with crude and boisterous comments, to applaud our embrace.

I stood up immediately if somewhat awkwardly and would have thrashed the male member of this party had Elsbeth not restrained me. And when they finally left, I of course apologized profusely for the liberties I had taken, saying that our momentary lapse in no way lessened my respect for her. I very nearly proposed to her then, not only because I loved her but to cast our moment of illicit passion in a salutary light. But I was afraid she would think I was only doing the honorable thing since, in all but the ultimate sense, our intimacies had begun. But a certain coolness had descended on Elsbeth's manner, which confirmed my sense of trespass. And the more I tried to apologize and accommodate her feelings, the more distant she grew until, back at the dance and emboldened by a few too many glasses of champagne punch, she blurted, with a crudeness she had developed of late, "Oh, for Christ's sakes, Norman, stop your damn whimpering."

The fact is I still cannot walk by the arbor in front of Bramble Hall, especially when the roses are in their glory, without a tinge of bittersweet regret. I have never gone back into the nooks and enclosures, which, I am told, are no longer safe, even during the day. And even if I did, I'm not sure I could find the exact spot where, uninhibited, our passion had such a brief and fruitless bloom.

Yes . . . Where was I? Yes, the article. Upon arrival this morning I went directly to the library. As I was about to enter the stacks in search of Frederick Hummer's *My Years at the MOM: A Life Preserved,* I noticed the shelves of *National Geographic* lining one of the reading areas. I resisted perusing them long enough to find the Hummer book, which is a trove of information about the museum in the early years of this century. But once out of the stacks I began a feverish browsing through the *Geographic,* starting in late 1969. Usually I never get very far in this worthy publication, the way its pictures and prose open up worlds so distant and various. This time I scanned only the tables of contents. In early 1971, I found what I was looking for. "Re-creating the Past in Loa Hoa." I nearly expected to find the article razored out. It wasn't. There was the island in all its pristine beauty, the plugs of extinct volcanoes standing like sentinels, the lush, deeply clefted valleys, the lapis sky. I flipped to the next page and a picture of a younger though still aggressively bald Raul Brauer, girded in a loincloth, his upper torso flamboyantly tattooed, his right hand holding a formidable blade worked in jade. I think my heart stopped for a second or two. For flanking him, also in loincloths, were a beardless Thad Pilty and a grinning Corny Chard. I read the caption to confirm what I could scarce believe. Sure enough, along with a few others it listed Assistant Professor C. Chard and graduate student T. Pilty. Corny's smile had something demonic about it, and there was a feral aspect to Thad's expression I have never seen before. Perhaps it was the long hair tied back in a swaggish ponytail or the intentness with which he looked into the camera.

I photocopied the article and brought it up here, where I have gone over it several times. Asked about ceremonies involving the eating of "long pig" (a Polynesian euphemism for human beings), Brauer is reported to have answered, facetiously it was assumed, that "short pig would have to suffice for the present." Needless to say, I feel plunged right back into the whole sordid business. Perhaps I should just call Lieutenant Tracy on Monday and show him this. Not that it constitutes, when you think about it, anything like proof.

Ah well. I did get some reading done in the Remick archive. It's a bit dry — business and family most of it — but I found George W. Remick's letters to his mother from the Union Army quite touching. Extraordinary how fervent he was in his patriotism, how ready he was to die for his country. I have also unearthed the log of the *Silver Fleece,* a Remick trader active about the time the museum was founded. It was captained for ten years by Reuben Remick Riley, a cousin from the Boston branch of the family. I suppose I should fly to Boston one of these days and see what's there. Which reminds me, if I'm going to drive up the Newhumber to Remsdale for a look at the old Remick homestead, I should have Don Tartley over at Bud's Garage give my old Renault a tune-up.

WEDNESDAY, JUNE 3

It is not very professional, it is even unseemly, to become obsessed with one's suspicions. But since finding that article in the *National Geographic,* I cannot escape a morbid fascination with the possibility that a deeply entrenched, highly dangerous cannibal cult exists among outwardly respectable people right under our noses here at the Museum of Man. Yesterday, as I was going into the archives on business having solely to do with the history, I ran into (not literally) Raul Brauer just as he was leaving. What a deadly look he gave me! And Mrs. Walsh seemed more flustered than ever, so I didn't pursue the matter of the missing files. Indeed, when I returned to my office I locked the door, unlocked my desk, and took out my father's revolver. Just feeling its precisely balanced heft in my hand reassured me. Perhaps I should take it out into the woods for a few practice shots, although, frankly, I cannot imagine myself pointing it at another human being, even at a bunch of ravening cannibals, let alone firing it.

Speaking of which, there was another meeting today of the Oversight Committee. The whole circus might have remained little more than that were it not for this pall of dread, which thickened palpably for me when Corny Chard started in with his particularly gruesome contribution to the proceedings. Randall Athol, his blond whiskers bristling around his precious pink mouth, set the tone for the meeting when he asked Thad Pilty if the models would be wearing furs. It took the good professor a moment to realize that the man's question was serious and another moment to realize it was hostile. Bemused and then amused, Professor Pilty replied, "Of course, but not furs in the sense of fur coats, rather clothing made of animal skins, including bits of fur." Well, that made Professor Athol rap his pencil on the table like a prosecuting attorney and say, "Then they will be wearing fur?" Before Thad Pilty could answer, Izzy Landes, God love him, interrupted with, "What do you expect them to wear, tuxedos and evening gowns?" But Athol, with that capacity for absorbing rebuttals that would silence better men, went on with some nonsense about promotion of the fur industry and all that that would imply.

Professor Pilty pointed out in response that the making of clothes from animal skins was undoubtedly a major step in man's (Professor Brattle: "and woman's") physical and social evolution. Without clothing, he said, we would have had to restrict ourselves to warm climates or grow thick fur all over our bodies. That image sent Mr. Onoyoko off into quiet laughter and caused Professor Landes to speculate on the amount of time one would have had to spend in barbershops as a consequence. Not to mention, Father O'Gould said, the cost of shampoo and treatments for dandruff. Corny Chard joined in, and you can imagine the rest of the persiflage — pattern baldness in sensitive areas, flea and tick problems, spring shedding, fur envy, postnuptial molting — until Professor Athol had only Ariel Dearth defending him with a portentous "I think Randy's trying to make a serious point here. We are assuming at least that the skins and furs will be synthetic?"

Professor Pilty conceded that they would be, if only because synthetics last longer, being resistant to the kinds of vermin that typically infest museums. Ms. Parkers of the Office of Outreach sensibly suggested that the signage could indicate that while "cave men," as she put it, wore animal skins, these particular furs were artificial. Athol said that would satisfy him and added that the informational material should point out that "these people wore furs because that was all they had to wear."

Dr. Gordon, after checking her watch, excused herself, and the meeting turned to talk about signage and signs, giving Professor Athol an opportunity to display all his specious expertise on the subject. He told the gathering that any informational plaques contemplated for the diorama would have to conform to the Wainscott Language Code. He said any use of the word *man* would need special scrutiny. Not to be outdone, Professor Brattle proposed that any literature about the diorama use the term *preherstory* instead of *prehistory*. In noting her remarks, I wrote her term down as "prehair story," which didn't make a whole lot of sense. I interrupted to ask for a clarification, and Professor Brattle explained, with a certain amount of condescending patience, the difference between history and herstory. Izzy Landes sat sputtering all through this before erupting into erudition. Eyes snapping over lowered half-frame spectacles, he pointed out that *history* derives from the Latin *historia,* meaning "narrative or account," which derives in turn from the Greek *histor,* meaning "wise," "a quality I still take to be gender-free." On the other hand, he continued, the singular masculine possessive is from Middle English *his* and has nothing to do with the word *history* or its etymology.

A kind of chastised silence settled on the meeting then, into which lull Professor Murdleston, speaking down his chin, began mumbling about depicting a "communal john." Murdleston, the occupier, as one wag put it, of an endowed stool, is known for his excavation of the Oberscheiss "latrine" not far from where the first Neanderthal was found in Germany. According to Murdleston, true civilization began with communal defecation. Site analysis showed, he said, the equivalent of a "four or five holer" that helped "foster a bond of trust and intimacy that allowed early man ("and woman" — Professor Brattle) to develop true civilization." I had the feeling that John has been bothering Thad with this idea, and Pilty probably told him to bring it up before the committee. I think Thad was surprised when no one objected to Murdleston's suggestion that several of the models be depicted "tunics up and squatting discreetly at one side of the camp." In fact, I think there was some murmured approval for the daringness of it all. Father O'Gould demurred, saying that showing the models at some form of prayer would be more edifying. Professor Murdleston replied that communal defecation may well have been an early form of prayer. Izzy Landes rejoined that sometimes it still is, however solitary. Personally, I don't know what it would add other than a kind of spurious realism for its own sake.

From defecation, the discussion moved to food. Professor Pilty mentioned quite casually that there would be a wild boar roasting over a simulated fire in the middle of the encampment. Professor Brattle asked if a man or a woman would be shown turning the spit. When Professor Pilty said they hadn't decided, Professor Brattle pointed out that to have a woman doing it would reinforce stereotypes that a woman's place was in the kitchen, however rudimentary the kitchen. Izzy Landes countered that to show a man tending such an impressive culinary chore might reinforce the impression that most of the great chefs of the world were men.

His remark set off a lively discussion about model roles and role models in the course of which Professor Dearth told Professor Pilty that he objected to the representation of a wild boar on the spit as it "would strike a very strong Gentile note." Professor Landes guffawed at that, saying, "Ariel, be serious. You'll want to show them observing *kashrut* next." An incredulous Professor Pilty asked Professor Dearth if he were really suggesting that the Neanderthals be portrayed as members of the Jewish faith. Undaunted, Professor Dearth responded that he was concerned about the impact the sight of a roasting pig would have on Jewish children visiting the museum. Izzy Landes wondered aloud whether Professor Dearth was thinking of the Neanderthals as a Reform or an Orthodox congregation and, if the latter, would they not have to wear yarmulkes made of fur, which Professor Athol would no doubt object to. This time Mr. Onoyoko's amusement reached the table-pounding stage. When Professor Pilty remarked that he understood many Jews eat pork, Professor Dearth replied that whether or not that was true, the presumption of "depicting a roasting pig shows precisely the lack of sensitivity that has this committee very concerned." Professor Pilty, with a shrug of helplessness, said that to show them roasting a bovid would offend Hindus. Professor Landes, who seemed nearly as amused by all this as Mr. Onoyoko, added that a butchered horse would offend some important alumni. Professors Dearth and Athol said nearly in unison that they failed to see the humor in what was being discussed. Professor Landes made a face and said, "Oh, for God's sakes, Ariel, we are descended from Gentiles." For that matter, Professor Pilty added, we are all descended from apes. In an aside that most of us heard, Professor Dearth said, "The apes I don't mind."

The matter might have ended there had not Professor Chard, with utter seriousness, proposed that "we show them eating another Neanderthal." He said there was good evidence from the Krapina excavation, a site in Croatia, "that Neanderthal man" (Professor Brattle: "And woman . . .") "yes, yes, of course, and woman, practiced systematic cannibalism." When Professor Brattle asked him if he was being serious, Professor Chard said that the diorama should be realistic, that it shouldn't distort man's . . . and woman's past. He said it would be instructive to show them butchering a body, perhaps cutting off strips to hang up for drying as jerky. He went into such gruesome detail — "the heart would be cut out and eaten raw by the priest-god in the manner of the Rangu on Loa Hoa or burned in an offering to the insatiable gods in the manner of the ancient Aztecs" — that we all listened in a rapt, horrified silence. I couldn't help thinking, as the bandy little man prattled on, that he was describing what he and perhaps others had done to Dean Fessing. Even the irrepressible Mr. Onoyoko stopped laughing as a morbid hush thickened in the room. Professor Landes, no doubt trying to lance the ballooning absurdity of Chard's speech, remarked that if these Neanderthal cannibals were going to be shown keeping a kosher kitchen, it might not do to have them eating a Gentile. Professor Dearth, with some real anger, said he did not find Professor Landes's remark funny in the least. But Mr. Onoyoko nearly had to be helped off the floor.

During this presentation I covertly watched Thad Pilty. Heretofore, I would have expected him to dismiss such suggestions as Chard's with a jesting remark. Instead he listened attentively, his glance keen, as though with some secret knowledge. There seemed something darkly significant in the look he exchanged with Chard when Ms. Parkers interrupted the latter's cannibal ramble with "Professor Pilty, what do you think about representing early men and women as cannibals?" I wasn't altogether mollified when he replied, "There's certainly some very suggestive evidence indicating cannibalism, even at the Lucille site. But I think the issue might best be dealt with on one of the informational plaques accompanying the diorama."

Professor Brattle said finally we would have to move on to other items, as "this whole line of discussion is in really poor taste considering what has happened to Dean Fessing." Ms. Parkers asked, Why couldn't the cave men be shown roasting a wild sheep? That, she said, should offend no one. Professor Athol said it would offend him, to which Professor Landes retorted, "Everything offends you."

In concluding the meeting Professor Brattle announced that she had talked to President Twill about having the committee address itself to "the underlying conditions at the museum that had fostered an atmosphere in which the tragedy could occur that had befallen Dean Fessing." She also announced that Professor Ray Mooney, a former associate of the Masters and Johnson establishment, and perhaps the Reverend Farouk Karoom would join the hearings in the future.

As I've remarked, it was all a waste of goodwill and good time. Despite that, I find myself, surprisingly enough, with more than a touch of sympathy for Ariel Dearth's position. While he is overly sensitive, I think, to criticisms, overt and insinuated, regarding his coreligionists, the depiction of an ancestor of *Sus scrofa* as standard Paleolithic fare does suggest a dietary orientation bordering on the invidious. His objections, surely, have more weight than those of Professor Athol. But even Athol's point about wearing fur shows what a minefield the diorama could turn out to be in this age of highly evolved sensitivities.

The fact remains, however, that the committee failed to address any issues of substance. There was no discussion about how the construction is going to disrupt the rest of the permanent exhibits; what it is going to cost; whether Mr. Onoyoko's support is in the best long-term interests of the museum; where the temporary exhibitions are going to be placed henceforth; and last, but by no means least, where exactly we are going to hold the Curatorial Ball. Really, I am more than half tempted to send a letter to the Board of Governors to arrange a special meeting with an agenda addressing exactly these questions.

I have to confess that, curiously enough, I missed the sore thumb of Bertha Schanke's presence today, even though I did manage to reach over and grab the Blueberry Filled before anyone else.

Ah well, the students, bless them, are gone for the summer. The rhododendrons have begun their dignified blaze. Honeysuckle, mock orange, and bridal wreath scent the air. Commencement culminates tomorrow with an impressive array of distinguished honorands and speakers. I will attend as usual (I am still, technically, a graduate student at the university), wearing my biscuit-colored linen suit and a rakish boater I reserve just for the occasion. My friend Izzy dismisses it all as an academic Mardi Gras, a sentiment to which I respectfully demur. I see it rather as a day when the members of the academy take a moment to acknowledge themselves and their achievements before withdrawing for the summer to retreats far and near for a well-deserved rest.

Speaking of which, I am determined to put this Fessing business aside for a long weekend whilst I take a well-earned vacation of my own to work, at home, on the history.

TUESDAY, JUNE 16

I returned to work this morning refreshed and inspired from having taken a long weekend off. It was a blessed relief to get away from the sump of suspicion and fear into which the Fessing case has turned this venerable establishment. I made and kept, with only a few lapses, a determination not to dwell on that grisly business. Perhaps, as some have ventured, the dean's demise was strictly an off-campus affair. And while one always wants to see the guilty brought to justice, I might not regret seeing the whole affair simply fade away.

It was a gorgeous time to take off. My roses are just coming into their own. I do nothing fancy, a few teas and a wall of climbers. The resident mockingbird is a regular Caruso. And the weather was like a mellow Beaujolais. It allowed me to spend most of the days in the shade of my garden sifting through, poring over, utterly spellbound by a banker's box full of diaries, records, letters, memorabilia, and so on having to do with the founding of the museum. History, or at least the history of the MOM, turns out not to be quite as tidy as I had imagined. In fact, I have made a most extraordinary discovery regarding the museum and fear my scruples will be tested if I am to render an accurate account of its origins.

As I related not long ago, I have unearthed the log of the *Silver Fleece*, which for some years was under Captain Reuben Remick Riley, one of the Remicks of Boston. Riley, it turns out, was an accomplished explorer and botanist in his own right (he corresponded with Darwin and Wallace and was an early advocate of the theory of evolution). In his log he relates a story altogether at variance with the official account of what happened to Nathaniel, who was thought to have gone down with his ship off Loa Hoa. In the winter of 1875 Riley had occasion to explore those same distant shores where Nathaniel's ship had come to grief. He reports in his meticulously kept log being treated "with exceptional civility" by the Rangu, "who showed me every courtesy, including the company of their choicest maids." It appears that this particular tribe were in the custom of venerating the skulls of their former chieftains, which they kept prominently displayed on raised platforms of stonework of considerable grandeur. Riley records his surprise at finding that one of the skulls "evinced a large gold tooth and prominent deeply clifted [*sic*] jaw that were distinguishing marks of my late and still lamented cousin." After much palaver Riley succeeded in trading "a spyglass, several rifles, a barrel of nails, and a quantity of rum" for the skull. He also reports hearing about a mountain village where blue eyes and sandy hair were common among the populace. His log recounts how they searched for this village up and down steeply wooded ravines "to the point of exhaustion and exasperation before returning to the *Fleece.*"

Not long afterwards, Riley came back from his expedition with the gold-toothed skull and stories about the blue-eyed natives. This began, from what I have been able to gather, a royal family row. Sarah, widow of Othniel, getting on in years and the "reigning matriarch," as one account puts it, would not hear of having this "heathen relic" interred in the family vault in Hope Cemetery. In a letter to her daughter Eudoxia that I chanced across, Sarah castigates Riley, saying he was not really a Remick but a Riley and "who are these Rileys, anyway?" Eben, however, was convinced the skull was that of his brother, a fact he noted several times in his diary and in letters to other family members, notably his eldest son, Thomas, to whom he wrote, "I know it to be Nathaniel and I cannot in good conscience, after these kindly, untutored savages have made him an object of veneration, simply stick him in the ground."

He decided not long afterwards to establish an institution "dedicated to the study of man and his artifacts, among the treasured objects of which will be my late brother's noble skull with the sole condition that it never be put on public display." From that unexpected grit, the pearl of this institution began. In making subscriptions among the first families of Seaboard to support and supply the museum, Eben dissembled its original purpose, i.e., as a place of honor for what remained of his brother's remains.

In this matter, I think my duty is clear. I must not quail in making a full account of the incident, if only because, without it, the museum might not have come into being. I have filled out a requisition for the skull and sent it to Alger Wherry, who is in charge of the Skull Collection. (The MOM has several thousand skulls, one of the largest cataloged skull collections in North America, if I'm not mistaken.) I will need to have it examined by Professor Duggerson, who, though retired now, was an eminent anthropometrist in his day. Surely he would be able to tell if the skull is that of a native of Polynesia or Seaboard. And surely a forensic dentist should be able to determine whether the gold tooth was fitted to the jaw where it is now or torn from the original owner by some warrior chieftain and stuck in his own mouth. I will have to deploy the most careful language if I am to be both honest and edifying in telling this part of the story. Why is it, I wonder, that there's always a fly in what we think is the purest of ointments?

Speaking of flies in ointments, I returned to find a most curious transmission from Pan House, ostensibly keyed by one of the beasts I can hear shrieking below in their exercise yard. Here, for the record:

CODE X443SRG CHIMPRITE ROYD WW64
aond amdnand
3333333333
vonnegutclapclapclapclapclap traptrap amdieuayb and *the* an c
akdahda *paths of* ZDAEanda dkanaoqund alks *glory* wuqyqbayak
yak ayk *lead* anappppamamfuiclk *but* toanandatoqna;pslamajd *the*
waman ajmamuck amucka *gravy* oaoian anaya ayesor no

I found time today to send a memorandum of my own — to Mr. Morin, who continues his strange ways, dragging his feet about hiring Ms. Pringle as press assistant. I put it in language as strong as I dared, given the man's curious vulnerability. Things are quiet now with the slow hum of summer looming; there's no telling what might blow up in our faces.

FRIDAY, JUNE 19

This Fessing case has me in its coils again. I smell a rat, or, rather, a whole nest of rats. The skull, or the Skull, as I think of it, is missing, and I think Alger Wherry . . . But let me explain. This morning, after I had taken the minutes of a general staff meeting, I went down to the Skull Collection, which is housed in a veritable warren of dim, low-ceilinged rooms in the sub-subbasement of the museum. I went down to pick up the Skull. (Being an officer of the MOM, I am privileged to request most any item from the collections for temporary study.) I found Alger, who is Curator of Skulls, ensconced in his office, a windowless room decorated with some of the more interesting specimens from the collection. He greeted me courteously enough, but with a tentativeness I had not noticed before. Alger, getting long in the tooth like all of us, is one of those perpetual graduate students who, with an air of defeat, haunt the libraries, laboratories, and collections of the world as though looking for something they know they will never find.

"Skull Number One," he said after we had exchanged civilities, "appears to have been temporarily misplaced."

"Strange," I said. "I would have thought there would have been . . . a place of honor." Something other than the surroundings sent a shiver down my vertebrae.

"It's been moved around a bit. Oh, it's here all right." A shortish man growing rather comfortable around the middle, Alger rose from his seat, came around his desk, and took me out into the collections as though he were going to take another look for the missing skull. But it turned into a kind of tour, complete with as much charm as the man could muster, as though to distract me. It wasn't difficult. What a strange and ungodly place! Like a library of death with narrow, dim passages between the stacks. The shelves seemed to go on forever. As I gazed on row upon row of lipless grins and hollow-eyed sockets, I saw each as a bulb that had once been incandescent with a million lights. All that consciousness!

The curator told me that the collection continues to grow and that much of it remains uncataloged. In a workroom lit with garish fluorescence he showed me some of the more recent acquisitions. I was more than a bit surprised to find the museum was still taking skulls, but perhaps I shouldn't have been. Wherever do you get them? I asked. He shrugged. "People donate them. Some come from the Medical School, some from the coroner's office. We used to take almost anyone, but now, with space restricted, we've had to be more selective." He showed me a specimen with a large, neat hole in the forehead. "Husband caught this guy with his wife." He spoke with a soft chuckle. "Wife's in here, too, somewhere. Shot her in the heart." Then, reaching for a specimen that looked unnervingly fresh, he said, "This one's Rick Royick's," and handed it to me.

"Rick Royick, the food critic?" I held the skull gingerly in both hands and felt guilty of a kind of trespass. "I knew him, Alger," I said and recalled how he had been known as "a fellow of infinite digestion."

"Not quite infinite," Alger said. "He died of uric acid poisoning, complications arising from gout."

"Yes, I'd heard he'd been ill. How do you get them so clean?" I asked, noticing the copious amount of gold in Rick's dental work and thinking of all the fine food those teeth had chewed, all the vintage wines that had graced this now unsensing palate.

"We use dermestids for the hard-to-get stuff and then hydrogen peroxide for the final degreasing."

We continued our tour. At the end of a poorly lighted passage we came to a door covered with green baize, an anomalous touch of formality in those stark surroundings. "What's in there?" I asked and tried the brass doorknob, finding it locked.

"Oh . . . storage," Alger said. Something in the tone of his voice, in the quick glance he shot with his usually averted eyes, made me experience a sudden, preternatural alertness slivered with dread.

And something else, something distracting me to near discourtesy as he showed me out, reassuring me that the Skull was there and would be located. I thanked him and in a state of fine-honed agitation took the uncertain elevator up to the fifth floor half-thinking how ironic it was to have established a museum as a place to keep an object only to have that object get lost. In midthought — a rumination on museums as the embodiment and practice of the science of ordering the things of the world — a realization crystallized that made me walk rapidly to my office, my hands unsteady, my heart palpably thumping as I unlocked the door and then the drawer in my desk where I keep my file on the Fessing case. There, in one of pictures in the *National Geographic* article, I swear, was a young Alger Wherry. The caption didn't list his name, and it was a wide-angle shot of a group erecting a thatch-covered native house. Had he also been one of Raul Brauer's students? Was he in the same group, the same cult, as Pilty and Chard? For a moment I contemplated ringing Lieutenant Tracy and telling him my suspicions. But, really, they're still . . . what? Far-fetched? I mean like a theory without data. Had Fessing turned up something, some documentation? I need to locate the file of that expedition to find out for certain. I need proof. And exactly what, I wonder, is behind the green door?

If only I had more time. I am driven to distraction answering phone calls. The Fessing case is back in the news. The clothes he was wearing at the time of his murder have been found in a Goodwill collection depot. (A charitable cannibal, it would seem.)

And it is an exercise in futility to appeal to Malachy Morin for help. The man never did do much real work, and now (according to Doreen, who told Sue, who works in Marge's office and told

Marge, who told me) he stays in his office all day with the door closed and insists on taking calls himself. When I telephoned him, he didn't recognize my voice and kept saying, "Who is this? Who is this?" When I told him, he said, as though immensely relieved, "Oh, Norm, you sound so official. Please call me Mal." I asked him what had happened to Elsa Pringle, a question that set him off into such incoherent burbling that I thought the man had taken total leave of his senses. Indeed, I hung up the receiver nearly feeling pity for the poor wretch.

MONDAY, JUNE 22

Oh horror, horror, such sweet horror! Malachy Morin has been arrested and charged with the murder of Elsa Pringle. Lieutenant Tracy called just moments ago to tell me that Morin was taken into custody late last night when officers, armed with a warrant, searched his home and found the poor girl's naked body jammed into a freezer in his basement. The lieutenant said that the body has been there several weeks and that, under the circumstances, Mr. Morin was being investigated as well for the murder of Dean Fessing.

I hardly expected this turn of events late last night when the lieutenant phoned me at home to ask when was the last time I had seen Elsa Pringle. I said that without my desk calendar I wouldn't be able to pinpoint it exactly but told him Malachy Morin and I had interviewed her sometime in mid-May. I asked why he needed to know, and he replied that the young lady has been missing for some time. When I related the contents, tenor, and results of the interview, he asked me was it for a position I currently occupy. I said yes but quickly disabused him of any proprietary claim on my part for the post. I said that Morin was responsible for following up the interview and that I had been hectoring him lately to hire Ms. Pringle as I wanted to get on with writing the history of the museum.

That, apparently, was the lead he needed. He told me Malachy Morin acted very suspiciously from the moment they arrived at his home just before midnight. When first questioned about Ms. Pringle, he pretended not to remember her name. Then he told the police, much more convincingly, that he was having trouble getting in touch with her. Finally, under repeated questioning, he led them down to the basement to the freezer. Lieutenant Tracy told me that Morin nearly fainted at the sight of the corpse and then tried, in a state of incoherence, to tell the police it was an accident. No one, of course, believes a word of his explanation. Lieutenant Tracy informed me in strictest confidence that they are sure they have found the murderer of Dean Fessing.

Imagine! Malachy Morin! I am flabbergasted. Murder, perhaps, but I would never have suspected that the man was capable of *haute cuisine*. But then, as Lieutenant Tracy pointed out, it's often surprising what we don't know about people.

The Seaboard Police Department is withholding public announcement of the arrest and charge on technical grounds until tomorrow or later. (The poor girl must be thawed, apparently, for an autopsy to be performed.) The press, of course, will have a field day with it, and I dread having to deal with the usual australopithecines of the media. I nearly feel sorry for Malachy Morin, the way I am going to have to cut him up in bits and pieces and feed him to the news hounds of this dog-eat-dog world.

I know, of course, that all of this is of little consequence compared with the fate of that poor young woman. And I am mortified, naturally, about what this will mean to the good name of the Museum of Man. But I cannot, for the life of me, control a most unseemly delight. Malachy Morin is gone! Gone! Whatever else happens, he is gone and will not be coming back. I wish I could resist the awful elation that keeps sneaking up on me and making me smile and smile when to smile is villainous. But it is not me that is smiling, it is the ape in me, the ape that is in each of us. And, I wonder, does Malachy Morin's exit really change anything? Thad Pilty will have his diorama. Damon Drex's chimps will go on to write the great American novel. Dr. Gottling will carry on whatever mischief he's up to in the Genetics Lab. And the Mr. Onoyokos of the world will own everything in the end. At least for a while.

Well, I have calls in to Dr. Commer, President Twill, Dean Scrabbe, and several members of the Board of Governors, as well as to Professor Pilty. And I suppose I should get busy and write a press release for tomorrow. How do you phrase it when a colleague has been arrested and charged with murder and cannibalism? How do you make it sound ... dignified? I think I'll just have all inquiries directed to the Seaboard Police Department.

On quite another subject, I received an invitation in my e-mail today that makes me realize how necessary it has become to make some real changes around here:

Dear Mr. de Ratour:

Dr. Drex and I would very much appreciate your company at a reception to meet the authors starting at 5:30 P.M., Thursday, June 25. An RSVP would be appreciated.

Respectfully,

F. Snyders

And, if nothing else, the removal of Malachy Morin opens the way for some direction, some new management, and some close, critical scrutiny of what's going on in the Primate Pavilion. On the other hand, can I be absolutely sure he's gone? Can he be fired on the spot? Is he not innocent until proved guilty? Are having the body of a missing person in your freezer and being charged with murder and cannibalism sufficient grounds for dismissal? We live in uncertain times.

TUESDAY, JUNE 23

As you may well imagine, the representatives of the media were as egregious as I predicted they would be. They swarmed all over the museum, at one point invading my office, harassing me with klieg lights and cameras and pointless questions until I insisted they leave. That awful woman Amanda Feeney asked me if I had ever noticed what Mr. Morin brought with him to work for lunch. They pestered everyone. Even poor Doreen, blowing pink bubbles of gum and snapping them with her teeth, was corralled by a reporter with a microphone and asked, I'm sure, all sorts of loaded questions. I came across one camera crew set up in front of Herman in Neanderthal Hall. For a moment I thought the reporter was interviewing the encased model, but he was apparently using the exhibit as a "backdrop," as he delivered a soliloquy to the listening camera. I heard something about "reverting to the days when our savage ancestors tore each other limb from limb . . ." Cornelius Chard, of course, was in his glory. "Cannibalism," I heard him telling one admiring woman reporter, "is nothing less than dining out at the very tip-top of the food chain." The *Bugle* got the story last night and ran a typically tasteless headline, something about an obese museum official arrested as the gourmet cannibal.

I must also report that Dean Oliver Scrabbe did not help matters in the least the way he pandered to the media, agreeing to answer, and elaborating on, their most poisonous, insinuating questions. "This kind of behavior," he said to one network reporter, "is precisely why it is imperative for the university to take immediate charge of all aspects of the museum." He was playing politics, of course, and I'm afraid that my attempts to control the damage only made things worse.

For all that, things seemed eerily normal once the news dogs left. There were a few summer visitors slowly circulating up and down through the exhibits. A docent from the Public Affairs Office was quietly explaining *metapes* (those marvelous Mesoamerican gristmills carved with zoomorphic ornamentation from solid pieces of volcanic rock) to a touring group from Japan. Marge was in her office dealing with the financial mess. And as I write I can hear the chimps yapping as usual in their exercise yard below. Speaking of which, I was the recipient today of another of those communications from the Genetics Lab. To judge from it, there may be a new public relations fiasco in the making over there, something I shudder to think about. I am entering it into this log, if only to keep a record.

Dear Mr. Detour [*sic*]:

I haven't sent you any messages in a while because I've been on vacation. Looks like they got the cannibal cook, but things are still happening over here. People were really ducking when I got back. Some joker substituted dog semen for one of the specimens in the sperm bank and messed up a whole bunch of experiments and the fur has really been flying. I'm more sure than ever that Project Alpha is still going on over here and has something to do with the pavilion but I don't know what it is. This morning I was adjusting the rotary evaporator in Professor Gottling's lab just outside his office and I heard him and Dr. Drex from the pavilion arguing about money. I couldn't catch it all but Professor Gottling got really mad. He accused Dr. Drex of bleeding the institute dry for a bunch of monkey tricks and those are his exact words. Dr. Drex also got mad and his English isn't that good but I think he said something like his monkey tricks were not only better than Professor Gottling's monkey tricks but legal. I know you can't do anything unless I get you some real proof but right now they are watching every scrap of paper and have just installed a new high-speed shredder and all kinds of codes when they enter data into the computer. They also tried to fire Charlene but she said she would sue if they did because of sexual harassment. I don't think anyone believes that because when you look at the tape carefully like some of us did last night on a monitor that's got a computer enhancement program it's Charlene who makes the first move. She was the one who unzipped Dr. Hanker's pants and started doing things to him with her hand. Everyone thinks that if Charlene gets fired Dr. Hanker ought to get fired too. Professor Gottling won't do that because he's afraid that Dr. Hanker who is one of the real insiders here might blow the whistle. I sometimes think I'm living right in the middle of one of those real-life thrillers you know the kind they have on television when they use the real characters from the crime and reenact the whole thing. But I can tell you're a good guy and will do something when the time comes.

Worried

I have been prepared all along to dismiss these communications as a kind of practical joke, but just this past week, Marge Littlefield informed me that for the last two fiscal years the Primate Pavilion has received large sums in its fees-for-service income account, mostly paid by checks from the Onoyoko Institute in the Genetics Lab. Now it is true that Damon Drex has received considerable support from the Ruddy and Phyllis Stein Foundation for his "research." But perhaps income from the Genetics Lab really is the source of funding for the wholesale renovation of the pavilion.

Not, I suppose, that it makes any difference regarding a possible connection to the Fessing case. But it does give Scrabbe and the powers that be at Wainscott one more pretext for seizing the museum. What I should do now is ask Dr. Commer to convene a meeting of the Board of Governors to deal with the situation. Whatever else Malachy Morin might have been, he was at least nominally in charge. Indeed, what I fear now is that I will, by default, have to decide and do more things myself, which means, I will not have the time to devote to the history of the MOM, which in any event appears to be coming to a bad end. I suppose I could always limit the time span, say, to just after World War II. But that might give the impression that the founding of the Primate Pavilion ushered in some bright new future when, in fact, it signaled, I think, the beginning of the decline. Well, maybe things will turn out better after this current mess is cleared up. Maybe that could be the happy ending. Happy ending. Another curious term when you think that every single one of us dies.

THURSDAY, JUNE 25

I have just survived a "literary" party of the kind I never want to experience again. The humiliation of it all! With that young man Snyders and some of the others nearly collapsing with laughter while Damon Drex extricated me from a situation at once too ludicrous, too frightening, and too embarrassing to describe. I can still feel the paws of the beast where it grabbed my person, and my hands, quite literally, are still shaking as I sit here trying to type while down below the noise and now, with this hot weather, the stink rises and . . .

Perhaps I should start at the beginning. Late this afternoon, more on a whim than anything else, I joined Esther and Margery in making an appearance at Damon Drex's "meet the authors" travesty in Pan House. I think we were all a little giddy with relief that Dean Fessing's murderer had been arrested, even if it turned out to be Malachy Morin. We naturally took the reception as a kind of joke, and had to suppress our tittering as we went through the gleaming new quarters and out into the exercise yard. I was surprised to see gathered there quite a few of the "regulars," the social core of the greater Wainscott community. Drinks in hand, they were chatting among themselves and mingling with the chimps. I waved to Thad Pilty and Corny Chard and said hello to Izzy and Lotte Landes, who reminded me (as though I needed it) that I was going to spend the weekend of the Fourth with them at their cottage on Mercy Island. A regular bar had been set up for the guests, and I ordered a gin and tonic while chatting to Pilty and Chard about how much relief we all felt that the Fessing case had been resolved even though it turned out in the end to be one of our own. Corny Chard allowed how the situation represented a unique research opportunity and how he had already petitioned the prison authorities for permission to hold a seminar with Malachy Morin for a few select graduate students.

The whole thing was, as you can imagine, quite surreal. Drex and Snyders were off to one side with what apparently were some of their "stars." A kind of receiving line was in effect, with some of the guests more or less lined up to meet the authors through their keepers. The venue certainly added to the fantastical scene. The gracious old courtyard, now enclosed on its open side by a high Cyclone fence topped with barbed wire, was lit with spotlights that threw everything into garish glare and black shadow. Thumpingly imbecilic music blasted from loudspeakers. And one had to step carefully around the liberal amounts of chimp scat of varying degrees of freshness, the sources of which were shuffling and scampering around with cans of beer in their paws from which they were drinking with great lip-smacking relish.

One of them, its can empty, tried to take my drink and made a horrible hissing sound when I refused to give it to him.

I hung on to my drink and my *sangfroid*, and a few minutes later I was "shaking" the long, hirsute appendages of Damon Drex's pongid literati. Is this safe? I asked. "No problem," said the young assistant, whom I thought I had just seen go back into the building. He seemed to nod his teeth at me. "Dr. Drex is absolute master of the chimps. If there is a Nietszche among the group he has no doubt identified Damon as the 'Superchimp.' " I must say the beasts bobbed and bowed around the man, Damon Drex, that is, as though he were the Messiah. F. Snyders did not try to hide his amusement as he made the introductions. It was he who gave the animals their whimsical *noms de plume* or, in this case, *noms d'ordinateur.* I met Royd, short for Hemmingroyd, "a pithy storyteller, a boozer, and a bully"; Impostor, "who likes to follow Royd around and imitate him"; Kupide, "our most accomplished stylist"; Ninny, "from the Paris Zoo, a femme fatale"; El Doc, "somewhat overrated, but not by himself"; Barleycorn, "who writes and writes and writes"; JH, "who writes and cooks with equal facility"; and Aych Aych, "a real character, ha, ha, with a fondness for *fruit vert.*" I mentioned to Izzy, who had wandered over, that I found it a bit unnerving to hear the authors described so frankly to their faces. At the few literary gatherings I have attended, I said, most people had had the politeness to disparage others behind their backs. Izzy was astounded, I think, beyond his usual bons mots.

At times I thought the chimps did understand what was being said. They do have the most soulful expressions, and I could not look at them for very long without recalling Damon Drex's awful remark about God being a chimpanzee. Still, the animals gazed back with such an unnervingly predatory relish that I thought, given the opportunity, they would tear us apart and eat us.

The actual interspecies literary chat was minimal, although

Mr. Drex did carry on some convincing ape talk using various hoots and pants rendered with indrawn breath. (There's been some rather vicious gossip over the years about Drex and some of his female charges, but really, it's too squalid for retailing here except to say that when Eva, one of the —) [*On the advice of counsel this portion of the Log has been excised — Ed. note*]

I have no idea what Mr. Drex and his simian friends were saying to each other, and no translation was offered. He appeared to be in the middle of a regular conversation with Royd, the "alpha male" of the troop, when his assistant, who seemed to be in several places at once, directed my attention to quite a different scene in another corner of the yard. There, in the full glare of a spotlight, Kupide was showing his slender, pink, and quite erect member to Ninny, who, judging from her inflamed hindquarters, was in heat. In any event, she seemed quite impressed by the display and turned her back end to the gallant Kupide. This exhibition of troglodyte passion had drawn an appreciative audience of young and old alike, the yaps and squeals of which, reaching Royd, sent him into an instant tantrum. His hair stood right on end, he threw down his can of beer, discharged a foul stream of excrement, and went in a determined rush at the mating lovers followed by 'Postor. But too late. Chimp lovemaking, apparently, takes only seconds, and by the time Royd got there, Ninny was already crying out her pleasure.

"Happens all the time," said the assistant. "But we have to make allowances for writers and artists, for the creative geniuses among us who live their urgent, passionate lives without the restraint of ordinary mortals." Then he laughed.

Poor Royd, I felt sorry for him right then, the way with nearly human dejection he slouched back toward us, picked up his empty can, and, with affecting pathos, begged for another beer. All the while Aych Aych was displaying his turgid apehood to and taking liberties with a young unattended female. What horrifies me in retrospect was the way, after a while, that it all seemed perfectly normal, as though the apes were a species of humans and the humans a species of apes.

With a mock earnestness lost on Damon Drex, his assistant told us the group was much like most creative writing workshops, in terms of social interaction and the quality of literary effort. However, the pongs, as he called them, were much less critical of one another's work than is usually the case in undergraduate or graduate writing programs. "But surely," Izzy Landes said, "the animals can't read." "That's true," he replied, "but you would be surprised at how many people who want to write these days can't read either."

I glanced at my watch and made motions to leave. I smiled and shook hands with Drex and his assistant. They didn't want me to go. Just then another fracas broke out among the beasts — Royd was cuffing and verbally upbraiding Ninny, who screamed and whimpered in a most distressful way. I hadn't realized there was so much violence among them. Young Snyders was talking at me all the time, something about achieving their original objective and starting a new program, Chimprite II, he called it. "It's a revolutionary way of teaching nonhumans what words mean."

I said I was sure it was nothing less than wonderful and glanced at my watch again. But with the prodding of Mr. Drex, the young man was not to be deterred. "When one of the writers types one of the five thousand or so words in the visual memory, bells go off and a visual representation of the word appears on the screen above the keyboard, with the word spelled out in big letters underneath it."

"And many candies," Drex added.

"Especially if they type the word over. Kupide already knows *boy, girl,* and *fuck.*"

"We know you help us, Norman, when time ripens," said Drex.

I murmured something noncommittal and was again consult-

ing my watch and making those polite noises that signal immi-
nent departure when Ninny, that Parisian *provocateuse,* came
ambling up followed by Royd, her cuckolded swain. She looked
me over with a none too subtle come-hither leer, which I might
have found comical had she not, with unequivocal and unmistakable intent, without the least warning and to my intense
mortification, turned and presented her livid rump directly to
me. I stood there, helpless with embarrassment, not knowing in
the least how to respond. Some lout in the group of onlookers
yelled, "Go for it, Norm." Well, when Royd saw this new display
of infidelity, he lunged directly at me, grabbing me by the thigh,
and no doubt would have sunk his bared canines into my pri-
vates had not Drex barked a sharp command and struck the
animal smartly upside the head. Still, it took them a moment to
free me from the clutches of the beast, and I tore this perfectly
good pair of new trousers in the struggle.

I cannot express how absolutely degrading it all was. And I did
not appreciate it in the least the way Drex's bucktoothed assistant
laughed and told me that I should feel honored, because "Ninny
is quite fussy about bestowing her favors, especially when it
comes to nonchimps." Lotte Landes asked me if I was all right,
and I assured her I was. But the humiliation of it all! Rubbing my
leg and watching where I was stepping, I beat a quick retreat to
the pavilion proper, accompanied by Snyders, who implored me
to stay, saying he hoped this "small incident" had not lessened
my appreciation of the important work he and his colleagues
were doing. I finally shook him off and quite literally fled back
here.

I must say I found it reassuring to climb up through the
collections. I nearly wanted to find Mort and have him open the
case with the Grecian terra-cotta figurines, so I could hold one,
just for a moment, in my hands. The experience, as you can well
understand, has left me quite shaken. I feel as though I have been

to hell, have had a glimpse of what we emerged from and to what, to judge from what I see and hear these days, we are returning as a species. I am now more convinced than ever that Damon Drex and his assistant are themselves bent on a hoax of stupendous proportions, and I mean to do everything in my power to thwart it.

My goodness, it's gotten late. I couldn't have gone to the Club anyway in these torn trousers. Perhaps I'll staple them up and stop by the Bon Vivant for a bite on the way home. The food's not much, but there's a waitress there who is always kind to me.

MONDAY, JUNE 29

I received in this morning's mail a snapshot taken with one of those cheap little flash cameras at the very moment that awful chimpanzee "presented" herself to me. It is not an edifying spectacle, to say the least, and the ribald note accompanying the picture from one of Thad Pilty's assistants is tasteless beyond words. The incident, in short, still rankles, and I am more determined than ever to see that the very existence of the Primate Pavilion be put on any agenda concerning the fate of the museum.

Strange how I find myself these days, to change the subject completely, thinking more and more of Elsbeth and how, really, I should perhaps have been more forward in my relations, I mean my physical relations, with her. Perhaps it's the time of the year; these languid summer nights recall other languid summer nights. Perhaps it's the memory of that summer day, many years ago, when Elsbeth and I swam together in Lake Longing, where her parents owned a cottage. (Personally, I dislike those tepid,

mosquito-ridden, squishy-bottomed, pine-fringed ponds left behind by the glaciers, but I frequented the place and even swam
there to please Elsbeth.) We had, on that afternoon, emerged
from the water and, as was our custom, sat on the little pier that
jutted hopefully out into the small cove just down from the
cottage. I distinctly remember how a certain agitation filled the
air that day. It may have been Elsbeth's playfulness in the water,
which left us both rather breathless as we dripped on the warm
wood and availed ourselves of bath towels. It may have been the
impending thunderstorm building to a boil of blue-black clouds
to the west. It may have been the mosquitoes, feasting on our
blood and leaving inflamed welts on our pale skin.

The mosquitoes and the coming storm finally drove us in-
doors. As we rose to walk up to the cottage, Elsbeth gave me the
most enigmatic glance and held out her hand for me to take. She
had undone the top strings of her swimsuit, and, really, I had to
avert my eyes to avoid seeing the full extent of her considerable
bosom. We had scarcely made the front porch, where her parents
sat reading, when the first big drops of rain came plattering down
and lightning licked and cracked at the far end of the pond. I
remained below with the Merriman seniors to chat and watch
the spectacular display of the storm while Elsbeth went upstairs
to shower and change for dinner. A short time later, I went up the
stairs myself, arriving at the landing just as Elsbeth came out of
the bathroom with a towel so haphazardly draped over her that I
could not avoid seeing her in a single flash, coincident, I remember, with a resounding near miss next to the cottage, quite, as
they say, in the round. With a little squeal of shock or delight or
both, she let the towel drop altogether as she swept down the
hallway and into her room.

Until that moment, which burned into my memory with
searing voltage, I had allowed myself to imagine the felicities of
the marital state with Elsbeth only as an aid to solitary release.

(Even now, some thirty-five years later, I can still see the full-figured contours of her striding form and hear that squeal of alarmed delight.) I had not even permitted myself to consider "doing it" until we were in fact married, an eventuality I considered somewhat remote in terms of time. I always thought it wise and proper for two people to become a union of souls before effecting a more physical connection, and still do. But with that incident at the top of the stairs, with the storm flashing and crashing all around the cottage, I stood ready in an instant to jettison my principles. I was shocked and aroused and had no defenses left against my imagination, which ran riot as to the possibilities of sexual intimacies. Trembling in the vivid aftershock of seeing her that way, I realize now that I didn't know what to do next. I thought of following her, of at least knocking quietly on her door. But what if she had let me in? What then? It is one thing to imagine something; it is quite another to do it. I retreated to my own room, where, pulling off my wet bathing suit, I found myself agitated into a quite palpable state of masculine readiness. I began to compose little homilies to speak to both of us. I was going to tell her that it had been a great and stirring privilege to see her like that, but that we should be careful as to the liberties we took with each other, whether accidental or not, as we were not even engaged. I planned to tell her that her charms were such that only the most stalwart self-control on my part could prevent advances that she might not welcome or that, if she did, might compromise her irrevocably.

Well, the very thought that she might welcome them, that she was, right then, in the next room, a thin wall away, quite as naked as I and perhaps, in her own way, as ready as I, spurred me to provide my own relief. But still, imagine my state of mind that evening at dinner with her parents. Albert Merriman, of Merriman Chevrolet, a stout, balding, mild-mannered, amateur myrmecologist — he had published several papers on the genus

Camponotus — grilled chicken for us on the outdoor barbecue, the somewhat charred remains of which we ate on the screened porch while the darkening world cheeped and chirped all around us. I was mortified, scarcely able to chew the potato salad or Rosalind Merriman's rather runny coleslaw, never mind the blackened, underdone breast of chicken, thinking that I had just seen the naked body of their daughter, who was only a junior in college. Elsbeth chatted on as though nothing had happened. Indeed, as though to be deliberately provocative, she wore a thin, strapless summer dress, white with red polka dots, that was quite revealing. It didn't help that her manner remained coy and teasing and that every once in a while she would glance at me significantly, as though she had seen me naked rather than the other way around. My particular disquiet persisted through two rubbers of bridge, during which I flubbed an underbid three no trump before the elder Merrimans (no doubt disgusted with my play) retired for the evening, leaving Elsbeth and me to the crepitating summer night.

It was not, of course, the first time we had been alone together under these circumstances, although Al and Rosie were usually good for three rubbers of bridge. But this night, as wraithlike moths pestered the porch light, I sat with Elsbeth on the rattan sofa that faced the fieldstone fireplace and shivered with an anxiety born of conflicting desires. Despite my earlier dissipations *à la main*, so to speak, the beast in me wanted to take advantage of the situation. I wanted to use the incident in the upstairs hallway to effect, in effect, a conquest. We were sitting rather close together on the sofa. The heat of the day lingered in the cottage despite the storm. And Elsbeth affected a distinctly sensual languor as she half-sat and half-stretched beside me. Oh, how I was tempted right then to make overtures, to tell her that I had found the sight of her ravishing, that I could not get the vision of her beauty out of my mind, especially when she wore such a low-cut, strapless dress, that I was, in short, a helpless, craven male utterly at her mercy!

But the other me, the decent, restrained me, perhaps the cowardly, self-relieved me, prevailed. With an effort, fighting the headiness of some new, provocative musk rising from her warm person, I inched from Elsbeth on the sofa. I held her hand and, as gently as I could, rebuked both of us for what had happened. I said that we would have to be more careful in the future, that I was not a man of infinite restraint, that we would have to work harder on the spiritual and intellectual aspects of our relationship if we were ever to think of building a life together based on mutual respect. Well, I had hardly finished my speech when Elsbeth, who had developed a surprising capacity for profanity, withdrew her hand and said, "Oh, for Christ's sakes, Norman, go to bed."

I know I did the right thing, even though I can see now, in the clarity of hindsight, that it might have been better had the beast in me prevailed. We no doubt would have married, perhaps, heaven forbid, have been forced to marry. My life might have been richer for it. I'm sure I would have been more successful professionally, perhaps as professor of archaeology at some small, respected university like Wainscott. It's extraordinary how much of life can hinge on the decision of one moment, how close I came that warm summer night to seducing myself into seducing her.

Oh, well. The summer school students have started to arrive, and Shag Bay is littered with sailboats. The museum is nearly deserted, except for the chimps, of course, who never go away. I was hoping to get some work done on the history, but I have been interrupted endlessly by phone calls regarding Malachy Morin. It's turned into a ghastly circus, and Corny Chard has not acted responsibly in the least. Marge Littlefield told me he was on one of those television talk shows, David Litterman or Latterman or someone like that. Chard apparently caused quite a stir when he asserted that the cannibalizing of Michael Rockefeller by natives in Irian Jaya back in the sixties resulted in the most expensive food ever eaten in history. I mean, that is precisely the kind of publicity we don't need.

Speaking of Mr. Morin, I had the most pathetic plea from him in the form of a nearly unreadable letter. The man is barely literate, a football scholarship student, no doubt. It seems all of his friends and colleagues have deserted him, and he's been unable to get a lawyer, other than a courthouse drunk desperate for work, to represent him. I frankly don't see why I should feel obligated to visit the miserable wretch. He never showed me one kindness or consideration during his tenure here. He's committed unspeakable crimes and owes a debt to society, which he ought to pay without whining. Besides, what could I do for him? Surely he doesn't expect sympathy from me? He needs a good lawyer more than anything else; the district attorney is looking for blood, and the whole community is in a lynching mood. And I do have to consider my position at the museum and in the Seaboard community. I am, after all, the Recording Secretary at the Museum of Man, and the name de Ratour has a long and distinguished history in these parts. I mean, if I were to be seen visiting him in the county jail and it got into the newspapers, what kind of a signal would that send?

In fact, with Mr. Morin's departure, I seem to have become the unofficial source of authority here at the museum, with all kinds of people seeking my advice and deferring to my judgment. It is not a role I have sought, but it is one I must fill to the best of my abilities as I assist in finding a suitable replacement for Morin or, better still, an energetic successor to Dr. Commer, which would obviate the need for the former position altogether.

But the man's letter is so piteous. And I call myself a Christian. And if everyone else has forsaken him, is it not my duty to recognize him as a fellow soul, however depraved his character and heinous his acts? Didn't Christ tell us we have to love our enemies? Oh, my, my. I probably will have to drive over sometime and see him. But I can't imagine what good that will do either him or me.

MONDAY, JULY 6

I returned this morning from a wonderful weekend with the Landeses at their cottage on Mercy Island, which is just north of Shag Bay. The Littlefields have a place there as well, and they joined us and Father O'Gould for Saturday night dinner. I'm starting to think that such gatherings may be all we have left of civilization, I mean as it was once thought of.

The Landeses were both, I must say, in excellent form. Lotte is a pale, freckled woman who wears her striking, coppery hair, which has just started to turn, swept up into a knot, which bobs back and forth when she laughs. Izzy is a smallish man with an elfish face, a white mustache, and a floccose ring of white hair that looks impishly like a fallen halo. They have been married now more than thirty years. Imagine that. When asked once to what he attributed the longevity of their "relationship," Izzy replied, "Because I have never confused marriage with tenure." But I think it's because of Lotte. I've been half in love with her myself for nearly thirty years. But then Izzy is known for his bons mots.

They have always treated me as though I were one of the family, and it's painful to admit at times that they are just about the only family I have. The Landeses and the others were most solicitous about what happened to me at that "reception" in the

Primate Pavilion. I assured them I was fine, when in fact I remain quite shaken by the incident.

But I must resist anything like self-pity. It was a gorgeous weekend. The cottage rambles along a headland that faces north to Hooker's Point, where you can still see a submarine spotting tower left over from World War II. The cove just south of the cottage sweeps back to a stretch of muddy shallows teeming with seabirds and shorebirds. The whole magnificent view can be taken in from their deck, to which we repaired early Saturday evening with good cheese and better wine.

Despite protestations from Lotte ("I came up here to get away from all that"), and efforts by the rest of us to avoid the subject, the conversation did drift inevitably to what was happening at the museum. Once Lotte had excused herself to see to the dinner, we all took a low, keen pleasure in shaking our heads with incredulity that it was Malachy Morin who had turned out to be the culprit. Only Father O'Gould, I think, refrained from appending a disparaging opinion of the man, though he joined in the general surprise that Morin was the Wainscott cannibal. I mentioned that he had written me a note denying he had murdered Elsa Pringle or intended to do anything unseemly with her body and saying that he had had nothing to do with Dean Fessing. I confessed that I was in a quandary as to how to respond to the man's pleas for me to come visit him. Father O'Gould reminded me that we don't have to like our enemies, we only have to love them. It was a comment that left me both chastened and encouraged.

Margery, resplendent in a suede skirt and green plaid shirt, her shapely legs crossed enticingly, her chin tilted up to blow cigarette smoke, remarked that "Morin certainly had a motive for getting rid of Fessing." She told us the man had so many crooked schemes going with suppliers and contractors, not to mention the fiddling he did on his expense accounts, that Fessing was sure to have called him on it. She recounted how, on her own initiative, she had spent nearly an afternoon with Fessing going over the details of Morin's fraudulent activities.

"Yes, but why cannibalize him?" asked Izzy, always the skeptic. Below us in the cove I noticed a raft of eider ducks bobbing in the swell.

"Corny Chard thinks it's natural," said the priest. "He claims human flesh is just another form of protein and the suppression of its consumption is another irrational human prejudice. I've heard him say that we think we're too good to eat."

"*Au contraire.*" Izzy laughed. "I think I would taste awful." He sipped from his wine. "On the other hand, I have been marinating myself in this stuff most of my adult life."

We all chuckled at that and turned to watch an unfamiliar black-sailed ketch running south. Into this silence Bill Littlefield, who hadn't spoken much during the conversation, remarked with effective portentousness that there weren't many left in the DA's Office "who thought that Malachy Morin killed Cranston Fessing."

"Why is that?" I asked. I felt oddly vindicated and fearful at the same time.

"They say it doesn't fit. The dean really was expertly cooked. And Morin's apparently something of a slob. They may still try to hang it on him in the public mind to clear the books, but it won't be one of the charges."

"You mean the Fessing case will remain officially open?" My question overlapped with that of Father O'Gould, who spoke at the same time, "Then who did murder the dean?"

Bill Littlefield said yes to my question and shrugged at that of the good father.

Izzy said, "I still think they should turn that Raul Brauer operation upside down. The man's been a charlatan from his first day at Wainscott."

And just as we were about to take up that gambit, Lotte called us to come in for lobsters, French bread, and salad.

That night, sleeping to the sound of waves, I dreamed a most realistic dream in which all the principals in the case — Malachy Morin, Lieutenant Tracy, Chard, Pilty, Brauer, Wherry, Drex, myself of course, Dean Fessing and Elsa Pringle, neither looking the worse for wear — were assembled in the Twitchell Room under the chairmanship of Constance Brattle to sort the matter out once and for all.

Early the next morning, I walked out with my powerful field glasses toward the shallows to peep on nature. Izzy and Father O'Gould accompanied me, and while I dwelt visually in that tremulous, prismatic world of spangled water and reedy grasses, I was able to eavesdrop on their conversation, which I always find edifying. They were immersed in that ancient and durable conundrum: man's place in nature. Izzy, who is the author of the award-winning *The Science of Science* and its equally brilliant sequel, *The Nature of Nature*, held forth on why it is both difficult and unwise for evolutionists to ascribe to organisms a qualitative order, saying that it is simply bad science or not science at all to assert that the frog is higher than the worm or that mankind is higher than the frog.

I had just spotted a greater yellow legs and would have let both of them have a look, only the bird is rather common on these shores even at this time of the year. Besides, Father O'Gould had begun his countering view, claiming that the scientific enterprise could not escape these kinds of value judgments. "The very people," he said, as we moved off the road down a path lined with late-blooming blackberries, "who contend there is no inherent superiority of man over the frog are perfectly willing to subject the latter to all kinds of grotesque experiments and even to eat its legs in restaurants. By those standards, are not cannibals and those doctors in the death camps the only ones who really see no difference between man and other forms of life?"

Izzy was shaking his head, and I nearly interrupted them, thinking I had found a *rara avis,* but it turned out to be only a common snipe. On this subject, Izzy said, there is much misunderstanding. "It is pernicious to both science and society to try to infer a moral order from the natural world or to examine the natural world through a lens distorted by social theory. The former leads to National Socialism and the latter to Lysenkoism and worse."

"But what of the brilliant medical student who forgoes what will surely be a lucrative practice to pursue a career in cancer research in order to relieve mankind of this scourge?" Father O'Gould asked.

"That medical student," Izzy responded, "may be propelled into the laboratory by his passionate humanity, but once he is there and in the process of comparing, say, the DNA of a frog's eyelid with that of a human being, it is of no use and indeed detrimental to the methodology of research to call one 'better' than the other."

We had reached the flats themselves, pungent at low tide with the smell of life, and we paused for a moment to watch a couple of egrets in courtship display. Our footgear squelching in the muddy sand, we moved on. Father O'Gould, I think, was leading Izzy on, waiting to spring his trap. We had left the flats and were ascending through a stand of wind-stunted oaks toward a brackish pond when he stopped walking and said, "If the scientist is willing to experiment on the frog in ways that he is not willing to experiment on human beings, then the scientist assumes absolute superiority right from the start, a condition that must color his research, whether he is conscious of it or not. The scientific method is anything but objective at its very basis, but in fact it assumes and depends on what might be called a 'higher objectivity.' "

Izzy was only slightly fazed. He muttered something about "the Uncertainty Principle" writ large. "Of course," he said, "to presume a value-free objectivity in science or any other field is in itself what I have called a 'necessary fiction,' objectivity being nothing more than another human contrivance, often colored by prevailing ideologies. But I would suggest very strongly that the effort to strive for such objectivity, however theoretical one may render it with philosophical discourse and ideological slumming and slamming, is an important one. Surely, the most skeptical deconstructionist and the most ardent feminist demonstrate absolute faith in the largely male science of aerodynamics when they board an aircraft to fly to one of their conferences. Such faith clearly transcends the rhetoric of rhetoric. And I would wager, S.J., that members of your own order would rather have that same airplane well maintained by an expert ground crew than prayed over by a thousand devout nuns."

"Indeed, Izzy, indeed." It was the good father's turn to concede, which he did with his usual graciousness. "But I think we both agree that the admirable tradition of scientific objectivity relies, at least in part, on an ethical tradition in which truth is valued for itself alone."

"Yes, yes," Izzy agreed. "And I will concede that I have little patience for those who hold there is no hierarchy in the scale of evolution — those who present themselves as hard-nosed, no-nonsense scientific tough guys but who are among the first to protest when the insights of sociobiology are even tentatively applied to our own species."

At that point, standing on the shore of the pond, I shushed them both. In my moist field of vision, perched on a low branch and doubled in the gleaming water, was a black-crowned night heron, looking almost jaunty with its long hindneck plume. "What we should never forget," I whispered as I handed them my binoculars to take a look, "is that nature is above all, always and forever, the supreme artist."

TUESDAY, JULY 14

Poor Malachy Morin. I am most thoroughly chastened. Never again will I gloat over the fate of another human being. I finally went this afternoon to visit him in the Middling County Jail, where he is being held on a million dollars' cash bail. What really has him frightened, though, was the announcement by the District Attorney that the prosecution would seek a first-degree murder indictment, conviction, and the death sentence in the state's newly refurbished electric chair. Newton Flanner has announced plans to run for Governor, which in some ways makes the threat even more real.

And I must say that the county jail, a large, granitic pile near the waterfront, a veritable Bastille, is a grim place. After an indecorous "body search" by a suspicious guard, I was taken to a room bare except for a table and two chairs. Malachy Morin, his limbs shackled, was brought in by another guard, who stood to one side of the table and watched every move we made. The poor man started to cry when he saw me. "Norman, Norman," he said. "You're the only one who's come to see me. Everyone else has deserted me." It seems all his friends from his football days and all the people he knows at Wainscott have forsaken him, and perhaps, because of the nature of the case, he has still not been able to find a competent lawyer to represent him.

Well, right off he started protesting his innocence. "Norman, I didn't kill her like they say. I wasn't saving her for . . . It was an accident, Norman. You have to believe me. Tell them, Norman, tell them I didn't do it. And you know I didn't have anything to do with Dean Fessing. I don't know what happened to him. I'm not a cannibal, Norman. I may be a slob and a glutton and a fornicator, but I'm not a cannibal. Please, Norman, you've got to help me."

I tried to calm him down, but when I reached to touch his shoulder, the guard intervened. But Malachy Morin is, I'm afraid, beyond comfort. He went on, blubbering out his soul to me, his eyes wide, red, and bulging, his mouth scarcely in control, his jowls aquiver. "You heard what the DA said yesterday, Norman. They want to execute me, Norman. They want to electrocute me. They want to strap me in that chair and . . . Oh, Norman, you know I've been afraid of electricity all my life. Doreen will tell you. I even make her turn on the lights in the office, and when there's a storm, I go down into the sub-subbasement. I've been treated for it, Norman. It's in my medical record. And now, now, they want to shave my head and attach an electrode and make me sit in that chair and . . . Norman, Norman, help me!"

I did what I could. I told him to get hold of himself. I told him that the District Attorney wasn't God and that there would be a trial, and that one had to have faith in the American criminal justice system. And he did eventually calm down, but only for a minute. He started in again, slowly, his distress building, his pathos naked on his face.

"They're so cruel in here, Norman, I can't tell you. The way they taunt me. One of the prisoners, a little runty guy, goes 'zzzzzzzzzzzzzzzzzzzzZAP!' every time I walk by his cell. And there was another one, a real wise guy, who called out, 'Hey, Fatty, they won't need to grease the chair when they fry you!' And the guy in the next cell has a balloon that he chafes until there's enough static electricity to make his hair stand on end. You can't imagine it, Norman. I never appreciated civilization until I came in here. It's like being in hell. And the guards are worse. Last night two of them pretended to be friendly. One was big and one was little and they stood outside my cell on their break. The big one told me I shouldn't worry because he had been up to see the chair in Ellsbank and said I wouldn't fit in it. Then the little one said they probably could squeeze me in but I shouldn't worry because the chair had been rewired and has all kinds of safety features to make sure no one gets hurt and that the first jolt knocks you out. They were pulling my chain, Norman, and I didn't even know it. Then the big one said his friend was right, that they give you about two thousand volts to stun you before they 'cook' you for a minute or two with four or five hundred volts and then hit you with another two thousand, just to make sure you're done. He said it was like doing a steak, you know, searing it on both sides and cooking it slowly in the middle. They were awful, Norman, awful to me. I tried not to listen, but I couldn't get away from them. The big one said to the little one, 'Did you tell him about the pan?' The little one said, 'Oh, the pan.' Then they acted like they shouldn't have said anything. 'What pan?' I asked, 'what pan?' I was terrified, Norman. 'Oh,' the big one said, 'the pan they put under the chair.' Norman, I nearly pissed myself. 'Why do they put a pan under the chair?' I asked. The little one coughed, and just when I thought I couldn't take it any longer, he said, 'It's to catch the juices.' Then they both laughed. Oh, Norman, I'm in hell. I'm in hell. You've got to help me. I'll never call you Bow Tie again, I promise. What happened with Elsa was an accident, Norman. I swear I didn't lay a finger on her. We were consenting adults all the way."

I have to confess I was relieved when the guard said our time was up. Morin said he was working on a "statement" with the lawyer he had and asked if I would read it over for him. I said I would and that I would also look for an attorney for him. And I told him not to worry about the electric chair, although I'm not sure I spoke with much conviction. I think I'll also write a letter to the warden suggesting that he somehow be separated from the other prisoners. I mean, the conditions he describes do sound inhuman.

Speaking of inhuman, I found upon returning a document in my e-mail that I will allow you, gentle reader, to judge for yourself.

Dear Mr. de Ratour:

Dr. Drex and I would like to announce that we have finally done it! As the verified transmission below illustrates, through sheer randomness and given enough time, members of the species *Pan trogodytes* are capable of producing a coherent line from the recognized canon. What remains for us to work through are the mathematical extrapolations regarding the numbers of operators and keyboard hours it would take for, say, our group of 19 text-producing units to achieve all of the world's great literature as compiled from standard reference works. Preliminary indications suggest that our group, working under the conditions pertaining to this ongoing effort, would take ten raised to the eleventh power hours to produce all the world's great literature.

However, we have very strong indications that our writing group is capable of far more than this kind of random effort. And while the number crunching will proceed with this project, we look forward to a far more revolutionary development in the near future — nothing less, as we have intimated before, Mr. de Ratour, than genuine pongid literature. But for now, here is the entry I mentioned above, and we do look forward to further communications with you regarding press releases, press conferences, interviews, etc.

Respectfully,

F. Snyders

CODE X443SRG CHIMPRITE BCORN WW234
aoodnasaoanm dna a-a0dma dal e=mc
squired, ecidn woo woo woo *Jesus*
nama, wappedamdna slept
ammmmpussnamandwinedwindwhinedlippedamdana,maw
ewanked[apad aqoneandlasaidthe
bishopsamslappedq9ea88a amam schleppedpp amd
sweptamdnama, as poapam *wept*

There were some real fireworks at today's meeting of the Oversight Committee, and I think Oliver Scrabbe has more than met
his match in Thad Pilty. Constance Brattle didn't help her own
cause when she took a provocative tone right from the start,
declaring that, given the arrest of Mr. Morin and other "ongoing
conditions at the museum," the committee would shortly extend
the scope of its inquiry beyond the diorama of Paleolithic life.
She then began to introduce Dean Scrabbe to the other members
of the committee as someone who would be "instrumental in
resolving the outstanding issues of the museum's operations."

Well, I don't think I have ever seen Thad Pilty so angry. Barely
controlling himself, his hands fisting and his jaw clenching, he
glared right at Professor Brattle and Dean Scrabbe as he interrupted her: "Excuse me, Professor Brattle, excuse me, please. I
find your last statement and the presence of Dean Scrabbe at this
meeting totally unacceptable. My original agreement with the
committee was that it would confine itself to suggestions regarding the form and content of the diorama itself. Unless Dean
Scrabbe excuses himself and unless this committee keeps to the
original agreement regarding its purview, I will have no choice
but to withdraw from this and any future meetings with the
committee."

I nearly clapped. I took inordinate pleasure in watching the
confusion into which Constance Brattle and her cohorts were
thrown. Randall Athol and Ariel Dearth started to say something, but she silenced them both. However, speaking as though
he were utterly in charge of the whole place, Dean Scrabbe told
the room that there was no way in which the finances of the
museum in general and the funding of the diorama in particular
could avoid oversight. He charged that aspects of the manage-

ment and policies of the museum bordered on the "criminally surreal," and that he was going to take the whole matter directly to President Twill and before the Board of Regents. With that he gathered his papers and stalked from the room.

As you can imagine, it took a few minutes for the group to settle down. After a session of whispering with members of the committee, Professor Brattle announced that they would proceed with the meeting as planned. Professor Pilty seemed reluctant but nodded and introduced Mr. Emmanuel Quinn, a representative of Humanation Syntectics, the company designing and manufacturing the models. Professor Brattle in her turn introduced the Reverend Farouk Karoom, a minister in the Islamic Baptist Temple of Zion. I was so taken by this gentleman's haircut, which I can only describe as topiary, that I nearly missed her characterization of him as a person "instrumental in agendarizing [or is it "agenderizing"?] community priorities [and who has] made multiculturalism more than another buzzword."

The Rev. Karoom starting right in malapropping — fittingly enough now that I think of it — biodrama for diorama. "I will insist," he insisted, "that people of color be given positions of power and dignity in any biodrama planned for the Museum of Man." Patiently, as though conducting a seminar, Professor Pilty told the minister that the people to be displayed in the diorama were Homo sapiens neanderthalensis. Puzzled for a moment, the Rev. Karoom replied that "the sexual preferences of the models are besides the point." It was Thad Pilty's turn to be puzzled. Finally, he said, "I should explain, Reverend, that neanderthal is a designation that we give to primitive man — " (Professor Brattle: "And woman"). At which point Bertha Schanke, working on the Boston Kreme, remarked as to how she considered all men primitive. Mr. Onoyoko, after listening to the ongoing translation by Ms. Kushiro, turned in Ms. Schanke's direction and smiled.

Professor Pilty waited for the room to quiet and then told the Rev. Karoom that the people to be depicted in the diorama were extinct. The Rev. Karoom nodded as though he understood and asked, "What does that have to do with minority representation in your biodrama?" Professor Pilty responded that they had considered making all the models dark skinned but thought that might be interpreted as racist in seeming to equate pronounced melanism with less derived morphologies. He went on to say that recent research on climate suggests that European Neanderthals were light skinned, perhaps even blond and blue eyed. Ms. Schanke interrupted him again, saying, "Why don't you admit you don't know and that the whole thing is a fantasy?"

Bobbing his amazing coiffure, the Rev. Karoom asked if the professor meant that there had been no "black Neanderthals." Before Pilty could answer, the minister went on in declamatory tones he undoubtedly deploys from the pulpit: "You mean to tell us, Professor, that there were no black Neanderthals when I have read in the newspaper about the African Eve. Your own colleagues, Professor, are telling the world that the mother of us all was a sister." When Professor Pilty started to explain about the European context, the Reverend cut him off. "You don't get it, Professor."

"What don't I get?" Pilty asked, showing just a bit of exasperation.

The Rev. Karoom allowed a moment of silence before pronouncing with a dramatic flourish: "That black people *invented* white people."

Well, that had Mr. Onoyoko mirthful again, and even Ms. Schanke joined in what was considered a good laugh at Thad Pilty's expense. The situation didn't improve much from there. Constance Brattle suggested that a compromise might be possible in that the models could be rendered in an intermediate shade, a kind of gray. Izzy Landes retorted that they would then look like they all came from New Jersey. Professor Athol opined that the problem with the diorama was its "Eurocentrism," to which Izzy retorted that, like it or not, we all, even Mr. Onoyoko, are part of European culture. Professor Ariel Dearth demurred, pointing out that Israel might be the best setting for the diorama given that whole families of modern-looking Neanderthals had been found in caves there. Professor Pilty then explained at some length that we were using a European setting because it was the one we knew the most about, because that was where he and his team had conducted their research. Which did little to mollify anyone.

All the while the Rev. Karoom sat back, gratified, I think, by the ruckus he had stirred up. Things had begun to settle down when Mr. Quinn, answering a question put to him by Professor Brattle, said his company could make the models any color they wanted. They could, he said, facetiously I'm sure, even make them spotted if that was what they wanted. The Rev. Karoom took the possibility quite seriously. He asked Mr. Quinn if that would be "black spots on white or white spots on black." Mr. Quinn replied that they could make them either way. But he suggested that a better solution to the problem of pigmentation would be to use stripes because, if they were done skillfully, it would be impossible to tell if they would be black stripes on white or white stripes on black. Rev. Karoom then asked Mr. Quinn if these would be broad stripes or narrow stripes. Mr. Quinn replied that his company could make them broad or narrow. He said they could even make them very narrow. He said they could make the models pin-striped, if that was what the committee wanted. In fact, he said, "We could give you a cross-hatched pattern, you know, a kind of plaid, or even a herringbone design, like a tweed." It went on like that, with discussions of piebald patterns, polka dots, and the like until Mr. Onoyoko was laughing openly and Professor Pilty was sitting with his face in his hands. It is just possible, I am beginning to hope, that he will rethink the whole project.

The meeting did give me a chance to buttonhole Ariel Dearth and tell him that Malachy Morin was having difficulty finding any kind of competent legal counsel. I must say he seemed quite surprised and intrigued, even when I told him that the museum would in no manner support any kind of defense fund. While I have my reservations about Ariel Dearth and his motives, he certainly would be better than the counsel Morin has now. Everyone else seems to have utterly deserted the man, although I have heard Amanda Feeney has dropped by to see him. But I suspect she's probably just looking for a story.

MONDAY, JULY 27

The nightmare continues.

Dean Scrabbe is missing, foul play is involved, from all appearances, and I am once again a suspect. Lieutenant Tracy came to my office this morning to inform me that the dean, after having spent part of the afternoon working at the museum, had not returned home yesterday. Very much a professional in his rugged trench coat, the lieutenant did not ask my permission to smoke but took out a cigarette, lit it, and began puffing. In a manner meant to intimate that I perhaps already knew what he was relating, he told me that the dean, after watching the first few innings of a baseball game on television, left his home to go to his office, the same one on the third floor that had been occupied by Dean Fessing. Scrabbe told his wife just before he left that he had come across some revealing anomalies in the finances of the museum and wanted to follow up on a hunch. When dinnertime came and went and he still hadn't come home, Mrs. Scrabbe called the dean's office and got a busy signal. At first she thought he was simply on the phone with a colleague, but finally she asked the phone company to check and found that the phone was off the hook. Alarmed, she called Wainscott security, who called the police.

The lieutenant paused as though to give me time to think it over. Then, his tone hard but not overtly hostile, he said, "The preliminary examination of his office indicates that a scuffle took place. His phone was knocked off the desk, and his computer looks damaged."

I was horrified, naturally, and still am, but I tried to remain ostensibly calm. "Well," I said, "this surely removes Malachy Morin as a suspect in Dean Fessing's murder."

The lieutenant remained noncommittal, and the ensuing silence was interrupted by the phone — reporters wanting to know if the Wainscott Cannibal had struck again. I informed the callers, with as much civility as I could muster under the circumstances, that I knew nothing about the dean's disappearance, that the dean was employed by Wainscott University, and that they should therefore call the Wainscott News Office. Of course, the calls were immediately referred back to me, and I parried by giving callers the office and home telephone numbers of President Twill.

It was during this flurry of calls and countercalls that I became aware that I was again, as they say, a prime suspect. What, Lieutenant Tracy wanted to know, had I been doing between the hours of three and seven Sunday afternoon? The notebook was out, and his tone bordered on the officious.

I told the officer that I had gone to de Vere Amphitheatre, which abuts the Marvell Gardens, to see a somewhat uneven production of *Julius Caesar* mounted by the Seaboard Summer Players.

"Was there anyone there who could vouch for your presence at the play?"

I thought for a moment. "I don't remember speaking to anyone there, although I saw, from a distance, several people that I know." I explained to him that this is not unusual, as many people connected with the university or the museum are away during the summer while a whole new crowd of summer students, tourists, and the like occupy much of Wainscott during July and August.

"When did the play finish?"

"About four-thirty."

"What did you do then?"

"I dropped by my office to pick up my newly restrung racquet before heading to the Club for a game of doubles."

"Who were the other players?"

"Let's see. . . . There was Bill Littlefield, Professor Punn of the Slavic Department, and Joe Dzhugashvili. He's Curator of the Armand Hammer Collection in the Frock."

"Is that like the baking soda brand?" He was taking down everything.

I said no and spelled it out for him.

"Mr. de Ratour, did you noticed anything out of the ordinary when you came into the museum . . . after the play?"

"Yes," I said. "I was in a hurry, but I couldn't take the elevator, because someone had propped it open on a floor above, a practice expressly forbidden by the fire ordinances in force in the building. As a result I had to go up through the exhibits and a thin scattering of Sunday visitors that were drifting down to the exit since it was near closing time."

"What time was this?"

"I would estimate about four-forty-five. I remembered having only fifteen minutes to get to the Club lockers and change for the five o'clock match."

Lieutenant Tracy asked if I would show him the elevator.

I said of course and with alacrity took him along the corridor to the ratterly old thing, if only to escape the phone calls. We rode it down to the third floor and paced the distance to Scrabbe's office, where a team of forensic experts from the SPD were going over the place for clues. They looked at me as though I was already handcuffed, and as a suspect once again, I could not help feeling a certain hideous kind of importance. In silence we continued to the basement, where there are storage areas for the various collections, and then down to the subbasement, which is just above the Skull Collection and which has more of the same and passageways connecting all three parts of the museum. As we were standing there, a technician from the Genetics Lab passed by on his way to the Primate Pavilion. I expressed some surprise to Lieutenant Tracy that the police had not looked at the elevator before and did not know that the subbasement passages were used to communicate between the two wings of the museum.

The observation chastened him a bit, and we returned to my office, where he continued to question me, but in a less aggressive manner. He told me that it was not good that I did not have a "watertight" alibi.

"One cannot live one's life as an alibi," I replied, but I wondered, in one of those daunting mental asides, if that wasn't what I had been doing for the past thirty-odd years.

The lieutenant's demeanor softened. It was as though he wanted to help me — or trip me up — when he asked, "Was there anything that happened at the play that was out of the ordinary? Something that you might have noticed and that could prove that you were there, at least for some of the time unaccounted for?"

The phone rang, and while I exchanged abuse with one of the worried people in Grope Tower, I racked my head about the play. At first I could recall nothing very unusual. There was the usual Sunday summer crowd, everyone casually dressed, the students more interested in each other than in what was happening on the stage. Then I remembered. "In Act II," I said, "the actor playing Brutus anagrammatically flubbed one of his lines. In that scene when the conspirators are talking about assassinating Caesar, Brutus said: 'Let's carve him as a dish fit for the dogs.' I almost missed it, but Cassius, a bit rotund and well fed for the part, snickered, because the rest of the sentence is 'Not hew him as a carcass fit for hounds.' "

Lieutenant Tracy nodded, then asked at what point it occurs in the play. I admitted it came quite early and racked my head for another gaffe as egregious as this one. Then I remembered. "In Act Five, Scene One, Antonius says to the assassins: 'You showed your teeth like apes, and frowned like hounds.' It should have been 'fawned like hounds.' "

"Is there any way you can prove this?" the lieutenant asked.

I made a gesture of helplessness. "You could question the actors. Perhaps they made a tape of it." I gave him my playbill.

"You know the play well," he said.

I quoted him: "I did enact Julius Caesar. I was killed i' the Capitol. Brutus killed me."

It appeared to impress him, but for only a minute. "That still leaves between four-thirty and five," he said.

"No," I replied, "between four-thirty and about four-fifty, which is the time I got to the Club. Really, Lieutenant, would I have been able, in twenty minutes, to murder and dispose of the body of a full-grown man?" I felt as though I had disappointed him somehow, as though he depended on me to be a good suspect.

Then he turned noticeably hostile. In rapid-fire succession he asked, "Isn't it true, Mr. de Ratour, that you had the same conflict with Scrabbe that you had had with Fessing about the future of the museum? Isn't the position of Recording Secretary obsolete, and wouldn't you lose your job if the university took over? Wasn't the animosity you felt towards Scrabbe aggravated by his offensive manner?" And before I could deny any of these charges, he informed me that I might want to have a lawyer present before answering any more questions.

I returned his hostility in kind. "I do not need a lawyer, Lieutenant Tracy, as I have nothing whatsoever to hide. You should realize as well that I cannot be bullied. I have had to stand up to bullying all my life, and I have become quite good at it."

A moment later he appeared to become conciliatory, then started in again as though that would be enough to mollify me. In that he was mistaken. When he began, as though thinking aloud, to go over suspects, Chard and Pilty again, the diorama, flipping back through his notebook, I stopped him. I said, "Lieutenant, I am perfectly willing to help you, but you are going to have to trust me. In fact, I would suggest you cultivate a flair for trust to go along with what I know is a necessary capacity for suspicion."

He gave me a most rueful glance. "Withholding evidence, Mr. de Ratour, could make you an accessory."

"Ideas are not evidence."

"But ideas come from knowledge."

"Or suspicions."

He sighed and smiled very faintly. "We checked Drex out. Around one-thirty yesterday he took a group of chimps in the pavilion van to the Middling County Zoo. He said that it was one of their regular Sunday afternoon outings and that they didn't get back until after four-thirty. He had ticket stubs with the time on them. The attendants at the zoo confirm his story."

I concurred that it made sense. Drex, I told the lieutenant, "is too obsessed with his chimps to go to the lengths that someone has gone to with Dean Fessing's remains. Besides, would he have eaten a whole dean by himself?"

"What about the chimps?"

"Chimps are frugivores and folivores for the most part, as far as I know."

"You mean vegetarians?"

"Fruits and leaves. But I'm not an expert, Lieutenant." After a moment of silence, I asked, "What about his assistant?"

He flipped through his notebook. "Frank Snyder?"

"Or is it Franz?"

"He gave both names. He was at the zoo as well."

I shook my head slowly. "There's something about that man . . ."

The lieutenant nodded. "I know what you mean, but he has an airtight alibi."

The phone rang again. Amanda Feeney. All but asking me if I had killed the deans. I got rid of her unceremoniously and turned back to the detective.

"What about this Professor Gottling?" he asked.

I shook my head and tried to dissemble the hair-raising prickle of suspicion I experienced at the mention of the name. I had stood and was glancing west-northwest, where I could see the glint of the Newhumber as it wound down from the Hays Mountains. "Why would the director of the Genetics Lab want to kill the deans?" I asked. I admitted there had been rumors over there for months about a very sensitive and controversial project. I was tempted to go to the computer and bring up the missives I had received from Worried. But I decided against it, in part out of my respect for "hard" science, which I take the study of genetics to be, but also because it seemed inconceivable to me that anyone exploring the mysteries of the genes would kill and cannibalize not one but two deans, if indeed that had been Scrabbe's fate. "Just a rumor. There are lots of rumors."

The lieutenant became instantly alert. "That's where you can help me. Where you should help me."

I shrugged and took a deep breath. "For years there's been a rumor about a cannibal cult centered on a retired professor . . . Raul Brauer."

"Chard's guest at the Eating Club?"

"Yes. He and some colleagues, it is said, while doing research in the Marquesas, killed and butchered a young volunteer as an exercise in ritual cannibalism." Voicing the canard so baldly seemed to reduce it to the absurdity it probably was.

"Who are his colleagues, the ones with him at the time?"

"Pilty, Chard, and someone named Alger Wherry. He's Curator of the Skull Collection. But I don't find it . . . credible."

"Why not?"

"Why two deans? Why not a plump undergraduate or a well-conditioned young athlete?"

"Could Fessing and Scrabbe have found out about the cult?"

"I suppose. If there is one."

"But you do think there's a plot of some kind, don't you?"

For a moment, as I looked across my desk at the intent, handsome face of the policeman, I felt that we were once again more like colleagues than antagonists, even if he maintained, with less and less conviction, despite his words, that I was a real suspect. "A plot?" I said. "I'm sure there must be one."

The lieutenant could sense, I know, that I was holding something back. And I might have told him about the missing archives from the Loa Hoa expedition and about the apparent disappearance of Skull Number One had I not suffered again from a strange hubris: the missing files were something *I* had found out about. They were *my* missing evidence. And as the interview, or interrogation if you prefer, wound down, I was inspired again to get to the bottom of these awful crimes myself.

Almost apologetically the lieutenant told me that, technically at least, I remained a suspect. "You have a motive, Mr. de Ratour. You don't have much of an alibi. And you admit being at the scene at the time of the murder."

"Disappearance," I corrected him.

"Yes," he echoed, "disappearance," and got up to go. He paused at the door to tell me, with a trace of facetiousness, not to leave town without informing him. Then the phone began ringing again. I ignored it. I opened my desk and took out the Fessing file, which I had presumed closed. I leafed through my black book. I couldn't get Thad Pilty out of my mind. I kept seeing and feeling the extraordinary anger he had shown at last week's meeting of the Oversight Committee. Then, on a strange impulse, I took out my father's revolver. I unloaded it, held it in both hands, aimed at the wall, and pulled the trigger several times, feeling the oiled mechanism click smoothly. Then, feeling the nugget weight of each deadly cartridge, I reloaded it.

Well, I think I have earned a good vintage with my dinner at the Club tonight. I don't imagine there will be much joking this time about how good or bad deans do or don't taste. I can already feel the fear rising around the whole place. We are all looking at one another with more and more suspicion. I must say I would feel more secure if I could carry the gun tucked snugly somewhere on my person.

THURSDAY, JULY 30

It has been only a few days since Dean Scrabbe's disappearance, and already it seems like an eternity. Everyone is on tenterhooks wondering what grisliness is about to be served up. The news media have been unmerciful, utterly unmerciful. They are assiduous in reporting every silly and grotesque rumor, including one about UFOs and cannibal aliens from outer space. Malachy Morin has been linked to a rumored "cannibal cult" among the faculty, that association with the professoriat conferring on the poor wretch a dubious kind of status. I cannot open my front door without finding some journalist or other waiting there with some imbecilic or gratuitously insulting question. Just last night I thought I heard one of them rooting around out in my trash bins. It turned out to be a large, bold raccoon, and I nearly expected it to start hectoring me. At the same time I confess to being relieved to see them, the journalists, I mean. The pall of fear that has settled on our little community is positively palpable. Each pair of averted eyes asks the same question: Am I next? To be murdered is bad enough; to be murdered, cooked, and eaten is simply *hors concours*. And if a full-grown man in all the vigor of his middle years can be plucked in broad daylight from his office in a public institution, are any of us safe?

Indeed, I have finally taken matters into my own hands and written to each member of the Board of Governors a detailed letter regarding the situation around here. I pointed out to them the clause in the Rules of Governance that not merely enables me to take such a step but in fact *requires* that, with or without the consent of the Director, I bring to their attention matters of paramount importance. I reiterated, of course, my respect for Dr. Commer, while pointing out that, if anything, that aging scholar's infirmities have grown more pronounced with time. I wrote that I was prompted to this act in part by the situation created by the (presumed) murders of Fessing and Scrabbe and by Malachy Morin's arrest and pending indictment, which has created more of a managerial vacuum than had existed heretofore. I stated that trends were developing which, if allowed to continue, could prove disastrous to the museum.

Another matter regarding the governance of the museum concerns me as well. I was the recipient this week of another communication through the e-mail from the Genetics Lab. I am glad now that I have entered all of these into this unofficial log, as they show a definite trend. Again, I will let the document speak for itself:

> Dear Mr. Detour [sic]:
>
> I can't tell you how crazy things are getting over here. I'm even thinking of leaving but I've been here a long time and I would lose a lot of benefits if I tried to switch jobs. I wouldn't be surprised if the stuff here had something to do with those deans getting killed. Someone around here is going to get killed the way things are going. Professor Gottling and Dr. Kaplan are barely talking to each other and when they do it's usually an argument. Dr. Kaplan kept telling Professor Gottling that he Professor Gottling I mean was trying to make a whole new Gino type, which sounds like some kind of Italian to me but then I don't understand all the complicated stuff they do here. Then Professor Gottling said it was only chimpanzees and why did Dr. Kaplan care. Dr. Kaplan kept saying it wasn't just chimpanzees because why did they need a human sperm bank in that case. Then they went around and around like that before someone saw me there and closed the door. I also heard from one of the secretaries that Charlene is pregnant and won't get an abortion because she's Catholic. It may just be gossip but Dr. Hanker sure does walk about with a worried look on his face. I don't know how it's all going to end but it's getting really tense around here.
>
> More Worried

Despite everything, I have, with effort, been able of late to find much comfort in researching the history of this marvelous place. What a boon, what a balm it has been to delve into the past! How simple everything seemed in those days! Among the family archives I have found some absolute treasures, including a bundle of letters between Othniel Remick and Sarah Goodfellow during their courtship. Extraordinary how civilized people were then, at least in the sentiments they expressed to each other. In a letter dated June 14, 1823, Othniel writes in part:

We are ashore on Isabela, which is a large island among the Galápagos. Here the wonders of the Creator never cease to amaze myself and my officers. Here might paradise have been, the wild creatures being so tame they light on one's shoulder and take feed from one's hand. Such is the bounty, we have provisioned ourselves with great land turtles that we secure on their backs for fresh meat many days from shore. God willing, I will arrive home before this poor correspondence that I am leaving in trust of Captain Bowdoin of the *Mermaid* out of Salem. You are never far from my thoughts, and I pray the Almighty will vouchsafe my return not for my life but for ours.

Reading that put in me mind of my own dear Elsbeth. It wasn't just Othniel's letter. Around this time of year I am particularly vulnerable to what used to a bittersweet melancholy one might call the blues — especially when I think of her. Just standing near the north window of my office, with its partial view of Shag Bay and the sailboats tautly propped against an onshore breeze, reminds me of other summers and of one in particular when I wasn't here. Elsbeth sailed her father's boat up on Lake Longing. I never took much pleasure in jibbing and tacking, coming about, being close-hauled, although I did like going wing to wing before the wind. But moving for its own sake never moved me. The illusion, I suppose, is that we are going someplace, not merely making the rounds of the inevitable circles, however ingenious, that we all revolve in. It was just about this time of the summer that I dropped out of her circles. It was the summer after she graduated from Wainscott. I should have proposed to her then, but I hesitated, not wanting, I told myself, to stand in the way of any career she might pursue.

Of course, I can see in retrospect that I was at least as concerned about the impact an engagement and subsequent marriage would have on my own career. Just that February I had been accepted by Professor Calloway to join the Wainscott team excavating the Greco-Roman levels of a site at Infra, which is just inland on the coast of North Africa. I had come to archaeology late, having taken my undergraduate degree in fine arts. Following my own graduation three years earlier and during the year I was at Jesus College, Oxford, studying under Blecky, I had begun to reject the notion of "fine arts" *per se,* a rather radical departure at the time. I saw that all art was "fine" provided it was competently done within its own terms: the finely etched boomerang of a naked aborigine is superior *tout court* to a mediocre oil from the Quattrocento. Having said that, I must insist that, where art is concerned, aesthetic standards should concede nothing to ethical or ideological considerations. Aesthetics constitutes a moral system of its own, and simply because a member of some "marginalized" group (awful terms they use these days) has made something does not endow it with any intrinsic value as art. Eskimos and Berbers are as capable of kitsch as the middlebrow Americans who, in buying such stuff, participate in its propagation.

But I have wandered from my subject. The fact is, I had at the time embraced archaeology with all the enthusiasm of youth, and I was full of passionate eagerness to join the team at Infra, having helped catalog some of the artifacts from earlier digs. It did not seem proper to propose to a woman and then leave immediately for nearly three months. Engagements, I have always thought, are a time of growing intimacy, when two people come to know each other by spending time together. Instead, I was spending less time with Elsbeth. As the mid-June departure date approached, I was in a veritable tizzy of preparation. I bought myself one of those Australian slouch hats that tie up at the side and the kind of shorts issued by the British Army in warm climates. I packed and repacked my kit. I suffered the necessary inoculations gladly. I read constantly. Elsbeth wasn't absent from my mind; indeed, I think in some ways I was doing it

for her. I imagined the snapshots of myself at the dig —
begrimed and bewhiskered, in slouch hat and shorts — that I
would send to her with long letters full of vivid details about
what we were unearthing from the past. I imagined returning to
her in September, sunburned and roughened, a man!

Our good-byes were quite tender. Although we were not for-
mally engaged, promises were made on the basis of which we
allowed ourselves intimacies previously denied, but which
stopped well short of any kind of consummation. I was moved by
her tears when for the last time we kissed before I boarded the
train at the old Seaboard station, a beautiful place since leveled to
make room for a slum. In grand Hollywood style, she stood on
the receding platform waving while I, from the open window of
my compartment, waved back.

Infra, I must say, exceeded all my expectations. Never before or
since has drudgery been such bliss. It is difficult to describe the
kind of exhilaration that comes when, digging on your knees,
sometimes with your bare hands, but always so carefully, you
unearth through the sand next to an ancient wall, as I did, a
charmingly simple clay jar complete with a fitted top and decorated with the red glaze characteristic of the region. With infinite
care, with my fingertips, I brushed away the grime of centuries,
put down its exact location, and then, in Professor Calloway's
presence, removed the top to find it half filled with clean, hard
grains of wheat. There I was, in the full brunt of the midday sun,
unearthing and fingering palpable history, resurrecting beauty,
making time disappear so that I was, for a transcendent, displaced moment, in a sunny courtyard millennia ago among
those early Greek colonists.

A more private bliss arrived with Elsbeth's first letter. It was an
unconditional declaration of love on her part such as she had
never made before. She missed me horribly, she said, and the
next few paragraphs made me nearly blush as she conjured in

quite graphic detail what to expect my first night back. I was deeply moved. I went out of my tent and peered up at the stars, which, in that high, dry air, were preternaturally bright. I decided then that we would build a life together, a strong physical, spiritual, and artistic life during which our periodic separations would only sharpen the passion. I wrote back telling her how much I missed her, how I thought about her in all her aspects, and how I had something very important to ask her when I returned. I enclosed a snapshot of myself in slouch hat and shorts that our resourceful photo technician, despite very rough conditions (we were at least a hundred kilometers from any sizable habitation) had been able to print.

I was somewhat perplexed but not alarmed when the post, erratic at best, failed to bring an answering letter from Elsbeth during the next couple of weeks. I was working, after all, from dawn until light failed in the evening. I had something of a small social life in the mess tent with the other members of the expedition, who were given to drinking great quantities of beer. I confess to a slight flirtation with an attractive blonde woman from California. It came to nothing, of course; I was irrevocably committed to Elsbeth. I was somewhat shocked but not entirely surprised to see this same young woman early one morning leaving the tent of Professor Calloway's chief assistant, a married man. (I'm not sure how they managed, since all of us, I know, had only those narrow army cots.)

Some weeks after her first letter, I received a second missive from Elsbeth, and I can still recall as though it was yesterday the mixture of anticipation and trepidation with which I took it to my tent to read. Even as I recall it here, my blood runs cold at remembering what I found in that cheap little envelope: nothing more than a hastily scribbled, scarcely punctuated "dear John" letter. She informed me that she had met "another man," a law student named Winslow Lowe. She said that they were "deeply involved" and that this was the "real thing." Into those trite phrases I read, of course, scenes of torrid voluptuousness; I imagined them in the most lascivious of embraces, indulging the very intimacies I had allowed myself to imagine with her. It was as though the passion promised in her first letter was now being lavished on another man. And the indulgences of my imagination returned to haunt my waking and sleeping hours in feverish visions.

I have never been so wretched in my life. Then did the desert, the desolation of which had so charmed me, turn to desert, reflecting back my inner desolation so that nothing was left in the world. The things I dug out of the sand became like so much detritus from a human past, the misery of which seemed as infinite as the sandy wastes and empty sky of my heart. I could scarcely eat and, while never heavy, grew gaunt. I could no longer dig during the midday heat and instead lay fitfully in my stifling tent afflicted by demons of loss and jealousy. The fever of my heart spread to my body, but even this I dissembled before the rest of the group until I became too ill to leave my tent, where a commode of sorts was improvised. My condition worsened, and when my temperature reached a hundred and five and I had become somewhat delirious, a decision was made to evacuate me to a hospital. However, my fever broke that night, and though still weak the next morning, I was much improved. A few days later I was able to resume work during the cooler parts of the day.

My heart, alas, never quite recovered. Where the fair sex was concerned, it had become a blackened, burnt-out stump. And while I gradually regained some interest in the work of excavation, analysis, and interpretation, I remained anxious and disabled in a way that has affected my entire life. I returned to Wainscott, and during a leave of absence from my studies, which had lost much of their flavor for me, I took a temporary position as assistant to Miss Vogel, whose own fragile health had begun to fail. I never wrote back to Elsbeth. I heard from her mother that she had taken a job in a New York insurance firm to be near Winslow Lowe, who was enrolled at Columbia Law School. I determined then never to think of her again, and in some ways I have been quite successful. In other ways, she is all I think about.

TUESDAY, AUGUST 4

I'm afraid I have become more involved in the fate of Malachy Morin than I ever intended to. Some of it, of course, is unavoidable. As the public spokesman for the museum, I continue to answer or brush aside all kinds of inquiries from the press, from people writing books, sensation seekers, and the like. I have to say a lot of it has been outrageous. Some national "humor" magazine is said to be proposing a "Cannibal Gourmet Cookbook" and has called the museum to get Morin's "recipes."

Surprisingly, to me at least, Dean Scrabbe's disappearance during Mr. Morin's incarceration has not been taken as a reason for exculpating the latter in the (presumed) murders of either of the deans. The current thinking, which was intimated to me yesterday during an interview with Lieutenant Tracy, is that a "cannibal conspiracy" may be extant in the larger Wainscott community and Mr. Morin may have served it as a "supplier." The lieutenant thinks the cult is centered on Corny Chard, which may be one reason I am no longer under active investigation. Corny, I must say, has not been helping his own cause in the least. Marge Littlefield tells me he's been interviewed on television and playing the anthropophagic gadfly to the hilt.

It also appears that through a simple act of Christian charity, my one visit to Malachy Morin, I have become his chief conduit to the world. Other than Amanda Feeney, whose motives certainly are suspect, I am apparently the only person with any interest in saving his neck, or whatever it is you save when you spare someone from the electric chair. With Ms. Feeney's help (I've heard she's angling for exclusive rights to his "story"), he has drawn up a statement setting forth his version of what happened to Elsa Pringle. This document arrived this morning, and, under the circumstances, the least I could do was to glance over it. I have not taken the time to enter it into the system. I have made a copy and will incorporate the text into the hard copy of this journal as a cautionary tale, to show what happens when the Rules of Governance are ignored, when politics becomes an end in itself, when individuals like Mr. Morin, whatever their prowess on the football field, are allowed into positions of power and discretion. [*NdR's comments in the following document have been incorporated into the text in brackets. Ed. Note*]

Statement by Malachy Morin Relating to the Accidental Death of Elsa Pringle

On or about seven o'clock on the evening of Sunday, May 17, Mr. Malachy Morin drove with Elsa Pringle for dinner at the Lobster Haul, a restaurant in Ellington, approximately twelve miles up the coast north of Seaboard. The purpose of this dinner was to discuss Ms. Pringle's prospects as press assistant at the Museum of Man. [I will try to get this changed to "his place of employment," so as not to compromise the good name of the MOM, but I'm sure he'll want to keep it for the stature it lends his case.] Miss Pringle had called two days before this dinner appointment concerning the status of her application to the aforementioned position. On that occasion, Mr. Morin took the opportunity to suggest to Miss Pringle that it might be advantageous for them to meet in a less formal setting to discuss the position in question in view of the complicated nature of the relationship between a busy [???] administrator and his press assistant. Mr. Morin said that he had found working with Mr. Rotour [*sic*] with the press had required all of his diplomatic skills. [I will insist that my name, misspelled and all, be removed, but I'm sure it's important to establish his motives in suggesting that he and Ms. Pringle have dinner together.]

Miss Pringle agreed to have dinner with Mr. Morin, and the latter drove in his vehicle, a Chrysler Le Baron, at or about 6:30 P.M. of the date above to her apartment at the corner of Elmsdale and Frothford. After a short social visit during which Mr. Morin had a Diet Pepsi and fixed a loose wire in Miss Pringle's stereo player, they drove up the coastal road to Ellington, arriving at the restaurant shortly after seven. During the drive, they talked about Seaboard and how, despite some of the newer developments along the coast, it was still a pretty part of the country. Miss Pringle told Mr. Morin that she liked it much better than Columbus, Ohio, where she grew up, or Gainesville, Florida, where she had gone to college. She said that she had decided to settle in the area after a summer internship on the Seaboard *Bugle*.

When they arrived at the Lobster Haul, they found the restaurant to be crowded. They did not, however, have a problem getting a table as Mr. Morin is a highly respected frequenter of this establishment and had called earlier to make a reservation. After some pleasantries with the hostess, the well-known country-and-western singer Lilly Laverne, Mr. Morin and Miss Pringle were seated next to the window with a charming view of Hooker's Point. For drinks Mr. Morin ordered a double Scotch on the rocks for himself and a strawberry daiquiri for Miss Pringle. During the meal they shared a bottle of *vin blanc de maison,* much of which Mr. Morin drank. For starters, Mr. Morin had a bowl of clam chowder and the garden salad with Roquefort dressing, and for the main course the two-for-one baked lobster special, which included steak fries and coleslaw, followed by blueberry pie ala [*sic*] mode and coffee with brandy. Miss Pringle started with a garden salad with the vinaigrette house dressing, the chicken special, which came with saffroned rice and glazed broccoli, of which she ate only small amounts, and coffee with lime sherbet. These details are attested to by the waiter and by the autopsy report. [Dr. Cutler, ever helpful, told me they were able to calculate quite precisely the time of death by the degree of digestion of the contents of Ms. Pringle's stomach — after they had thawed her out, that is.]

During the course of the meal, Mr. Morin and Miss Pringle discussed the press assistant position in considerable detail as Mr. Morin was desirous of communicating to Miss Pringle the importance he attached to the job. In this regard he stressed that he wanted someone who would be proactive rather than reactive. He told Miss Pringle she would be responsible for compiling a local, national, and even international list for the press releases that would project the Museum of Man in a favorable light. They discussed what kind of assistance Miss Pringle would need. They touched on salary, and while a minimum was agreed to, Mr. Morin said he would see about getting her more as he believed in equal pay for equal work. Mr. Morin told Miss Pringle that as far as he was concerned, the job was hers, but that he would still have to see to a few technical details involving personnel, accounting, payroll, and so on, and hoped there wouldn't be any snags.

After dinner, at or about 8:45 P.M., Mr. Morin and Miss Pringle exited the restaurant. At that point, Miss Pringle asked Mr. Morin if he wanted her to drive because of the amount of alcoholic beverages he had consumed on the premises. Mr. Morin replied that he was capable of driving them back. He said that for him it had been something of an abstemious evening where alcohol was concerned. She asked if he was offended by her concern, and Mr. Morin said, on the contrary, it demonstrated to him her sense of responsibility. As they sat in Mr. Morin's vehicle in the parking lot of the restaurant, they got to talking as people will, and Mr. Morin informed Miss Pringle that he found her very mature for her age. He said he found her congenial and thought they could work well together at the museum and that he liked her as a person. In saying this, he took Miss Pringle's hand in what was meant as a purely platonic, reassuring gesture. Miss Pringle then leaned towards Mr. Morin and kissed him in an entirely voluntary way. Following this kiss, Mr. Morin, who was completely sober at this point in time, drove them in his Chrysler Le Baron back to Seaboard along the coastal road without incident. Out of sheer habit, Mr. Morin drove to his own home, one of the former faculty houses on Shade Lane, where he has lived since being divorced some six years ago from the former Mrs. Morin. At this point, Mr. Morin thought it would be impolite not to ask Miss Pringle if she would like to come in for a cup of coffee or a drink. Miss Pringle agreed entirely on her own volition, with no undue pressure on the part of Mr. Morin. Upon entering the house at approximately 9:20 P.M., Mr. Morin turned on his stereo and put on a compact disc featuring light classical music. And, as the evening was chilly for the time of year, he then proceeded to start a fire in the fireplace, which he had arranged earlier in the day. For refreshments, Mr. Morin went into the kitchen, where he poured and drank a straight Scotch before pouring another for himself and a sherry for Miss Pringle.

Mr. Morin and Miss Pringle sat together on the couch facing the fireplace, listening to an orchestral version of *West Side Story,* and resumed the conversation they had had during dinner and their ride back to Seaboard concerning Miss Pringle's duties as press assistant at the museum. Mr. Morin told Miss Pringle that she could, time permitting, contribute articles to the MOM *Newsletter.* He told her he thought she would find the museum a congenial and collegial place to work. He told her again that he was impressed with her attitude and that what she lacked in experience could be made up in hard work. Mr. Morin also told Miss Pringle that Mr. Ratour [*sic*], although a bit of a stick [!!!], would be able to help her considerably. Miss Pringle asked Mr. Morin if it was all right to smoke, and he said it was. At that point in time, Mr. Morin left the living room to get himself another Scotch and Ms. Pringle another sherry and an ashtray.

After Miss Pringle had finished her cigarette and drunk about half of the second glass of sherry, she and Mr. Morin exchanged another kiss of a purely voluntary nature. Gradually they became more intimate in a natural and physical way. In the course of these intimacies, Mr. Morin told Miss Pringle that, despite the apparent differences in their ages, interests, and so on, he found himself very much drawn to her. When their mutual fondling had reached a sufficiently intimate degree, Mr. Morin told Miss Pringle that despite his reputation as a ladies' man, he often had difficulty in achieving and maintaining an erection. This information appeared to goad Miss Pringle, because at that point in time and on her own initiative entirely, she unzipped Mr. Morin's trousers and with her hands and mouth soon resolved Mr. Morin's difficulties in this regard. Shortly thereafter, in a state of high mutual arousal, an initial attempt at conventional intercourse was made on the couch, but it faltered when one of the corner supports snapped. Mr. Morin suggested that his bed would be more comfortable and that they should go upstairs. Miss Pringle agreed to this, and after Mr. Morin had refreshed their drinks, and turned up and set the stereo to play another disc of show tunes done in a classical mode, they went upstairs to the king-size bed in Mr. Morin's bedroom.

After both had undressed and lay down together, Miss Pringle found it necessary to apply herself again to Mr. Morin's person. After considerable exertions on her part proved successful and after several attempts in various positions, during which time Mr. Morin's rigidity began to falter, insertion was achieved with Miss Pringle in the superior position. Mr. Morin, though very much a masculine man, deemed this position appropriate given the relative proportions of the parties involved. However, in the course of the next few moments, what with the twisting and turning that naturally attend vigorous intercourse and with an understandable resurgence of masculine pride on the part of Mr. Morin, they more or less revolved into the standard missionary position, that is, with Miss Pringle underneath Mr. Morin.

The record should show that, despite Mr. Morin's reputation as a lover, it had been some time since he had successfully had sexual congress with a woman. The record should also show that while Mr. Morin has a considerable capacity for alcohol, the amount he had drunk and the excitement of expectation had begun to take their toll. In short, it took him considerable time to achieve ejaculation after intercourse with Miss Pringle commenced. Moreover, the record should show that the prospect of *not* achieving ejaculation, and all that meant to his self-esteem, to Miss Pringle's view of him and through him her appreciation of the museum, drove Mr. Morin to great and preoccupied lengths in his lovemaking efforts. The record, in short, should show that in the sway of his passion, his sense of duty, and the magnificent music crashing all around them, Mr. Morin got carried away. It was in this context that some time after Mr. Morin and Miss Pringle had arranged themselves in the missionary position so called, Miss Pringle, all but hidden beneath Mr. Morin's considerable bodily bulk, began to move in a very pronounced way, squirming and kicking. Mr. Morin took this to be the very throes of sexual excitement, which excited him to ever more strenuous efforts. These culminated a few moments later in what Mr. Morin took to be one of those wonderful mutual orgasms he had read about in books, particularly judging from Miss Pringle's final, convulsive shudderings.

Mr. Morin recalls quite clearly that they lay together for some time. The clock on his bedside table read 10:35 P.M., making it about 10:30 P.M., as the clock is about five minutes fast. Miss Pringle at this time lay there in what Mr. Morin took to be a drowse of postcoital bliss. Although Mr. Morin does not smoke, he went downstairs to get Miss Pringle's cigarettes and brought them back to the bedroom with another sherry for her and a double Scotch for himself. Not being sure that Miss Pringle wanted to stay the night, Mr. Morin called her name softly, asking her if she wanted him to call her a cab. At first he thought she was just a deep sleeper and continued to try to rouse her. Then he noticed there seemed to be something strange in the way she lay there, her head bent to one side and her legs still splayed. He called her name several times quite loudly and nudged her arm. Gradually and with deepening horror, Mr. Morin realized that Miss Pringle was unconscious. Then, with even more horror, he realized that she seemed not to be breathing. He took a small mirror off his bureau and held it under her nose. It did not fog. She appeared, in short, to have died.

Mr. Morin's first impulse was to dial nine-one-one and ask for help. He is a faithful fan of the television show named after that emergency number and was aware of the nearly miraculous resuscitations paramedics and others had effected in the course of their work. But in his panic he quickly drank the Scotch he had brought up for himself and then the sherry. He dialed nine-one-one but out of a nameless dread put the phone down before anyone answered. He did not know what had happened to Miss Pringle. He was afraid. Whatever the cause of her death, he knew there would be a scandal, that it would bring shame on himself and on the museum as well as Wainscott University. Mr. Morin had several more drinks. He is not sure how many. He tried to think. The horror of what had happened kept engulfing his sense and senses. The record should show that he sat down and cried like a little boy. He wondered if she had had a heart attack. He thought of putting her clothes back on and calling the police. But all the time he was growing more and more confused. Mr. Morin considered calling a priest or a minister. But he knew they would only tell him to call the police.

In his desperation and confusion, Mr. Morin decided what he really needed was time. But he knew he didn't have any time. Every moment made it later at night. In his whirling thoughts he contemplated the nature of time and its relation to life. He recalled hearing somewhere that there is no time without motion and no motion without energy and that only at absolute zero does motion cease, all of which led him to think of the freezer in the basement of the house. Mr. Morin did not want to conceal anything. He merely wanted time to think and to present the situation in a more appropriate setting. In the mental state he was experiencing then, he imagined he could keep Miss Pringle intact until he could arrange for it to appear that the accident had happened in the afternoon, with all of her clothes on.

It was on that basis alone that he decided to put Miss Pringle in the freezer, an upright Kenmore that had been in the basement for years. To do this, he had to remove the shelving and some of the things on them, including a twenty-pound turkey that had been there since his wife had left him. When Mr. Morin had accomplished that, he went back upstairs to the bedroom, hoping to find that through some miracle Miss Pringle had come around. But she lay there, exactly as before. He lifted her up and took her down into the basement, where, in a sitting position, knees up, she fit into the bottom of the freezer. He was able to fit some of the upper shelves back in along with some of the food but had to discard the turkey.

After that, Mr. Morin went upstairs, turned off the music, and drank himself to unconsciousness. The record should show that never during this whole time did Mr. Morin, who was only trying to do his job as a highly respected museum administrator, compel Miss Pringle in any one of her actions. The record should show that what happened was an accident, a tragedy for Miss Pringle and a tragedy for Mr. Morin, whose only mistake was to fail to report to the proper authorities in a timely fashion what had happened.

Well, I'm not sure what to make of this document. It sounds plausible enough in not sparing us the awful details. On the other hand, I know Mr. Morin to be capable of imaginative mendacities, and the threat of the electric chair is a real one. And the circumstantial evidence for the charge of murder and cannibalism (I mean, keeping that poor girl in the freezer) is certainly strong. I will, in any event, pass a copy of this document on to Ariel Dearth. With the disappearance of Scrabbe, there appears to be considerable commercial potential for anyone even peripherally connected to the case. Malachy Morin, in short, might now be able to afford Mr. Dearth's services.

On an entirely different subject, as I have leafed back through these unofficial entries, I found them to be a bit more auto-biographical than I intended. Not that I object to autobiography as such. I simply wouldn't want these diaristic leavings to sound like contemporary fiction. So much of what is offered these days is consciously and self-consciously about what are called "rela-tionships," a horrible hybrid of a word that sounds like it comes from a manual on pathology. It all stems, I suppose, from what might be called the therapeutic ethos. What I certainly don't want these entries to sound like, what I cannot abide myself, are accounts by faculty members about what goes on in their institu-tions, especially dreary accounts of the petty politics involved.

Not that it makes much difference what I include or exclude. I can't imagine anyone besides myself or a future historian of the MOM reading this account.

MONDAY, AUGUST 10

I feel like a juggler who has gotten one or two too many balls going in the air. I have heard from Dexter McFarquar. It appears a tentative date has been set for the Board to meet. His response, as usual, was most gracious, but he hinted at reaching "an ac-commodation" with the university. I suppose I should expect that.

I did receive what may be some good news. Ariel Dearth gave a press conference Friday announcing that he will undertake the legal defense of Malachy Morin on a *pro bono publico* basis. In practice that means he will charge only three hundred and fifty dollars an hour for his time. More important, from now on I will have all calls concerning the Morin case referred to Mr. Dearth's office at the Law School, which, apparently, he runs like a regular law office. Dearth called asking me to coordinate any of the museum's public relations efforts with the strategy he and his "team" will develop over the next few weeks. I told him I would take the matter under advisement. You have to be careful with lawyers. The next thing you know I will be listed as codefendant.

But there are still some grace notes left in life. The Reverend Lopes dropped in this morning, making a pastoral visit, both bringing and seeking comfort, or at least advice. He offered quite generously to conduct a prayer service at the museum if I thought it would help the staff cope with Dean Scrabbe's disappearance. I am ashamed now to admit that I discouraged it, that I dissembled with vague remarks my real objection: to have the Wainscott Minister presiding at a service in the MOM might be seen as a legitimization of the university's claim to the museum. We passed over the matter quickly. He said he was in fact stumped as to what to do for the larger community. "I can't, Norman," he said, holding the cup of tea I had brought him from the cafeteria, "hold a memorial service when the poor man is simply missing. He could show up any day, the victim of amnesia or a bizarre kidnapping." He went on to say that Scrabbe's disappearance raised for him a more fundamental theological problem: "To disappear like that, Norman, makes us all seem, well, ephemeral."

I quaffed my coffee. "Alfie," I said, "it is only our mortal form that is ephemeral; and I am more and more convinced of that every day." I went on to suggest that he hold a vigil service in Swift Chapel for the whole community. That, I said, would acknowledge the dean's disappearance, signal the hope of his eventual return, and constitute, in retrospect and in the eventuality that the dean's fate never comes to light, a kind of standby memorial service.

Alfie replied that he and his staff had considered doing just that. The problem, he said, is that given the nature of vigils — their being acts of faith and hope — they are easier to initiate than to terminate, especially when the object of their observance remains unresolved, as might happen in this case. He confessed to me that he was deeply disheartened by what was happening to the museum, to the university, and to the city. "When these things happen, Norman," he said, picking up his straw boater and preparing to leave, "it takes some time to restore our faith in the possibility that we are transcendent beings."

He left me feeling small that I had caviled about his holding a prayer service at the MOM. It is summertime, after all, and there's really no one around to notice. And Alfie is such a benign presence. Indeed, I felt uplifted all morning by his visitation. I was brought back to reality by the presence of a police officer at the main entrance. We now have a member of Seaboard's finest stationed at the door twenty-four hours a day, although what good that will do is beyond me. It certainly has done nothing to dispel the sense of doom that pervades this beautiful old place.

My own investigation, at the expense of my historical research, I must say, has continued apace. I have decided to enlist old Mort in getting behind the Green Door. I have a feeling I will find the Skull, the missing archives, and God only knows what else there. I have called over to the Wainscott Personnel Office to have sent to me the CV's of several — I won't call them "suspects" so much as individuals on whom I am starting dossiers. "Human Resources" at Wainscott helps us keep employee records, especially for the lab, the pavilion, and professors with joint appointments.

I am also starting to take more seriously the communications I have been receiving from the lab. Upon my arrival this morning I found another communication from Worried:

Dear Mr. Detour [sic]:

I am writing to tell you that I have found out important information about what Professor Gottling and the others are up to with Project Alpha. I was talking yesterday with a friend who I haven't seen in a long time who works at the pavilion part-time and he told me they have a really restricted area there that you need a special badge to get into where they keep eight chimpanzees. He says three of the chimpanzees are males and five are females and that the doctors come over and go through these special procedures to get the eggs from the females and milk the sperm from the males. It sounds disgusting to me but my friend says they bring the sperms and eggs over to the lab here to mix together and then they bring them back and put them back into the females. He says they come back after a few weeks and give the females an abortion. Then they take the fetus back to the lab to study. He says they are doing it in secret because there are really tough state laws about experiments with animals even with rats. We now have guards at all the entrances around the clock. I don't know if it has to do with Project Alpha or with Charlene's mother who came in last week and disrupted a big meeting that Dr. Hanker was having in his department. One of the secretaries who was there told me that she came in and started screaming at Dr. Hanker saying she had seen the tape and knew what he had done to her daughter and that he was going to pay. Then she went right up to him and punched him right in the face and had to be restrained. Poor Dr. Hanker was walking around all week with a big bandage over his nose. I've also heard that his wife wants to divorce him. She's supposed to be rich and good looking and bored with Seaboard anyway. I told my friend at the pavilion that I was writing to you and he said he would try to find out more. Maybe he can get some solid evidence to send to you. I don't know but I'm starting to think that this all has something to do with what happened to Professors [sic] Fessing and Scrabbe.

                                            Very Worried

Of course, Worried may only be some disgruntled lab technician or a graduate student playing a sophomoric prank, as graduate students are wont to do. I would show these communications to Lieutenant Tracy, but they hardly constitute real evidence. He says they get crank calls all the time down at headquarters. My real worry, frankly, is the press. Even if there is a small sliver of truth in these allegations, the *Bugle* would blow it out of all proportion. The story or some mangled version of it would get into the national and international press, and we've had enough of that what with the cannibalizing of Dean Fessing and now Dean Scrabbe's disappearance and Malachy Morin's involvement in the death of Elsa Pringle. Speaking of which, Marge told me yesterday when I saw her at the Club that Morin and Amanda Feeney have become something of "an item," even though he's still in jail. Wonders never cease.

What I should do, of course, is confront Professor Gottling with these accusations. There's no one else left, not even Scrabbe, who didn't have any official authority in the first place. If Gottling is involved in anything remotely like the experiments Worried accuses him of, a Board of Inquiry will have to be convened. The Rules of Governance allow for that, of course, given "just cause on the part of any museum principal or employee." It's all so tiresome and complicated. I am sorely tempted at times to take early retirement. I could retreat to my own study at home and dwell on the beautiful past. I won't, of course. It would be the coward's way out. And there comes a time, sometimes more than once, when a man has to stand and face things even when he's not sure what it is he's facing.

And it's more than that. I have something of a small confession to make. At times, especially in the summer, when the days are long and I have this old place all to myself, I wander down through the galleries, very nearly inhaling the light from the setting sun that fires the skylight above with scarlets and amethysts, tinting the glass on the cases with paler hues, especially up on the fifth floor. I linger there over the terra-cotta figurines, miniatures of Attic perfection, one of which, a full-bodied Aphrodite in clinging, diaphanous gown, reminds me of the Elsbeth of my youth. Or, for the thousandth time, I stop by the case of netsuke, never failing an inner smile at the contorted antics of Ashinaga and Tenaga rendered in elongated detail in one inch of ivory. I grow nearly breathless under the sway of a wonderful, eerie sensation: this place, where the beauty of the past is gathered and venerated, is the *afterlife;* this temple to man's propensity to create beauty is where our spirits go to dwell, and I fervently believe that if only one particle of one's being could survive and persist here, it would be enough.

FRIDAY, AUGUST 14

My hands are unsteady as I type this entry. I may just have solved this whole bloody business! This afternoon the Wainscott Personnel Office faxed me several of the CV's I had asked for. I was puzzled to find two CV's, one for Francis Snyder and one for Franz Snyder, identical except for their present employment. Perhaps he had more than one job. The former is listed as working at the pavilion and the latter in the creative writing program in the Wainscott English Department. But when I read the attached stick-on note, I felt that bristling that comes with the pulse of adrenaline. The note simply stated they couldn't decide which of the twins I meant so they were sending me both CV's. Twins! I called over there at once to ascertain if the twins were identical. I was bumped up the line to someone with sufficient authority to inform me that she couldn't say for sure if they were identical but it certainly looked that way judging from their file photos, the ones they use on their identity cards. Identical twins! If one of them doesn't have an alibi, then neither does! I also learned that the brothers were owners and operators of a restaurant in Boston called something like Dri (P? B?) rat . . . sten — something German, I think, but I couldn't make out the name because of a typographical distortion in the transmission. So they would know about cooking!

What a confusion of delight and fear I experienced at this discovery. The delight of *knowing,* of finding this crucial fact before any of the police did. I had to resist the unseemly pleasure of suspicions confirmed, if only because this inner smirk was accompanied by a distinct presentiment of danger. There are two of them, after all, big, strong men both, and who knows how many more are involved. Drex, perhaps, persons unknown in the Genetics Lab. The missives from the lab began to take on a new, darker significance.

I called the SPD and was patched through immediately to Lieutenant Tracy when I told the dispatcher who I was and what I had to relate. How gratifying it was to hear the lieutenant say, "Good work. We'll get on it right away." Once the arrests are made, I think I'll turn my whole file over to the police.

Needless to say, I feel positively triumphant. I feel like calling Elsbeth and telling her what has happened. I'm not sure why. To make her feel proud of me, I suppose, although I don't know why I should want her to be proud of me after all these years. Just yesterday, in going through my desk drawers as part of a preliminary reorganization of my office, I came across a piece of paper with Elsbeth's phone number scribbled on it. For a moment I couldn't place it, even though in a premonitory way my pulse had already begun to quicken. I gazed at it for several moments until, just like you see in the movies, the scrap of paper dissolved into a scene some fifteen years ago on a blustery wintry day outside of Waugh's Drugstore, in the old downtown part of

Seaboard. I was just emerging from the pharmacy with a prescription for a sinus infection, I think, when whom should I literally bump into but Elsbeth. I scarcely recognized her. I hadn't seen her, after all, in more than fifteen years, and in the meanwhile she had put on some weight. But she was still quite attractive, and seemed to take genuine pleasure in meeting me. In the sway of those large, shining eyes, time skidded to a stop, reversed, and went careening backwards. I stood on the wind-plucked sidewalk trying to gather enough wit to say something civil and intelligent while the old passion, a Lazarus of infinite tendernesses, aches, and yearnings, rose from the crypt of my heart.

In the humdrum present she told me that she and her family were now living in a suburb of Philadelphia. Strange, I said, I was to fly to Philadelphia in about two weeks on family business. (An old uncle, Ivan E. Abbott, after whom I was very nearly named, had died, leaving a small estate of which I had been appointed executor and colegatee.) Well, she said, you must come over for dinner. She scribbled her number on a scrap of paper she took out of the jaws of her crocodile purse (the details we remember!) and handed it to me. I took it, thanked her, and walked on with the shaky step and gauzy pain of someone who has been resurrected from the grave, only to be told he is going to die again.

I don't think I slept an entire night for the next two weeks. I was torn between calling her before I arrived to arrange for the promised dinner or simply letting it lie. I can't help thinking sometimes that the past is as full of hazards as the future. Perhaps that is why we have museums: to organize, label, and tame the past, lest it rear up and devour us. On the other hand, I thought it might be purgative simply to go to dinner, meet her family, acknowledge her actual existence, and get on with my own life, such as it was. Besides all that, I admit to having had a nearly morbid curiosity. What kind of life had she distilled for herself from the alembics of time and chance? What had I missed?

So a few days before I left for Philadelphia, I called the number she had given me. A young girl answered, and at my request bawled out, "Mawww!" I perhaps should have hung up then, but I don't think I've hung up on anyone in my life. The arrangements went forward. Carrying a rather expensive bottle of Château Latour and a bouquet of yellow roses, I took a taxi to a prosperous suburb of the city and a mock-Tudor house with quarreled windows, steep roof, and sloping lawn.

I am not sure, in retrospect, whether I felt, in the course of the evening, more sad than disappointed. Actually, I was quite appalled. The two children, a boy and a girl as far as I could discern, had scarcely the rudiments of civility. They squabbled loudly the entire time I was there, fussing and whining and interrupting without the least censure from either parent. Winslow Lowe turned out to be the most ordinary of mortals, a plump, sallow man with a rather obvious toupee who served up the conversational banalities of someone who is bored with life and may not realize it. He was of a piece with the house, the relentless Tudor details of which (mostly fake, I'm sure) jarred with the wall-to-wall carpeting of a uniformly bright colorlessness that flowed down the staircase to spread evenly throughout the place. There was, I remember, a television set in nearly every room, even the bathroom off the kitchen, where a telephone hung on the wall next to the toilet. But I could find no piano, no *lieder!* There was a wall of fancy electronic equipment, but most of the discs, as far as I could tell, were show tunes, pops favorites, the kind of stuff rich lawyers listen to. There were scarcely any books in evidence. I forget what adorned their walls, if anything.

After cocktails, cheese and crackers, small talk — mostly about "good old Seaboard," as Elsbeth laughingly dismissed it (as though Philadelphia and its environs constitute the epitome of high culture) — we sat in a dining room furnished down to the last tittle with a matching set of reproduction Hepplewhite complete with a bowl of wax fruit. Without the continual disruption of the children, I'm not sure we would have gotten through a truly awful meal: an overdone lamb roast on which my excellent Bordeaux was wasted, accompanied by chemically vivid peas and slightly burned scalloped potatoes that also came out of a package.

Elsbeth seemed terribly flustered and very much under the heel of her husband, who alternated between fake smiles and inexplicable frowns as he directed her with stares and sharp, disapproving nods, his conversational contributions coming in awkward bursts of pomposity. Disparagement of Seaboard and Wainscott provided only so many conversational gambits. The children refused to eat any of the meal, and when Elsbeth voiced the smallest reprove, she received one of her husband's glances. They were finally excused to go watch television. Silence congealed with the lamb fat and the industrial cheese on the potatoes. The brownie à la mode was excellent, I must admit, and we managed to talk about that for nearly five minutes. With feigned affability, for I could tell he was something of a domestic tyrant, Mr. Lowe excused himself, saying he had work to do. He has an office over the garage, where he works on his stocks, Elsbeth explained to me with such evident embarrassment I wanted to reassure her that I didn't mind.

We lingered at the table a bit more, and God knows I tried to break through the facetiousness with which she dissembled her shame. I can't believe I made her nervous. We were finally reduced, when the silences positively boomed, to the living room, an enormous television set, and a police drama involving lantern-jawed men with extraordinary teeth, young women wearing skirts that barely covered their pronounced rumps, and much chasing around the hilly streets of a West Coast city in screaming cars. At least the children, dabbing on the carpet at fish fingers and french fries Elsbeth had heated for them, were quiet.

So there was no *tête-à-tête* about the old days, no perspectives on the trajectory of life that you might get at a class reunion or when you meet an old friend. Elsbeth knocked back a sizable brandy or two and got a little tipsy, I thought. When she yawned at the end of the television drama, I took it as a signal to leave. The taxi came mercifully soon after I had called it, and there was minimal time, what with good-byes to the children — "Say good night to Mr. Ratour" — who scarcely responded, and the usual pleasantries — "It was so good to see you again . . ." "Yes, likewise . . ." — to say anything else. I felt keenly for her plight, and it may only have been my imagination, but I thought I detected more than a hint of pleading in the final look she gave me. Or was it apology, an admission of a mistake? As the taxi pulled away, she was still in the peaked doorway, and I felt a deep, deep pity for her and for her life, which to me, in its personal and philistine dimensions, seemed a vision of hell.

Still, when I got back to the office the following Monday, I took that scrap of paper from the haphazard archives of my life (we should all take more time to curate our collections), and carefully filed it away. Despite everything, I was still very much in love with her. And as I sit here enjoying what may be a small moment of triumph, I feel like calling her and telling her. Because through all these years she has remained for me a kind of internal audience, even if it has meant that, all along, I have been playing to an empty house.

TUESDAY, AUGUST 18

It turns out I won't have anything to report to Elsbeth after all: the second twin has an ironclad alibi. Between 4:15 and 5:30 P.M. of the afternoon Dean Scrabbe was abducted, Francis Snyders was in the Northside substation of the Seaboard Police Department. His car, apparently, had broken down nearby, and he needed to make phone calls and wait for a towing service. Lieutenant Tracy told me it's in the logbook in black and white, and the desk sergeant on duty remembers the incident very well. I still can't help feeling there's something decidedly fishy going on with those twins. It's all too neat, somehow.

Nonetheless, there is significant other news to report. The Board of Governors has finally met and taken action, but I find myself in as great a quandary as ever. The members have asked me to be acting Administrative Director pending a thorough evaluation and overhaul of the present management structure. Naturally, I was surprised and somewhat flattered, and I told the Board I appreciated their confidence in me. I said, however, I would need time to consider their request.

I don't think they were quite expecting that response. Indeed, they became openly craven in their pleading, embarrassingly so, especially old Dexter McFarquar, who once asked me, while I was taking the minutes, what I did at the museum. I hid successfully, I think, the strange mixture of trepidation and vindication that agitated me when they pressed me as to my hesitations. They said there would be a commensurate increase in salary. They said I would play an important part in any restructuring. Robert Remick, scion of the Remicks of Remsdale and as always the worldly gentleman, told me that he spoke unofficially but for the other members of the Board in telling me that they were all very grateful for the indispensable services I was performing during a very trying period and that I had in fact already assumed many of the duties of the post they were offering me. I didn't really know what to say. I managed some platitudes about needing time to think through the conditions necessary for me or anyone else to fill effectively the "managerial" gap left at the museum by Mr. Morin's incarceration.

They decided right then and there to meet again in September, the first time in the history of the museum, I believe, that the Board has ever held two meetings so close together. I am to get back to all of them individually before that meeting and let them know what I have decided. If I decide not to take the position, then I am to try to find candidates they might consider worthy, which makes me, whether I want to be or not, responsible.

As I sit here now, I am nearly tempted to write them all a letter saying that I categorically will not serve as acting anything. For one thing, I am opposed in principle to the very position they want me to assume. If the museum had an effective Director, it would not need an Administrative Director and the panoply of special assistants, make-work, and general bureaucratic aggrandizement that inevitably attend such redundancies. I feel like telling them that what they need to do is simply face the unpleasant reality of informing Dr. Commer that it is time he retired. Then they should start an immediate search for a Director who will direct. That is their responsibility. They are the Board of Governors. They are supposed to *govern*. But really, is it my role to tell them what their responsibilities are? I suppose I might try to have lunch with Robert Remick, if he's available. I'm afraid, though, that Dr. Commer is sacrosanct precisely because he is one of them — a geriatric case, to be blunt about it.

And really, what would they expect me to do as "acting" Administrative Director? Why not Director? Acting Administrative Director? The very term smacks of responsibility without power, of obligations without resources. But I am sure they would want me to make the Malachy Morin scandal disappear, find Dean Fessing's murderer, locate Dean Scrabbe, keep Wainscott from swallowing us whole, prevent Damon Drex from making a spectacle of us before the world, send the Oversight Committee packing, rein in whatever mischief Professor Gottling and his cohorts are up to, and balance the budget. It is not just a matter, as some of them seem to think, of improving relations with the press.

Besides all that, who will take over as Recording Secretary? The one time I have been sick for more than a few days — I had my appendix out in 1969, the weekend of the first moon landing — the person they brought in made a complete mess of the records. It took me nearly a month to straighten everything out. And what about the history of the MOM I am determined to write? It will take thousands of hours just to research it properly. I am not about to waste my time doing one of those "official" histories that no one ever reads. The Museum of Man deserves better. I am, indeed, tempted to inform them of my feeling now, but then I did tell them I would think it over, and think it over I will.

The possibility, by the way, of Damon Drex making a spectacle of himself and the museum is very real. I received a transmission from his office in my e-mail this afternoon that left me dizzy. Not content, apparently, with claiming to prove that old saw about monkeys, time, and typewriters, he would now have us believe that one of his apes has climbed Parnassus. His assistant requests in a prefatory memorandum that I set a date for a press conference and send over to him a list of all "the print and electronic media" to be invited. The communication included, in addition to "a short lyric" purportedly written by that veritable beast Royd, the text of a press release and "an appreciation" by one Professor Reader of the English Department, all of which is to be part of a "press packet" to be distributed at a press conference. The final draft is to be printed on "Pan House" stationery, and I am to get back to them with suggestions or changes. Drex himself appended a note:

Dear Norman:

You will from papers see we have succeed on the other side of day light dreams. Royd that you meet at our jolly hour has made poem. I know how enthusiasm you have for our program. Now together we tell world. It will be bannered day for Museum of Man and Chimpanzees (my little joker) and for us.

Well, I am going to can the whole thing. The press release claims "a major breakthrough in interspecific communication," and "[t]he first recognizably literary production from a nonhuman source." The quotation in the press release from a Fergus McFergus: "It's obvious that these mere 'animals' have established a new level of writing, one that could well be emulated by the far more numerous 'higher' primates writing today. The simplicity and clarity of the syntax, the unadorned and powerful diction, the sparseness of sentiment, and the hypnotic cadences of the words impart to this short piece a nearly quadrupedal surefootedness. . . . We could do worse than to heed what might be called the sense of pongid urgency that this short work achieves with such convincing effect."

The release goes on to say that Professor Jack D. Reader (I've never heard of him) has generously contributed "a more formal appreciation of the poem, placing its significance within the framework of contemporary literary theory." (I know, kind reader, that you think I am making this up, but I am not. As incredible, as fantastic as it may seem, I have it right here on my video screen, as real as the cursor pulsing with a perfect beat.) *Ecco Simius:*

Chimp Champ
by Hemmingroyd

Me chimp champ
You chimp chump
Chimp champ
Chomp chomp
Chimp chump

It gets worse. It gets awful. I tried twice to read what Professor Reader wrote, but I have to confess, I can scarcely make head or tail of it. (Why is so much that is written about writing unreadable?) At the same time I feel constrained to place Reader's remarks in this journal as part of the record, not, frankly, that I can imagine anyone, even a historian, wanting to read it.

Paleonymics and Hierarchical Reversals
in the Pongid Realm
by Jack D. Reader

Though not the first pongid utterance of record, this short lyric constitutes the first record of a consciously "literary" expression by a species other than *Homo sapiens*. This fact alone, on its surface *(surface)*, foregrounds the necessity of reconsiderations of interpretive strategies now in place for more conventional textual artifacts. Hemmingroyd's ostensible project posits in a closed structure a paradigmatic scheme of intraspecific relations very nearly Foucaultian in its effects. And while the formal program of the piece appears simple, perhaps even simplistic, a close analysis of the tensions and contradictions underlying the binary oppositions will disclose, in the matrix of a rudimentary language *(langue)*, the grit of words *(parole)* around which the empowered reader *(lecteur envoulant)* may accrete the layered pearls of his own miscomprehensions, setting the stage, so to speak, for a reversal of hierarchies. The missing copula, for instance, in the first two lines not only heightens the effects of recursive intonationality but foregrounds questions that are anything but stark. While the provided lack of any form of the verb "to be" in traditional analysis might be interpreted as an "apeing" of cigar store "Indian talk" *(parler de peau-rouge de magasin de tabac)*, raising the possibility that Hemmingroyd is employing a self-parodic mode not to parody Amerindian speech but to align himself with a marginalized group, thus politicizing this utterance with an economy little short of breathtaking. (As a member of *Pan troglodytes*, Hemmingroyd, by definition, is absolved of both the Europhallogocentrism that has marked so much of the received canon and the anthropocentrism typical of literary production generally.)

However recondite, such an approach provides a mere sniff *(odeur)* of the interpretive plenitude to be gleaned from the cracks and crevices of this seemingly seamless text. Whatever its other possible sociopolitico stratagems, the forgone copula in the first line establishes for the reader of Indo-European copulated languages an ontological uncertainty that is repeated, affirmed, and deepened in the second line, where the introduction of the I-thou configuration escalates what can only be called the epistemological risk. At the same time, the problematics of the missing copulas is attenuated if not obviated by the use of the objective case in the predicate, the ambiguity of the *you* notwithstanding. Is, in short, this small but in no way trivial jump *(salter)*, this Nietzschean escape from grammar if not language, this objectification of the first person that fuses it with and transforms the nominal predicate nominative, even as the formal elements of speech remain graphically separate on the page *(page)*, rendering the nonexistent copula into the active voice, i.e., being as existence rather than as equation, a move to fuse and therefore eliminate the subject-object dichotomy? Or is it simply that the dropped copulas *(copules lachées)* represent a deliberate creation of places of indeterminacy *(Unbestimmtheitsstellen)*, into which the aroused reader *(lecteur amoureux)* is invited to supply his own copulation?

Perhaps, but the dichotomy persists in what remains a structure of opposing valences, mitigated, it is true, by a play of monosyllabic graphemes that, whatever their signification, change meaning with single vowel variations. The question for the scrutinizing language theorist locates itself in this instance in the relations between the binaries *chimp* and *champ*, *chimp* and *chump* and the double binaries *chimp champ* and *chimp chump*. In this first instance, does *chimp* modify *champ*, or is *chimp* substantive while *champ* remains adjectival, i.e., supplemental? Or does the reverse pertain? Or does it make any difference? In any case, a larger issue establishes itself regarding the double bind of the double binaries noted above. It is possible, in an algebraic move, to factor out the *chimp* from both sides of the equation (leaving aside for the moment the issue of the active verbs that link subject and object), privileging the question: what distinguishes *champ* from *chump?* (Some language theorists will object to this line of inquiry as a valorization of the obvious. A more productive approach, they will contend, would be to examine the oppositions *chimp* and *chomp,* however problematic the former's status as a substantive. They will ask, how do you tell the chimp from the chomp? For a discussion of this issue in general terms, see A. J. Denny's analysis of the de Man dance/dancer conundrum. *Viz.* "Effects of a Vitiated Stream of Protons on a Fabricative Arcanum" (*Wordlings and Other Orphans,* Boston: Orange Press, 1985). A conventional interpretive strategy would devolve on the role played by the compound (perhaps even squared) verb *chomp chomp. Chomp,* according to the *Oxford English Dictionary,* is an Americanism or dialect for *champ,* a resonance that further links subject and verb, particularly as the word as verb belongs "to a primary *chamb,* app. [ears] closely connected or identical with JAM *(jamb),* and *jamble,* to squeeze with violence, crush." Leaving aside the possibilities of "enjambment" or the communicatory "jamming," the ostensible object of Hemmingroyd's project consists then of a constative speech act followed by a performative, assuming an elliptical *will,* resulting in an apparent hierarchy of a dominant champ over a chomped chump.

A more resourceful reading, a more radical hermeneutics, however, reveals other, different, deferred possibilities. The tropographical spareness of the work (despite the inferable allusions to jam making, enjambment, and jamming), provides, in what might be a deliberate irony, an interpretive toehold: words, *per se,* are not words but traces of words, traces of traces of words, a veritable ichnology of meaning, conglomerates of paleophemes, fossil phemes mineralized over time from the precipitates of many meanings. It is possible to decode, therefore, with paleophemic instrumentality, a range of alternative significations. When the overlay of the *ch* is dissolved from the work, the resulting schema, 'Me imp amp/You imp ump/Imp amp/Omp omp/Imp ump,' while retaining the thrust of its declarative force, reveals an underlying text open to a diversity of interpretive modalities.

Imp in this construction can be taken as its primary definition, "child," or its secondary, "demon." Similarly, *amp*, short for *ampere* (after André-Marie Ampère, 1775–1836, French mathematician and physicist), is a measure of electrical force and stands for power *(pouvoir)*. This construction gains credence when it is recalled that in Saussurean ([dino]Saussurean?) theory, words can only mean in their relation to difference with other words. Thus is *amp* amplified as "power" when contrasted with *ump*, short for *umpire*, the personage wearing the Egyptianate chin ornament who squats with shield and shin guards behind the catcher in American baseball adjudicating balls and strikes. "Power" thus confronts "right," or, more likely, "demon power" does something (does something) to "child right," and even at the paleophemic level the tension of the binary oppositions holds.

Omp may appear at first glance more problematic. Further reduced to *om*, it takes on a decided Zen/Ginsbergian coloration. *Om*, however, despite its suggestive power, forgoes the transitive force required in this context. At some risk to consistency, the *h* of the dropped *ch* could be reintroduced at the terminus of the paleopheme, producing *omph*. In this move, "imp amp omph omph imp ump," suggesting, again in the Ginsbergian context, a transcendental fellation of right by power. A more fruitful appreciation retains the origin pheme and anagramizes it to *pom*, resulting in *pom pom*, the tasselated hand object shaken by short-skirted cheerleaders at American football games. To pom pom, in short, is to cheer, to encourage, to affirm. And while the possibilities abound and the ambiguities are profound, a more radical reversal of hierarchies is difficult to imagine beyond the infinite regression entailed in all such analysis, and the resulting euphoric ap(e)oria makes all the *différence* in the world.

Well, there you have it. I am nearly tempted to help them arrange a press conference and see what happens. The worst they could do is make a laughingstock out of the museum. No, the worst they could do is be taken seriously. And the way the world's going they probably would. I can imagine Damon Drex surrounded by his charges on the cover of *Time*. "The New Voices," the headline would say. And who are we to judge?

In another rather interesting development, Malachy Morin has been cleared of murder charges related to Dean Fessing. He's still being held in the death of Elsa Pringle, however, despite a good deal of legal maneuvering and public posturing on the part of Ariel Dearth. Amazing how much airtime and newsprint that man manages to garner for himself. He had the presumption to ask me for a deposition attesting to the "sound moral character" of Malachy Morin. I sent him a note saying that I could not, in good conscience, make such a statement.

Enough. I am closing up for the night. I am going to wend my way over to the Club and order myself a large whiskey. Although, as Kevin says, quoting some Irishman, there is no such thing as a large whiskey.

MONDAY, AUGUST 24

Why are nightmares always worse the second time around? Dean Scrabbe has been found. Or his decapitated head, at least, was found yesterday at the Humboldt Museum. Someone with a demented sense of the macabre placed it in the glass case where the demestid beetles have been demonstrating their services to science. A group of residents from a halfway house were standing around looking at the case when one of them, realizing what was there, started screaming. The rest, apparently, began pointing and lurching and laughing hysterically. I can't say I blame them.

I did not see it myself, thank God, but a shaken Dr. Cutler told me that the "gnawed brain" of the language theorist, "putrid and crawling with maggots and beetles and things I couldn't describe," was the worst mess he had seen inside a human skull in nearly forty years of forensic pathology. The dean was killed, apparently, by a blow to the head, although Dr. Cutler told a hastily convened press conference that "the discernible trauma to the right temple" could have been made postmortem. He reported that no postcranial remains had yet been found.

Again, sadly, the university tried to evade all public relations responsibility. I was adamant with the press: "Dean Scrabbe," I said in a written statement that I gave to them, "was a Wainscott dean, and he was found, his head, anyway, on Wainscott property. Any other questions would have to be directed to Wainscott authorities or the police." I finally got tired of the whole sick circus, came up here, and closed the door. When the phone started ringing, I disconnected it. Something evil is happening in this community, and something needs to be done to stop it. I have said it before and I will say it again: The murdering and mutilating of sitting deans strikes at the very heart of civilization as we know it.

Lieutenant Tracy arrived not long afterwards very much in need of a cooperative witness. He said a thorough investigation of the custodial staff at the Humboldt had turned up nothing. I told him that Alger Wherry uses demestids in the final preparation of fresh skulls.

"And who is Alger Wherry?" he asked, turning officious.

"He's Curator of the Skull Collection."

"The Skull Collection?" He was taking notes.

"The museum has one of the largest skull collections in the country. It's located in the sub-subbasement."

"I think you should have told me this before, Mr. de Ratour."

"I just found out myself. About the demestids, I mean. I didn't think them relevant until Dean Scrabbe turned up the way he did. Even then I thought your own investigation would have discovered at least the existence of the Skull Collection." And although I responded in kind to his tone, there lingered in the air that subtle sense of something held back. Indeed, I was thinking about the collection and about what might be behind the Green Door. And again I refrained from disclosing my suspicions out of a strange, proprietorial instinct. I was determined now, more than ever, to go and see for myself. With Mort's help, of course. Unless the police got there first.

The lieutenant sensed it right away, but his importuning, for that's what it was, came as a watchful silence, which deepened between us, exerting a subtle, nigh irresistible pressure on me. With an artful sigh and some uncanny duplicity, I reached into my desk and drew out, as red herrings, the e-mail messages from Worried. "I perhaps should have showed you these earlier, Lieutenant," I said, "but I thought you burdened with enough crank calls and false leads."

He read them over quickly, shuffling through them with evident agitation. In a cold, level voice, he said, "Why were you hiding these?"

"I wasn't hiding them, Lieutenant. I merely thought them irrelevant."

"And why is that?"

"As a matter of principle I dismiss any communication addressed to me without a name. If someone is unwilling to sign what they write then they are free to write anything." I did not go into the fact that I had, from time to time, been the object of some rather nasty anonymous communications.

He watched me intently for a moment. "You could be charged with withholding evidence, Mr. de Ratour."

"I would hardly think that what I've given you, which is just a kind of rumor and gossip, hearsay really, constitutes hard evidence."

He stood to go, the set of his face conciliatory again. "You're right, Mr. de Ratour. Rumor and gossip are not hard evidence, but they are the heart and soul of an investigation. If you know anything else like this, if you've heard anything, if you hear anything, I don't care how implausible, please let me know." Standing there in his rain-stained mackintosh (it's been pouring all day), he said whoever was dispatching the deans would strike again unless apprehended. "You can," he said, "count on it."

He was just about to leave when the door opened and Damon Drex came in, carrying in the crook of his arm an infant chimp in a diaper. Introductions were difficult to avoid, and I must say the lieutenant immediately evinced a charm I had not suspected him capable of. Boy or girl? he asked Drex. And it wasn't until later that I realized he may have taken the chimp to be Drex's child, as young chimps in fact look quite human. I then had to endure twenty minutes of pressure from Drex regarding the press conference he wants to stage. I know I should have told him then and there what I thought of the whole project, but the lieutenant's visit and accusations had left me quite chastened. I told Mr. Drex that I was simply too busy even to consider his request at the moment. When he tried to construe that as a commitment, I simply said I had work to do, and that he was in violation of museum rules in bringing an animal into this part of the building. He left abruptly, offended for some reason. But I am not going to worry about him.

I may, however, have to worry about Ariel Dearth. He called to say he wants to meet with me to coordinate a large fund-raising event at the museum to help defray Malachy Morin's legal costs. The man is one of those obliviously insistent people who don't hear what you're telling them. I was particularly exercised by and vehemently dismissed his suggestion that "the museum bears some responsibility for the accident that befell Mr. Morin in that it occurred when Mr. Morin was acting on behalf of the museum." It was a threat in the form of an insinuation, and all my instincts about lawyers and the law — a rigged game run by knaves as far as I can tell — came to the fore. I could not shut the man up. I put the receiver on the desk and let him babble on until there was a silence, a click, and the dial tone.

As though this wasn't enough, the Oversight Committee plans to meet again in the near future. I've never seen morale lower at the museum. People are talking in hushed tones. Doors are closed and faces averted. There's been more than one resignation since Scrabbe disappeared, and now I suppose there will be a virtual exodus. I have to admit that I am seriously thinking again about retirement myself. I am at times dispirited to the point of despair. I am also afraid. I have no wish to be fodder for the grisly mill of whoever is perpetrating these outrages. More than ever I would retreat into history, but now even history seems utterly blighted by what is happening in the present.

THURSDAY, AUGUST 27

A most extraordinary thing has happened. Indeed, I cannot wait until evening to record the event and am writing about it now as I pick at a crab salad sandwich in my office. I have just received a long letter from Elsbeth Lowe, informing me that her husband Winslow died of a stroke nearly a year ago. She writes that she was quite at sea about the whole thing but lately has started to put her life back together. Family business, she says, will bring her to Seaboard. The old cottage out at the lake, it seems, is in a state of near collapse from an infestation of carpenter ants. She asks if I would like to meet her for lunch or dinner.

While surprised and delighted, I find myself tortured by old quandaries and new possibilities. What am I to do? I have asked myself, pacing my office with her scented letter in hand, the faint, unmistakable musk rising from it, a heady elixir out of the past. I grew angry. Does she want me now, at the eleventh hour, after more than thirty years of emptiness? But that passed quickly, as I am not given to vengeful self-pity. I will, of course, meet with her. But I can't imagine what she wants. Will she expect overtures from me? And if I *don't* make them, would she find someone else again? I am utterly dithered by the prospect. What if we were to flirt with each other and it led to an understanding, where would we go? It would not be good for her reputation to be seen going into a hotel with a man, even with me, or especially with me. Under no circumstances could I think of taking her to a motel. Then I began to worry about whether I would want her to come to my house, as charming as it is in its own way. I have only single beds, except for the sad, sagging old thing in Mother's room. The bed in my room is a large single, it's true, but a single nonetheless. I thought about ordering a double bed. There would be room for it if I moved out the wing chair where I read and shifted some other things around.

I then realized how absurd is all this thrashing about. Elsbeth is a bereaved widow who is just being nice to someone she knew years ago. We will probably have lunch someplace like the Club or A La Descartes in town. We'll talk about old times and the people we used to know. We'll stand up at the end of it and shake hands or she'll give me a peck on the cheek. She probably already has another man lined up. One of her husband's law partners, no doubt, a distinguished member of the bar, a widower who has always admired her from afar. I imagined they had already planned an intimate wedding with a few close friends, after which they would fly somewhere for a couple of weeks before returning to lead a life of quiet wealth.

So sitting here, glancing out at Shag Bay, pacing, I have been thinking it through. Even if she had marriage in mind for me, I thought, I really shouldn't be too hasty to line up for it. I do, after all, have a settled way of life. Having another person in the house is not something to be gone into lightly. She may want to cook dinners at home, and she's not much of a cook. I have gotten used to going to the Club. Everyone knows me there. It wouldn't be the same if Elsbeth came along. And she wouldn't want to go every night, anyway. Women crave variety. She would want to go to other places, those fashionable new restaurants in town that serve food no one's heard of and charge a small fortune for bits and pieces got up to look like bad art. Perhaps I should drop by and talk to Alfie. For all his spirituality, he is a man of the world. He might be able to give me some perspective, especially as it relates to the question of premarital relations.

Then there's this murder mess. Any association with me would drag her willy-nilly into its coils, could even put her in danger. Indeed, since what remains of Scrabbe has showed up, I have gotten the feeling from time to time that I am being followed. "Shadowed" might be the better word for it, because I can't quite be sure if the anonymous-looking people — sometimes it's a man, other times a woman — are actually *following* me. It's more as though they are simply there. For instance, this morning I increased my stride walking to work, apparently "shaking" one of these elusive pursuers, only to find what looked like another one disguised as a derelict waiting for me as I came through the Memorial Gates in the arboretum. I can't tell whether I'm being threatened or protected. I can't be sure it's actually happening. I would ask Lieutenant Tracy about it, but he would probably just deny it. If that's the case, how could Elsbeth and I "get away" for some privacy without going through some elaborate and probably futile machination to "lose" whoever might be following me?

It's a most unnerving sensation, and it's hardly a situation into which to introduce a woman of standing. Whatever I decide, I will certainly have to write back to her. I suppose I'll have to see her when she arrives, at least for a cup of coffee. Anything else would signal an animosity that I simply cannot feel.

TUESDAY, SEPTEMBER 1

You may imagine my shock and chagrin when I arrived at work this morning to find Malachy Morin standing outside his old office and sounding off as though nothing had happened. "Bow Tie!" he bellowed at me as I stood there dumbfounded, unable to avoid his reaching hand, which gripped and crushed mine, nearly pulling my arm from its socket. *Sotto voce,* beneath the boom of his commonplaces, he proceeded to thank me for my help during his "troubles." "Lining up Dearth, Norm, the way you did, was a stroke of pure genius. The guy's amazing. So, hey, how are they hanging?"

"What are you doing here?" I cut in coldly after I had extricated my bruised hand from his grasp.

"What do you mean, what am I doing here?" A brief shadow of suspicion darkened his visage as he blustered on. "My job, Norm, old buddy, my job. Stuff's really piled up. Too bad, by the way, about old Scrabbe. But you know, I always knew that guy would come to a bad end. I mean, he was always trying to make things more complicated than they are."

As he hulked there in the hallway, sweating in a seersucker suit, his presence still unbelievable to me, I said, "I mean, aren't you supposed to be in jail?" almost adding, where you belong.

"Oh, that. Well, I'm out on bail, but that's only a technicality.

Ari's filed a motion to have the bail requirement rescinded. Hey, listen, we're contending that it never should have been imposed. In fact, I never should have been arrested in the first place. The whole thing was an accident. Could have happened to anybody. But this guy Ari! Hey, Norm, you got to see this guy work. I mean, he's got the judge eating right out of his hand. Think of it, Norm, ha ha, a few weeks ago I was worried about the chair and here I am now."

"But surely you've been fired," I countered, as an awful possibility occurred to me. We were just outside what was still, technically, his office, into which he motioned me with a conspiratorial gesture. I stepped inside the door but would not sit down as invited as that might have seemed to constitute a recognition of his right to be there.

The man stood behind his desk and drew himself up to his full, imposing height while giving me his most daunting managerial scowl. "What do you mean, I've been fired? No way, Norm, no way at all. On what grounds would they can me? Why would they even want to? Through thick and thin I've been holding this place together and you're talking about my being canned because of a misunderstanding with the cops about something that happened to a little . . . I don't know what you're talking about, pal. I've gotten no indication from anyone about any of this. What have you heard? I mean, I've been getting my paycheck right through it all. You know that raise I put in for in April, well, that just kicked in and I got paid retroactive back to July first. In fact, Ari told me to check with that . . . with Marge Littlefield about having the museum pick up some of my legal costs."

"Good God!" I said, too astonished for more.

"But it's okay, Norm. Everything's going to be okay. We'll get the old team up and humming like the old days. In fact, Norm, I've been thinking of appointing you to the executive committee. I mean, you were there for me when some real shit was going down, and I think it's time we recognized your contribution. You know, over the years. You know, to the museum. But you're going to have to play ball, Norm, I mean, like everyone else."

I simply shook my head, turned, and left the room. Of course! No one, in all the confusion, had bothered to go through with a formal dismissal. That would have been Dr. Commer's responsibility, but I keep forgetting the man is all but comatose. I will have to do something. But what? I fear that if Malachy Morin is allowed to remain on the premises, never mind being put back in charge, I will use my father's gun for more than self-defense.

Dear, dear, dear. How do you sigh in words? For I am sad and sighing as I sit here. It's not just Malachy Morin. Of late I have not been sleeping well. I have been brooding on the fate of the museum and what to do about Elsbeth's letter. There are times when, moment by moment, I must resist the temptation to tender my resignation. How weary, stale, flat, and unprofitable seem to me all the uses of this world. I want to say fie on it. I want . . . I know not what. For it seems to me these murders will never be solved. And even if they are there will be more murders, murders till the end of time.

Enough of that. I received today another communication on my e-mail from Worried. I'm entering it here for the record and sent a copy to Lieutenant Tracy, for what that's worth.

Dear Mr. Detour [sic]:

You must have finally tipped off the cops because this place has been crawling with fuzz lately and Professor Gottling looks fit to be tied. Anyway, I think I've finally found out what Project Alpha's all about and why there's been so much secrecy. This morning I heard Professor Gottling and Dr. Kaplan arguing again. Professor Gottling kept saying like he had before that it was only chimp sigots [zygotes, no doubt] he was working with. But Dr. Kaplan kept waving a long printout in the air and saying and these are his exact words that the sequences were from the human geenome [genome, no doubt] or something like that. He said this had been done with batches A27, A31, A42, and A53. Professor Gottling told him the human and chimp sequences were practically identical so that it didn't make any difference. I didn't hear any more because I didn't want them to see me hanging around the door even though I had a work order to check on one of the synthesizers not the way things are going these days. I asked my friend about it and he said they're fertilizing the sperms and eggs of chimps and splicing in bits of human DNA. The fertilized egg is then put back in the female chimp for one or two months. Then they give it an abortion and study the thing. I don't know if that's true but I know it's not regular research because I heard Professor Gottling shouting at someone later who kept saying that they were going too far and that if word got out about what they were doing it would ruin all their careers. I don't know if you heard or not but Charlene is suing Dr. Hanker for patrimony and a whole lot of other things including damages and someone in the cafeteria yesterday said it was better than getting AIDS but I don't think Dr. Hanker thinks so. I don't really know what's going on but I think you should find someone who might have the power to investigate. I will keep you informed as best I can but I'm getting scared.

Really Very Worried

SATURDAY, SEPTEMBER 5

It is nearly five o'clock in the morning. I have been here since just before three composing my letter of acceptance to the Board of Governors. I awoke around two from the most horrendous nightmare of my life. Dean Scrabbe's decapitated head, horribly disfigured, but human and weeping all the same, spoke to me through torn lips. "Avenge my death," it intoned. "Avenge my death," the voice echoing in a dull boom as though out of eternity. When I tried to back away, it grasped me somehow, not with arms but with its violated ears, or something like ears. It pulled me down next to its horrible, suppurating mouth, and while thick amber tears flowed from its hideous, bloodied eyes, it wailed at me that I would be next unless I acted now. With a shout the neighbors might have heard, I sat bolt upright in the bed, and as I type this, my hands still shake.

I know it sounds corny. I know it sounds like something out of a novel, but the dream shook the scales from my eyes. I am not doing this lightly. I am not doing it out of ambition, although fear and horror can generate a sense of purpose akin to ambition. Who was it said that in nightmares begin responsibilities? Anyway, as I sat there in the darkness with these thoughts and myriad others whirling through my head, I asked myself who would act if I didn't. It is not easy for me. I have had to admit something to myself, something personal and embarrassing. Ever since the meeting of the Board, a catered luncheon in the Twitchell Room as is traditional, I have been inwardly blustering and fuming at them for asking me to do their dirty work. I have been reaching high and low to find reasons to turn them down. And slowly, grudgingly, a humbling and horrifying possibility has been afflicting me: I am hesitant to take responsibility. I lack the courage. By courage I don't mean a lack of fear, however noble fearlessness may be. Izzy Landes said it best: courage is doing something difficult or dangerous when you don't want to do it. All my life I've been avoiding the difficult and the dangerous. I have denied it all along, of course.

But I realize now that I have been afraid of the world ever since Infra. I came back from North Africa like a wounded beast, crawled into this little niche, and here have licked my wounds ever since. Oh, when I think back to it! For months I couldn't even leave Seaboard; I was so afraid something catastrophic would befall me. I've scarcely been away from the museum for more than a week at a time since then. And each time, especially early on, the absence was a cruel torment of worry about whether everything was all right or not. Professor Calloway asked me twice more to go on digs with him, and twice I refused. And while I have kept up with the literature in a desultory way over the years and have even managed to build a small collection of my own, any real interest I once had in archaeology withered like a corpse in the desert.

Two years after I returned from Infra, I met Margery Littlefield, O'Donovan then, with hair like a flame and that marvelous laugh. She was still at Smith and spending the summer as an intern at the museum. I think she was attracted to me. She came by my office several times for information she could have gotten elsewhere. We had coffee a couple of times. But I lacked . . . I was so afraid. Of what I'm not sure. That if I reached out and tried to do something again the world would come crashing down on me and tear me limb from limb. Oh, I've put on a good show. But mostly I've kept low, hiding behind others, telling them with my little memos what they ought to do.

I can see now that Elsbeth broke more than my heart that summer; she broke my spirit. And all these years I have denied it and I can deny it no longer. But I don't blame her. If we are not responsible for ourselves we responsible for nothing. Still, I fear that knowing all this is not going to liberate me from it. I am shaky. It takes courage to have courage.

Only now, if I don't act, I may never get another chance. Not, mind you, that I don't think the office of Recording Secretary is not an important one. Indeed, it's a position I want to keep and have included it in the conditions I am setting forth to accept the position. You see, I am finally able to admit all this to myself because I have decided, regardless of the consequences, to take the position and act and thereby attempt to redeem, in some small measure, what's left of my life. If there is one metaphor Christianity has left us that is worth keeping, it is that of redemption, however circumscribed.

For a start, I must face some facts. Were it not for the awful scandal in which we find ourselves roiled and soiled, it is entirely possible that the university would have moved to effect a consolidation in a way that the Board of Governors, even if it were so inclined, would have been unable to resist. These dreadful events have provided the breathing space whereby a *modus vivendi* might just be possible that will leave the museum with at least some shreds of autonomy and honor. At the moment the university is putting as much distance as it can between itself and the museum. All calls regarding Deans Fessing and Scrabbe are still being directed to me, even though both of them were deans of Wainscott. Once things settle down, I presume the university will again try to sort matters out, provided, of course, that it can find another dean brave enough to try.

In any event, I have drafted a reply to the Board, setting out the conditions under which I will accede to their request to act as Administrative Director for the interim. Briefly, I have asked that funds be raised to endow the position of Recording Secretary; that this position remain intact regardless of any affiliation with Wainscott; that Malachy Morin's executive committee be disbanded; and finally, that a committee, chaired by me, be formed to study the status of the Primate Pavilion and the possible transfer of the Genetics Lab to the university. And, of course, one of the first things I will do is fire Malachy Morin, although I didn't mention that in my reply.

I concluded my letters to each of the board members by informing them that I am prepared to meet and discuss these terms at any time and would, in the meanwhile, without formal power, continue to monitor the operations of the museum to the best of my capabilities.

That is not all I have done. When I had finished, addressed, and stamped the envelopes, I sat for a while thinking about Elsbeth and the letter she had written to me. I still had not written back, and I was undecided what to say. I was of two minds. Part of me wanted to send her a brief, dismissive note the very courtesy of which would be a rebuke. The note, in short, would effect a final break, more for myself, of course, than for her. But another part of me wanted not merely to welcome her but to welcome her warmly, with an unselfish largesse that would signal, at the least, that all was forgiven and, more hopefully, that we might rekindle the old flame. Because this may be, I told myself, the last chance I will get to sit, however belatedly, at life's feast. I am tired of sipping pale wine and cowering before oblivion. I want, while there is still time and chance, to drink of headier stuff and reel before the sun.

So, using a real pen with real ink, I have written, telling Elsbeth I would be delighted to meet her for lunch or dinner when she comes to Seaboard. I have told her that I will drive her out to the cottage by the lake and that if she happens to be here in December, I would love to take her to the Curatorial Ball, which, with my new powers, I will see held as before.

Now, more than ever, I am determined to get to the bottom of these macabre murders.

TUESDAY, SEPTEMBER 8

When I informed Lieutenant Tracy about the Skull Collection, I expected him to carry out a thorough investigation. He did little, apparently, other than go down there and question Alger Wherry, who told him nothing. I found myself somewhat per-

turbed when I learned this during an interview with the lieutenant yesterday morning. I was irritated in any event by the continued presence of Malachy Morin, and I may have acted out of
frustration when I decided, finally, to do some looking around
myself.

It happened quite by chance. Last evening, after dinner at the
Club, I had stopped back in the office to pick up my umbrella
since a cloudy sky had turned decidedly leaky. As I was coming
down the corridor, I ran into old Mort wheezing his way up the
last steps of the stairway. On a sudden impulse I said, "Mort, do
you have the key to the Skull Collection?"

Mort, one of those Down East types, sighed and said, "Eyeah."

"Could you open it up for me?"

"Eyeah."

"*Would* you open it up for me?"

"I don't see why not."

As we walked to the elevator together, the trepidation began.
As we went down and down, farther down than I thought possible, I became positively fearful. The low, dank corridor was
scarcely lit. Mort switched on his club of a flashlight, and I was
suddenly very fearful of him for some reason, thinking peripherally how disturbing it was that a source of light could be used as
a weapon. But not by old Mort, I thought, not old Mort. That
wouldn't make sense. But little seemed to make sense anymore.

"Looking for anything in particular?" he asked as he checked a
massive ring of keys for the right one.

"The Skull and few other things," I replied, trying to keep my
voice steady.

"Uh huh."

The peculiar odor of bone, of subterranean mildew and preserved death assailed my nostrils. It didn't help matters in the
least that the lights wouldn't turn on. Mort explained that they
were probably on a timer as they had to be on during the day

anyway. I confess I hesitated and thought of turning back. I shuddered audibly when the stab of his light crossed a row of japing bone faces. I heard or thought I heard something. I whispered for us to stop and be still for a moment. But there was nothing but the silence of death and the painful thumping of my heart.

My sense of direction is not very good, and we must have walked through the entire collection, a review of the dead, so to speak, before we came to the Green Door. My resolve nearly faltered there, as though I had used up all the courage I could muster. I was relieved when Mort, upon inspecting the lock, muttered about it being one of the old ones. At least we had tried. Then he produced from his jacket a large object that looked like a stage key. "The old master," he whispered. "I carry it around because they didn't change over some of the doors." The key fit, turned, tumbled the tumblers. The door creaked open.

I was not disappointed as Mort aimed his stab of light around the small, oblong room. Dismayed perhaps, not a little frightened, but not disappointed. There was a solid antique table of the kind that abounds in institutions set short side against the narrow wall, thereby forming a kind of projecting altar. Several chairs of like vintage were arranged around the table as though meetings were held there. Meetings or even ceremonies, for, at the head of the table, against the wall, which was hung with brown bark cloth worked in geometric symbols, stood a squat stone statue, the features in low relief, of a man sticking his tongue over his lower lip while holding his belly. On top of this, the gold tooth gleaming, was the Skull. There appeared nothing else of note until I found, under the table, several banker's boxes with the missing archives of the Loa Hoa expeditions in them. Just behind them was a plain wooden box. I lifted the lid and found a rubberized poncho, several books on mysticism, some little pipes, and a photograph of a young woman that looked like it came from a high school yearbook.

All of which, I knew, as I heaved the boxes onto the table and started to go through them, proved nothing. I leafed quickly through the contents as Mort held the light for me. I found the usual materials — copious notes, sketches, diagrams of sites, samples of cloth, photographs of artifacts, correspondence, typed reports. All quite routine. Perhaps Brauer, a man of eccentric habit, simply used the place for a study. But why? I asked myself, my detective's instincts aroused. Why the Skull? Why hadn't Alger Wherry simply gone and retrieved it for me when I asked for it? Why wouldn't Mrs. Walsh know where the files were?

I stood, ready to give up, when Mort, with the flashlight, pointed out the drawer in the table. I tried to open it and found it locked. That didn't faze Mort. He took out a smaller ring of keys, and on the fourth or fifth try unlocked it. With some trepidation I lifted out a binder-size black zippered case. I lay it on the table and opened it carefully, with Mort again holding the light. The loose-leaf paper, running about fifty pages, was filled on each side with encrypted entries. It seemed to be a journal of sorts.

I was frustrated again. I was also in a quandary. Should I confiscate this notebook and turn it over to the police? It probably wouldn't take them long to break the code. Or should I just put everything back the way it was, alert Lieutenant Tracy, and have him come with a search warrant to carry it all off legally? While thus musing, I noticed a slight bulge in the side pocket of the case. It was a slim package of photographs, five by seven in black and white. As I began to go through them, my heart beat so violently I had to sit down. In the shaky illumination of the flashlight I saw, arranged against a dramatically rising precipice and filling the foreground of the photograph, Raul Brauer, Corny Chard, and Alger Wherry, all holding, quite distinctly, pieces of a human body. Chard had a foot, Wherry a forearm with attached hand, and Brauer what looked like a heart. One of the other pictures showed the three of them sitting on a mat with natives of rank actually eating these things! I was glad I was sitting down myself, for my vision blurred for a moment and I thought I would pass out.

A moment later my head cleared and I acted decisively. I replaced everything exactly as I had found it. I rang the SPD from Wherry's phone and was patched through directly to Lieutenant Tracy. I explained exactly what I had discovered and suggested that he obtain a search warrant. He agreed immediately, and we arranged to meet him at the main entrance to the museum. Extraordinary, really, how soon the sirens began and with what flashing fanfare several cruisers and one unmarked car pulled to a wrenching halt in front of the museum. I have to confess I had been very gratified by the note of respect in the lieutenant's voice as he showed me the warrant and asked that I lead him to the room with the Green Door.

Mort found the override switch, and we got the lights turned on. There were the usual nervous wisecracks from the team as we made our way through the collection. Mort opened the Green Door again, and the police, carefully, with gloved hands, removed every item, with the exception of the table and chairs, from the room. They took the Skull, and I asked the lieutenant that it be treated with every respect. At my suggestion, he called in and got a supplementary warrant to go over the prep room. All the while the lieutenant deferred to me, asking my advice, putting in an occasional question. The supreme compliment came when, taking one of the more egregious photographs, he asked me to accompany him to Brauer's residence to help with the questioning.

It had started to rain and it was getting late in the evening, but I agreed, if not with alacrity then with a keen, disquieting anticipation. I must say I was glad that I was not doing it alone and that the lieutenant was armed.

Brauer lives a ways out of town in what looked like a converted

barn set well back from the road. We hadn't called, and I told the
lieutenant he might not be at home as he still traveled a great
deal. But there were more than a couple of cars in the yard and
several lights on. Under an umbrella we stood together and
waited for someone to answer our knock. We were greeted by a
very striking young woman with a fetching combination of
Polynesian and European features, especially the thick black hair
that fell over her shoulders. When the lieutenant asked to see
Professor Brauer, the woman turned and called up a nearby
stairwell, "Dad, someone to see you."

Brauer, in a dressing gown of flamboyant scarlet silk worked
with zoomorphic forms in black, came down the stairs with the
face of a man half anxious and half irritated. The lieutenant
introduced himself, shook hands, and said, "You probably already know Mr. de Ratour. He's assisting me with the investigation of the murders of Deans Fessing and Scrabbe." Brauer
nodded curtly at me and led us down a hall into a barn-beamed
study hung and set about with a collection of Polynesian art and
artifacts — jade weapons, bark cloth, wood carvings, statuettes
— worthy of any museum. The considerable computer equipment in evidence didn't seem out of place, even with the rain
tattering clearly on the roof above. From behind a desk of in-
tricately carved rosewood, he produced a bottle of Dalwhinnie,
offered us a drink, which we both declined, poured himself
several fingers, and asked, in an impressively deep, confident
voice, "What can I do for you gentlemen?"

The lieutenant was silent for a moment, as though preoccupied. "You can tell us about the contents of a room in the Skull
Collection at the Museum of Man that has a green door."

Brauer's face paled, and the hauteur of his expression, seemingly innate, collapsed into uncertainty, even fear. But only for a
second. He sipped his single malt, which appeared to restore him,
and said, "Some files and a few artifacts. I go there sometimes to

study and to . . . contemplate. There's no phone and" — he allowed the lieutenant a confiding laugh — "and not many people come looking for you down there."

"Have you ever indulged in cannibalism, Professor Brauer?" I asked, surprising myself but not, strangely enough, the lieutenant.

The professor all but sneered at me. "What would give you that idea?"

With exquisite timing and with a gesture nearly threatening in its authority, Lieutenant Tracy produced one of the photographs and handed it to Brauer.

The anthropologist was silent as the blood drained again from his face, showing suddenly a sad man gone jowly with age. He drained his glass, but the whiskey didn't restore him this time. In a slow, clear voice, he began to talk.

"I want to make it understood, Lieutenant . . ."

"Tracy."

"Lieutenant Tracy . . . and Mr. de Ratour, I want it understood that I have had nothing whatsoever to do with the murders and what happened afterwards to Fessing and Scrabbe. I also do not think any of my immediate colleagues has had anything to do with the murders of the deans. But they can answer just as well for themselves. I can explain that picture and the others you no doubt found with it. Where were they, by the way? I've been scouring the museum and this house . . ."

"In a pocket of the zippered case," I said.

He nodded ruefully. He reached behind him to a cabinet and pulled out a loose-leaf binder. "Here is an original, an unencrypted version of what's in the other notebook. It's an account of what happened offstage, so to speak, during the nineteen-seventy expedition to Loa Hoa, as you might already have guessed. Are you sure you won't have a drink?"

I accepted, and the lieutenant asked if he might smoke. Brauer poured me a generous tot of the malt and found an ashtray. All the while he spoke, his voice, though rueful and world-weary, gained confidence, perhaps from the relief of confession or the rebound of his arrogance. "There was, in fact, as rumor has had it, a young man, a drifter of sorts, not quite sane, not that any of us were in those days. We did joke one night around the camp-fire, while he was off chanting in his tent, about killing him and eating parts of his body to re-create one of the important and more or less suppressed rituals of the Rangu. But it was a joke. We were all a little drunk on honey beer and far gone on the kind of potent marijuana that grows at high elevations. We were joking, but I'm afraid that one of our local helpers, who hap-pened to be very devoted to us and would do, it turned out, literally anything for us, took the joke seriously."

"What was his name?" asked the lieutenant, who was taking notes.

"Freddy Hiva. It doesn't matter. He's dead now. Anyway, the killing and eating of Bud, short for Buddha, as he called himself, became a kind of running joke. He even joined in, made wise-cracks about how he would taste. He was a blond fellow, of medium height with a slight build. One of those harmless, clue-less creatures. I was, naturally, quite horrified when, coming back to camp one afternoon, Freddy told me there had been an accident. Bud had fallen off one of the nearby cliffs and been killed."

He stopped and poured himself another measure of whiskey. "I was both horrified and excited. Once a philosopher twice a pervert, I have always thought. Not that, in those days, I didn't welcome the second appellation as well. When I asked Freddy if he had done it deliberately, he gave me a look of mock horror and said, no, no, no! It was against the law. I know I should have contacted the authorities, but I fancied myself an outlaw scien-tist, a Nietzschean for whom no experience was taboo, not even the eating of human flesh. And I still do." He glanced up at us defiantly. "I did it for research.

"We had to act quickly. I told Freddy to keep the news absolutely secret. I immediately informed Chard and Wherry about what had happened and how we now had an opportunity to recreate one of the basic rituals of the Rangu culture. They agreed, and together we approached Thad Pilty, all the while keeping up the fiction that it had been an accident. Thad wanted nothing to do with it. He said as far as he was concerned he had heard nothing and he wanted to hear nothing more about it. We left him in charge of the camp and, taking some supplies, including the camera, went to the site where the body lay. Bud's neck was broken, but he appeared otherwise unhurt by his fall. I didn't question Freddy about it. What was done was done. With help from a few trusted locals, we tied the body to a makeshift litter and headed over a rough trail deep into a high valley where few if any whites had ever penetrated. It took us nearly a day. We arrived at a taboo site made of large stones forming a sizable platform. It wasn't easy, being accepted, I mean, by the local chiefs. But I knew the language, and in native dress with my tattoos I could pass.

"It's all in the notes that I took, the magic chants, how Bud's heart tasted. But you should know it wasn't an exercise in depravity. It was enormously exalting in a way, not just a symbolic sacrament but the real thing. It was only later, as the significance began to sink in, that the doubts started. We all dealt with it in our own ways. My misgivings have been minimal. I would do it all over again. Poor Alger shriveled into his little morbid job. Corny tried to joke and rationalize his way out of it. We would meet and talk about it. We couldn't publish anything about it, of course. Without perishing. We began meeting in the little room in the Skull Collection. We called ourselves the *Société de Couchon Long* as a kind of joke. I think it was as much a shrine to Bud as anything else. We never did find out who he was. The wooden box contains everything he had. Some books on Buddhist teaching and drug paraphernalia and a picture of a girl."

"That's why you didn't destroy anything," I said.

He nodded. "I have nearly finished a book that I planned to have published posthumously."

The lieutenant glanced up from his notes. "Was anyone else involved with the group?"

"We tried to interest Thad Pilty at one time, but he wanted nothing to do with it."

"Did either Dean Fessing or Dean Scrabbe know or learn anything about this incident?"

"I don't think so."

"Did they know anything about your . . . society?"

"I don't know. But someone knew about it."

The lieutenant raised an eyebrow. "Yes?"

"We keep a very fine thread fixed over the green door, which we replace every time we go in there. Some time ago we found that it had been broken."

"Why did you keep the Skull in there?" I asked.

He sighed, looked weary. "As a kind of fetish, I suppose. A surrogate Bud. I don't know."

We got up to leave finally. I could tell the lieutenant was skeptical. "Thank you, Professor Brauer," he said with stiff formality. "I would like to have a team come here this evening and do a thorough examination of these premises and those of your office at the museum. If you would grant permission, it would save our having to get a search warrant."

Brauer bowed his affirmation of the request. "I have nothing to hide. But I would prefer you did it in the morning."

"I'm afraid that won't be possible. Do you mind if I use your phone?"

It was all very businesslike. The forensic team showed up.

Brauer signed some forms and gave the officer in charge the key to his office at the museum. I called Mort to tell him to let the police back in. As the lieutenant drove me home, I could tell that he was disturbed. "I don't understand . . ." He shook his head. "People with the kind of education . . ." We parked for a moment outside my house. He said, "I think he's lying about Fessing and Scrabbe not knowing. They knew something, and I think Brauer knew they knew."

I demurred. It was a possibility. I said I thought Chard the most likely suspect if that group had anything to do with the murders.

As I got out he thanked me. "That was a real piece of work, Norman."

I thanked him in return and asked a favor: could he do everything possible to keep this out of the press until there was more conclusive evidence that the suspects were involved?

He told me he would do all he could but added that word about such things leaked out pretty quickly.

Well, I'm heading over to the Club for dinner and, I hope, a postprandial with Izzy and Lotte. It'll be all I can do not to tell them about the room behind the Green Door. I find I'm quite proud of what I've done. I wish Elsbeth was here already so that I could brag a little to her. Although, to tell the truth, I wish I could be as certain as Lieutenant Tracy that we have found the culprits.

MONDAY, SEPTEMBER 14

There is a bit of wisdom, of rabbinic origin if I'm not mistaken, that states you must choose carefully what you think you want in life because there is a good chance you will get it. At the conclusion of an impromptu teleconference on Friday, the Board of Governors announced that Dr. Commer would step down as Director to become Director Emeritus and that I was named, effective immediately, "Director, with extraordinary powers for the duration of the present crisis at the Museum of Man." At the end of the meeting, Robert Remick called to tell me that he and the Board had complete confidence that I would "get to work and clean up the mess."

The first job I assigned myself, of course, was firing Malachy Morin. How many times I have dreamed of doing just that I cannot tell you. There have been nights when merely the thought of seeing the last of that man has kept me going. But now, granted the power and the cause to fire him, I find I have little stomach for it. I suppose I should have done it right away, immediately after the meeting, when he was still in a state of stupefaction at what had been announced. The way he looked at me, with that awful smile, his jowls quivering, fear and surprise mingling in a kind of low-grade, grudging respect. The fawning way he grabbed my hand, and his pathetic words of congratulations. I should have smothered all his overtures with a quick and decisive meeting in my office. But it was after four-thirty, and I did have a five o'clock tennis match at the Club.

I remained nervous all night, thinking and dreaming about it. And it was worse when I arrived here this morning. How do you kick someone who is licking your boots? How do you shoot a cringing dog? I did at least tell him there would be a drastic reorganization and was about to intimate that his position was at best tenuous when he interrupted me, saying we had worked well together in the past and would make a great team in the future. It was not an auspicious start for my career as an administrator.

I found it nearly as difficult to be straightforward with Thad Pilty. I met with him just after lunch and told him that I planned to write a letter to Constance Brattle to let her know there would be no further meetings of the Oversight Committee regarding the diorama of Paleolithic life. Well, you would have thought I was interfering with the affairs of the museum rather than the committee. I kept my course, however, and his tone grew more conciliatory. He implored me "for political reasons" to allow the upcoming meeting, set for next Tuesday, to go forward as planned.

In acquiescing to his plea, I mentioned that I personally had reservations about the diorama — not so much its form and content, which I said struck me as original and instructive, but its usurpation of space traditionally reserved for temporary exhibits. After a rather stiff silence, he said he would be willing to meet with Edwards, the likable and resourceful young man in charge of exhibits, to see how best to make the exhibition removable and storable. He added, however, that unless the diorama was established "on a semipermanent basis," he would go to the Board himself and even hinted that he might offer it to the American Museum of Natural History in New York. I simply nodded, saying nothing about the Curatorial Ball. But I have in fact called around to arrange a meeting of the Ball Committee, so that we can get things rolling, as they say.

I scheduled a meeting of all MOM staffers in Margaret Mead Auditorium, with coffee and sweet rolls laid on. I am going to tell them what has happened and to apprise them, as far as is prudent, about what steps I will be taking to improve security and boost morale, which has hit an all-time low, at least in my tenure here. I also want to hear what they have to say.

Of course, to accomplish this there will be some toes, some well-protected toes and some quite precious toes, that I will have to step on. I may have to bring in an expert consultant to straighten out the financial mess. I have in mind a joint Wainscott-MOM committee to consider the status of the Genetics Lab. If the future of that establishment has had anything to do with the murders of Fessing and Scrabbe, then a committee would be the best instrument to effect change. The murderer or murderers would have difficulty, one presumes, with dispatching a large and active committee. I have sent a note to Professor Gottling informing him of my appointment and requesting a meeting as soon as possible to discuss a range of issues, not least the relations between the lab and the pavilion. Closing down that latter entity will, by itself, save enormous amounts of money. (Speaking of which, I returned to Damon Drex his draft "press packet" with a note telling him that he ought to have a thorough check done on his computer and his programmers.)

Last, but by no means least, I must press ahead with my own investigation into the murders of the deans. I am naive, perhaps, but I still do not share the lieutenant's belief that one or all of the cultists are implicated directly in the crimes. The cultists certainly fit into the larger puzzle that is slowly coming together in my mind. I may be wrong, of course, and I must say I find it troubling that Thad Pilty is the only other person with a motive who knew about what happened in Loa Hoa. A thorough search and examination of the Skull Collection and the residences of Wherry and Brauer has turned up no incriminating evidence, or none that Lieutenant Tracy has been willing to share with me.

I am also pursuing some hunches of my own. I do not want to reveal what they are even in this journal as it's possible that the perpetrators, who appear to be omnipresent, may have access to material in the mainframe, even that protected by a password. Suffice it to say that I have retained at my own expense a reputable detective agency to do some research for me. It may or may not be a long shot. In the meanwhile I'm going to have to keep my wits about me if I'm not to end up, quite literally, in the same pot as Fessing and Scrabbe.

I have yet to receive a reply from Elsbeth, and it makes me think that I was perhaps overly warm in my response to her. In my worst moments I think there might be a farcical replay of the awful little missive I got from her when I was at Infra. But I have no regrets. As it is said, nothing ventured, nothing gained.

WEDNESDAY, SEPTEMBER 16

What is it about our age that inverts so many expectations? Here I was, daily expecting another grotesque media circus when the news of the Brauer cult and those incidents in Loa Hoa so far and so long ago leaked out, as I knew they eventually would. The story "broke" the day before yesterday as the lead article in the *Bugle* under a byline by Amanda Feeney, who has her own sources in the Seaboard Police Department. Except for the headline, "Cannibal Cult Uncovered in the MOM," it was a reasonably straightforward account of what Brauer had related to Lieutenant Tracy and me. So I braced for the usual spate of calls by reporters asking loaded, insinuating questions, for visitations by the television types, trailing through with their gear as though they owned the place. And there have been a few calls, tours of the Skull Collection and that sort of thing. But instead of pariahs, Brauer and company have been made into national celebrities.

A story in this morning's news reports that Brauer is on the point of signing a three-point-two-million-dollar contract for a book and movie deal. Marge told me there's already a lot of speculation about who will play Brauer. She mentioned some names that I didn't recognize, but then I've never been much up on popular culture. Corny Chard has been utterly irresponsible. I tuned in Mother's old black-and-white television set last night, and the man seemed to be on just about every channel, saying things about how human flesh tasted to him like lamb. I wonder sometimes if this is the way civilization unravels.

All of which pales, I must confess, next to what's happened in my own life. Elsbeth called this morning to tell me she is arriving on Thursday, October 8, and plans to spend at least two weeks here. She told me she is looking forward very much to seeing me and asked if I would drive her out to the cottage. She said she was utterly delighted that I had written back and couldn't wait to see me and "dear old Seaboard."

Her call has me walking on air one moment and the most miserable of wretches the next. The sound of her voice turned my knees and my heart to mush. The way she said "Norman" made more than thirty years of life and time simply disappear. She sounded so pleased, with a note of something like relief in her voice. Then I think, is she merely being polite, was there not also a kind of condescension in the voice, the expectation that I will act like a dog she has well and truly whipped? Am I just an old boyfriend to her while to me she is the object of a lifetime of painful obsession? What will we say to each other? What will we talk about? Will I even care? Will she be little more than a plump suburban matron *d'un certain âge* who will, with some thoughtless banality, snuff out the flame I have been carrying lo these many years? Or will we, however decorously, fall into one another's arms? Will she rescue me from what I admit has been a stunted bachelor existence? And do I really want to be rescued? Will that not make a mockery of most of my adult existence? On the other hand, I have to admit that even these torments are better than those that would have come from a tepid or cold response, from the prospect of nothing.

Not unexpectedly, perhaps, the prospect of her visit has made me resolve to get to the bottom of this murder business once and for all. I mean, if Elsbeth is bent on some arrangement, something more than a casual meeting, then I can scarcely expect her to remain in a situation where my life and perhaps hers would be in danger. It is time, in short, to act.

FRIDAY, SEPTEMBER 18

I should have had more faith in Malachy Morin, more faith that he would give me cause not merely to fire him but to fire him with something akin to relish.

Until late this morning he gave me little to complain about regarding his behavior since getting out of jail. Indeed, his demeanor and his pathetic attempts to find something useful to do have all been exemplary. There is nothing really against him other than the fact that he is implicated in the suspicious and unseemly death of an innocent young lady and the fact that, quite simply, he is not needed here. I certainly have no plans to retain him as an executive assistant.

Anyway, it was getting on toward noontime when it happened. I had just gotten back from an exhausting meeting with Marge Littlefield. My head was quite spinning from the sheer amount of raw and confused data regarding the museum's finances. Small wonder Fessing and Scrabbe had difficulty pinning down just where the money comes from and where it goes. Marge claims to "have a good idea" about what's happening, but frankly I could make neither head nor tail of it. She didn't object openly when I told her I would be retaining a consultant to go over things, only I could tell her nose was just a bit out of joint. But I'm afraid it is going to take a veritable Theseus of an accountant to get through that fiendish labyrinth, and I shudder to think what Minotaur of finances will be found at its center.

It was in this state of mind that I received a call from Mr. Morin asking if I would come down to "go over our strategy" in the Pringle case with Ariel Dearth. I demurred, saying I was very busy. Then he mentioned that I might be interested and helpful as part of their defense would involve the museum's policies. With that bit of information my ears pricked up and I betook myself with dispatch down to his locker room of an office.

I found Mr. Dearth at his officious best when I entered. "I'm glad you could make it, Mr. de Ratour," he said, snidely insinuating that it was the least I could do under the circumstances. Then, his mustache twitching as he spoke, he began by blithely assuming I would serve as a character witness for "your esteemed colleague, Mal." I had just sat down in one of those spindly wooden armchairs so common in institutions like ours. I shook my head and was about to voice my refusal as candidly as possible when he barged on obliviously, taking up other areas where my "support would be useful." He and his team, he said, would establish that what had happened to Elsa Pringle was nothing more, technically, than an "industrial accident." The defendant sat there nodding his head (he's starting to put on weight again, I noticed) and said, "Happens all the time."

But that, Ariel Dearth announced with a flourish, standing and pacing in his best courtroom manner, was only the beginning. "Malachy Morin," he declaimed, gesturing in the direction of his client, "is nothing less than the victim of widespread prejudice against persons with aberrant morphologies. Indeed, we are a society racked by a deep-seated and broad-based adiposephobic bias." Pacing, turning dramatically, framed in the aura of the wood paneling, he went on in that vein, talking about the "millions of victims suffering in heavy silence" while "a multibillion-dollar diet industry feeds on them." I was surprised, to say the least, when the learned counsel stopped in front of me in a pose meant to convey deep thoughtfulness (head bent forward, chin in hand, other hand crossed over holding elbow) and said, "Tell us, Mr. de Ratour, is there or has there ever been a program in place at the museum to counsel and help individuals like Mr. Morin come to terms with their configurative conflicts?" Objection, I nearly said, but before I could recover from my utter bemusement, he strode away, turned, strode back, and whirled on me. "Is it not also true, Mr. de Ratour, that the system failed Mr. Morin to the extent that the museum did not have in place any programs to counsel and help its sexually vulnerable employees? Was any effort made to identify and help the morally impaired among you? Was there even a pamphlet available to help them be conscious of and cope with situations of interpersonal conflictual stress? And is it not also true, Mr. de Ratour, that at the time of the accident, Mr. Morin, in the wake of Dean Fessing's murder, was under intense pressure from the museum to secure the service of Ms. Pringle as a press assistant?" He turned again from me to a putative jury. "I would suggest, ladies and gentlemen of the jury, that it was under just such pressure that Mr. Morin, utterly unprepared by the institution he was to suffer so much for, felt obliged to take extraordinary measures in his efforts to enlist Ms. Pringle's services for the Museum of Man. Ladies and gentlemen of the jury, let me sum up for you by pointing out that the real victim of this tragedy, the person who has had to live and endure unimagined pain and suffering, is none other than the accused, Mr. Malachy Morin."

To the applause of the defendant, Dearth sat down in a chair like mine. I didn't know where to begin. I was ready to go upstairs, unlock my top drawer, take out my father's gun, bring it back down, and shoot them both. But before I could get a word out, Dearth stood up again and resumed his lawyering. All of the elements he had mentioned, he said, constitute not merely a defense "but the basis for a civil suit against the museum, which as an institution had been derelict in its responsibilities to those employees susceptible to victimization by the system." He went on to claim that Malachy Morin "in making his extra effort at the behest of the museum had, knowingly and with incredible courage, not only put himself in great moral and physical danger but risked heart attack, stroke, or worse." Indeed, he said, Mr. Morin was to have a complete checkup at the infirmary to see what damage had been done.

When he had finally finished, I stood up. I was so angry I was trembling. I told them both that I had not heard anything so preposterous in my life and that if they attempted in any way whatsoever to malign my museum, I would see to it that they were countersued for millions of dollars. Well, both of them were flabbergasted in turn. Sounding a note of strained patience, Dearth started to explain that what he was proposing was now standard practice and that they had checked and found the museum had insurance coverage for just such eventualities. I became quite uncivil. I told him not only that I found his proposed suit outrageous but that his conduct was subverting a grand and honorable profession, that he was making the law into the disorder of which it purports to be the relief. As he sat there sputtering, I turned to his client and said, "Mr. Morin, you are fired. You have exactly one half hour to remove your personal effects from this office and turn over any keys you have to Doreen. You will receive written confirmation of this dismissal in due time. Whatever traces of you are not gone by one P.M., I will personally escort to a Dumpster. And if you present any diffi-culties, I will call the police and have you arrested for trespass." I then turned and stalked out the door.

"Mr. de Ratour, Mr. de Ratour," Ariel Dearth called after me, "you are making a great mistake. You are acting without due process. You are in contempt of litigation . . ."

I ignored him. And when I poked my head in shortly after one, Malachy Morin and his stuff were gone. Doreen sat there looking somewhat bewildered, and I told her she could stay on as my secretary but that she would have to stop chewing gum or at least stop inflating and snapping those obscene little bladders in front of her mouth as she does so.

TUESDAY, SEPTEMBER 22

Edo Onoyoko died suddenly today under unusual circumstances, and we will have to await the results of an autopsy to find out if foul play is involved. In the meanwhile the media have descended like a plague of locusts, gobbling up what few stalks of information I have been able to throw them. I was present when the old gentleman died, and for reasons of propriety, I have refrained from telling members of the press exactly how it happened.

I should, I suppose, start at the beginning. I had planned to announce at today's Oversight Committee meeting that I had been named Director of the MOM, and that this was to be the last "hearing" about the diorama to which the museum or its representatives would be party. Then I remembered my agreement with Thad Pilty and decided instead to let the meeting proceed as scheduled. And it did proceed, opening as has become customary with a long statement by Constance Brattle that tested my resolve to see the thing through. She spoke darkly of what had happened to two Wainscott deans while serving at the MOM. She said the discovery of a "cult of cannibalism" in the museum made it likely that the committee would undertake "full and open" hearings into "these dark events in the Museum of Man."

On the other hand, I was encouraged by the number of absentees. Ariel Dearth wasn't there; he was hard at work, I assumed, perverting justice on behalf of Malachy Morin. Corny Chard didn't make it; he has become quite a public figure as an advocate of what he calls the New Anthropophagism. Father O'Gould also failed to appear, and Bertha Schanke came late, giving me a chance to grab the only Blueberry Filled. Mr. Onoyoko was there and seemed his usual self, bowing and smiling to everyone in anticipation of another good laugh. Two newcomers arrived in the persons of Professor Ray Mooney and Ms. Jackie, a model brought along for demonstration purposes by Emmanuel Quinn of Humanation Syntectics. As habits die hard, I took out my notebook to keep the minutes.

Mr. Quinn's technical show-and-tell began sanely enough. Ms. Jackie turned out to be the upper torso of a model from what he called their "standard line." As a demonstration, he proceeded to dismantle the model. We were all impressed, I think — as much as a committee in academia is ever impressed — by the way Mr. Quinn lifted the lifelike fair skin and glossy brunette hair of the model, a comely young woman, to reveal the array of tiny servomotors and miniaturized hydraulics that gave her such a living presence. I heard some stifled gasps of incredulity when, restored by Mr. Quinn to her original state, the young woman, who was dressed in a modest blouse and a business suit jacket, began to speak. Her lips moved in remarkable synchronization with her words, and she made appropriate gestures with her hands and face as she told us, in a pleasant, natural voice, that she was available to work at trade shows, shop windows, specialty displays, and any other place where her services would be useful.

I should point out that Ms. Jackie, as she introduced herself, was set on a base on a chair in such a way that she appeared, for all the world, just like another person at the meeting. After she had finished her little talk, Mr. Quinn activated a switch on her base that put her in what he called an "active/passive mode." She appeared most attentive the way she blinked her eyes from time to time, furrowed her pretty brow, raised a finger to her mouth in a thoughtful gesture, and even glanced around with a winsome, attractive smile. I fully expected one of the attendant activists to tell Mr. Quinn to put away his distracting homuncula, but they, like everyone else, seemed quite taken with her.

There were, of course, the usual hostile questions. Professor Brattle asked Mr. Quinn in a bristling voice why his company had decided to use female models for demonstration purposes. Mr. Quinn replied in an unoffended tone that they had found that when they used male models for presentations at universities and other nonprofit organizations, someone, usually a woman, invariably protested that female models weren't being used instead. Ms. Schanke, polishing off donuts with her usual panache, asked how much each model was going to cost. Professor Pilty took that question, saying that while final costs had yet to be determined on the "package" they were negotiating with Humanation Syntectics, he estimated that each model, with a five-year maintenance contract, would cost around thirty thousand dollars. Well, that created some reaction, and Ms. Schanke opined that there were many other causes on which the university's money could be better spent. Forgetting myself for a moment, I interjected that the funds in question belonged to the MOM, not to Wainscott. Everyone seemed surprised that I had spoken up, and my reminder produced some murmured demurrals, but I think the point went home, and I felt the better for having made it. Mr. Onoyoko, serious for a change, made it known through Ms. Kushiro that all of the microchips and precision servomotors were designed and produced in Japan. Izzy Landes provided a needed note of levity when he remarked that it would be worth the money to have such a model of himself to send to faculty meetings.

At that point a strange quiet descended on the room and its large circular table. It was, I think, the presence of the robot lady that fascinated us all into silence. Even Professor Athol, who speaks when he has nothing to say, remained silent, taken, like everyone else, with the beguiling Ms. Jackie. Professor Murdleston began to mutter something about seeing her "lower parts" when he was interrupted by Professor Mooney, one of the lesser lights in the Biology Department. He asked what was being done in the diorama to depict the sex life of the Neanderthals. I should explain that Professor Mooney, who came of age in the sixties, is a thin, beamish man with a wispy beard and a ponytail to match who walks around in a celebratory haze and used to be considered ever so daring for the graphic lectures he gives on mammalian reproduction. He is one of those people who still wants to free us all from our oppressive Puritan past.

Professor Pilty said in reply that some consideration had been given to a tableau in which a Neanderthal woman would be shown giving birth. Professor Mooney snickered openly at that and said, in that knowing way, that he was talking about sex, real sex. Thad Pilty was clearly unprepared for this. He cleared his throat and mentioned something about the number of children who were expected to visit the diorama. Ray Mooney, of course, was waiting to pounce with all the usual arguments about how we protect our children from the facts of life while foisting on them the most graphic images of violence and murder. Professor Pilty was about to respond when Professor Athol weighed in with his expertise, saying that the depiction of the sex act could be ethically sanctioned provided it was done tastefully in the context of a "long-term committed relationship." Professor Landes pondered aloud if Professor Athol might provide the committee with a description of tasteful sex.

I know the good man was simply trying, with his needling wit, to puncture the ballooning absurdity of the whole thing, but his jab, in fact, only moved the discussion from "whether" to "how." (No one, including myself, I have to confess, stood up to denounce the idea for fear of being labeled a prude.) Professor Athol said the couple might be situated "in one of the darker recesses of the planned cave," where they would be engaged in "a standard sexual act." "You mean the *a priori* position?" Professor Landes asked. Professor Athol did not know what *a priori* meant, and it had to be explained to him in terms of the contrasting notion of *a posteriori*.

Well, at this, just about everyone around the table wanted to get in their two-cents' worth, with the exception of Mr. Onoyoko, whose smiles had given way to head-shaking laughter. Ms. Jackie seemed to be smiling ever more brightly, while Mason Twitchell's likeness, perhaps because of the way the sunlight struck the oils, appeared to glower. Thad Pilty tried to diffuse the issue by explaining that little or nothing was known about the sexual habits of the Neanderthals. He noted that in the popular fictions of Jean Auel and Elizabeth Marshall Thomas, couples of the Late Paleolithic are depicted *copula more canun*. However, he went on to say that Desmond Morris and others had argued that, for physiological and psychological reasons, face-to-face copulation had probably evolved early among hominids. He cited Frans de Waal's study, *Peacemaking among Primates*, in which *Pan paniscus*, the pigmy chimps, have been observed to mate face to face with considerable frequency.

Professor Mooney asked Mr. Quinn if there would be any difficulty arranging to have a couple of the models depicted having sexual intercourse. Mr. Quinn asked if the professor wanted "the genitals engaged." When Professor Mooney expressed surprise that they had models with genitals, Mr. Quinn described what he called the Erotomax Series, a line of sexually active models. He said with some pride that his company was installing "a raft of them right now in an indoor theme park in Vegas for Panthouse Enterprises. I've seen some of the mock-ups. I mean, they've got everything, threesomes, clusters, the whole nine yards." Professor Landes asked, facetiously I'm sure, if they had Aretino's wheelbarrow as well. When Dr. Commer asked, "Whose wheelbarrow?" and Izzy explained it to him, even Constance Brattle smiled, and Mr. Onoyoko was all but banging his head on the table.

When the room settled down again, Mr. Quinn said that what he was trying to say was "that if you people want to have a couple of these Neanderthals getting it on, I'm sure we could modify a pair of our Erotomax models, I mean with all the hair and the faces and the short legs." Izzy said it was starting to sound like the Paleobscene, getting a nod from Professor Pilty, who asked how expensive it would be. Mr. Quinn said he would price it out for us but thought it might even cost less as the hydraulics of the Erotomax line are "kind of elementary, with the servomechanisms mostly in the jaws and hips."

At that point Professor Brattle said that, before they went any further with this suggestion, "I think it is important from the standpoint of the committee's concerns that the position of any female partner in any depiction of sexual congress be given careful consideration." Mr. Quinn agreed saying that, when it came to sex, position was everything. Professor Brattle said that she meant that she was opposed to having the couple engaged "doggy style" as that necessarily put the man in the superior position. Mr. Quinn said they could have them lying on their sides. Professor Mooney objected, saying that that would be boring. Mr. Onoyoko was wiping his eyes. Professor Brattle ignored him, although her eyes were rolling like those of someone suddenly stranded in a high place. She said that, whatever was decided, she wanted to make sure that the female model not be shown in an inferior position. Ms. Marlene Parkers, who had remained silent until then, said that if this "scene" was really going to be necessary, why not have them alternate positions? Professor Mooney asked Mr. Quinn if that were "technically feasible." Mr. Quinn said that we were going to need a technician to come and "switch them over," but as the contract calls for someone to come in every six months for general maintenance it could be done then. Professor Landes slapped the table. "My God, six months in the same position. Now that does sound boring. I mean, won't the parts . . . wear out?" Mr. Quinn, ever the professional, said they would eventually, but that the "moving parts" on the Erotomax were made out of "really high-tech stuff."

Ms. Schanke, who had been furiously eating donuts all this time, put up a powdered hand. "Let's just hold on one minute," she said. Then, after swallowing a mouthful: "I don't see why consideration isn't being given to showing two women having sex. Why do we always have to subscribe to phallocentric domination?" Mr. Quinn shrugged. "We can do that, too," he said, turning to the chairperson. "And that solves the problem about who to put on top." Meanwhile Mr. Onoyoko nearly gagged with laughter, as Professor Pilty declared with evident exasperation that there was no evidence of lesbianism among Neanderthals. Ms. Schanke countered that there was precious little evidence of anything among Neanderthals, so what difference did it make? Professor Landes countered, asking how, without heterosexual activity among our forebears, did we get here?

Well, it degenerated from there, if you can believe it. Ms. Schanke was hurling epithets at Professor Pilty so special as to constitute another language. It was a shame Father O'Gould was not there to point out that the graphic depiction of the sexual act would ruin the whole diorama because in fact that's all most people, including the children, would notice. I am not a prude, but I think there are limits, and I had decided to step out of character again to voice not merely my objections but a veto on any such tableau in the diorama. As I waited for a suitable break in what was becoming an increasing acrimonious debate, a sudden lull descended on the room, in which the only sound was the staccato voice of Ms. Kushiro and the convulsive mirth of Mr. Onoyoko. I cleared my throat and was just at the point of speaking when Mr. Onoyoko's laughter took on an ominous gargling sound. I glanced over to see that his normally pale face had turned a most unwholesome green. A moment later he collapsed with a thud on the table and, to the horror of us all,

gurgled a bit and slid to the floor. Ms. Jackie continued to smile
and gesture while the rest of us gathered around the fallen
benefactor. Strangely enough, it was Dr. Commer, more alive
than I have seen him in years, who rose to the occasion. Amid
the usual cries of "give him air," Dr. Commer knelt beside the
stricken man, felt for his pulse, and announced, "He no longer
needs air."

I asked everyone to remain calm and not to leave the premises.
I delegated Izzy to go to an adjoining office and put in a 911 call.
When Professor Brattle glanced at me quizzically, I explained to
her that I was now Director of the Museum of Man and under
the circumstances in charge. I surreptiously took the half-filled
paper cup of coffee Mr. Onoyoko had in front of him and, using
a napkin, placed it on a high bookshelf. Repeating that everyone
would have to remain until the police arrived, I left the Twitchell
Room and its buzzing occupants and from an adjoining office
put in a call to Lieutenant Tracy. I was patched through immediately, and he asked me to return to the meeting and keep
everyone there until he arrived. I told him I had already done that
and had secured Mr. Onoyoko's coffee cup. He rang off saying he
was on his way.

By the time a team of emergency medical technicians arrived,
it was apparent that Mr. Onoyoko had entered the long night of
history. Shortly thereafter, the lieutenant came in with a team
of his own, and I helped arrange rooms for interviewing in some
of the nearby offices. The lieutenant assured everyone that the
questioning would be strictly routine, but that if anyone wanted
a lawyer present it could be arranged. Even Ms. Schanke was
subdued by what had happened, and no one put up any particular fuss, except Professor Athol, who appeared excited at the idea
of being a suspect.

I spent some time with Lieutenant Tracy going over routine
details — who sat where, who said what, and so on. I'm not sure

he fully comprehended what I was saying when I tried to convey to him the topic and tone of the meeting. It was gratifying to have him ask me if I thought Onoyoko's death could be linked to the murders of the deans. I told him I had yet to give it much thought. At first glance the man's demise didn't fit any logical plot. Unless, of course, the Japanese businessman had become privy to a conspiracy conducted in his name and had moved to stop it. In that case the Genetics Lab and the communications from Worried might take on real significance. We agreed it was useless to speculate until we had the results of an autopsy. He said he would keep me informed.

The fact is, I am not myself in the least distressed by Mr. Onoyoko's death. Indeed, it may be the key to solving a lot of our problems. That is to say, without his beneficence we will not be able to afford the Primate Pavilion or the Genetics Lab. They will simply have to go.

Ah well, there goes the phone. I'm going to ignore it. I am going to the Club for a bit of self-indulgence. Strange how, with my new position, there seems a bit more respect in the air when I make my entrance there. I can't say I don't enjoy it. And just imagine, in seventeen days, barely more than two weeks, Elsbeth will arrive.

FRIDAY, SEPTEMBER 25
_____

It is late. I am tired, and I must go home to dress for the annual dinner of the Seaboard Historical Society, an event that, for the first time, I do not look forward to with much anticipation. I mean, there will be the same food, the same faces, the same things said. But then my life has taken on a new zing of late, and my capacity for boredom has diminished accordingly. Still, I feel obliged to record the events of the past few days as they relate to my investigation into the murders of Fessing and Scrabbe.

First, I have had another disquieting communication from Worried in the Genetics Lab. As per usual, I will reproduce it here.

Dear Mr. Detour [sic]:
  I am very afraid as I send this to you. I think my life is in danger sending you this stuff. I would not be surprised if Professors [sic] Fessing and Scrabbe met their horrible ends at the hands of one of Professor Gottling's assistants or maybe even Professor Gottling did it himself. They are all fanatics except maybe Dr. Kaplan and he is scared of the others. They all want to go down in history. There's been even more police around asking questions since Mr. Onoyoko died and my friend who really knows what's going on says they're hurrying things up for this big experiment code-named Mary Shirley or Shelly or something like that. He says they're going to take a couple of fetuses out of the chimps and add some human genes and grow them in a special glass box. I'm not sure this is a good idea. I think someone out there ought to know what's going on before we have a lot of little monsters running around and maybe getting loose. I almost forgot to tell you that Dr. Hanker has left the lab. Before he left there was an out of court settlement with Charlene that came from Dr. Hanker's wife who is rich. Charlene has been wearing an engagement ring from her regular boyfriend who knows all about Dr. Hanker and has even seen the tape. He's going to marry her to give the baby a real father although some people are saying he's doing it because she really got a load from Dr. Hanker's wife and that the kid is probably the boyfriend's anyway because he's been seeing her all along.
                                                 More Worried Than Ever

When Lieutenant Tracy dropped by this morning to tell me that the autopsy on Mr. Onoyoko's body proved negative — he died of a heart attack — I showed him this latest missive from Worried. The lieutenant didn't seem in the least perturbed and repeated back to me what I had told him about information received anonymously.

"Have you spoken to Gottling?" I asked.

"Oh, yes. He showed us around the whole facility. He's a most impressive man."

"What did he have to say about this series of e-mail communications I've received?"

"He said they were nothing more than ridiculous fabrications and insisted on seeing the originals."

"Did you show them to him?"

"I didn't. But I doubt very much, Norman, that Professor Gottling had anything to do with the murders."

His enunciation of "Professor" made me raise my eyebrows. "Not personally, perhaps, but he does have people working for him."

The lieutenant's expression was comically pained. With some exasperation he said, "I know, I know, but he really is too — "

"Important?"

"Perhaps. Serious might be a better way of describing him."

I allowed myself a slight smile. "But, Lieutenant, you are the one who has taught me that the most respectable of people are capable of the most heinous of crimes."

He smiled back, and his *"touché"* had a most endearing uncertainty about it.

Still, I am going to pursue my own investigation into the Genetics Lab. I have sent Professor Gottling another note, this time telling him that I am to open discussions with Wainscott regarding the future of the lab. If that doesn't get a response, I'm afraid nothing will. There's nothing much else to report. Ariel Dearth's office has called several times, but I have refused to take his calls or call back. Damon Drex has also been plaguing me. He wants to have a "meeting of the brains."

Ah well, Elsbeth arrives in less than two weeks. I'm having the kitchen done over at a quite exorbitant cost, but the results are already manifest and gratifying. Amazing, isn't it, the gadgets available today for cooking and disposing and whatnot. I microwaved, if that is an acceptable verb, my first frozen dinner last night, beef something or other, and it really wasn't all that bad with a bottle of good California zinfandel. Yvette's coming a week from today to give the whole house a thorough cleaning. But I'm still not sure about investing in a double bed.

WEDNESDAY, SEPTEMBER 30

I have succeeded in meeting with Professor Gottling, and what I learned today has left me quite disturbed and, frankly, in a quandary as to what to do. I am convinced he has a motive for getting rid of the two deans if they were beginning to find out not only about the arrangements between the Genetics Lab and the Primate Pavilion but about the nature of his experimentation and research. At any rate, when he called me this morning it was more to put me off than to arrange a meeting. He told me that he had gone over everything with the police, and that if they were satisfied, why wasn't I. When I mentioned Project Alpha he said it had been canceled. I informed him that my sources told me differently and that, as Director of the MOM, it was my responsibility to meet with him about this matter. He turned brusque and said he was a very busy man and did not have time to placate every administrator worried about rumors. I said in return that I would then have to call on the museum's counsel to summon a Board of Inquiry as provided for in the Rules of Governance. After a bit of blustering about, he finally, and not very graciously, acquiesced to a meeting.

To prepare for the meeting, I reviewed the CV the Wainscott Personnel Office had obligingly sent me some time ago. I don't need to reproduce it here. Suffice it to say that Stoddard Gottling was born fifty-six years ago not far from Boston. He received a Ph.D. in cytology and biochemistry from Harvard at an early age and worked at the Biological Laboratories there, Cavendish, and Cold Harbor, before coming to the MOM some five years ago. It's probably not coincidental that, at about the same time, Edo Onoyoko arrived and began taking an active interest in the research of the Genetics Lab. I will not pretend to understand the work he has been doing. He is an expert, I know, in the slicing and splicing of genes and has an enzyme insertion technique named after him, for which, apparently, he has been short-listed several times for the Nobel Prize.

Thus informed I went, a little after two this afternoon, through the labyrinth of tunnels in the subbasement that connects all three parts of the museum. (Because of the increasing number of restricted areas in both the Genetics Lab and the Primate Pavilion, ordinary access through the upper floors has all but ceased.) I was left to cool my heels in the office of his secretary before the eminent geneticist emerged and ushered me through several labs into his book-lined, paper-strewn office. He tried to be cordial, but I could tell it was not something that came easy for him. Almost immediately, he asked me if I had brought copies of the reports I had been receiving.

I told him I had brought along a summary of the reports, which I gave him in a manila envelope. I did not tell him that I had omitted some important accusations, which I thought best to bring up personally during our discussion. Professor Gottling appeared disappointed to the point of anger, but he hid it well enough as he glanced quickly over my summaries.

"This is preposterous," he said finally, lighting a cigarette and setting up a veritable smoke screen. All the same, I think he was badly shaken. "I've gone over this already with the police. Certainly we are working on gene therapies. Everyone is working on gene therapies. But, really, it is quite another thing to be designing a new human genotype, as this person, whoever he is, alleges."

It was the words he used and the way he reached for a fresh cigarette with one burning in the ashtray and caught himself just in time that made me think, with a flash of genuine horror, that he was lying. He insisted on seeing what he called "the original documents." I refused. I told him that they had been sent to me in confidence and that it would take a court order to pry them loose. I think it was the word *court* that brought blood to his face. He is a tall, pale man with short-cropped graying blond hair, eyes the color of ice, and the kind of loose lower lip given easily to disdain. I do not think he is used to having people disagree with or refuse him. His agitation reached such a pitch that for a moment I actually thought he might strike me.

"Professor Gottling," I said, "it doesn't make any sense not to be frank with me. I need to know in detail the extent of your experiments, how long you have been doing them, and the results to date, insofar as a layperson such as myself can comprehend them."

"What do you need to know for?" he asked, exuding so much smoke he might have been a volcano about to erupt.

I repeated that I was Director of the museum and might be for some time. As such, I said, "it is my responsibility to know what is happening in all departments of the museum so that I am able to report with competence and completeness to the Board of Governors. "Furthermore," I continued, "the person who is sending me these reports will surely start giving them to the newspapers in the belief there may be some connection between what's going on in the Genetics Lab and the murdered deans."

In retrospect, I find it difficult to describe the nearly satanic glower that lit his cold eyes when I mentioned the deans. I could almost think him insane, and did think the unthinkable: it was he who had dispatched Fessing and Scrabbe or had some devoted underling do it for him when they started asking the same questions. Despite a shiver of fear, I pressed on. I told him I needed to know the exact arrangements and conditions under which he was using chimpanzees from the Primate Pavilion for his work. I needed to know the number of animals involved, what he was doing with them, and for how long. I pointed out that state regulations in this regard were very strict, involving not merely fines for infractions but criminal prosecution.

Again he blustered, demanding to see the reports I had received, saying the lab had nothing to hide, that they were "serious and very busy people." He went on in that vein, but I did not relent. I told him I needed "a detailed accounting of all monies paid to the Primate Pavilion for services rendered." He denied that the Genetics Lab had paid anything "for the few specimens we have collected from time to time from a few of the animals." What about the funding of programs in the Primate Pavilion from the Onoyoko Institute? He waved his cigarette at me. He denied he had anything to do with the institute's funding policies. It was an outright lie. I took out another document I had had the foresight to obtain before coming to the meeting: the last annual report of the institute, which, while vague about where most of its monies went, listed its officers and the members of its disbursement committee, the chair of which is Professor Gottling. Presented with that, he belched more smoke and said that "out of heuristic considerations" he might have sanctioned funding a project or two in the pavilion, but these were details others attended to. The baldness of his lie embarrassed both of us; if department heads pay attention to anything in academia, it is to who and what gets funded.

He stood up and sat down, snubbed out his cigarette and lit another. "Why is this so important to you?"

"Because I am responsible ultimately for what goes on in the Museum of Man."

"Why don't you ask Drex about where he gets his funding?" he asked in a sneer.

"To be perfectly frank, I am not convinced that Mr. Drex is altogether sane."

The man's laugh and smile were not pleasant, but for a knowing moment we were in some agreement. I persisted, however. I repeated that if he were not forthcoming in all necessary details I would convene a Board of Inquiry. I also said that while I was loath to have the press meddle in any affairs of the museum, I was not above using the media if it came to that.

The man's expression was such that for a moment once again I could believe he had something personally to do with the deaths of Fessing and Scrabbe. His suppressed rage, his clenched jaw and clenching fists were such as to suggest madness barely under control. "Who told you about the chimpanzees?" he demanded to know with a fury that belied his assertion that the lab used "animal material" from the pavilion merely as a convenience. "Listen, Mr. . . . ."

"De Ratour."

"De Ratour, the animals happen to be right here. We can get the same thing from other sources on a routine basis."

I ignored this lie and began to get specific. "I have heard, Professor Gottling, that you are planning to grow a couple of chimp fetuses modified with human genes in a glass box. It's code-named Mary Shelley."

His face blanched, his lower lip trembled. Again he demanded that I show him the original documents. He wanted to know who had sent them. "There has been a major breach in security," he said, catching himself to amend it to "I mean, a breach in confidence, in the kind of trust we need for our work." He went on, as though speaking to himself, expostulating about human frailty, about how he already had enough problems with the death of Onoyoko, about how he couldn't even get a call through to Onoyoko's son, "a playboy who has taken to decadence with typical Japanese diligence." I interrupted him finally to say that, unless he wanted to speak to me now in an open and candid way about his operations, I would immediately begin an internal investigation in a very thorough manner. When he hesitated, I stood up and turned toward the door.

I don't think I have ever seen a person change personalities so abruptly and radically. "Mr. de Ratour," he began, in a quiet, nearly humble tone, "please sit down." He indulged in some preambulatory flattery about how he knew I was a man of culture and vision and how I had the best interests of the museum and the labs at heart. I imagine he had used the same applied charm on Lieutenant Tracy. I complied with his request, sitting down, while he paced, smoking continuously. "Mr. de Ratour," he repeated, as though my name pleased him, "I am going to tell you some things in the strictest confidence, and you must promise not to tell anyone else." I told him I could not make that promise. He smiled. "Good," he said. "I know I can trust you." I think now that it was a streak of hubris that made him confide as much as he did. He told me first, however, that any announcement or public discussion of what they had done and were doing would have to be couched in the most careful terms. He conceded that there could be "major repercussions" if what they were doing was misconstrued by a public "wary of science." I waited, not committing myself in any way to an implicit collusion.

"First tell me, Professor Gottling," I said, "have you been using chimpanzees for experiments?"

"We are pushing to the limits the concept of gene therapy. We are using pongid zygotes to — "

"Then you admit to using chimps experimentally."

"Well, it's against state and federal law to use human fetuses."

"But," I insisted, "the protocols for using animals like chimpanzees are also very strict."

"Drex has been most understanding . . . for a price."

"So you have been dealing with Damon Drex?"

"Drex and his minions. They're all batty if you ask me."

"Is that what those restricted areas are all about?"

"Of course. Who do you think is paying for all of those renovations in the pavilion and for those inane experiments? The man belongs in an asylum."

The pot calling the kettle black, I thought, but said, "The Stein Foundation?"

He very nearly laughed at me. "They provide a mere pittance." He remained silent for a moment and then glanced at me with a look meant to convey significance. I think he was just on the point of confessing something horrendous, but he veered away. "We can say," he said, as though composing a news release, "that our work is right on the cutting edge of applicable genetics, perhaps even over the edge here and there. We have from time to time made a few speculative forays . . ." His voice trailed off and his eyes grew distant.

"Is there any truth whatsoever," I asked, "in the notion that you are tinkering with the human genotype?"

His distant gaze refocused on the present with what might be called a wry smile. "Self-speciation? Not yet. I'm afraid we're years from that, Mr. de Ratour. People have no idea how complicated we are. It's going to take years and billions of dollars just to sequence the human genome. How can you start making alterations unless you have the blueprint? We've . . . pushed the envelope, but . . ."

"With the chimpanzees?" I asked.

"With the chimps, with the . . . the little monsters . . ."

"Then you've tried?"

"Not really. A few shots in the dark, a few hunches. I was

hoping we could at least initiate some basic procedures, areas of intervention, a beginning of the beginning . . ."

"Then you are talking about eugenics," I said, scarcely reassured by the note of disappointment in his voice.

"Eugenics?" He nearly spit the word back at me. "Eugenics is old hat. It's farmyard stuff. Tinkering. No, Mr. de Ratour, when we get the tools, and we will, there's going to be nothing less than a long overdue restructuring of the human genotype, perhaps a whole new species, *Homo superbus.*"

I sat there utterly dumbfounded. I kept expecting him to sound a cynical laugh, signaling that he had been joking. "You're serious?" I said.

"Of course I'm serious."

"But that's monstrous." I said. "It's . . ." I could not find words to describe how I felt about what he was telling me.

"Oh, but think about it, Mr. de Ratour. Do we really want to leave human evolution to mere chance? Or worse, to a committee?"

"Chance hasn't done that badly so far," I said, but without a whole lot of conviction.

"Come, come, Mr. de Ratour. Look at us as a species. We are never satisfied, are we? We murder, we lie, we cheat, we covet, and we steal. How much farther up the evolutionary ladder do you really think we are from Mr. Drex's friends? We don't even kill each other for food. Oh, no, we kill each other for sport, Mr. de Ratour, for sport. Nothing fascinates us as much as a good murder unless it's a good mass murder. We like to think that Hitler and Stalin and their less efficacious imitators are the exceptions, Mr. de Ratour, but they are the rule. We can't admit to ourselves that human history is one long bloodbath. We rage in our hearts and smile at those we would destroy. We lust after each other like goats. We whine and bitch and want what cannot be. We work and sweat and build for what? To die miserable, lingering, tortured deaths. Toads live happier lives, Mr. de Ratour.

"And quite aside from what we do to ourselves, look at what we are doing as a species to the planet. We are overrunning it at a prodigious rate, and the only hope, a massive nuclear war, is now receding with the end of the Soviet empire. But the very nature we would despoil with our greed and technology answers us with AIDS and Ebola, and AIDS and other viruses, Mr. de Ratour, are only the beginning. We are going on six billion people, each one of us a little laboratory for the evolution of diseases that will make AIDS and Ebola seem like the common cold. And if we don't, in the meantime, melt the ice locked up on Antarctica and flood most of the world's coastal cities, we will strip the atmosphere of ozone and wreak havoc with crop production. Thus is man, the paragon of animals . . ."

"What will you make us into?" I asked. With credulity came a horror I could scarcely contain. In that man's presence I felt threatened not only personally but as a species. "How," I asked him, "do you see man as man would re-create him?"

The man's caution had given way to enthusiasm. He leaned forward, his cold eyes warming like sunstruck ice. "*Homo superbus,*" he said, "will be smaller, perhaps much smaller, darkly complected for protection from ultraviolet light, probably hermaphroditic, more fuel efficient, with each individual perfect in his own way. She/he will be healthier, with individual differences reduced to the incidental. We will all be perfect. And perfectly happy."

"How can you be perfect unless you know imperfection?" I asked. "How can you be happy unless you've been unhappy?"

"We will find the panoply of genes that affect our happiness and alter them accordingly."

"Professor Gottling, please understand that if there is any truth in anything you are telling me, I will not cease until this whole operation is exposed and brought to a halt."

His smile sent a chill through my whole being. "You are being naive, Mr. de Ratour. I can and will deny everything other than bending the rules a little perhaps on using chimp gametes for research. Everything else is standard research on gene therapies. You will turn yourself into a laughingstock." Then, bringing himself closer to where I had sat down, he grew chummy in a way that made my innards crawl. "Think about the possibilities, Mr. de Ratour. We can save the planet without resort to disease, starvation, and war. Everyone would be intelligent, disease resistant, long lived. Think of what a perfect human being would be: the same as others, yet different, self-confident without being arrogant, spontaneous but not flighty, sensual but not depraved, proud but not smug, daring but not foolhardy, kind but not weak, respectful but not groveling, cautious without being timid, well informed but not pedantic, spiritual but not superstitious, artistic without being arty, discriminating but not finicky, amusing but not silly, witty but not cruel, genial but not fawning. Think about it, Mr. de Ratour, no more crime, no more disease, no more death. We will all be perfect."

"No, no," I cried. "Perfection is death. Without our pains and our imperfections and our struggles to overcome them, we will be less than human."

"No, Mr. de Ratour, we will be more than human. We will re-create ourselves in our own best image. We will finally become our own Gods."

I had so many questions, so many objections, I sat mute. Because what could I say in rebuttal to this brave new world? That most of us live lives that are a series of mistakes out of which we try to make the best? That our imperfections, the knots and barbs embedded in the thickening years of existence, are precious because, for most of us, they are, finally, more our own, more us, than anything else we have or will have?

I got up finally to leave, having promised nothing about what I was going to do. I reiterated that I expected a complete report from his office regarding the expenses and activities of the lab, especially its dealings with the pavilion. I was nearly in a state of shock as I made my way up through the collections. Never had they seemed more threatened to me. Never had the divinity I have always found here seemed so spurious. Beauty, I had said in desperation to Gottling when he finished detailing the monster he wanted to create, what about beauty? Oh, he said, beauty. Yes, we'll find the genes for that as well. Everything will be beautiful. Beautiful. God is dead. Nature is dying. Are we next?

I have been sitting here for a long time. I might have succumbed to the worst kind of depression. But Elsbeth arrives in just a few days, and that prospect has me filled with hope and trepidation. Love, I wanted to shout at the professor, what about love? But he probably thinks he can find genes for that as well.

FRIDAY, OCTOBER 2

I have begun "packing" my father's revolver in a shoulder holster smelling pleasantly of new leather. It is snug against the left side of my rib cage, weighty and reassuring. And right now I need all the reassurance I can get because I have, I think, quite inadvertently, set a trap with myself as the bait.

It began late this morning when Damon Drex came into my office and started that obsequious fawning he passes off as Old World charm. "Norman, I bring you again our pressed release," he said. "How does it come that you neglect me? No words about news conference you promised." He waved that absurd "pressed release" in my face. "Frans publishes this in *Trog*." As he spoke, his mask of geniality tightened into a strange fanaticism.

I was actually prevaricating when I said, "Before we discuss anything at all, Mr. Drex — "

"You are pleased to call me Damon."

"As I was saying, Mr. Drex, before we discuss anything to do with anything, I need to know what arrangements the pavilion has had with the Genetics Lab regarding the provision of chimpanzees and any other animals for experimentation."

His smile was toothy and false. "That is professional confidentials. . . . Little potatoes for you. We will talk big things."

"Mr. Drex — "

He waved a sheaf of papers in his hand. "We talk pressed release — "

"No."

"What you mean, no? You promise — "

"The fact is, Mr. Drex, I never once promised I would sponsor a news conference regarding your experiments in the Primate Pavilion. Any interest I might have evinced in your 'work' was in large part professional courtesy that one colleague shows another. And simply because the material you have produced for the press conference is to be published in some in-house publication in no way gives it the legitimacy of having research 'published.' " I went on to tell him that rather than being awestruck by the material he had sent me, I had been convinced that he was either the perpetrator or the victim of a huge hoax, perhaps by someone who knew about his "program" or by someone with access to the codes in the mainframe memory. "I think, Mr. Drex, you should check on your assistants Frank or Frans or whatever they call themselves."

"Frank! Frans!" he screamed at me. "Frank and Frans like sons!"

I watched as his face went blank except for his yellowish eyes, which stared out from under his heavy brows with the most malignant expression I have ever seen on a human face. But I was not to be intimidated. Indeed, I got my back up enough to tell him that not only would I not sponsor a news conference but, as

Director, I would prevent his holding anything like a news conference on the premises of the MOM and that, should he hold one elsewhere, I would issue a statement disavowing any museum involvement with his "experiments." I began to enjoy my indignation, which is always dangerous, because I got carried away and dropped, as they say, my bombshell. While he was sitting there regarding me with an expression I can only describe as homicidal, I told him that, given the museum's uncertain financial condition following the death of Mr. Onoyoko, my own predispositions, and the falloff in experimentation with primates because of new and stricter state regulations, I was proposing to the Board of Governors that the pavilion be closed and that the animals be sold or given to other institutions. I told him quite frankly that I did not regret the prospect.

Mr. Drex said not a word more but regarded me in the most, how shall I put it, feral manner. He stood up and left my office.

When he had gone I locked the door and took out the revolver. I emptied it of bullets again, aimed it at the coatrack hung with my overcoat, which I pretended was Damon Drex, and pulled the trigger several times. I know this is not like me. Heretofore I wouldn't have dreamed of holding a gun, much less practicing using it against another human being. But I feel I am right on the verge of solving these murders, and I must remain alive if I am to do it and if I am ever to see Elsbeth again.

TUESDAY, OCTOBER 6

This will be a very important entry in this log. I have much to relate, and I need to do it carefully, as what I say will now constitute part of the official record. (Incidentally, I am using the terminal in Malachy Morin's old office, cheap paneling and all, since mine won't be habitable again for a while.)

Where to begin? Or rather, how to end? The events leading up to this denouement began auspiciously enough. When I came in yesterday morning to work, as I have been doing for more than three decades, I found a large manila envelope in my mail slot from the detective agency I had retained. I took the envelope into my office, closed the door, and sat down at my desk. Carefully, with the pearl-handled letter opener I inherited from my mother, I slit it open. What it contained made me slap my forehead. Of course! I should have picked up on it before! I had, finally, the last pieces of the puzzle.

I immediately put in a call to Lieutenant Tracy and left him some detailed instructions in the form of suggestions. He is a professional to the tips of his fingernails and did not cavil in the least at the role I assigned him. I then placed a series of phone calls, talking to or leaving messages for Damon Drex, Corny Chard, Thad Pilty, Raul Brauer, Alger Wherry, Stoddard Gottling, and the Snyder Brothers. I told them there would be an emergency meeting in the Twitchell Room regarding the murders of Deans Fessing and Scrabbe. I told them that nonattendance would be viewed dimly by both the Seaboard Police Department and the Museum of Man. I called Public Programs and instructed them to close the admissions desk at one P.M. for the afternoon. Scheduled groups would have to be rescheduled. I had Doreen call each department in turn and tell them to give all nonessential personnel the day off. I called Izzy and Father O'Gould and left messages that they might want to make the meeting, which I set for two.

I then sat back to marshal the evidence and my thoughts. I knew, of course, that the whole thing could literally and figuratively blow up in my face. I knew I was taking a risk. I had moments of doubt. Why not just turn it all over to the police?

That was their job, after all. Because win or lose, but especially lose, wouldn't what I was about to do be taken as grandstanding on my part? But anything like personal glory was the farthest thing from my mind. This murderous mess had begun in the Museum of Man, defiling everything it stands for and striking at the very foundation stones of civilization. I was determined that here, in this museum, this horrific plot would be exposed and brought to an end. To this purpose I telephoned the *Bugle* and left word for Amanda Feeney to be in attendance. For once, I thought, I would use the press rather than be used by them.

An unusual calm appeared to descend on the museum. I noticed it when I went down early to the cafeteria for a sandwich and lemonade to bring back to the office. Gottling called to ask, "What is this all about?" and I told him to be there if he didn't want his name taken in vain. I let him sputter on for a while.

The calm grew to silence after the museum emptied around one o'clock. The silence, which I could hear through my open door, became positively eerie. I made a few phone calls. I paced about a bit. The day being warmish, I opened my window and regarded the blueness of the ocean and the thick rug of forest stretching to the Hays Mountains. Its foliage was well past its gaudiest flamboyance. While thus musing, thinking how I prefer the more mellow browns and yellows of this time to the reds and oranges of the week before, I heard a sudden eruption of shrieks and hoots from Drex's chimps. But from within, not from below, the noise coming through the open door. I went down the hallway and peered into the exhibition galleries. Damon Drex, followed by a troop of his scampering apes, was making his way up through the exhibits. My first, rather foolish impulse was to yell down to him that museum regulations expressly prohibit, except in the case of seeing-eye dogs, the presence of live animals in the exhibition or conservation areas.

Then I knew!

I raced back to my office, afraid not so much for my life as of what I might have to do to preserve it. My door, a venerable thing, did not lock from the inside without a key, which I didn't have time to look for. I closed and chained it with an old brass thing that's been there since ever I can remember. If nothing else, it bought a precious few seconds. I retreated behind my desk and took the revolver from its holster. Not a minute too soon. The beasts came howling down the corridor.

"Call them off, Damon!" I yelled. "Call them off or I'll shoot them." The door jerked open, and two hairy paws curled around the edges. Again I called out, saying I was armed and ready to shoot. In vain. With a terrific crash, the door was pushed inward with such force the frame gave way. "Stop!" I shouted and pointed the revolver at Royd, for that's who it was, his ape's mug contorted with naked rage. Drex stood beside him and smirked at my gun. It was that smirk that made me stand up just as Royd started for me, aim the revolver with two hands, and shoot. What a sensation, the way the revolver jolted to life in my hands. I had missed and might have been overwhelmed had the noise not made the animal hesitate for an instant. It screeched horribly and lunged for me again across the desk. I fired again, and the shot must have hit him near the heart because he collapsed onto the floor, blood pluming from his chest. Another large chimp came toward me bipedally, his torso bobbing from side to side. I winged him with a shot to the shoulder, making him howl and skitter away.

"Call them off, Mr. Drex, or you will be next." I aimed the revolver directly at his head and cocked the hammer. He had turned white. He snarled at me like one of his beasts. "Don't make me kill you," I said, amazed at my own calm, which sprang from a deep, cold anger. Was this how poor Fessing had met his end — pulled apart by deranged apes in the sway of a madman? For several seconds, as we stood eye to eye, the issue was in doubt. Then Drex staggered, covered his face with his hands, and leaned against the wrecked doorjamb. The animals milled around behind him as though confused. "Take them downstairs and lock them up," I said when he had recovered some composure. "I'll be walking right behind you."

Something of a crowd had gathered at the bottom of the staircase in Neanderthal Hall. "Everything's under control," I said to the upturned, alarmed faces. By then I had slipped my gun back into its holster under my jacket. I could tell from the utterly crushed Drex that I wouldn't need it. To Sergeant Lemure, who just happened to have come in, I said, "Officer, make sure this man locks up these animals. One of them needs medical attention. Then arrest him and bring him to the Twitchell Room. Lieutenant Tracy, who'll be arriving shortly, will show you where it is."

"What's the charge?" he asked, skeptical.

"Assault with deadly animals. Attempted murder." Then I turned and headed back up to my office to retrieve some papers I needed. Royd lay on his side, and I might have felt some pity for the beast were his eyes not open and his fangs bared and menacing even in the stillness of death. I stepped around the carnage, picked up the papers, and left. Downstairs I told a uniformed officer that there was a dead chimp in my office and it was to be treated as evidence in a murder case. He said he would inform one of the detectives.

By two o'clock, to my grim pleasure, all of the parties I had called were present. Thad Pilty looked quizzical. Raul Brauer, his baldness gleaming, appeared restored to his usual self. Corny Chard joked with one of the several uniformed officers in attendance. Damon Drex sat handcuffed and pale faced. Amanda Feeney arrived, bustling in with a somewhat better groomed Malachy Morin in tow. Ariel Dearth followed them, his expression decidedly officious for the occasion. The Snyder brothers, dressed identically in black, looked like mirror images of each other. Alger Wherry was his usual, averted self. Izzy, accompanied by Father O'Gould, showed up, a half smile playing around his eyes as he regarded me with puzzlement. Professor Gottling came at the last minute and demanded to know if it would take long. I told him he could leave now if he wished. He flustered about and finally took a seat, glowering at the ceiling. Others had gotten wind of the meeting, and the room started to fill up. I noticed Marge and Esther had come in, along with several of the curators. Lieutenant Tracy arrived last, nodded imperceptibly to me with the faintest of smiles, and closed the door behind him.

Precisely on time I began, a quiet anger subduing my nervousness while slowing and deepening my voice. "I have called all of you here because for the past eight months we have been subjected to a reign of terror that has been horrible in its gratuitousness and insidious in its effects, a threat to the very basis of a civilized order. For the longest time this grotesque plot, for that is what it is, has baffled the best minds of the Seaboard Police Department and frustrated my own, admittedly bungling efforts to get to the bottom of it. Much of the difficulty has arisen from the initial grit of irrational inspiration around which this rough, dark pearl of evil has accreted itself. Some of our failure has stemmed from the human predilection to see things in black and white. In fact, there is black and white in this case. But there are also lots of grays, dark, somberly tinted grays as well."

I looked up into the circle of faces and took them in in a long sweep, eye to eye. I cleared my throat. "Most of you now know that there has existed, right under our noses, right here in the museum, a cult of cannibalism." Corny Chard smiled. "Professor Brauer did indeed carry his 're-creational' practices to their grisly extremes during one of his expeditions to Loa Hoa. The proceedings of the Société de Couchon Long will prove interesting reading not so much to anthropologists as to students of abnormal psychology. And the spate of ensuing books will no doubt pander to a public taste for such things. But even if these materials were found earlier behind a locked door in the Skull Collection, along with what might be called the founding skull and paraphernalia of a kind associated with juvenile behavior, it would not have led to a resolution of the case. Cannibalism itself isn't a crime in our beautiful state. I presume that our aversion to the consumption of human flesh is so deeply a part of our ethos that there has been no need to outlaw it as such. Therefore, I can accuse Raul Brauer, Corny Chard, and Alger Wherry, and any of their fellow dupes, of nothing worse in their abominations than the worst possible taste.

"No, ladies and gentlemen," and here I paused for effect, "the real culprits are not the members of this ludicrous, grotesque cult but a person or persons who knew about the cult. This person or persons, possessed of uncanny knowledge and access to all aspects of the museum and university, knew that the presence of the cult would divert attention away from them. This conspiracy, more hellish even than that of the long piggers, blossomed like poison fungi in a petri dish under the corrupt and lax administration of Malachy Morin, a man whose own brutish self-indulgence not only resulted in the death of an innocent young woman but sidetracked the investigation of the murders for several critical weeks." I glanced in his direction, but he was smiling, as though glad for the attention. "This poison blossomed rankly in the lack of oversight of the Genetics Laboratory and the Primate Pavilion, where ambitions silly and profoundly disturbing were let fester unchecked.

"I fault myself as well. There were hints and clues that I should have followed up. I should have been more sensitive to names. My German has never been very good. Had I investigated the diet of chimpanzees I would have found, as I did within the past week, that they hunt monkeys and other small game in the wild, and even indulge in cannibalism. I should have asked Dr. Cutler to examine more closely the gnaw marks on Dean Fessing's remains. I'm sure they'll prove consistent with the dentition of *Pan troglodytes*."

There was a stir of ohs and ahs.

"Still, I do not accuse Damon Drex, even though, because I would not sanction his hunger to bask in the bright, false light of media attention, he tried just before this meeting to unleash his chimps on me. Whether a willing or an unwilling accomplice, Mr. Drex was little more than a dupe, a puppet strung along like one of his hairy charges.

"Nor do I accuse Professor Gottling, who was funneling large amounts of money from the Onoyoko Institute to the pavilion in return for access to animals for experiments in the human genotype, experiments that will be placed under close and immediate scrutiny."

"You don't know what you're talking about," the geneticist said, rising from his chair.

"Perhaps, Professor Gottling. But as we speak a team from the state Attorney General's Office is in your lab starting their investigation."

Professor Gottling immediately left.

I waited for the room to quiet, looking down at my notes before glancing around at my audience. But I did not need any notes. It was all inside me, poised like a verbal dagger.

"As you can see, none of these parties is completely innocent. But neither are they guilty of the murders of Cranston Fessing and Oliver Scrabbe. No, ladies and gentlemen, that guilt lies" — I stopped and pointed — "directly with the Snyder Brothers."

They started, as though they might attempt to flee.

"It's useless to try to escape. Every door of the museum is secured with heavy police guard."

"We have alibis," they said in unison. "You have no proof."
And they smiled their wicked smiles.

I smiled back. There was a hubbub of hushed voices. Amanda
Feeney was scribbling furiously. I waited until order was restored.

"Yes, of course, I know both of you have airtight alibis for the
time Dean Scrabbe was knocked on the head and taken from his
office. Too airtight for my liking. That one of you was at the
Northside police substation precisely at that time asking to use
the phone was overdoing it just a bit much. I called the garage
that towed your car, and they said they found nothing wrong
with it. And I fault myself for not getting a better copy of the CV's
the Personnel Department faxed me. The reference to the restaurant you owned at 333 Backbay Street in Boston came over
graphically garbled as *Dri Brat* or *Prat* and something *sten,* the
best I could make it out. *Dri Brat Worsten?* It didn't make sense.
Even when I called for and received a clean copy and saw the
name of the restaurant was Drei Bratwursten, I still didn't catch
on. Drei Bratwursten. The Three Franks. That's right, not just
two Frank Snyders but three. Identical triplets."

To another outbreak of exclamations and murmurs, Lieutenant Tracy opened the door, and the third Snyder brother came in,
handcuffed to a large uniformed officer.

"The Three Franks," I repeated when order once again had
been restored. "Franz, Francis, and Frans, born in Baltimore
thirty-four years ago. And practical jokers, right from the start.
Am I not right?"

"We're not saying anything until we talk to a lawyer," they all
said in unison. Then they laughed, identically, creating a creepy
effect.

"You worked your way up the coast, playing games, a habit
that started early, harmless enough at first, this ability to be a
single, a double, and especially a triple. People gaped and gawked
and couldn't believe their eyes. You got thrown out of college for

cheating when you didn't have to. You were arrested in Philadelphia for running a con game with old ladies in a retirement home. You won endurance bets, dance contests, even a marathon in New York. Not for money, just for a joke.

"And when you came here after the Health Department in Boston closed you down for having cats, raccoons, and a dog as well as 'unidentified meat products' in your restaurant freezer, you found a situation ripe for the hoax of your wildest dreams. You found Damon Drex allowing Professor Gottling to have chimps for experimentation for practically nothing. So you started the biggest practical joke of your careers. You launched the program, funded by the Onoyoko Institute, to teach chimps how to write. And just when the joke was coming to fruition, Cranston Fessing showed up and, being the shrewd old dean he was, smelled a rat, or three rats in this case. At that point you decided to take the joke one ghastly step further. You killed and cooked the dean and fed him to the chimps. And when your murder and mutilation of Fessing didn't deter the university, you repeated your ghastly joke, using Scrabbe's skull to point suspicion at the Skull Collection and the antics of the Long Piggers. All the while you could barely stop laughing. You were able to get away with your wretched pranks because you were one person in three, miraculously capable of being in three places at one time. Or, more to the point of your hubris, three persons in one, which made you think you were invincible, a veritable god. What you didn't count on, what all murderers big and small don't count on, is that a civilized society will only take so much. You carried your joke too far, and your pride went before your fall.

"I think, Lieutenant, that you'll find the third triplet has no alibi for the time Dean Scrabbe was abducted. I think a thorough search of the Snyders' place of domicile and the facilities of the Primate Pavilion will turn up sufficient material evidence for an indictment. I also think that Mr. Drex will prove a most cooperative witness."

Lieutenant Tracy officially arrested the triplets, read them their rights, and had them led off. They were followed by a quick-stepping Ariel Dearth, who was trying to give them his card. Amanda Feeney, after telling Malachy Morin to wait for her outside, asked me many questions, but in a respectful manner. Corny Chard tried to congratulate me, but I would not shake his hand. I watched Raul Brauer slip away quietly. I sat around for a while and chatted with my friends, remarking cryptically that I hoped "Worried" felt better. Then Izzy, saying he had just stocked some excellent champagne, suggested we retire to the Club for a well-earned tipple. So, surrounded by these good friends, so relieved as to be weak, I walked out into the brilliant October light.

FRIDAY, OCTOBER 9

As I sit here making this quite personal entry into this unofficial log, I find myself a different, a transformed Norman Abbott de Ratour. Curiously enough, it has almost nothing to do with the resolution of the murders of Fessing and Scrabbe or with the ensuing and rather gratifying notoriety it has won for me. Suffice it to say that I am older, I am younger; I am sadder, I am happier; I am more serious, I am scoffing at myself; I am infinitely wiser and as obtuse as ever; I am much more confident, but of what I am not sure. I should start at the beginning, yesterday morning, to be exact, when I drove to our modest little airport to pick up Elsbeth. I had scarcely slept the night before. I nicked myself shaving and bled like a martyr. I could not find matching socks. I considered putting on a suit, then settled for a rugged corduroy shooting jacket with a leather patch on the right fore shoulder, an off-white shirt, and my club tie, which I rejected in favor of an

indigo silk cravat with a paisley design. But it was all a front. I
didn't know what to do with the bouquet of yellow roses I had
picked up. I put them in the car. I took them back into the house.
I went and retrieved them. I nearly ran over Mrs. Norris backing
out of my drive.

At the airport I paced the waiting room like an expectant
father. I wasn't disappointed. When she came through the double
doors, three decades disappeared. She was her old self, her smile
radiant under short, neatly coiffed, still lustrous hair. She strode
toward me in a pleated tartan, suede jacket, button-down oxford,
and rakish cravat nearly matching mine, her short heels clicking
decisively, her smile a picture of delight. We kissed chastely, a
peck on the cheek. What a eruption of sensations swirled around
and through me! Though hardly slender, she had become positively svelte and appeared, if anything, to have grown younger
since that awful encounter in Philadelphia. She had one of those
pull-along suitcases, so I had nothing to do with my big hands,
which felt like encumbrances as I helped her through the door
and out to the parking lot.

I was altogether too light-headed with uncertain elation to do
more than smile and nod rather idiotically as I drove her in my
newly tuned and polished Renault to the Miranda Hotel, our talk
along the way carefully small — the flight, the weather, how
Seaboard had changed. She checked in. I waited like a swain of
old in the lobby while she freshened up in her room. We had the
whole day to ourselves, and as I paced the faux Iberian lobby, I
wanted to escape into the faded murals of seascapes and white-
washed villages, a march of stylized olive trees, stick-legged don-
keys, and azure skies. I wondered what on earth we would do.
Lunch, of course, and a trip to the lake no doubt. But lunch
where? And what would we do at the lake? What would we talk
about?

Above all, as she stepped from the elevator, having changed

into slacks and turtleneck, I was determined not to reveal my heart. I knew I would not survive another rejection and felt supremely foolish even thinking in those terms. Somewhat stiffly, I think, I said, "I suppose you'll want to go out to the lake first," the "first" implying other activities of which I hadn't a clue.

"Oh, do let's go and see what's become of old Bramble." She laughed, and the sun, playing hide-and-seek behind high, wistful clouds moving in a fresh, sea-scented breeze, came out for a glorious moment. We became tourists of our common past, and the day began to take care of itself.

She took my arm as we mounted the porticoed steps of what had been, in more genteel times, a ladies' residence hall. The double French doors were locked, but a student with a key didn't object when we entered in his wake. It was unrecognizable at first. They had vandalized the gracious old lobby, covering the flower-swirled plaster ceiling with sound-insulating stuff and installing what looked like stage lighting in place of the glassy chandeliers. Gone were the chintz-covered chairs and sofas, the drapery and dainty tables. They had been replaced by what looked like inflated life rafts and chunky wooden things, making it seem more like a room for children than adults. We did find the nook with the battered upright Vose almost intact. To the bemusement of some of the lounging students, all of whom looked not a little seedy, we bungled our way through a couple of *lieder*. Indeed, before we finished there had gathered something of an audience, which applauded us and asked for more.

On that note we left and proceeded through the sadly neglected Marvell Gardens. In the little enclosure where we had embraced, we found an apologetic homeless man sheltering as best he could. Elsbeth reached into her purse and gave the man a five-dollar bill. At my raised eyebrows, she said, "Oh, I've got more than I'll ever spend. Winslow was good in that way."

"Yes," I said, distracted by her remark even as I explained how I felt something amiss both when I gave and when I didn't give to beggars. *Winslow was good in that way.* But not in other ways? Was it a disparagement of her husband? Had I heard a subtle emphasis on the *that?* Or was it just a remark? And why on earth did she seem so happy to be with me? Pale, tremulous hope stirred in me like one of those fantastic desert plants that lie dormant for decades and then bloom into life at the first touch of rain. But if she were giving me an opening, I did not know how to take advantage of it, or lacked the courage to. She talked in a self-deprecating way about the work she was doing in a shelter for homeless families in Philadelphia, and I listened with the silence of one muted with love.

It was Elsbeth's suggestion to take a picnic out to the cottage. When we stopped at a delicatessen for sandwiches and fruit, and at a wine shop for a bottle of chilled white wine, how well she organized it! How I welcomed her brisk efficiencies! On the drive there, we remarked how, while suburbs had thickened around the periphery of Seaboard, much of the farmland had reverted to forest. We talked about what had happened at the museum. She said she had read and heard about it in the national media. She told me she had seen me on television and I was very telegenic. Then, placing her hand on my shoulder, she said she hoped fervently that I was now out of danger. What I can't describe is how, as I talked to her about it and as she listened, watching my eyes, that whole absurd, grisly business fell from me like a great and cumbersome millstone. Or, more accurately, I think, she imperceptibly moved closer as though to take some of the weight. But I couldn't see her eyes, which might have been pitying or admiring or wary. Was she throwing me some little sop of life but gingerly, the way you give a scrap to an abused dog?

We turned off the state highway onto a single-lane road and wound our way up through a needle-carpeted evergreen forest, the past turning into the present, or vice versa, I'm not sure which. We came to a forking dirt road and a turnoff I always used to miss and almost did again. The drive, sloping down to the cottage, was blocked by a growth of hemlock saplings. It wasn't much of a walk, the lake water all adazzle through a screen of leafless lilacs.

She took my hand as we approached, as though for balance. We were both surprised to find the cottage looked largely intact, at least from the outside, surprising as well a porcupine sleeping under the side of the porch facing the lake. It awoke and rattled off with slow dignity. The perspective from there — the bristle of pines on Barkley's Point, the old railroad bridge and embankment on the distant shore, the sweep of blueberry shrubland to the right — seemed scarcely changed at all, an impression reinforced by the call of jays coming through the sharp air. The cottage itself listed decidedly to starboard, and we found, under the skirting of lattice, one of the sills and some of the uprights eaten away by ants. We went in, continuing our time walk. Elsbeth moved about, exclaiming, touching things, finally crying, so that I had to comfort her. "Why," I asked, "did you never come back here?" I wanted to kiss away her tears.

"Win never wanted to, and we always did what Win wanted. Right from the start." Bitterness curdled the sadness in her voice.

I didn't encourage an elaboration. I didn't feel particularly vindicated. It was too late for that. And, anyway, revenge is a dish that grows cold. "I'm sorry to hear that," I said. "Although I suspected as much . . . when I came out to visit you."

We were in the kitchen, the cobwebs straining the cold light on the steel sink, the four-burner gas stove, the oilcloth on the table where a few dead flies lay, when she put her arms around me, collapsing against my chest. She was sobbing again, whispering, "Norman, Norman, please don't hate me . . ."

I held her in my arms and let her sob, patting her back, saying twice or three times, "Of course I don't hate you, of course . . ."

while wondering with a poignancy too exquisite for words whether forgiveness was all she wanted from me.

Indeed, she recovered her composure so quickly I was just a little put out. She suggested we have lunch on the porch, now bright with sunshine. She found a corkscrew and some glasses while I arranged a card table and a couple of chairs. We toasted with our glasses of wine, exactly what I still wasn't sure. She ate and spoke avidly, waiting to swallow, then talking, one hand moving just a little bit, as though conducting herself, the way she always had. She elaborated, seemed positively anxious and relieved to talk about her life with Winslow. She knew she had made a terrible, terrible mistake, she said, after they had been married only a few months. But by then, through carelessness, she was pregnant with their first child, and in those days you didn't automatically get a divorce. She elaborated on her late husband's smallness, his need to control everything, his growing preoccupation with money, his golf. I listened, nodding, wondering what all this had to do with me, when she said something so extraordinary I had to put down the ham and Swiss on rye I had been toying with. "During all those years, Norman, I thought about you every day. I thought about you every night, especially those nights when . . ."

"When what?" I asked, obtuse to the end.

"When Win wanted to make love."

"Oh, dear" was all I could manage and sipped my wine. I held her hand. It was as though, through all those years, we had been making love after all. But I couldn't tell her that, not yet.

A cold wind came off the lake. We went inside and started a fire in the fieldstone fireplace to take the chill off the air. We sat on the wicker sofa in front of the fire and watched it roar and dance. We kissed.

I won't, gentle reader, even in the privacy of this journal, go into details after she whispered that we should go upstairs.

Suffice it to say that what ensued on her cleanly sheeted and only mildly mildewed bed was touching, passionate, and in its own way hilarious. Elsbeth simply couldn't believe I had waited.

She has made a complete man of me, and I am so happy that I scarcely resent all those lost years. Because I think all of us, in a way, carry around ghost lives, lives we could have lived with others, in other places, doing other things. But we can't regret not having lived them, even when they rise up and come back to claim us.